Plain Dane: Dawn of Power
By: David L. Schlaufman

ISBN-13: 978-1-7328676-0-4

i

For my family.
You are all my superheroes!

Author's Note

Good and evil. One cannot exist without the other. They are opposites, and yet brothers divided by only two factors.

How many people in the world would actually identify themselves as "evil"? Would they not make the case that their mission is simply different from others who have been deemed "good" by society? Think of a character, real or fiction, who bears the label of "evil." Look at their story. Where was the turning point in their life that sent them down a darker path? Look at how they got to where they are. What was the catalyst and the thought process brought on by this event that steered them in this direction? Look at the actions that have given them their label of "evil". Are these actions brought on by a need for self-defense? Adequacy? Revenge? "Pure evil" does not exist. Instead, the existence of evil is something that is created out of a good soul stricken by negative occurrences. Still, everything is not simply left to chance. The two major factors that separate good and evil? Love and strength.

Now I urge you to think about someone on the side of good. Think of their background and what got them to the height of their story. Is it not true that most, if not all of them have also faced a catalyst event at some point in their life? In many cases, this event has even pushed them to become better and more driven in their fight to help others. So, why did they not turn towards evil like the others? Why did the event steer them in the completely opposite direction? The answer is love. We talk about love all the time as a feeling we have towards another, but what is it about love that can alter someone's destiny so much as to turn them against everyone, or do the exact opposite and create a hero?

Every single human being ever has possessed love. Love for our family, friends, significant others, pets, objects, sometimes people we don't even know. Along with this love comes the ability to be a hero, or to become evil. When that love is threatened, or taken away there is something deep within us that swells to the surface:

strength, and it is strength that will send us down one of those two paths: It will take the love that we wish to protect and use it to make us stronger, ready to fight for what we believe in while still containing the love we have for others. The other path is vengeful, disregarding of others, and reckless in our fight for what we love. We are all stronger than we know, and the peak of our strength will always display itself when love is on the line. It's what you do with that strength and the love you use it to defend that will give you your title: Hero or Villain.

As someone who grew up watching, reading about, and pretending to be superheroes I always admired how they were different in many ways, but always shared the characteristics of love and strength. I have always worked to build my own personal strength in its various forms, not only physical (but let's be honest, I'll be ready for the Zombie Apocalypse!), while also trying to always show love for those around me, even if they can make that a very hard thing to do at times. In the end, what is the deciding factor when an unstoppable force meets an immovable object? Love. Heroes see the good in everyone, even when it's deep beneath the surface, and they understand that they were meant to use their strength to protect it. If you are reading this book, you are a fan of superheroes too and you may have grown up admiring them and pretending to be them as I did. My advice to you is to remember what drew you to them when you were younger, and what still draws you to them today. Always remember to love. Continue to grow stronger. Though it may look different, the fight against evil is just as real as it is displayed in comic books and movies, and the world needs heroes.

The world needs you.

Chapter 1

The flash of a cape, an explosion, the piercing sound of police sirens. From the rubble a villain is apprehended and a hero emerges victorious. Cheers and applause erupt from anyone lucky enough to witness the scene, but the hero wi l exit without even the smallest sense of obligation to the crowd of unfamiliar faces. This was his duty, he was chosen for this. Fade to black, cue the horns.

With wide eyes and mouth agape, a child looks on in wonder and excitement, his fuzzy brown head of hair glowing in the television's light. He stands in front of the glowing box in his underwear and a tablecloth cape. Filled with hope he clenches his fingers tightly as his fists find their way to his hips, puffs his chest, and raises his eyes to the sky as the superhero on the screen in front of him darts in and out of monstrous, white clouds and into the horizon to await his next calling. At this moment the boy is poised, standing tall, ready to take on any foe that may threaten the common good of the world...

"Dammit, Dane! I told you to go put some clothes on!" a woman sweeps into the room, bypassing his imaginary super-senses, and pushes him from in front of the television.

"Awww, Mom! It was almost over!" Dane whines.

"I don't care! We're going to be late if we're not out the door in three minutes!" she pushes him up the stairs. "Now put something on other than your underwear...AND NO CAPE!!"

"Dang it...Amazing Dane's one weakness, Krypto-mom" the boy mutters to himself as he reaches the top of the stairs. He walks into his far-from-tidy room untying the makeshift cape that flows behind him and tosses it on the bedpost over top of the previous three days' worth of dirty clothes, then makes his way across the room. He grabs some jeans off the floor in front of his dresser, then pulls a blue shirt with a bolt logo across the front out of an open, clothes-spewing drawer and throws it on. Grabbing his favorite action figure off the desk and hugging it tight under his arm he makes his way towards the door, but stops catching a glimpse of himself in the mirror. A confused look on his face, he takes a step back in front of it to get a better view, immediately hanging his head and letting out a sigh of frustration as he turns back towards the dresser, a small cape he hadn't realized was attached to the shoulders of the shirt flowing behind him.

Downstairs, Mom is waiting by the door, bag in hand, looking at the clock on her lit-up smartphone. Finally, Dane comes bounding down the stairs flying the action figure with his outstretched arm.

"Hey, Captain Slowbutt, I said 3 minutes. Let's go, we're gonna be late!" Mom says impatiently and ushers him out the door to the car.

The Eatonville Elementary School sits atop a hill just outside of town, a winding driveway leading up to it. The parking lot, sandwiched between the front of the school and the football field that sits down in a small ravine, looks out over the houses and buildings of downtown Eatonville as if they were Monopoly pieces. Everything, though, even the school, sits under the looming figure and watchful eye of Mount Rainier. Past the football field, past the town, through woods and streams and lakes sits the black giant with the white, snowy cap that, on most days, threatens to pierce right through the clouds and into the blue sky above.

Inside the school, the cafeteria is teeming with kids and their parents. Some kids are running around shouting and chasing each other while others have been corralled by their parents at cafeteria tables across from teachers. At the far side of the room Dane and his mom are seated at a table next to each other and across from an older, grey-haired woman with a flowery blue and green blouse. In front of her on the table sits a name card, "Mrs. Thurman: 3rd Grade Homeroom". While the two grown-ups are deep in conversation, Dane continues to occupy his own little world playing with his action figure.

"You see, Miss Denson," says the older woman, "it's not only that his grades are suffering, but there's a social aspect to it too. He's sort of made himself the outcast from the other kids because...well, look!" She gestures over to Dane, who stops abruptly and looks up at her nervously "He just wants to play by himself with his action figures, or he pretends everyone is a bad guy. He's either by himself, or he's against everyone."

They both look over at Dane disappointedly. Feeling their gaze, he looks up at his mom, then over to Mrs. Thurman, then back to his mom. "Invisibility, GO!!" he shouts closing his eyes and clenching his entire body tightly as if this will cloak him from their hostile conversation. After a couple of moments of silence he peaks one eye up towards the grown-ups, scanning from one to the other and back again. Mom lets out a sigh as she rolls her eyes and shakes her head.

"I'm so sorry Mrs. Thurman," she says across the table to the teacher. "I knew he had a vivid imagination, but I didn't know it was becoming a bad thing. And I definitely didn't know it was affecting his grades!"

"Well, that's why I wanted to discuss it with you, it really is!" the teacher says sternly. "I think it's more than an issue of having a strong imagination. I catch him daydreaming, doodling superheroes and sneaking comic books into his desk far too often. To be honest, I think it'd be a good idea to get this checked out professionally. We could be dealing with an ADHD situation and I think it's best to head it off as soon as we can."

"Yeah, ok..." Mom says uneasily, glancing back down to her son who has resumed playing with his action figure, then continues with Mrs. Thurman, who has now pulled out tests and assignments to show her.

Sensing a disturbance in the area, Dane looks up from his toy and across the room as the adults' critical conversation fades to a low mumble in the background. On the other side of the cafeteria two young boys point over at him. They laugh mockingly as they pretend to fly around each other and shoot each other with imaginary laser beams from their hands. Standing against the wall next to the two boys, an adorable little girl with straight blonde hair pulled back into a half pony tail watches and chuckles at them. As her bright blue eyes shift across the room and settle on Dane, her smile suddenly glows with empathy and Dane quickly averts his gaze back down to his action figure. He tries his hardest to keep his head down as the boys continue to mock him and wrestle with one another, but slowly, he raises his eyes back over to the group, where the little girl still looks in his direction. She is still smiling at him as her eyes flutter, but suddenly the two boys run into her, breaking the connection. She recovers her balance and yells at them, pushing them both away playfully. Dane sadly reverts his attention back to the conversation between the grown-ups.

"Well, thank you for everything," Mom says. "We're going to get this under control, aren't we sweetie?" She runs her fingers through Dane's soft, brown hair and looks at him with wide eyes, fishing for some involvement on his part. He looks at her blankly, then shrugs his shoulders. She looks back to the teacher who has her compassionate eyes fixed on Dane. "Yes, we are. Thanks again, Mrs. Thurman. C'mon Dane." She grabs his hand and leads him away from the table.

As he is dragged from the cafeteria he passes by the group of rowdy kids. The two boys are now lost in a smartphone game as the blonde girl looks on. She looks away from the phone towards Dane as he reaches the door and raises one hand to wave at him. Embarrassed, he quickly looks away again and is pulled into the hallway. The little girl lowers her hand looking sadly at the doorway for a second, then goes back to watching the boys play on the phone.

Outside of the cafeteria Mom looks inquisitively on a business card that Mrs. Thurman had given her. After a moment of nervous thought she stuffs it in her pocket and slingshots Dane around in front of her, bending down to his level to look him in the eyes. She sets her hands softly on his shoulders as he looks up to meet her gaze. "Dane, we've gotta fix this. What's going on with you?"

Dane fidgets with the toy in his hands, "I dunno."

"You've gotta talk to me, sweetie!" She urges. "If you don't tell me anything then I won't know how to help you. What do you want me to do?!"

He shrugs his shoulders again with frustration, "I don't know!"

"Well, we've gotta do something!" Mom says sternly as she stands. Reaching down she pulls the action figure out of his hand.

"NO!" he screams as he reaches for his toy. "Mom, give it back!"

She turns to him and shakes it in his direction. "No more of this! I'm making you an appointment with this doctor tomorrow." As Dane continues to scream and jump for his action figure, she turns away and tosses it in a nearby garbage can. Dane's eyes widen and glaze over with tears. He screams and rushes towards the garbage can, but is stopped in his tracks and wrapped up by his mom's arm as she lifts him from the ground. He feels completely powerless but continues to scream and reach out for the trashed toy as he is carried away, the blurry view of the garbage can getting further and further until the front doors close behind them and it is completely out of sight.

Back at home, inside the window of his 2nd story bedroom Dane sits on his bed next to a large cardboard box, shoulders slumped, trails running down his cheeks from the tears, defeated from what had just occurred at the school. As he sulks, Mom rushes around him collecting action figures off of the dressers and shelves, rolling up posters, snatching masks, capes and other articles of clothing from his drawers and off the floor, and collecting all of his superhero movies and video games into the box, scolding him and throwing her hands up in frustration as she goes. Dane never looks up from his somberness, even as his mom approaches and strips the logo-brazen shirt off his body. She throws it in the box as well and finally picks the entire thing up and storms out of the room. Dane is once again powerless. He can do nothing but sink his face down into his hands and continue to cry.

Chapter 2

Eleven years later, through the seemingly endless waves of snow, jutting rocks and wind-blown trees, a small shack stands at the end of a long, winding trail lonely on a very calm and sunny June day. Smoke rolls from a small, metal chimney coming off the side of the building as if to signal someone's presence. The frosted windows are only transparent through the middle of each pane of glass revealing a light glowing from inside.

Light streams from the slightly thawed windows into the shack that is otherwise only lit by a small desk lamp. The walls of the room are almost completely hidden by stacks of computer towers and equipment with hundreds of small, multicolored lights, some steadily lit, others blinking rapidly. A small desk stands in the middle of the room, which is also teeming with devices and monitors as well as the lamp. Against the back wall the only open spot between the equipment is a door, visible in the darkness only due to the illumination coming from its creases with the wall and floor.

"Uuuuuggggggh!" comes a loud grunt from behind the door. "Uuuuuuuughhhh, God!" After a couple of seconds of silence a toilet flushes loudly, followed by the running of water. The bathroom door disappears into blackness as the light that had outlined it goes black. "Damn processed food!" A broad shouldered man with messy, black hair swings the door open with frustration. It slams against one of the computer towers causing it to power down and go dark and silent. "SHIT! I've gotta stop doing that!" he shouts at himself as he starts flipping switches and pushing buttons trying to get it back online. As a last resort he lets out an angry scream as he throws his fists against it and kicks the side of the tower. It promptly returns to life and lights back up. "...piece of shit." He utters.

From the desk, a light on a walkie talkie lights up red as it beeps loudly, followed by a woman's voice, "Kurrt. Kurrt, do you read? We need your updated readings...KURRT!"

Kurrt leaves the tower and sighs as he slinks over to the desk and grabs the walkie talkie, "Yeah, yeah, I'm here," he grumbles as he falls into a desk chair and reclines back nonchalantly.

"Well?!" the voice on the other end urges impatiently.

"Well, what!?" snaps Kurrt. "I keep telling you guys, there's no changes going on up here. The seismic readings are the exact same as they've always been and you refuse to look into the radiation level, so…" he trails off in frustration.

"I've told you before, Kurrt, you're not up there to do radiation tests. You're strictly there to test the fault-lines and see if it's progressing or not." The female voice urges, "Besides, do you think we'd send you into a radiation zone, anyways?"

"Yeah, I do think that, you bossy bitch," he grumbles under his breath rolling his eyes in the direction of the walkie talkie. He then lifts it to his mouth reluctantly and pushes the button on the side. "No, of course not. I'm just saying, there is way more happening with the radiation readings. I mean, the readings are still extremely low and insignificant, but the seismic readings haven't changed a wink since I got here 2 weeks ago. So, there's your update, I guess."

"Listen Kurrt, just do what you're up there for…" the woman urges as Kurrt rolls his eyes again and mouths the next words along with her, "Monitor, then report. Got it?"

"Yeah, I got it" he grumbles.

"Good, we'll check in later," the walkie talkie gives a quick squeal then turns to static. "Ugh, whatever." He grumbles as he tosses it on the desk and slumps back into his chair taking a drink from a can of Monster Energy. He sets the can down on the desk and taps it with his finger a couple of times before reaching over and pushing the power button of a small computer monitor. As it slowly glows to life, Kurrt's face, illuminated by green light, shows deep concern. Different levels of green, blinking lights display themselves across the screen with the largest, brightest one in the center. Nervously, his unblinking eyes stare intently at the obvious pattern they draw on the screen in front of him: a mountain.

Chapter 3

In Eatonville, cars fill the parking lot in front of the school. Mount Rainier stands tall in the distance covered mostly in green shrubbery and trees, aside from its rocky, snowy peak. Inside the school, the halls are empty and quiet, as if the whole building were completely abandoned. In an instant, with one piercing bell ring, a seemingly endless flood of students flows from the classroom doorways into the hallway and replaces the silence with shouting, laughing and cheering.

A skinny boy approaches locker #638, his small frame making his plain, blue t-shirt look a half size too big as light brown hair falls over his forehead above his blue eyes. He enters his combo, 08-41-19, and pulls on the handle to swing the door open. The bottom of the locker is filled with Pepsi bottles and candy wrappers while a backpack hangs on a hook and books fill the shelf at the top. As he rustles through the books under his arm he is startled as the door is suddenly slammed shut in front of him. An arm wraps itself around his neck and violently pushes him up against the locker. "Gimme all your lunch money, ya little shit!" says a deep raspy voice behind him. "Yeah, pony up JANE!" says a higher pitched voice mockingly.

He forcefully pulls the arm off of him and turns around to face the two boys who just attacked him, unable to keep a smirk from finding his lips. "Nobody carries 'lunch money' anymore, idiot." He corrects the taller, stocky boy with the London Fade haircut who grabbed him, then turns to the skinny kid with the spikey, black hair who slammed his locker shut, "and 'Jane'? That's the best you could come up with?" he mocks him as he reaches out and shoves the kid's shoulder. "Now I have to do my friggin' combo again, jackass!"

"Chill out, Dane," urges the stocky kid, "it's the last time you'll ever have to do it! LAST DAY FOR SENIORS!!!" he cheers loudly with his hands raised in the air. He turns and pumps his fist with a huge smile on his face and points to a group of girls gathered at the locker across from them. The girls scoff and turn away with disgust. "Hm, looks like the juniors who have two weeks of school left are a little JEALOUS!" he finishes the sentence loud enough for them to hear, earning him a glare, before they return to their conversation. "Pfft, whatever," he says mockingly, "they won't be getting an invite to 'Gavin's Summer O' Fun'!"

"'Gavin's Summer O' Fun'?" questions Dane, "All you want to do is go up to the Rainier camp site, get shitfaced and pass out in a bush, you've been talking about it for weeks, right Tim?"

"That's exactly what he defines as a 'Summer O' Fun'," says the other boy, making good use of air quotes. "What else would you expect from a 'Summer O' Fun', created by this guy?"

"Summer O' Fun!" Gavin shouts excitedly throwing his fists up in the air again.

"Ok, fine. Can we please stop saying 'Summer O' Fun'?" Dane urges them as he reenters his locker combination and pulls it open for a second time. He pulls out his backpack and begins removing all of the locker's contents and stuffing them into the bag.

Gavin pulls a round can out of the back pocket of his jeans where a faded ring has worn itself into the blue denim and stuffs a wad of chewing tobacco into his lip. "Yeah, we can't get too ambitious just yet," he says through a puffed out bottom lip as he drops a hand on each of the other boys' shoulders and squeezes. "We may be done with school, but we've still got some business to take care of, right boys!?"

"Yeah, the rivals are in town tonight!" Tim chimes with a big smile on his face. "I was talking to coach earlier too and he said if we beat the Hurons tonight we only need to win one more of our last three games to go to districts!"

Dane grabs the last thing out of his locker, an orange pill bottle, off the top shelf and slams the door shut loudly turning to his two friends with a look of determination on his face. "Well, I guess there's only one thing to do then..."

Gavin and Tim are taken aback at Dane's sudden change of demeanor and look at each other nervously, then back to Dane and immediately burst into laughter. Dane's previously tensed shoulders drop and the seriousness in his face fades to a look of disappointment as Gavin gives him a shove, "I love when Dane tries to be serious! It's hilarious!" He laughs with Tim as they turn away from their friend and begin to walk towards the light streaming in the double doors at the end of the hallway.

Dane raises his arms to his sides and shrugs his shoulders, "Hey, I tried...I'll see you guys at the field!" he shouts to his friends. Tim turns and throws his head back in agreement while Gavin just throws up two fingers in a peace sign without turning around. Shaking his head Dane just smiles and turns to walk in the opposite direction, his bag slung over one shoulder. He pushes and maneuvers his way through the hordes of students, some clamoring to empty out their lockers, others standing in small groups with their friends laughing and goofing around, celebrating their newfound freedom. He suddenly turns a corner into an empty hallway and stops realizing that was his last walk through that crowd. He gives a look back over his shoulder to the chaos and the noise, then turns and continues into the silence. Pushing through a heavy door near the end of the hallway, he is bombarded by sunlight. He puts one hand on his forehead like a visor and squints as if he's been kept in dark isolation for years. Once his eyes adjust and the parking lot comes into view he crosses to his old, beat up, grey Saturn. He throws his bag in the back and drops into the drivers' seat, giving the school one last look before speeding off down the winding driveway.

As he turns out of the driveway and heads through downtown towards home he reaches down and turns up the radio. His eyes go wide with excitement and he begins dancing in the driver's seat while rapping along like he's on a concert stage.

"...I am known to do the Wop, WOP! Also known for the Flintstone Flop, FLOP!! Tammy D gettin' biz on the crop, CROP!!! Beat-see Boys, known to let the beat....." he prepares for the big "DROP", suddenly disappointed as the radio cuts out with a loud sustained beep. "What the hell?!?" he shouts as an intense, symphonic tune blares from the speakers, "They cut off the best part!!"

"Breaking news into the newsroom today coming out of Los Angeles." begins the deep voice on the radio as Dane listens on with a confused look on his face. "InCorps, The world's leading drug distributor has issued a massive recall on all distributed medications. Anyone currently taking medications distributed by the company are urged to stop use immediately until more information comes forward. Again, a worldwide recall has been issued for all medications from the medical distribution giant InCorps. Please stay tuned for further updates."

As the radio switches to resume playing music, Dane gazes out the windshield, deep in thought. Suddenly, he reaches blindly behind him feeling his way into his bag and retrieving his orange pill bottle. He gradually pushes down on the brake pedal as he rolls up to a stop light and is able to look down to his hand. He rolls the pill bottle over revealing its label with his name, "Denson, Dane" on top, "Ritalin HCl: Methylphenidate" written in red letters underneath and the large InCorps logo stamped in the upper left-hand corner.

"Shit…" he mutters to himself as he drops the hand holding the bottle into his lap. He turns his eyes out his driver's side window and stares off into the distance as he thinks. With a concerned look, he diverts his attention back to the pill bottle as if to check that he had seen it correctly the first time. Suddenly a loud "HONK!" comes from behind him, snapping him back to reality. He quickly tosses the pill bottle onto the passenger seat, looks up, and guns it through the green light.

At home, Mom is in the kitchen with the makings of a sandwich spread out across the counter. The loud rumble of a bad muffler outside the window over the sink draws her attention as Dane pulls up to the front curb, causing a smile to come over her face. She turns back to pile the turkey and veggies in between two slices of bread, grabbing a knife and cutting it diagonally in half as Dane gets out of his car outside, retrieving his bag from the backseat. He shuts his door and turns to head towards the house but is suddenly startled by a loud bang across the street. He turns quickly to see a backhoe pulling huge heaps of dirt out of the middle of his neighbor's yard and dumping it onto his concrete driveway. Dane raises an eyebrow, then turns back to head up the walkway to the house.

As Dane enters the house, he swings the door shut behind him and takes the quick left into the kitchen, where Mom is stuffing the sandwich into a plastic bag. "Hey, sweetie!" she says with a smile on her face. "How did the last day go?"

Dane throws his bag onto a stool at the counter and props himself up onto the stool next to it. "It was fine," he says offhandedly, obviously distracted. "Did you see that Mr. Logan is getting a pool?"

"Yeah, I heard all of that going on over there. I guess someone's really upgrading their summer plans this year, huh?" She says with a smile. "Maybe he'll let you go over there and use it from time to time before you head off to college!"

Dane gives her a cynical look, "I dunno, he's kinda...lame. He always thinks he's so hilarious."

"Yeah, you're not wrong there, but, for some weird reason, I've always liked the guy." she looks out the window momentarily at the construction in progress, "Well, maybe you can just use it when he's not home then!" she laughs, coaxing a smile out of her son as well.

Dane shakes his head looking down into his lap. His eyes gaze over to his bag and he remembers the radio report in the car. "Hey, did you hear anything about the medication recall?"

Mom stops sealing the Zip-lock bag abruptly and looks up at him, "Recall? On what medication? Yours!?"

"I think so," Dane says calmly, hoping to curb her worry enough that she won't freak out. He reaches over into his bag and digs around blindly. "It's the same company they were talking about on the radio." He pulls the large orange bottle out of the bag next to him and slides it across the counter to her where it hits a groove, falls over and rolls onto the floor.

Mom finishes zipping up the plastic sandwich bag and tosses it on the counter in front of him, "Nice try there, 'Cocktail'," she quips with a smile as she bends down and picks the bottle up off the floor. As she stands, she rolls it over in her hands and looks over the label. "Hmm, InCorps...when did you last take them?"

"Not since this morning. I was going to take one before the game, but then I heard the radio on the way home. They didn't really give any details, just said the company's name." Dane informs his mom of what he knows.

"Alright," she says nervously. "Well don't take any until we know more. I'll turn the news on while you're getting ready and see if they've got any more information. Now, go get ready! This is a big game tonight, right!?" she pulls on the handle of a drawer to her right and pulls out a remote control. She points it towards the TV on the far counter and pushes the power button, causing it to flicker on and glow to life. She begins scanning through seemingly endless channels, looking for the news.

"Yeah, I guess," he mutters. "We'll see if I even play."

"Oh, I'm sure you'll play," Mom encourages quietly, obviously distracted with trying to find a news network on the TV. It finally lands on a man in a suit with well-combed grey hair sitting at a large news desk. She hits the volume button a couple of times and sets the remote on the counter as she returns to cleaning up the ingredients left behind from her sandwich making. "Now go get ready!"

Dane grabs his sandwich off the counter and his bag off the stool next to him and exits the kitchen, heading up the stairs to his room. Mom's attention is drawn back to the television as her cleaning slows down significantly. The banner on the bottom of the screen reads **"MASSIVE RECALL FROM GLOBAL MEDICATION GIANT INCORPS"** while updates troll across the bottom of the screen on a ticker. The grey-haired news anchor continues his reporting as Mom reaches for the control and pushes the volume button a few more times.

"...which is the world's largest commercial drug distributor, are recalling up to 25-30% of the medications that are in the hands of their patients right now. Reports coming in are speculating that, due to a slow-leak incident over the past three to five months at one of the company's main factories, some of the already distributed medications may have been exposed to small amounts of dangerous chemicals. A press release from InCorps has stated that they believe all medications are safe, but precautions must be taken to ensure the safety of their patients. Representatives from the company will be traveling the country over the next two weeks, making stops in all major cities to test currently distributed medications, replacing any that are found to be contaminated."

Mom's eyes are wide with concern for her son as she looks back down to the big orange pill bottle in her hand.

__Chapter 4__

Crowds gather at the baseball field in the middle of town, sitting and standing in the small curb of grass between the field and the road and filling the small section of wooden stands, cheering on their team. On the mound, the Huron's pitcher peers over the tip of his glove at Tim standing ahead of him, bat cocked over his back shoulder, awaiting the pitch. He shifts his gaze down between the knees of his catcher to see the signal for a fastball, nods to confirm the call, and prepares to throw. Gavin, behind him taking a leadoff from second base, claps his hands loudly to attract attention.

"Let's go, Timmy. Bring me in, kid! Little rip, eh!?!" he shouts, then turns his head and shoots a large, brown trail of spit onto the ground next to him.

The pitcher checks the runner at second, then raises his leg up in front of him, turning his head back towards the batter, kicks forward, and winds up the small, white ball behind him. He then launches forward, releasing the ball with all his might towards the catcher's glove. Tim lifts his leg in front of him and pulls the bat even further over his back shoulder preparing to put everything into his swing. As the ball approaches he launches himself and throws his hands forward, sending the barrel of the bat towards the ball. The fastball rises up and to the inside part of the strike-zone and "SMACK", it pops into the catcher's glove as Tim finishes his swing, immediately turning and slamming his bat against the ground in frustration. As he heads off the mound towards the dugout the pitcher grits his teeth and pumps his fist. The deflated crowd groans then gives a slow, supportive clap. Gavin rips off his helmet and slams it with his free hand as he slinks back to the dugout to rejoin his team, which has crowded around their coach in front of the doorway. A look at the scoreboard shows the Eatonville Cardinals ahead by one run over their rival, the Mount Rainier High School Hurons in the seventh and final inning.

After a quick pep talk by their coach followed by a team cheer, the players gather up their gloves and head out to each of their positions, except for Dane. He entered the dugout with his team, but does not leave towards the field as they do. Instead he heads towards the end of the bench and plops down, grabbing a bag of sunflower seeds out of his back pocket and pouring about half the bag into his mouth as he watches his team warmup. Tim stands tall on the mound awaiting the first batter as his teammates chatter behind him for encouragement.

"Let's go, Timmy baby! Let's shut these ladies down! Here we go guys, solid D! Solid D!!" Gavin's voice carries out the loudest from shortstop. With the batter setting himself into the batter's box, Tim confidently steps up onto the white strip of rubber and gazes towards his catcher to get the sign. The catcher goes straight for the two-finger sign for curveball, and Tim agrees nodding his head once.

In the dugout, Dane stands and leans forward, spitting sunflower seeds through the chain-link fence. Tim goes through his wind up and heaves a big, slow, hanging curveball towards the batter, who hitches at the speed of the pitch, then swings anyways, connecting and sending a slow-roller out into the field.

Gavin charges in from shortstop and calls for the ball, diverting the third baseman away as the batter drops his bat and runs a do-or-die sprint towards first. Gavin adjusts his feet, extends his bare hand towards the ground and cleanly scoops up the ball throwing it off-balance towards first base and sprawling to the ground. The ball smacks into the glove simultaneously as the batter's foot stomps on the corner of the base and, for an instant, all is quiet at the field as everyone awaits the call. The umpire emphatically throws his arms out straight at his sides, "SAAAAAAAAAAAAFE!!!!!" he screams loudly as the Huron's dugout explodes and the home team players and fans groan and shout angrily in the direction of the umpire.

"Damn..." Dane slams his open hands against the fence, then turns and sits back down on the bench. The game ahead of him continues, but he is overtaken with boredom. His mind begins to wander. As he watches each shell he spits towards the ground, he begins to see them as meteors hurtling towards a city set ablaze by the disaster.

The game in front of him fades and disappears as the imaginary, fiery rocks rain down from the sky towards the buildings and bridges. People scream and run in all directions seeking shelter. A young girl stands abandoned in the middle of the street crying and looking all around her frantically. "Mommy!!" she screams through her sobs as she looks up towards the sky to see a gigantic, fiery rock dropping straight towards her. "MOMMY!!"

As the scream reverberates through the destruction from street to street, many miles away Dane's ear catches the faint sound and he looks over his shoulder in her direction. He turns quickly, entering a runner's stance and his hands and feet immediately begin to vibrate in their place as if ready to be unleashed. Slowly, he raises his head with an intense glare and instantly disappears.

He speeds through the streets at supersonic levels towards the young girl. The meteor screams ever closer, striking the top of a building and continuing on its destructive path as if nothing had gotten in its way at all. The girl falls to her knees and covers her head preparing for the impact. Dane rounds a corner, sliding to a halt that sends pieces of concrete flying from under his feet. He spots the origin of the scream and the meteor that is only moments away from crushing her. Without hesitation he shoots forward even faster than before, screaming as he reaches his hand out. Fully outstretched and traveling at speeds previously unknown to mankind, he is just about to pull the girl from her sure demise...

"DAMN IT!!" the coach yells, bringing Dane back from his daydream. He slaps his hat against his thigh out of frustration and yells towards the field, "Let's go boys, settle down and focus!" Shaking his head, he replaces his hat and looks across the dugout. "C'mon Dane, get your head in the game, huh?"

In the time Dane has been lost in his imagination Tim had walked the next batter, putting runners on first and second base. Dane stands from the bench and grabs the chain-link fence to display involvement in the game. Tim's next pitch is a big hanging curve that trails down into the strike-zone, drawing a swing from the batter. It strikes the top of the barrel of the bat and shoots high into the air and towards the right side of the field. As the right fielder settles under the pop-up, the runner at second prepares to take off towards third on the catch. The ball pops into the fielder's glove who, without hesitation, grabs it out of the leather and heaves it at full force towards third base in hopes to beat the runner for another out.

The ball bounces in to the third baseman, who catches it on the hop and looks quickly towards second base where the runner has stopped and retreated to safety, but a blood curdling scream shifts everyone's gaze immediately towards right field. The right fielder is lying on his back, holding his right arm against his body as if he were cradling a child. Dane's grip on the fence tightens with fear as he looks on in dismay for his teammate. Without hesitation, coaches, players and umpires rush towards right field.

After a few minutes, the crowd tending to the boy parts and he is lifted to his feet to slowly walk off the field still clutching his arm tight to his body. As he walks past the dugout Dane catches a glimpse of the boy's forearm sitting at an odd angle, both bones having clearly snapped while making the throw.

"Holy shit!" Dane exclaims quietly as he turns away and puts his hand to his mouth to prevent himself from throwing up. He takes a couple of deep breaths, still facing away from the field, then sits on the bench and puts his head in his hands to recover. They lead the player outside of the fence to the passenger seat of a car and rush him away to the hospital.

The coach reenters the dugout, a pale, sick look on his face, "Alright, Dane, you're in. Get out there!" he says in a shaky voice. Dane looks up with his own sick look on his face. "Let's go! We've got a game to win!" the coach urges sternly. Dane urgently grabs the glove off the bench next to him and jogs from the dugout.

"Alright, Dane! Solid D out there kid," Gavin encourages his friend as he jogs through the infield. Dane simply nods, still trying to figure out how to get this disgusting visual out of his head so he can focus on the game.

He arrives at his position in the outfield and takes a couple of deep breaths. Tim steps up onto the mound to face the next batter. He keeps his eye on the runner at second, winds up and pitches. BALL! The catcher tosses it back and Tim resets on the mound, eyes the runner, pitches. BALL! The catcher returns the ball again as Tim catches it angrily with his glove. He curses under his breath, steps back onto the mound and goes through his routine again. BALL! He takes his hat off his head and runs his fingers through his matted down hair cursing in frustration. After a couple of deep breaths, he returns his cap to his head and steps up on the mound to redeem himself. He checks the runner, kicks, throws. BALL! The runner confidently makes his way over to first base, tossing the bat towards the dugout on his way past as the crowd groans.

As the next batter approaches, Tim curses himself under his breath and the crowd increases their cheering to get their team back into it. Dane looks on from right field, hands on his knees, awaiting some action. No action would occur during the next batter as Tim would duel with the kid to finally strike him out after eleven pitches. With bases loaded and only one out left to get the win, Tim digs his foot into the dirt in front of the white rubber strip and turns to face his final opponent. Once he gets his signal, Tim heaves the ball and the batter doesn't move. STRIKE! As the ball returns to the mound, they both prepare once again. The pitch comes in towards the heart of the plate enticing the batter to swing, then drops at the last second. STRIKE!

"Let's go, one more strike Timmy!" Gavin shouts through his wad of chew.

The next couple of pitches would miss the plate while Dane continues to stand, prepared, with his hands on his knees...

One more fastball comes in hopes of striking the last batter out and winning the game. The ball approaches the plate as the batter's eyes go wide and he puts everything he has into a swing. "TINK!!" The aluminum bat solidly connects with the ball and sends it screaming out into right field. Dane is jolted into action as he turns and runs towards the fence, tracking the ball over his shoulder the entire way. Realizing he is approaching the outfield wall, he leaps and stretches his glove high above him in a final ditch effort to save the game, and...POP! The ball smacks into the webbing of his glove! Dane squeezes tightly onto the ball and closes his eyes, bracing to hit the fence, but no impact occurs. After a couple of seconds, he slowly opens his eyes and looks upwards. He sees his outstretched glove gripping the baseball with the sky behind it, but shifting his eyes downward, he suddenly realizes the reason the collision never happened. He is IN the sky!! He is flying!!

He looks down to see the field far below him, everyone standing silently and staring up at him in awe. He pulls his hand down to grab the ball from his glove, causing him to slow to a stop and float in midair. Still confused, he retrieves the ball with his free hand and rolls it around, then glances down at the baseball field below. With an excited smile he reaches out the ball towards the field, propelling himself downward as he screams "WOOOOOOOOOOOOO HOOOOOOOOOOOO!!!"

As he approaches the grass of the outfield he angles the ball up sending him shooting only a couple of feet above the ground. He flies within inches of Tim, brushing him back a couple of steps before exiting the field and shooting up towards the clouds. The entire crowd and field is silent as he disappears into the distance. Tim then looks down into his glove and sees the ball. Confused but excited, he grabs it with his bare hand and holds up into the air as he screams, "YEEEEAHHHHHHHH!!!!!!" The crowd sees his reaction and explodes into cheers as his teammates charge the mound and begin celebrating with him.

By this time Dane is miles away, flying at amazing speeds, ducking and dodging clouds as he laughs and screams with excitement. Breaking through the top of the clouds the sunlight hits him. He closes his eyes and is enjoying the wind hitting his face...

"TINK!!"

Dane is startled as the batter's swing connects with the ball. He is jolted back to reality once again and realizes the ball is headed in his direction, but was not hit as well as the one in his daydream. He springs forward towards the pop up as the runners begin to round the bases at full speed. He keeps focused on the ball as he plants his foot, grits his teeth, and thrusts himself forward through the air. With his glove out at full extension towards the ball, he closes his eyes and, "SMACK!!"

With his body now at rest in the grass, Dane opens his eyes and sees the ball lying in the grass about five feet from his glove. His stomach drops as the center fielder arrives to pick up the ball and heave it in towards home plate. Unfortunately, the second runner crosses well before the ball arrives and the Hurons begin to celebrate their win. Dane buries his face in the grass and curses at himself as his teammates slowly sulk towards the dugout. Dane pushes himself to his feet and pulls his hat down over his face.

As he jogs in towards his team he catches a glimpse of a beautiful blonde girl in the crowd that he hadn't been able to see from the dugout. She talks sullenly with her friends, obviously upset by the outcome of the game, as Dane hangs his head in disappointment and misses the sympathetic gaze her bright blue eyes send his way.

After a deflated post-game team meeting, Dane gathers up his equipment in his bag and heads towards his car quickly to avoid ridicule from his friends. He throws his bag in the backseat and climbs in and stares out the front window for a moment. He pulls his hat off his head and runs his fingers through his brown hair then looks down at his hands, which are shaking slightly after all the excitement.

"Man, that was weird…" he says to himself as he returns his hat to his head and rubs his fingers into his eyes. He breathes heavily again reaching down to the shifter, puts the car in drive and speeds away towards home.

At home, Mom has been glued to the TV to get as much information about the recall as possible when Dane slumps in the door and tosses his bag on the floor loudly. He immediately heads towards the stairs without acknowledging his mom on the couch in the living room.

"Hey kiddo, how'd the game go?" She asks, finally taking her eyes off the TV. "Did you guys win?"

"No, we lost by one." he sulks, stopping on the first stair. Hoping this is the end of the conversation he turns back to the stairs and begins to climb again.

"Hey!" Mom manages to stop him one more time as she turns down the TV volume. "Are you alright, sweetie? Did something happen?"

"Well…" he hesitates, "Collin broke his arm. I saw it, it was disgusting. I still feel a little nauseous." he lies trying to keep the talk as short as possible so he can retreat to his room.

"Oh my god, that's terrible!" she gets up from the couch and walks over to console him at the bottom of the stairs. She reaches over the railing and brushes off the grass-stained front of his jersey and smiles. "I see you got some playing time!" Dane is not amused and shrugs as he pulls his hat lower over his face. "Well, go get cleaned up and relax for a bit and you can sleep in tomorrow since it's your first day of summer!"

"Ok, I think I'm just going to go to bed now, so I'll see you tomorrow." Dane says as he climbs the stairs.

"Alright, sweetie." Mom utters quietly, then attempts to stop him one more time. "OH! I found out more about your medicine. We can talk about it tomorrow, just don't take it for now and let me know if you start to feel crappy, ok?"

"Got it." Dane says over his shoulder without stopping, then disappears into the darkness upstairs. Mom stands at the bottom of the stairs looking up with worry in her eyes, then shifts her gaze back to the TV which displays footage of people in lab coats being led out of a large building by men in yellow Hazmat suits and the heading ***"INCORPS RECALL: LABS BEING EVACUATED ACROSS THE COUNTRY"*** emblazoned across the bottom. Mom quickly makes her way back to the couch, pulling both feet underneath her and covers her mouth as she turns up the volume.

Chapter 5

The weekend passes and Sunday morning finds Dane slumped into the couch concurrently flipping through channels on the TV and playing games on his cell phone. Still unsure of what had happened at the baseball game and upset by the outcome, he hadn't left the house all weekend. Even Mom's sporadic updates about his medication recall have drawn minimal response from him. She had done her best to let him relax on his first couple of days off from school while keeping herself updated as more news came in. She walks into the living room with a big bowl of tortilla chips and sets them on the table in front of him.

"You ok, sweetie?" She asks, pulling his eyes away from his cell phone. "You haven't said much all weekend..."

He tosses the phone onto the cushion next to him and picks up the remote, looking away towards the television. "Yeah, I'm fine."

"Dane, I've known you for a little while. 'Fine' is Dane-ish for 'Not Fine, But I Don't Want To Talk About It'." she urges him. "You sure you're feeling ok without taking your pills?"

Dane had not told her about the daydreaming or his shaky hands afterwards because he didn't want her to get worried. He had also not had either of the symptoms since, so he had all but dismissed them at this point.

"Yeah, I'm ok. I promise." he encourages her. "I dunno, I just wanna be lazy for a couple of days."

"Alright, well InCorps is sending reps to all the major cities to do tests on peoples' medications starting tomorrow, so I'll have to go in to Seattle for a little bit, but hopefully they'll be ok and you can start taking them again." she assures him, hoping to get a response. After a moment, she leans into his view of the television, "Do you need anything for now?"

"No, I'm fine..." He senses a glare from her. He looks over and gets confirmation, instantly backpedaling, "I mean, I'm good, I promise. Thanks." A small smirk breaks through the side of his mouth.

She sends a smile back, "That's better. I'll be doing some writing in my office if you need me to help cut off those roots you're growing." She reaches out and runs her hand through his hair lovingly, then turns and exits the room. Dane returns to channel surfing, but is suddenly startled by a loud "BANG" from outside. He stands and makes his way to the window curiously. Across the street he now sees a large cement truck parked on his neighbor's lawn pouring cement into the huge hole that was dug over the previous two days. A second truck is parked out on the street and workers push dollies of crates up his driveway and stack them alongside the house. "I wish we were getting a pool." Dane utters under his breath as he heads back over to the couch, grabs a handful of chips and plops back down. As soon as he's settled on a TV show his phone vibrates and lights up. He looks at it from the corner of his eye then hesitantly grabs it and presses the power button, seeing a text from Gavin. He enters his password and opens the text.

Incoming Text: Gavin - Mountain Time, Bitch!!!

"Ugh, great!" Dane utters, rolling his eyes then swipes his thumb around the screen.

Outgoing Text: Not feeling so great...you'll have to do mountain time without me

After a few seconds, his phone vibrates and lights up again.

Incoming Text: Gavin – Still off the meds? You've been a hermit all weekend

Outgoing Text: Yeah, getting them checked tomorrow...we'll see.

Incoming Text: Gavin - Well, you kinda owe us for losing the game the other day, but it's all good ;)

Dane rolls his eyes as he reads.

Outgoing Text: Right, thanks for reminding me. Later

He sighs as he tosses the phone back onto the couch and turns back to the TV. After flipping through a few pages on the Channel Guide he doesn't see anything that interests him and tosses the remote to the side as well. After a moment, he looks over at his phone, sighs, and picks it up flipping open the cover and swiping his thumb around the screen again.

Outgoing Text: On my way!

He closes the case and shoves it into his pocket as he heads up to his room to get ready.

Dane pulls up to the parking lot of the Mt. Rainier National Park identifying a couple of his friends' cars and finds his own space to park. He turns the car off and gazes out the windshield ahead of him at the trail that leads to the camping site where they usually meet and sees the beautiful blonde girl from the baseball game walking and laughing with a couple of her girlfriends.

"Sherri...shit." He curses under his breath nervously as he looks down. In his lap, his hands are shaking once again. Bewildered, he holds them up in front of himself and rotates them, studying them as if he had never had hands before. He cups them together tightly, then shakes them out, but the involuntary trembling doesn't subside. It had gone away last time, so he decides to ignore it and unbuckles his seatbelt, once more glancing up at the girls walking up the path. "Shit...ok, here we go." he pep talks himself as he forces his arm to throw open his door and exit the car to go meet his friends.

A little ways up the trail a bonfire blazes high in the middle of a campsite as groups of young boys and girls gather around it, some roasting marshmallows in the flames, others standing in groups drinking from cans of beer and laughing. Dane stands off to the side with Gavin, Tim and a few other guys, but his eyes keep shifting towards the large log next to the fire where Sherri is seated with a couple of her friends.

Gavin reaches over in Dane's direction and snaps his fingers twice in his face. "DUDE! We losing you again? I said kill that beer, we're all doing a Jell-O shot!"

"Oh, sorry." Dane apologizes shaking his head, then throws his head back letting the cold beer shoot down his throat.

"At least this time it didn't cost us a baseball game!" he laughs with his friends as he punches Dane softly in the chest causing him to spit out a little of the beer he had just chugged. He grabs the can out of Dane's hand and tosses it off into the bushes, then hands him a small plastic cup filled with green Jell-O.

"Ha Ha, friggin' hilarious!" Dane says sarcastically once he's swallowed. He looks at the shot in his hand and notices it shaking around, even more than before and quickly grabs his wrist with his other hand in hopes of calming it down.

Tim hoists his shot cup in the air leading everyone else to follow suit, "Cheers fellas. Here's to the 'Summer O' Fun'!"

Dane laughs, "Oh, Jesus, 'Summer O' Fun' again? Really!?"

"SUMMER O' FUN!!!!" the boys all exclaim in unison and proceed to throw back their shots. His head tilted back, the cold Jell-O hits the back of Dane's mouth. He opens his eyes to the sky and sees large, fiery meteors falling in all directions. Startled, he almost chokes on the shot and immediately drops to his knees covering his head with his hands. After a second, realizing he hasn't been engulfed in a terrible explosion of fire, Dane opens his eyes and looks upward. The pit of his stomach drops as he sees no meteors, only five guys looking down at him with confused looks on their face as they finish swallowing their shots. He slowly stands up looking around the group and smiles nervously, "Um, strong shot!" he jokes, hoping to avoid any ridicule.

The boys look around at each other as Gavin reaches out and grabs Dane's shoulder and squeezes, "You're such a pussy, dude! We gotta get you out here more often, toughen you up!" he jokes creating a laugh among the group.

Dane joins in the laugh and shakes his way out of his friends' grip. He reaches into a cooler to grab another beer and glances across the clearing towards the bonfire, catching Sherri's gaze. He freezes and looks away nervously, but his eyes wander back one more time, catching another glance from the young girl. As he reaches to pry open the beer he realizes the can is shaking all over the place. He steadies it with his other hand and slowly works his fingers onto the tab to pop it open. Unsurprisingly, it explodes in all directions and white foam comes pouring out of the mouth. As he looks at the puffy, white foam, he suddenly finds himself in the sky again ducking and dodging through the clouds, rolling up and down in the bright sunlight like a bird with the speed of a fighter jet...

"I don't think you're supposed to shake them up first!" a small, melodic voice startles him, bringing him back down to earth. "Sorry, I didn't mean to sneak up on you!"

"Sherri! No, no, it's fine." he says nervously, still holding his wrist with his other hand to steady it. "So, uh, what's up? What's going on?"

"Nothing really!" she says with a bubbly smile, her bright blue eyes shine in the natural sunlight. She tucks her curly blonde hair behind her ear as she reaches down and grabs a LaCroix from the cooler. "Just chauffeuring for a bunch of drunk high school girls all night...SAT's in the morning."

"That sucks!" Dane spouts emphatically, doing his best to hide his distraction, but he keeps glancing down at his left hand holding tightly onto his right wrist so the beer doesn't splash out of the can. "Where did you, uh, say you were going? Like, for school next year?"

"Well, that's the thing. I got accepted to State already, but I'm trying to get into George Washington, so I had to schedule another SAT appointment for tomorrow morning." she gives him a nervous half smile. "I need to add another two hundred points to my score or there's no hope, and drinking doesn't necessarily have a positive impact on the awesome all-nighter I have planned for myself tonight!" she jokes sarcastically bringing the cute, crooked smile back to her face. "What about you, I don't think you've told me what you're doing!"

"I haven't!? That's weird!" Dane acts surprised, knowing full well that he has actively avoided Sherri since the second grade. The shaking in his hand is slowly getting worse, so he grips his wrist as tight as he can to keep it wrangled. "I'm just doing CC first, Green River. Lucky me gets to live at home for a couple more years..."

"No! That's great!" she tries to comfort him. "You'll save money not having an apartment, it's close so the commute will be easy...and I'm sure your mom's happy she'll still have someone home with her for a couple more years..." she trails off as if she had misspoken.

Suddenly, Dane's hand shakes out of his own grip causing him to drop his beer. Hitting the ground it shoots upward like a fountain between them, causing Sherri to jump back. Dane looks up at her with surprise and embarrassment.

"Dane, I didn't mean…anything about your dad, I just…" Sherri begins to apologize.

"No, no, no! I, uh," Dane's eyes dart around as he avoids looking at the young girl. "I've gotta go!" He looks into her bright blue eyes one more time, then turns and darts up a dirt trail behind him.

"No, Dane!" Sherri reaches after him taking a step forward. "I'm…I'm sorry." She finishes the sentence under her breath as Dane passes through the trees and out of sight. She looks sadly up the trail and breathes out a big sigh, brushing the beer droplets off her sundress and slowly turning to rejoin her friends.

Dane stumbles a few hundred feet up the trail away from his group, his vigorously shaking hands finding a large boulder to hold onto. As he rests against the rock, he finds himself unable to breathe, pain in his temples begins to accompany flashes of his daydreams and a feeling of being underwater, thrashing and fighting for air. He bends forward to put his head in his hands and rocks back and forth, gripping his head tightly as if to squeeze out the pain. The pain and his gasping for air worsens and he lets out a desperate scream that carries into the trees and disappears into the distance.

And then, with one final bright, green flash in the midst of his scream it all stops. Still bent over gripping his head, he slowly sits upright and inches his hands away to uncover his eyes. He cautiously begins to look around, then down at his hands, which have completely stopped shaking. Confused, he peers up through the trees at the snow-covered mountain top, then back again to his surroundings. It's gone. He feels totally normal. Was he daydreaming again? He waits a couple of minutes just to be safe, and realizes that whatever had happened, it wasn't coming back just yet. He lifts himself up and begins walking back to his group, still unsure what to think.

Giving one final, confused look back at the boulder he continues and disappears towards the campsite. Suddenly, a squirrel appears out of the woods and runs across the trail. Sniffing around the bottom of the boulder, it abruptly perks up nervously and looks around. A low rumble sends it darting away into the woods and a small crack appears in the ground behind the boulder emitting a glowing, green light.

Chapter 6

Monday morning, Dane is sound asleep in his room. Mom peeks in to check on him before she heads in to the Seattle doctor's office to have his medicine tested. He had come home the previous night without hardly a word to her and had been sound asleep since. With one last concerned look at him, she quietly closes the door and heads down the stairs to the front walkway, stopping only to grab her purse, keys and Dane's orange pill bottle off the table from next to a picture of a young man standing tall and steadfast in an Army uniform. She locks the door behind her, hops in her car and speeds away towards the city.

Dane, hearing her car door slam, slowly sits up in bed and rubs his eyes then stretches his way through a huge yawn. He squints his eyes towards the window, which is allowing in a bright stream of sunlight onto the floor in the middle of the room. He lazily rolls himself out of the bed grabbing a hoody off the closet doorknob and throws it over his head as he makes his way out of the room and downstairs. Grabbing the remote control off the coffee table, he points it at the TV screen, hits the power button and tosses it onto the couch along with his phone and makes his way to the kitchen for some breakfast. As he pulls a box of Cinnamon Toast Crunch out of the cupboard, the sound of a news program on the TV resonates from the living room.

"...the increasing amount of seismic activity over the years in the areas around Mt. Rainier reminding us all that it is an active stratovolcano and leading some to believe that we might be due for an increase in small rumblings from our gentle giant, but what about the possibility of an eruption? Though this is something that has not occurred since 1894 when multiple small explosions at the mountain's summit alarmed people of the surrounding areas, but caused no damage or casualties, our scientists say it is not out of the question to believe it could happen again and that we could, in fact, be overdue."

Dane reenters the living room while scooping an overloaded spoonful of cereal into his mouth, dripping milk down his chin and focuses his gaze to the news program on the TV. By the time he reaches the couch and plops down the report has changed over to a story about a yellow lab that helps old people cross the streets in downtown Seattle. "Ugh, such stupid stuff all the time." Dane utters to himself as he reaches for the remote, noticing the blue notification light on his phone blinking. Leaving the remote where it is, he grabs his phone and opens it up to see a text message from Mom. He unlocks it and views the message.

Incoming Text: Mom - Headed into Seattle, left 1 pill in your bathroom in case they're ok. Will text soon!

Dane runs his thumb around the keyboard on the screen

Outgoing Text: Ok, thanks. Don't text and drive :P

He stands and walks over to the window, gazing across the street to his neighbor's house, where contractors are spread out around the top of the pool, some measuring, some hauling equipment and boxes down into the open hole. Mr. Logan stands on the far left edge pointing at blueprints being held by another contractor and giving orders to the men. The phone vibrates in his hand, startling him.

Incoming Text: Mom - I sent that before I left, smartass. Besides it's bumper to bumper right now. Could be a while. I'll let you know

Outgoing Text: Ok

Dane sends his response and returns to his spot on the couch with his cereal and begins flipping through channels.

After a few hours in traffic, Mom pulls into a parking spot across from the doctor's office in Seattle. She puts the car in park and looks out her driver's side window towards the big building to see a line of people all the way out onto the sidewalk. "Ugggggh, dammit!" she utters, immediately assuming she'll be there all day. She reluctantly shuts off the car and exits to feed the meter with as much time as it will allow, then makes her way across the street to get in line.

After an hour and a half of spaced-out shuffle steps she has finally made it to the entrance of the office lobby. A nurse stands in the doorway, a tired smile on her face, reaching into a large, unmarked box with every person that files past her. As mom approaches, the young nurse flashes her a smile, reaches into the box and hands her a white bottle. "We're so sorry for the inconvenience. Thank you for your patience." she recites as if it's already the one millionth time she's said it, and Mom thinks to herself that it very well might be. She rolls the bottle in her hand to view the label, emblazoned with "InCorps: Super Multivitamin" and chuckles at the name, stuffing it into her purse

The spacious waiting room is packed wall to wall with annoyed-looking people and kids, some of whom are sleeping on their parents while others entertain themselves with cell phones. She files in slowly with the others in line and comes into view of the receptionist's window where a couple of nicely dressed, overweight ladies are organizing seemingly endless amounts of paperwork. Behind them, men and women in white coats bustle around with charts, already looking exhausted. Suddenly, a woman comes into view that she recognizes. She takes a step closer, "Judy?!" The receptionist looks up through her dark framed bifocals with surprise.

"Hey! What are you doing here?" she asks with an overabundance of happiness, which fades quickly to concern, "Oh no, is it Dane's meds?"

"Yeah, just playing it safe. What are you doing here?" Mom inquires.

"They called all the surrounding area doctor's offices for extra help for the next two weeks while they're running all the tests for the recall," she says with a stressed look on her face that quickly switches to a smile, "I'm getting time and a half plus using my PTO in Eatonville!!"

"Wow, that's great! Looks like they definitely need it," Mom motions to the chaos behind the receptionist.

"Yeah, it's been pretty crazy all morning." Judy rolls her eyes, "luckily all of the medications have come back negative so far, so it's been a lot quicker than expected. Hey..." she stops and takes a look around at the other receptionists and doctors, "Lemme see Dane's pills. I'll push you through to the next round of tests, get you outta here a little quicker!"

"Really?! Are you sure?" Mom looks around at all the other people in the waiting room, then back to Judy. "I mean, that would be amazing, but I don't want to get you in trouble."

"It's fine, I promise." Judy assures her. "They're so scatterbrained back here they'll never know."

Mom pulls the pill bottle out of her pocket and sets her purse on the counter as an obstruction, quickly slipping the pill bottle behind it. As soon as it hits the counter Judy folds it into a chart and pulls it behind the window. "Thank you so much, Judy! You're a life saver!"

"Think nothing of it, they brought me here to help right!?" Judy confidently shoots her a smile. "It should be less than an hour and they'll call you back."

"Thank you!" Mom graciously smiles at her and turns to hopefully find an open chair somewhere in the waiting room.

Behind the window, Judy walks the pill bottle in the chart back through the hallways of the doctor's office. She approaches a small wooden transfer window on a wall and gives a quick look each way as if she were crossing a street. She pulls the door open to reveal 4 other pill bottles and quickly adds Dane's to the mix, closing the door and heading back towards her reception area.

About a minute and a half later, two nurses come by gossiping loudly as they open the door and take the medications out. They put them on a metal tray and head towards the waiting room, stopping at a small fold-out table containing about 50 other bottles of medication. They set the bottles on the table and head back down the hallway, chatting and giggling as they go. After a few minutes, a doctor appears from a nearby room and approaches the table with a clipboard. His six-foot-five frame seems like it should be lanky and awkward, but his broad shoulders hold up his large, square-shaped head strongly making him look even taller than he is. Adjusting his dark framed glasses, he takes a seat at the table and begins organizing the names from the pill bottles onto a sheet marked "Clean/Return to Patient"

In the waiting room, Mom has lost track of how many times she's seen the doctor come out, announce names and take groups of people back, but every time he lurched through the doorway she thought he looked more and more like he would make a great Bond villain. Assuming she will probably see him another ten times or more she works slowly through a People magazine and doesn't even acknowledge his presence the next time he lurches through the doorway.

"...Denson, Dane..." the man belts over the patiently-waiting crowd, catching Mom by surprise. She stands quickly, setting her magazine on the table next to her, and heads towards the door with the other people he had called. As they get through the doorway, the doctor has a seat behind the table and sets 10 pill bottles out in front of the group.

"Alright, thank you all for coming today," the doctor avoids eye contact with any of them as he begins speaking very robotically, obviously having done this routine quite a few times today. "Looks like this group is all good. Go ahead and grab your medications, you can resume taking them immediately without any worry of contamination. InCorps would like to apologize immensely for the inconvenience and any worry this has caused. We greatly appreciate your business and would like you to know we are taking any and all steps necessary to right the current situation and ensure that it never happens again." He looks up at the group for the first time, "Thank you, and have a great day."

The group all make their way to the table and pick up the pill bottles with their respective names on them. A few of the people head towards the door, but some linger, seemingly confused by the situation.

"Wait, so that's it!?" A large, balding man with his daughter at his side exclaims with frustration. "My daughter has been off her medication for 3 days waiting for you guys to get here. This is a serious situation and you're just going to say 'Sorry, have a nice day'!?"

A couple others begin to show their anger as well causing the doctor to stand, towering above everyone in the room, and attempt to calm them down. Not wanting to take part in the scene that was escalating Mom looks at the pill bottle in her hand and works her way towards the door from which she had just come. On her way through the waiting room she sees Judy behind the window and waves, mouthing the words "Thank you!" to her. Judy simply smiles and waves at her.

As she exits through the front door she peers down the sidewalk, noticing that the line is now three times as ong as it was when she had gotten there. Relieved, she crosses the street and hops in her car. She pulls her phone out of her purse and types a text.

Outgoing Text: Meds are A-OK!

Back home, Dane's phone vibrates and lights up as he gets her message. After reading it he heads upstairs to take the pill she had left him. He flips on the bathroom light, which shines across the small white pill on the counter displaying an evanescent hint of green. He tosses the pill into the back of his mouth and angles his head under the faucet to get a small amount of water in his mouth, swallows it down and returns downstairs to continue watching TV. As he reaches for the remote his phone vibrates and lights up again.

Incoming Text: Mom - Get off your butt and do something...

Dane lets out a huge sigh and rolls his eyes. He grabs the remote and powers the TV off then reluctantly pushes himself up off the couch. "I swear she's got a camera somewhere in this place." he grumbles to himself as he grabs his phone off the couch cushion, sends her a quick "K" and heads up to his bedroom. He steps in the doorway of his room to be greeted by clothes, food wrappers, Pepsi cans and more displayed in a very post-tornado fashion. He tiptoes through the mess to his computer and opens up his ITunes, clicking on his favorite Yellowcard album. With a sigh, he takes one final look around and begins tackling the mess one shirt at a time.

In the small, isolated shack Kurrt stands in the middle of the equipment-cluttered room, shoulders hunched and head down. The only sound that can be heard is the whistle of the blistering cold wind sneaking through the cracks in the wooden walls and tin roof.

"He's accomplished so much in his career, there is really nowhere to go but down," he whispers quietly, taking a deep breath in that raises his shoulders, then out as he hunches back downward and goes silent. "This will end it all..." He slowly swings his arms to the right, then back through to the left creating a small thud that sends a small white golf ball rolling steadily across the wooden floor boards towards a tipped over water glass against the wall. As it approaches, his eyes go wide and he clutches his fists preparing to celebrate. At the last second the ball strikes a slightly protruding nail and veers to the right clinking off the rim of the glass.

"GAHHHHHH, DAMMIT!!!" Kurrt drops the putter and shakes his fists into the air with frustration. Just then the walkie talkie crackles, diverting his attention.

"Come in Kurrt, status report," the female voice says sternly. "What are we looking at?"

Kurrt throws his head back and lets out a sigh as he slinks his way over to the desk. He plops down in the chair and grabs the walkie, bringing it up to his mouth. "A pot on the stove, that's what you're looking at! I'm telling you, nothing's changing up here...no boil."

"Don't get cute, Kurrt." the woman scolds.

"Hehe, cute Kurrt..." he chuckles to himself.

"Just send us the data for the week and your final assessments of the area. I wanted to inform you..." Kurrt's eyes go wide and he cuts her off.

"Wait, did you say final assessments?" Kurt has a sudden liveliness to his voice.

"Yes...as I was saying, I wanted to inform you that you're being removed from Mt. Rainier and reassigned. We should be able to have you back to the facility in 3 days." she informs him.

Kurrt throws his fists up in the air again, this time emphatically with happiness and starts dancing around the room as the woman continues.

"We will just need your final report today, then for you to continue your normal monitoring of the area. As normal, any fluctuations in the data must be reported over those 3 days and you are to gather your things and prepare for your extraction..." she goes quiet waiting for his response. Kurrt is on the other side of the room dancing and kicking the tall machine next to the bathroom door that has given him so many issues. "KURRT! Do you copy?!"

He stops his celebration with an annoyed look on his face, raises his hand in front of him with his middle finger up in the direction of the walkie talkie and heads back towards it. "Copy, 10-4, roger that. Yes, I got it...Over, and OUT!!" he shouts with excitement and makes his way back to spinning around the room with his hands over his head, laughing and cheering.

Chapter 7

"Bring on the college chicks!!!!" Gavin shouts with a huge smile as he lunges down and flexes a bicep across his body. Behind him, Tim stands tall pointing his fingers in a Usain Bolt sort of stance. Ahead, kneeling in the grass, Mom laughs and snaps pictures of them goofing off in their graduation gowns in front of the house. They change poses a couple of times as she continues to shoot, then Tim stops for a second, "Where the hell is Dane?" Mom lowers the camera from her face and looks up to his window with a smile.

In the upstairs bathroom, Dane is struggling to adjust the collar of the shirt underneath his gown. As he becomes frustrated and gives up he hears Mom shout through his open bedroom window. "DAAANE!! Let's go, get a move on!!"

"YEAH DANE, MOVE YOUR ASS...sorry Miss Denson." shouts Gavin.

Dane chuckles and shouts back, "CHILL OUT, I'M COMING DOWN NOW!" Leaving his crooked collar, he fits his cap onto his head and grabs his pill bottle from next to the sink. He shakes a little white pill into his hand and throws it back. He had felt much better in the week that has passed since he started taking his medication again. The daydreams have subsided and he has had a little more energy, though he had still avoided going out as much as possible. With one more quick look in the mirror he throws his draping sleeve across his nose like a caped crusader. "So stupid..." he says with a laugh and takes off down the stairs. As he reaches the landing he sees that his friends are now inside running around the living room as they laugh and joke. Entering the room with a smile on his face he realizes that they are actually playing with an action figure, flying it around the room and tossing it back and forth. His smile fades as he realizes it is the same action figure that Mom had thrown away at parent teacher conferences 11 years earlier.

"Oh, save me Captain Awesome!!" Gavin shrieks in a high pitched woman's voice as he cowers behind the couch. "You may be super small, but I've always believed it's not about size, it's how you use it!"

"You are correct my dear," Tim bellows while holding the action figure up in front of him and moving its arms as if it were talking. "I shall save you from the clutches of the evil Couch Blob and we shall retire to my hidden lair so I can prove it to you! WHOOSH!!" He tosses the figure at the couch like a dart while providing the flying sounds.

"HEY!!" Dane shouts as he enters the room and quickly makes his way to the couch to retrieve the toy. His friends have smiles on their faces as he picks it up and looks it over for damage.

"Dude, Couch Blob? What kind of bad guy is that?!" Gavin jokes with Tim, who can only shrug and smile. "I didn't even know you were into action figures, Dane. You hiding a nerdy side from us all these years?"

"No, I'm not...I mean, not anymore." Dane has a confused look on his face as he rolls the figure over in his hands. "I actually didn't even know I still had this..."

"I found it in the cabinet drawer." Tim points to the entertainment center that houses the TV. "Your mom needed another memory card for her camera. You alright dude?" He reaches out and puts his hand on Dane's shoulder.

"Yeah...sorry. It's just...my dad got it for me before I was born..." Dane trails off, then snaps himself out of his thoughts and smiles nervously at his friends, whose demeanors have changed entirely.

Mom bursts through the open front door breaking the awkward silence, "DANE, what's the holdup!? You've gotta be to the school in 15 minutes and I don't have a single picture of my own son in his graduation gown! Let's go!! Move, move, move!" Dane stuffs the action figure into his oversized gown pocket as she ushers the 3 boys out the door to the front yard stopping only to forcefully fix Dane's collar.

After she has shot a multitude of pictures of the three friends, they gather up all their stuff and rush to Gavin's car parked on the front curb. "Dane, hold up a second." She holds him back from his friends and embraces tightly. "I want you to know that you've done such a great job pulling things together over the years and I'm very proud of you," she chokes up for a second as tears well up in her eyes. "and I know your dad would be too. He'd disguise it by cracking ridiculous jokes the whole time, but I know he would be."

"I know Mom," Dane hugs his mom in comfort, "I wish he were here…"

"Me too sweetie." As she pulls back from the hug, Dane pulls the action figure out of his pocket and looks back into his mom's eyes for an answer. "I had to go back and get it…I know how much it meant to you." She smiles through the tears. "You're my real-life superhero, Dane."

Dane looks down to the figure in his hands to hide his tears. With a big sigh, he looks back up to her, "Thanks, Mom."

He reaches out to hand it to her, but she pushes it back with an open palm. "Keep it. That way he'll be with you today." she says with a loving smile. He reciprocates her smile as he stuffs it into his pants pocket under his gown, turns and runs towards the car where his friends are waiting.

"Jesus, dude, did she change your diaper too?!" Gavin razzes him as he climbs into the car, not thinking Mom can hear him, then flashes her a huge smile. "Bye Miss Denson, we'll see you soon! Did I mention how lovely you look today?" She lets out a laugh and waves as the car guns away from the curb and down the street.

"3 days...that bitch. She told me 3 days..."

Kurrt sits on the floor of the wooden shack spinning the walkie talkie in his hands, staring intently as he waits for the device to make a noise. The luggage on the floor around him has been opened and some of the clothes and food that had once been neatly packed are now strewn about the floor. It has been nearly a week since he has heard the woman's voice on the other end.

"I can't believe I didn't see this coming..." he continues talking to himself while shaking his head, the anger swelling up inside of him. He sets the walkie talkie on the floor in front of him and runs his hands over his face and through his hair and lays his head back against wood behind him. He closes his eyes letting out a sigh and slowly grips his hands into fists so hard in front of him that they begin to shake. "This is RIDICULOUS!!!" he shouts thrusting his head back against the wall in anger, but catches a jagged nail sticking out of the wood slicing a deep gash into the back of his head. "GAHHHH, dammit!!" he screams in pain immediately reaching up to cover it with his hands as he brings his head between his knees. After a few seconds of moaning, he sits upright and brings his hands in front of his face slowly, seeing them covered in blood. "Son of a BITCH!!" he shouts as he returns his hand to his head to apply pressure, pushes himself off the floor and moves quickly to the bathroom.

He turns the knobs on either side of the shower faucet and ducks his head under the spewing water to wash the blood away from the wound. As the water rushes over his head and he continues to scream obscenities he is unable to hear the beeping from the computer at his desk begin to quicken. On the screen, the green shape of the mountain begins to pulse inward, lightly at first, then more intensely, pushing the glow towards the center of the map.

"Ugh, not another one mom!!" Dane sighs with frustration as his mom motions with her hands for everyone to pack in tightly, then ducks behind her camera. A group of about 10 of Dane's classmates squeeze in tight, arms around each other and huge smiles on their faces as she snaps a few pictures. As soon as she releases her finger from the camera, most of the kids disperse in different directions, laughing and joking with each other and finding their families. As Dane turns from his friends to head towards his mom, he stops short realizing she is being hugged by someone in a long, silver gown. "Dammit..." Dane's nervousness builds up inside of him, the sunshine shimmering off the girl's golden hair as if to taunt him. He forces his feet to continue on their intended path and, as he approaches, Mom and Sherri separate with big smiles on their faces.

"I'm so proud of you guys. You'll all have to keep in touch this next year and let Dane know when you're back in town!" she encourages with one hand on Sherri's arm. "Oh, Dane, hi sweetie! I just told Sherri that maybe you can go over and help her dad load up the heavy stuff when she goes to college later this summer!"

Dane forces a nervous smile, "Yeah, uh, for sure!"

"Ugh, that would be so great." Sherri brushes his arm with her hand causing Dane's synapses to fire all the way down into his toes. "He's been giving me such a hard time about moving away. It would probably ease his mind a little to have some help."

"For sure!" Dane winces realizing he had already said that. "Uh, hey, do you want to get a picture?"

"Yeah! Cool! Let me just get rid of my hat." Sherri bounces away towards her mom and hands her the square mortarboard.

"Oh, NOW you want to take another picture, huh?" Mom jokes with a proud smile on her face.

"Yeah...shut up..." Dane smiles and looks down to the ground with embarrassment.

Sherri returns and wraps her arms around Dane's shoulders as his mom gets into place. Slowly, Dane puts his arm around her, trying not to create too much contact, and smiles as best as he can while his mom begins shooting.

With water still cascading over Kurrt's head the beeps on the computer screen have increased to a rate that could almost be perceived as one constant tone. Next to the computer, the seismometer has also begun to go crazy as the pen moves violently from side to side when, suddenly, a small thud causes everything to go quiet.

Kurrt turns off the faucet and emerges from the bathroom with a towel pressed to the back of his head. "Dammit that hurt." he groans, wincing in pain. After a second, he stops and listens curiously realizing it is completely silent in the shack. Confusion masks the pain that radiates from the back of his head as he walks in front of the desk and an amazing green glow from the computer screen illuminates the worry on his face. Still clutching the towel tightly against his injury, he thumps his free hand on the computer tower hoping to hear a beep. Quickly, he shifts his focus over to the side of the desk where the seismometer sits, drawing nothing but a calm straight line across the recording paper. "There's no way...it's just...gone." he whispers to himself as he forces his eyes to look in the direction of the computer screen. What used to be an entire outline of the mountain is now one bright green nucleus glowing brighter than ever before.

"No. There's no way..." he repeats as he drops the bloody towel to the ground and bolts away from the desk. He grabs a large case and yellow jumpsuit off the wall and rushes out the door, slamming it shut behind him. "This isn't possible!!"

After seconds of silence, the seismometer pen shows a little life again with a small spike...then another slightly larger spike...then, as an ear-piercing tone erupts from the computer tower, the pen spikes and breaks right off the machine, falling onto the wooden floor.

Mom continues to snap pictures of Dane, Gavin and Tim from a distance as they celebrate their milestone with their friends. For a moment, she stops to proudly look upon her son. Dane glances in her direction and can't help but smile back at her as she stands in the open parking lot smiling at him. Suddenly he is blinded by a flash of light from behind her. As he drops to his knees with his arm over his eyes, the entire crowd lets out a gasp, then...

BOOOOOOOOOOOOOOOOOOOOOM!

Everyone is jolted off their feet to the ground by the force of the explosion. After a few seconds of shock, people begin to push themselves back to their feet and look in the direction of the sound.

"What the hell...AHHHH, I can't see!!" Dane's voice is muffled in his head by the ringing in his ears. As he pushes himself to his knees, he removes his arm from his face and squints to attempt to refocus them on the blurs that dash around him. Other noises begin to come through the ringing as he begins to realize that people are running past him screaming and shouting. "Mom!!" he shouts as he reaches out his hand for something to hold onto and attempts to stand. "Mom, where are you!? Gavin!? Tim!?"

Suddenly, an arm wraps under his armpit and pulls him to his feet. His eyes begin to refocus on the figure in front of him as a voice pushes through the ringing. "Dude, are you alright!? ...Dane, you alright man!? ...DANE!!!" Tim shouts trying to get his friend's attention.

Dane's eyes finally focus in on the mayhem around him. Parents and kids in graduation gowns are screaming and scattering desperately in every direction with frightened looks on their faces. "Dude, what the hell happened!?" he shouts at Tim, still unable to hear his own voice clearly.

"I don't know man...look!" Tim shouts pointing over Dane's shoulder causing him to turn. Fear rushes to the pit of his stomach as his eyes go wide and his mouth hangs open in disbelief of what he sees in the distance. He can barely even hear Tim scream, "What the hell is that!?"

Chapter 8

Terrified, screaming people scramble in every direction on the school lawn attempting to find their loved ones. The principal of the school is on the graduation stage yelling into the microphone, attempting to calm everyone down and usher them to their vehicles. Some have stopped and pointed their smartphones in the direction of the mountain to take pictures and videos of a scene that seems like it is straight out of an apocalyptic movie. The once calm, snowy-white peak of Mount Rainier is now almost completely gone and has been replaced by a huge cloud of black smoke billowing hundreds of feet into the air.

"MOM!!!" Dane forces himself past person after person as his eyes scan the faces that rush past him. "MOOOOOM!!" He stops moving and stands as tall as he can to see over the crowd. Just as he is becoming frustrated he spots her near the stage calling out to him while trying to stay out of the way of the panic-stricken crowd. She looks up in his direction causing their eyes to lock and he can see the immense fear they display. "STAY THERE!!" Dane shouts while pointing to her, then pushes through the chaotic crowd in her direction.

He finally reaches her and she immediately embraces him, "Dane! We have to get out of here!" she shouts over the noise.

"Is it a volcano?" Dane looks back over the town to the mountain in disbelief.

She scans the mosh pit for the safest way through, "I dunno, sweetie. Let's go!" She grabs his arm and pulls him along the stage to get around the crowd and they rush to her car. As Dane is climbing into the passenger side he glances across the lot to see Sherri ducking into the car with her parents. He feels a small bit of relief in knowing she is ok and jumps in the car, slamming the door behind him.

Pulling out of the school the only sound in the car is their heavy breathing as they stare straight ahead attempting to process what they had just witnessed. As they pull up to a stop light, Dane looks over to see tears forming in Mom's eyes. He reaches over and grabs her shaking hand, startling her, but she immediately squeezes it back, and smiles through the fear.

"I'm scared too, Mom." he comforts her with a soft smile. "Should we get out of town?"

"I...I...I don't know." She stammers shakily, "Ummm, maybe we should check the news when we get home?" she takes a deep breath, regaining herself, and wipes the tear trails from her cheeks. "What do you think?"

"Yeah," Dane agrees, "that sounds-"

He stops short as a red sports car zooms past his window like a blur. As it flies through the intersection ahead it swerves and, with a sickening metallic crash, is struck by a truck going through the cross street. They both stare in shock as the car flips in the air over the curb into a gas station lot and lands on another parked vehicle. In the intersection the truck is hit directly by another car, which in turn is rear-ended. People begin getting out of their cars and rushing towards the accident to make sure the drivers of the wrecked vehicles are ok. Dane throws his door open and stands up, surveying the disaster and suddenly hears sirens in the distance. With one last look, he sits back in the passenger seat and slams the door behind him turning to Mom, who still has a look of fear on her face.

"It's ok, Mom," he comforts her, "I heard an ambulance heading in this direction. I'm sure they're fine." Her eyes never leave the accident in front of them and she doesn't say a word through the shaking hand that covers her mouth.

Just then, the sound of sirens overtake their ears and Dane turns to see an ambulance turn the corner recklessly and accelerate towards them. "See, Mom, they're...wait, what the hell!?!"

Dane and his mom both cower back into their seats and cover their heads as the ambulance continues to accelerate towards the middle of the accident. The people who had exited their cars to help scatter in all directions, pulling each other and the injured drivers to safety. At the last minute, the ambulance swerves slightly and careens through the vehicles sending the truck spinning through the intersection towards Dane and Mom. It comes to a stop just before reaching their car and the ambulance accelerates on its path past them without stopping. After a few seconds of shock, Dane and Mom sit up tall in their seats, "What the hell is happening?" Mom asks in a shaky voice. More sirens arise as 2 police cars and a large black SUV with lights on top fly through the hole in the accident made by the ambulance. She looks over at Dane with wide eyes.

"Let's get home!" Dane urges.

Mom shifts the car into drive and they speed off through the accident towards home. Dane turns around in his seat to watch the chaos through the back window as Mom's eyes stay locked onto the road ahead, glazed with tears.

As the mountain continues to shake Kurrt stumbles out of the trees and into a snowy clearing not far from where the peak used to be. He looks up with fear to see the black cloud of smoke almost as wide as his entire line of vision that pours into the sky over the trees on the other side of the clearing. He throws his case down into the snow and flips it open to reveal measurement devices. He then tosses the yellow jumpsuit onto the ground and steps into the foot holes, zipping it up to his waist. Before pulling the rest of the suit over his upper body he kneels down in the snow and begins to pull the devices out of the case and set them up. The first is a seismometer, which begins going crazy as soon as he flips the power on.

"Oh, no DUH!!" he shouts at it with frustration as he begins to work on the other device, a radiation detector. He extends the antennae from the top, then reaches down and pushes a large yellow power button. The screen lights up green, then slowly fades to black as it begins to beep very slowly. "Oh, thank god..."

Propping it up in the snow against the seismometer he grabs a pair of goggles out of the case, fitting them over his eyes. He closes up the case and stands to finish putting on the rest of his radiation suit. He reaches back and pushes his hands through the heavy, reflector-covered sleeves and into the attached gloves. As he reaches down to zip up the front of the suit, he stops. The radiation detector begins to light up brighter with each more rapidly occurring beep. Before too long, its rate is so fast that it is just a loud, shrill, piercing tone with a solid green screen. Suddenly, sparks shoot from the device, the beeping stops and the screen goes completely black. With his hand still on the zipper he slowly raises his head to look in the direction of the smoke. His eyes go wide behind his goggles as a wall of green light hurtles through the snow covered trees and across the clearing. With one large, green flash he is blown backwards off his feet and onto the ground unconscious.

"You can slow down a little, Mom." Dane reaches over and touches her arm softly. Though they are out of the downtown area and the traffic is much lighter she continues driving well above the speed limit.

She looks over to him, looking away quickly as the tears stream forward down her cheeks. She looks back towards the road as she wipes her face with her forearm. "I know, sweetie...I know." She trails off, slowing the car down to heed his request. Dane looks out the passenger window, seeing people loading up their vehicles with luggage and other possessions, rushing out of grocery stores with jugs of water and other necessities and boarding up their house windows and doors.

After a few minutes they pull onto their street and up to the curb in front of their house. Getting out of the car they look up across the street to the mountain. The black smoke spewing from it has covered up most of the blue sky above them and black ash falls like large snowflakes. They hurry up the walkway and burst through the front door, unsure of their next step. Dane pulls his flowing black gown over his head as he makes his way hastily into the living room. He grabs the TV remote and hits the power button, bringing the screen to life on a national news channel. Mom finds her way in behind him, gripping the back of the loveseat in fear of what they will hear.

"...reports that Mount Rainier near Seattle, Washington has actually erupted like a volcano..................................re advised to seek shelter as soon as poss...........................no previous reports of seismic activity......overhead pictures......nothing but smoke coming from the peak of Mount Rain........"

Suddenly, the ground shifts below them shaking the entire house and causing the TV to go completely black. Mom grabs tighter to the loveseat to stay upright while Dane leans against the couch. He regains his balance and violently attempts to turn the TV on again with no luck.

"We need to get out of here..." he says to Mom, who agrees silently with a nod of her head. They rush back towards the door, where Dane stops abruptly. "Go to the car, I'll be right there!"

Mom rushes out the door and down the walkway as Dane turns and rushes up the stairs. At the top, he leans into the doorway on the left and reaches in, grabbing his pill bottle off the bathroom counter. He stuffs them in his pocket and lumbers back down the stairs and out the front door without shutting it behind him. Halfway down the walk he is startled and ducks his head as two helicopters roar very low overhead swirling the descending ash in every direction. They roar into the distance towards the mountain as Dane uprights himself and gazes around in fear. People in their neighborhood pull their possessions from their houses and load them into their vehicles while some hammer boards over their windows preparing to ride out the disaster.

He refocuses himself and rushes the rest of the way across the yard, reaching the passenger door. He yanks on the handle, swinging the door open, but stops and looks around curiously.

"Dane, what is it!?" Mom says with urgency. "What's wrong?"

"I thought I heard something…" he shouts as he surveys the neighborhood. "I thought I heard my name."

"…DANE!!……….DENSONS!!…….OVER HERE!!"

Dane spins around with confusion then looks directly across the street to see the top half of his neighbor, sticking up from a hole in the ground waving his arms wildly.

"Dane, we have to go!" Mom urges from the driver's seat.

"Mom, wait…look!" Dane points towards his neighbor's yard in shock causing her to look through the driver's side window. "Mr. Logan wasn't digging a pool." He exclaims with a smile on his face. "It's a bomb shelter!!"

"Oh my god." Mom brushes the hair out of her face to get a better look. "C'mon, let's go!!" She pushes out of the car and follows her son across the street and up into Mr. Logan's yard. As they reach the entrance, the lanky old man with the messy white ponytail moves to the side, allowing them room to climb in.

"Man, I'm glad I saw you! I was just about to close up." He exclaims as they climb in. "Hurry, the tremors are getting worse!"

Once they are making their way down the ladder below him, he takes one last look around at the chaos and pulls the metal door shut behind him and locks it down. In the distance, through the black smoke that billows into the sky, a green wave can be seen traveling down the mountain passing through the trees in all directions. In an instant it bears down on their neighborhood, shaking everything for a moment as it passes through, continuing on to Eatonville and beyond.

Chapter 9

"OW, dammit!" Dane exclaims as pain suddenly radiates from his foot. He reaches blindly into the darkness with both hands trying to figure out what he just kicked. "Mom!?"

"I'm over here." Mom responds softly from a few feet away where she is feeling her way along a concrete wall towards Dane's voice. "Where's Mr. Logan?"

"Sorry guys...sorry, sorry." his voice comes out of the darkness along with the sound of him climbing down the metal ladder and shuffling across the concrete. "Just ooooooooooooone..." the sounds of a generator rumbling to life startles the two stowaways and a few bright bulbs flicker on overhead revealing their new home, "...sec." he finishes with a smile as he looks up at the lights. "Weird, the blast must have knocked t out. Oh well, welcome to 'Logan's Lair', as I like to call it." He looks back and forth between them for a response, but they look unimpressed, still shaken by what had happened above ground. He just shrugs his shoulders and heads past them into the living area, "I thought it was kinda clever..."

Mom makes her way over to Dane and wraps her arms around him in relief. "Mom, what about everyone else?" Mom pulls back and looks him in the eyes with sadness as she brushes the ash out of his hair. "Gavin, Tim...Sherri. Do you think they're ok?"

"Oh, sweetie, I'm sure they're fine." She embraces him again, "I'm sure they all got out of the city with their parents as fast as they could. John, do you have a radio or anything to let us know what's going on up there?"

Mr. Logan has made his way over to a small kitchenette and is organizing some of the shelves that were jolted by the blast. "Of course!!" he exclaims with excitement, leaving the disheveled makeshift kitchen and rushing to a large, wooden storage cabinet on the adjacent wall. "Bunker Survival 101: Maintain Contact!" he exclaims, pulling open the right cabinet door and retrieving an old-looking radio with a retracted antenna.

Dane and his mom make their way over to him, taking in the contents of the small, concrete room as they go. The kitchenette, composed of a full-sized refrigerator and freezer chest, a small sink and a hotplate on the counter with the open shelves above displaying plastic drinkware, plates, silverware and lots of Tupperware, sits along the right side wall next to two large cylindrical water tanks. The left side of the room resembles a grocery store aisle as it is entirely metal shelving that is loaded up with canned goods, bottles of water, bags of rice, labeled Tupperware, and more necessities. The wall straight ahead where Mr. Logan has pulled out the radio contains the storage cabinet, which also has other electronics and devices, a box of gasmasks and what looks like hunting gear on the open side. Next to the cabinet is a stack of boxes marked "clothes", "bathroom stuff", and "other stuff". An old couch sits lonely at an angle to the corner as if set up in front of an invisible television. Behind them, past the shelving, a dark corner holds a hanging curtain on a round track open just enough to show part of a toilet with a tiled area that has a shower head above it.

"Hopefully they're still doing news reports." Mom says quietly as they approach Mr. Logan, all of their eyes fixed on the little grey box. He pulls the antenna out as far as it will go and turns the volume knob on the front, which causes a small red light marked "Power" to light up. As he brings the volume up, static is the only thing that comes from the speakers. He leaves the volume knob and begins to turn the tuning knob.

"Oh, don't worry," Mr. Logan says confidently, "if they stop running the news I have a CB radio too, though it probably won't reach more than a few miles through these thick walls." he motions around the room at their solid concrete surroundings. "It goes quiet and we'll see if we can reach anyone...if anyone's left by that time."

Dane and his mom look away from the radio, their wide eyes focusing on their host, then each other.

"Hey, sorry," Mr. Logan puts his hands up in the air as if someone had just aimed a gun at him, "not trying to freak you out! Let's just say I've got a page of this book most people don't know exists. Hence, the bunker!" He drops his hands back down to the radio and keeps turning the knob looking for a voice to come through. "The only thing I don't get, though, is why it looked like it was only smoke coming from Rainey..." he mutters to himself.

"That's what the reporter said on the news before the power went out." Dane interjects. "There wasn't fire, or lava, or anything but smoke."

"Yeah," Mr. Logan responds quietly as if talking to himself, still distracted by the radio, "it doesn't make sense..."

"MAKE SENSE!?" Mom exclaims with frustration startling the man and causing him to stop messing with the radio and look into her angry face. "If you knew, why didn't you tell anybody something was going to happen!? Now you're making it sound like people are going to die and you've been over here building this bunker for weeks to save yourself and NOBODY ELSE!?"

Mr. Logan, surprised by the sudden outburst, stares back at her like a toddler in trouble, "I saved you guys..." he says softly with a shrug of his shoulders.

"OH! You're the man of the year!!" Mom screams facetiously throwing her hands over her head. "Don't give me that shit! We were in the right place at the right time and you know it!" She turns away angrily and begins pacing the concrete room looking at the things on the shelves he has stowed away in secrecy over the past few weeks. "Millions of people could die, or already be dead, and you knew all along, but that's fine because you always knew you'd be safe and sound down here in your little hole eating..." she grabs the first things she sees off the shelf and studies them, "BABY FOOD!? Oh, and I should've known...Twinkies!!" she shakes the dessert cake in his direction.

"What!?" Mr. Logan goes on the defense, "There's a lot of necessary nutrients and fiber in baby food and Twinkies are just damn good!" Dane sees the glare this statement earns him and slowly retreats back towards the kitchenette. "Listen," Mr. Logan becomes more stern, "I wasn't ABLE to tell anyone. I was under surveillance! I even had to purposefully make this thing look like it was going to be a pool until the last couple of days or I wouldn't have even gotten the chance to save myself...OR YOU!" Now Mr. Logan's voice gathers some angry volume, making Dane nervous. "I didn't bring you down here to ridicule me! Call me a bad person! Point fingers at me!" He takes a step closer to Mom, causing Dane to perk up protectively. "I think it was a pretty nice thing I did considering the circumstances!"

He takes another step forward causing Dane to rush in between them defensively. "Don't come near my mom!" he shouts up at the old man with as much confidence as he can muster.

"Take it easy, kid. We're just talking." Mr. Logan says more calmly turning to make his way back to the radio. "Besides, I wouldn't want you to sic your little friend on me." He motions towards Dane's pocket with a smirk.

Dane looks confusedly down to his left pants pocket to see the feet of the small superhero sticking out. He had completely forgotten that it had been there since they were at the house taking pictures. He pulls it out and slowly rolls it over in his hands sadly.

Mr. Logan looks from the radio back to the young man, "It's the only thing you've got left." Sympathy comes over him as he watches Mom put her hands on Dane's shoulders to comfort her son. "Ok, ok. Let's all just calm down a little. We're all pretty stressed out over this whole thing." He takes a step towards them, reaching out to hand the radio to Dane. "Why don't you try to find something on the radio, I'll make us some coffee and tell you what I know." Dane takes the radio out of his hand and Mr. Logan makes his way over to the refrigerator, pulling the door open. "Dane, Capri Sun? Or, I guess there's never been a better time if you want a cold beer...if it's ok with you of course, Miss Denson?"

She shoots him a glare, still upset from the previous exchange.

"The juice is fine...thanks." Dane says quietly as he stuffs the action figure back into his pocket. Mr. Logan tosses the juice pack at him, which he catches with his free hand and heads towards the couch with the radio.

The pure night sky looms above sending snowflakes floating softly down to the ground. The air is crisp, but not bitter and there is not a single sound in any direction, creating an amazing moment of tranquility. With a couple of blinks to focus his vision, Kurrt's first thought is that he could lay here looking into the black sky forever...except, as his eyes adjust, he realizes that it's not the sky sprawled above him. Confusion sets in immediately and the rolling layer of smoke becomes visible behind the falling flakes, which he now realizes is ash, not snow. Suddenly, everything flashes back to him. The eruption, running up the mountain, the wall of green energy. He attempts to sit up quickly, but can't move. Realizing first that his head is restrained, then also his arms, legs and waist, he begins to struggle in an attempt to free himself. His senses having fully reawakened he now notices movement around him. His eyes strain to the side to see people all around him in yellow Hazmat suits scanning the area and gathering up his equipment.

"HEY!! HEY, GET AWAY FROM MY STUFF!" He screams as he thrashes against the restraints, "WHAT THE HELL IS THIS!? LET ME GO!"

As he yells in the direction of his equipment, a gloved hand softly lies on his opposite shoulder startling him and diverting his attention. "Kurrt, I need you to calm down, we're here to help." a woman's voice comes calmly out of the helmet of the Hazmat suit. Inside he sees a middle-aged Asian woman, her face is beautiful while still displaying a certain toughness and wear. "We think you've been exposed and we need to get you out of here immediately."

"Holy shit…" Kurrt utters in shock, "it's you. From the radio…you're here!" His disbelief calms him down for the moment as he attempts to process the information at hand.

"Kurrt, I need you to focus." she says back sternly, now using the same tone he knew her so well for over the walkie talkie. "How do you feel? Any nausea? Hallucinations? Anything abnormal?"

Rage overtakes him again as he snaps out of his state of shock. "I mean, I'm feeling pretty ANGRY right now! Is that abnormal!?" he snaps sarcastically at her and begins to struggle again.

With a look of disappointment, the woman moves her attention away from Kurrt as she stands. "Alright, let's get him in the chopper." she gives her orders to a group of men off to the side, causing them to head in her direction. She turns and makes her way towards a small, two-man helicopter sitting in the clearing with a pilot waiting inside. Seeing her coming he starts up the engine and the rotors begin to spin. She turns back towards the scene around Kurrt, "Get this cleaned up and get out of here…LET'S GO!!" she barks out her orders to the seven suited men.

Kurrt's formerly peaceful view is now invaded by these alien-like figures as they lift his stretcher from the ground and begin to carry him towards a larger helicopter. His mind races with a million different thoughts and questions and fear quickly overtakes him. "You guys left me up here for THREE WEEKS and you didn't listen to a word I said! I told you there was radiation up here and YOU DIDN'T LISTEN!!" He screams, hoping the woman is still within earshot. "LET ME OUT OF THIS THING!! AHHHHHHHHHHHHHHHHHHH!!!!!!" he screams with such force his body arches against the restraints.

As the painful scream leaves his mouth his stretcher suddenly halts to a complete stop in midair, causing the men to stumble slightly. With bewilderment they look at each other, and attempt to pull it along again with no success as Kurrt continues to scream and struggle to get free. One of the men turns in the direction of the woman, "Hey, uh, Doctor?" he shouts with a nervous, unsteady voice, "We...ummm...we've got an issue."

The woman is a few feet from her helicopter when she stops and turns around slowly, "What is it?!" she shouts with irritation. The stern look on her face melts when she sees Kurrt throwing himself around on the stretcher that now mysteriously hovers about 4 feet off the ground.

"I don't know..." the man motions towards their captive with confusion, "he's just...stuck!"

"What the..." the woman utters under her breath as she takes a step in their direction.

Suddenly, Kurrt's screaming stops, his eyes roll back into his head, his struggling stops and his body goes limp on the stretcher, which immediately falls and lands in the snow and ash. The woman runs across the clearing at full speed pushing her way through the men and pulling out a device with a node that she quickly plants on Kurrt's temple.

"I've got nothing!! Get me the oxygen mask and AED!" she shouts with panic as she rips the node off his head and puts the device in her pocket. "C'MON," she orders as she looks around to the men behind her, "what are you waiting f-"

Her sentence stops abruptly as, one by one, all of the men around her in the clearing crumple to the ground. She slowly stands and turns watching with confusion and fear as the bodies collapse around her, then her eyes roll back into her head and she drops to the ground dead.

Chapter 10

"...seems to be a natural disaster of some kind, but it's really a weird situation happening at Mount Rainier."

"I've got something!" Dane shouts with excitement as a voice finally projects itself out of the static from the small radio. Mom rushes over from the kitchenette where Mr. Logan is pouring coffee into two small mugs and sits next to Dane on the couch. "It sounds like a political show or something."

"I mean, there hasn't been anyone affected, to our knowledge, and everything we're hearing says it's just a bunch of smoke shooting into the air over the surrounding areas and Seattle. There's no lava. There's no fire. Hell, there was barely an explosion!"

"I thought it was a pretty decent explosion..." Mom mumbles under her breath as she stares intently at the radio like it's a TV. Mr. Logan draws her attention away for a moment as he approaches, handing her a cup of coffee, then pulls a foldable lawn chair out of the cabinet and sets up next to the couch.

"The big question is, what's in store now?" a second voice comes through on the radio, *"We're lucky there's been no destruction that we know of yet, but we still don't even know what this is. We don't know if it's over, we don't know what the longer-term effects are. We just don't know!"*

"You're totally right," continues the first voice, *"we're not even sure if this is an act of nature or something brought on by humans...or terrorists!"*

"Oh, you would bring up terrorism!" frustration engulfs the voice of the second reporter, *"Are you kidding me!? Why the hell are terrorists going to blow up the top of a mountain in one of the least populated corners of the US? That's ridiculous..."*

"You're ridiculous to think they wouldn't!" argues back the first reporter. *"It could be a warning shot, but you know the government is just going to play it off as some sort of experiment-gone-bad or something…"*

Mom, Dane and Mr. Logan look away from the radio to each other with judgement. "Well, they don't sound like they know anything. Let's try to find something other than a Fox News wannabe, huh?" Mom suggests sarcastically to Dane and takes a sip of her coffee.

"…Idiots." Dane sighs and goes back to work on the tuning knob.

"So, John," Mom shifts her attention back to their host, "Word is you know a little more than we do about this situation. Care to share?"

"Well I suppose now is as good of a time as any." he says calmly, leaning back in his lawn chair and bringing one leg up onto his opposite knee. He closes his eyes as he takes a sip of his coffee and swallows, enjoying as the hot liquid runs all the way down through his chest. He reopens his eyes to see Dane and Mom staring at him, intently awaiting his story. He uncrosses his legs and leans forward in his chair, "It was a dark and stormy night…"

"UGHHH!" Dane grumbles loudly as Mom rolls her eyes in frustration

"Would you just be serious for TWO MINUTES!? Please!?" she exclaims wiping the grin from his face.

"Ok, ok, fine." Mr. Logan recovers from the sudden barrage of anger. "It actually WAS a dark and stormy night, though! I was working for TechGo, a company that delivers computers and other tech equipment to labs and facilities across the country. One of our regular drop-offs was at the Geological Society of America in Colorado since they do so much work with seismometers, computer tracking and reporting, and other stuff. That place it totally geeked out, it's awesome!" he exclaims momentarily, then quickly continues to keep his audience from flipping out on him again. "I was there to drop a few crates of the newer model seismometers and pick up their old ones to be recycled. I'm telling you, these new ones are really cool, not like those old 'needle and paper, jagged line when you accidentally kick the leg of the table' seismometers. These new ones look like IPads that have laser projectors so you can do readings almost anywhere, and…"

"JOHN!" Mom yells, then raises her eyebrows in a silent urging to get on with the story.

"Sorry," he apologizes with a small laugh, "I'm a geek at heart. So, anyways, we load everything up and take off to our next drop at InCorps way back down in LA. Let me tell you, that place is HUGE!! I lost my way, like, 3 times trying to find where their friggin' crate of computer monitors were supposed to go, but I finally found it. On my way back I got lost again, go figure, and I end up in this large white hallway with big doors, all closed…except for one. I park my lift and go to ask how to get the hell out of there and I see two guys in suits in the room talking in front of a huge display. On the screen is a gigantic map of the US with different icons over some of the major cities, which I assume is just their medication distribution map or something…

"Would you just get on to it, Howard?" a large man booms in a deep voice. He is taller than Howard, dark skinned with big, broad shoulders and stands with his hands folded behind his back spinning a ring on his left hand. "Is it at dangerous levels?"

"That's exactly what I'm saying. It's only a matter of time before the radioactivity causes the core to implode…" exclaims Howard, "…or explode, we don't really know. A whole lot of people could become exposed, and we don't know what that means…we just don't know much at this point!"

"Now I don't know anything about medicine," continues Mr. Logan, "but I'm pretty sure nothing in their field requires radioactivity, or cores, so I had no idea what they were talking about."

"I want a clean-up plan put in place by tomorrow and get with the GSA. We just bought them all those new toys, have them get me a timeline by noon tomorrow." orders the first man. "If we can't contain it, then we have to be prepared to control the result…whatever that may be."

"Yes sir," Howard agrees. "I will have-"

"HEY!" shouts a loud voice from down the empty white hall. "What are you doing down here? You can't be on this level."

With the commotion in the hallway, the two men become alerted and rush towards the doorway to see what is going on. As they reach the hall, a security guard has made his way to Mr. Logan and restrained him by his arm. Mr. Logan looks nervous as he is suddenly surrounded by men in suits who do not look very happy.

"Hey, hey, hey." he tries to smooth over the situation. "Just got a little lost, fellas. Can anyone tell me and Ol' Betsy there how to get back to the loading dock?" He smiles, motioning to his lift parked down the hallway.

"Get him out of here." the first man motions to the security guard, his voice so deep it seems to rattle the walls of the hallway. "…nearly gave me a heart attack." He folds his hands behind him again as he and Howard turn and walk back into the room.

"Says the big, fit guy! You're a beast, you'll be alright!" Mr. Logan lays on the charm. "I really do apologize guys, thanks for the help. Let's go Jeeves!" he sends a big smile the security guards way, which does nothing to break the sternness on his face. The large man turns momentarily to look back at the doorway with a suspicious eye, then returns to studying the large display on the wall.

"So I grabbed my lift, the guy escorted me to the dock and I left. No big whoop, right?" Mr. Logan shrugs his shoulders and takes another drink of his coffee. "So I thought..."

"The accident at the InCorps plant in Los Angeles! The chemicals!" Mom exclaims.

"BINGO!" Mr. Logan points at her.

"Bingo?" Dane has now completely given up on the radio in his lap and is completely enthralled in Mr. Logan's story. "Bingo, what?"

"Let me help you out kid...I got one last look at that map on the screen before the security guard dragged me away. Do you want to venture a guess where the only two pulsing red dots were located?" Mr. Logan leads him towards a realization and waits for his response.

Dane looks down to the floor in thought, "Los Angeles..."

"Aaaaaaaaaaaaand?" Mr. Logan ushers him along.

In a moment of realization, Dane looks up to Mr. Logan in bewilderment, "...Mount Rainier."

Mr. Logan shrugs his shoulders and grins at the young man in front of him, "Bingo." he says calmly taking another sip from his coffee.

Mom, who has been staring off into the distance trying to process the information during their interaction interjects, "But you said radioactivity...and that must mean the core they were talking about..." she trails off.

"You got it," Mr. Logan says with confidence, "the Earth's core."

"How is that even possible?" her voice raises as she begins to show some anger. "InCorps is a pharmaceutical company, not a radioactive waste company! Are you sure, John? How do you know that your information is even correct?"

Mr. Logan gets a defensive look and begins scanning the room emphatically, "Did you forget where we are!? We're in a goddamn doomsday bunker!" he lifts his hands up to once again display the concrete surroundings. "Please let me know if you have anything else that might explain our reason for being here and I'll be sure to give it good consideration." he says with frustration as he stands from the chair and makes his way back to the kitchenette to pour himself more coffee.

Dane and Mom share a worried glance as they replay the information in their heads. Mr. Logan faces away from them at the kitchenette in silence. After a minute goes by Dane begins to work with the radio tuning knob again.

"The thing I keep thinking about though..." Mr. Logan, still facing away from them, finally breaks the silence. "...is that I don't know what caused it, but it sounded to me like they were trying to fix it. I walked out of there thinking InCorps is probably the good guys, but then I started to notice things. Black cars at the end of the street, weird things happening with my cell phone and computer...they knew I saw something, and they were keeping an eye on me."

"I'm so sorry, John." Mom apologizes. "I didn't mean to imply that you were lying, it's just a lot to take in. Plus, we still have no idea what it all means."

"Yeah, I may know too much already, but in a weird kinda way I wish I knew more." Mr. Logan says quietly without turning around. "It's like having a key, but no door to use it on." He turns and Mom sees some fear in his eyes for the first time. "What good is it, ya know?"

She feels an empathetic connection with the old man, but cannot find any words to comfort him, instead forcing a small smile with a nod of her head. He turns back around to his coffee on the counter and loses himself in thought. She turns to Dane, who still looks worried. With the same grin, she reaches over and rubs his back with her open hand as he returns to scanning through the stations for any noise other than static.

Later that night, the bunker is dark and quiet aside from the small flicker of a battery powered candle on the kitchenette counter and the low sound of static coming from the radio that lies next to Dane on his blow up mattress. Mom is curled up in a blanket on the couch and Mr. Logan has set up a nest of blankets on the floor next to her. All sleep deeply, exhausted from the long day they had just had. In the sink, dirty dishes pile up, remnants of their first meal together in their new home.

Suddenly, out of the static comes a voice,
"Thank... *static*...tuning in, this is Frank Al... *static*...News 10 reporting on the current state... *static*...from the Mount Rainier explosion. We are still seeing no immediate effects or damage and the government has yet to comment on the state of the nation as the President still has not emerged from the White House bunker...wait a second. We're getting a breaking report coming in. It sounds as if someone has just reported a mass suicide...or mass killing at St. Leonitus Hospital in Enumclaw. We are still waiting on details of how many are dead or injured but it is a suspected poisoning as there were not gunshots or explos-" a thud is heard from the radio. "Oh my god, Rebecca?! Rebecca, are you ok? Our producer Rebecca just passed out...Greg, I'm not getting a pulse, call 911, NOW!" Another loud thud occurs. "Greg? Greg, are you ok? What the hell is happ..." one final thud is heard, then silence surrounds the sleeping inhabitants of the dark concrete room.

Chapter 11

"Welp, here we go." Mr. Logan leads Dane and Mom up to the metal stepladder that leads to the bunker's hatch. The three exchange one last nervous look. Mr. Logan breathes in deeply and releases it through pursed lips, turns and starts up the ladder. Dane follows with Mom climbing right behind him.

As Dane reaches the halfway point of the ladder Mr. Logan pauses just above him and begins releasing the locks on the hatch. He finally reaches for the wheel release that will open the hatch and pauses to look over his shoulder at the two nervous faces gazing up at him. "Be ready for anything..." he warns them and turns back to open the hatch. Gripping both hands tightly on the wheel lock he muscles it a half turn counter-clockwise and a loud metallic thud is followed by a hiss of hot air and bright light that shoots down into the bunker causing them all to shield their eyes. Dane, with his head still turned away from the sun's glare that his eyes have not been exposed to in almost two days, very slowly opens his eyelids allowing his eyes to adjust slowly. By the time he is able to turn his gaze upward again, Mr. Logan is gone. He shoots a nervous look back at Mom, who is still squinting up towards him.

"You alright, sweetie?" she asks in a shaky voice. Dane just nods his head then turns back around to begin his climb. "Here we go..." Mom repeats Mr. Logan's words nervously.

A few steps up the ladder and Dane pulls himself above ground. Standing in Mr. Logan's grassy yard there is no wind and the air seems hot. A greenish hue from the sun breaks through the mountain's smoke, which covers the sky as far as Dane can see. Everything is still and quiet and Mr. Logan is nowhere to be seen.

He turns around and bends down to help Mom out of the bunker grabbing her hand and forearm. With one good heave, she joins him on the grass with a "Thank you." Suddenly, her eyes become fully adjusted and she begins to look around, "Oh my god..." she utters as she raises her hand to cover her mouth.

"What's wro-" Dane turns to follow her sight and sees something he hadn't noticed until now. In the yards, in the street, on the porches of the houses are people, lying motionless. "Are they..."

"I don't know, sweetie." Mom says through her shaking hand.

As they begin making their way cautiously across the street they look for any signs of movement from the bodies. Suddenly, Dane stops, his eyes fixated ahead of them across the street.

"Dane, what is it?" Mom asks quietly, unable to break his gaze. "Dane! Dane!!"

Sadness and confusion grow within him as Mom's voice fades away. In their yard lies a small body facing away from them, its curly blonde hair resting in the grass. As tears begin to glaze his eyes his sadness turns to rage. He begins to think about Mr. Logan's story, InCorps, the fact that he was saved while his friends perished. His teeth clench in his mouth. His fists clench at his sides and he feels a heat swelter inside his palms. He feels the emotions overtake him. He raises his clenched fists in front of him to realize that they are on fire! The fire burns a bright orange from a green center in his palms and begins to work its way up his arms. In fear he regresses backwards as if to escape it, but his heel hits something causing him to trip and fall onto the concrete, which also extinguishes the fire on his arms. Confused he pushes himself up onto his hands and turns to look behind him. He is startled as he realizes that he had tripped over another body. Lying there, motionless, eyes wide open in his direction is Mr. Logan.

He spins around with surprise, "Mr. Logan?" He reaches out and taps the man's arm to draw a reaction. "Mr. Logan, are you okay?" Still getting nothing, he is suddenly gripped by fear. "MOM, Mr. Logan needs help!" he shouts quickly getting his feet under him. As he begins to stand, he realizes there is someone on the ground behind Mr. Logan. "No..." Dane utters quietly as the body becomes more visible. "No, no, no..." he attempts to convince himself. Now fully standing, the lifeless body of his mom becomes fully visible. Sadness fills his heart. Anger fills his mind. Tears begin to fill his vision but a green flame ignites deep in his eyes. The heat grows in his entire body as he succumbs to the greatest pain he's ever felt, causing small flames pop up all over his body. He raises his clenched, fiery fists once more and, as the fire overtakes his entire body, the scream that has been building itself in his lungs explodes forth...

"NO!!" Dane jolts himself awake. The dark covers him like an ocean as he sits on his airbed in confusion. In the soft light of the candle he rubs his eyes and looks around, waiting for them to focus. He stays still for a few minutes, breathing deeply and trying to process what was dream and what was reality.

It all felt so real.

"Dammit!" he suddenly exclaims to himself, realizing that he hadn't taken his medicine before bed the night before. He scrambles in the dark towards the edge of the bed where his jeans lay on the floor, now also seeing that he had fallen asleep while tuning through radio stations, as displayed by the illuminated red Power light. He turns off the radio, frustrated with its lack of help, and sets it on the floor, then grabs his jeans. He reaches into a pocket and pulls out his orange pill bottle, but then realizes there is something in his other pocket. He reaches in and, with a sigh of frustration, realizes he had completely forgotten in the chaos that his cell phone was in his jeans. He pulls it out and pushes the power button, not expecting anything to happen, but the screen lights up displaying that it is 10:37am. "Damn, we must've been tired." he utters to himself. With only 13% battery and no signal, he powers down the phone in case it is needed later. He uses the last flickers of light to find the juice pouch Mr. Logan had given him the day before and sucks out the last of it to flush the pill down his throat.

He throws his jeans over his legs, zipping and buttoning them at his waist and sits on the edge of the bed rubbing his eyes, trying to force the dream from his vision. After a few minutes with his eyes closed trying to slow his heartbeat he makes his way through the dark to the kitchenette and flips on a small light above the sink. He pulls a glass from the cabinet and a jug from the refrigerator and pours himself a glass of water. As he sips he looks over the bunker, the shelves of food, the makeshift living room with his sleeping roommates, still trying to believe they're even in this situation.

Suddenly, the deaths that occurred in his dream finds its way back into his mind and his stomach turns over with fear. He sets the glass of water on the counter and makes his way over to the couch where his mom is silent and still.

"Mom," Dane whispers as he approaches. Mr. Logan also doesn't stir. "Mom!" he whispers a little louder as he reaches the back of the couch. He reaches over and touches her blanket-covered arm and shakes it softly, "Mom, wake up," he gets louder. Immediately, fear consumes him and he forcefully grabs her arm and yells, "MOM!" She jolts out of her sleeping state and sits up abruptly on the couch.

Mr. Logan also gets startled and appears over the front of the couch looking confused, "What the hell...did we die?" he utters.

"What is it!? What happened!?" Mom asks in a panic looking around the mostly dark room.

"You weren't waking up...I got worried." Dane says, somewhat embarrassed at thinking she might have been dead.

"Oh...Jesus...ok. Yeah, I'm ok" Mom works on coming down from the moment of shock and reaches up and rubs his arm to comfort him. "What time is it? Oh, wait..." she realizes they don't have a way of knowing.

"Yeah, yeah, I know, I forgot the clock." Mr. Logan groans as he lies back down on the floor to go back to sleep, "Let's pretend it's three in the morning..."

"Actually, it's about eleven, I found my phone in my pocket this morning." Dane informs his mom.

Mr. Logan's head pops back into view from the floor, "11am!? Holy shit, we slept for..." he tries to do the math in his head, "13 hours? Is that right?"

"Yeah," Dane confirms with him, "I think we all might have been a little stressed out, huh?"

"Ha, ya think?" Mom agrees with him as she works her way off the couch to make some coffee for her and Mr. Logan. "So, what's on the agenda for Bunker: Day 2?" she asks sarcastically.

"A whole lot of the same?" Dane rivals, looking to Mr. Logan for confirmation. "I'm on the radio, I'm guessing?"

"Make it happen, kid." Mr. Logan says, grunting his way off the floor and stretching out as he reaches a standing position. "Coffee time!"

A nonchalant smile breaks onto Dane's lips and he makes his way back to his bed to find the radio, powering it on and scanning through the static as Mr. Logan and Mom work on breakfast.

Breakfast becomes lunch, lunch becomes dinner. They sleep, they wake up, they talk, they pace, they laugh, they argue. Over the next 3 days Dane feels like he has scanned the entire line of radio stations a million times and Mr. Logan has also had no luck with his CB radio. Though their theories of what is going on above them have ranged through seemingly hundreds of possibilities and they have discussed what their next move should be multiple times, Day 5 in the bunker brings a lot of the same.

"Dane, don't eat another Twinkie. I'm getting dinner ready right now!" Mom scolds her son who is now eating out of boredom while playing with his action figure on the couch. A crinkling noise causes them both to look over towards the cabinet where Mr. Logan has his back turned to them. He immediately turns looking like a deer in headlights, a Twinkie sticking halfway out of his mouth. "Goddammit," Mom utters in defeat. "Why do I even make these meals when you guys can just eat processed junk all day!?" The guys look at each other and chew slowly with no response then go back to what they were doing before being scolded. "Ugh…" she scoffs and continues cooking.

Dane sighs as he tosses his action figure over onto his airbed and makes his way to Mr. Logan and the cabinet to see if he's finding anything on his CB radio. "Any luck over he-"

He's cut short by a quick slam of the cabinet door, though the right side remains wide open displaying its contents. Mr. Logan turns to him slowly as Dane looks past him to see the CB radio off and untouched. "Hey kid, what's up?" he says nonchalantly.

"Nothing, I just…thought you were on the radio…" Dane trails off now wondering what Mr. Logan was actually doing in the cabinet. It's at this moment he realizes the left side of the cabinet had not been opened since they got there.

"Oh…no, I tried that earlier and was going to try again before we head to bed tonight." He then attempts to divert the attention, "Hey, have you tried your radio yet today, that one's the better bet. Longer range."

"Yeah…um…I guess I'll go try again…" Dane slinks away from the awkward situation, now suspicious of what Mr. Logan seems to be hiding in the cabinet. He plops himself down on the couch again, grabbing the radio from the floor and scanning through the stations slowly. From the kitchenette, Mom looks over her shoulder at him and flashes him a smile. He catches her gaze, but, as his mind wanders, he can't find it in himself to return the smile.

Darkness creates a slow cover over the world above as the night sets in. Four eerie days of silence have gone by as pale, lifeless bodies scatter throughout neighborhoods, cities, and streets around the world. TVs left on have turned to static with nobody to control the feed. Animals have begun to work their way into once populated areas, drawn by left out food. Cars that haven't crashed have idled to a stop and run out of gas while many boats of all sizes have either collided with the shore or still float aimlessly. The smoke that continues to billow from the top of Mt. Rainier has worked its way across most of the US creating the same overcast that had covered Eatonville the day of the eruption.

Suddenly, on the top of the mountain, a hand twitches under a thin layer of snow and ash. Slowly, each finger begins to move shakily as the hands turns over and comes to a rest with the palm facing upward. From the fingertips a green current grows in brightness as it snakes its way down each finger, converging in the palm. A glowing orb appears in the center of the currents and slowly builds, reaching a blinding intensity, then is slowly hidden away as fingers clench into a fist over top of it and, with a blinding green flash, the restraints that hold the arm down are blown away.

Chapter 12

With dinner in their stomachs and a couple of card games in the books the trio settles in for another night in the bunker. To Dane sleep has become a welcome relief from the repetitious daily routine. Mom and Mr. Logan continue to try to keep the spirits up in their small containment, but time is beginning to wear on everyone.

"If I never have to use a radio ever again I would be totally happy..." Dane scoffs as he climbs under the sheets of his airbed, "and I'm never going anywhere without a phone charger again! At the very least I could play Candy Crush all day!"

Mom and Mr. Logan chuckle from the couch where she is reading the "Doomsday Bunker Cookbook" and he is checking the filters and seals on his gas masks. Mom closes her book, setting it on the floor next to the couch getting ready to lay down for the night. Mr. Logan takes the hint setting his gas masks aside and moves down to his nest of blankets and pillows on the floor.

"Well kiddies," he exclaims while tucking himself under his blanket, "how are we feeling about tomorrow?"

Dane lets out a loud, frustrated grunt from under his comforter. Mom pokes her head back up over the back of the couch and smiles in his direction. "Well that's a pretty clear answer," she jokes, "but I'm actually excited to try some of these recipes! There's a Chicken Pot Pie that's flavored with Peas and Carrots baby food and has Twinkie breading!"

"UUUUUUUUUGGGGGGHHHHHHHH..." the two guys in the room can't hold back their disgust.

"Can't wait Mom..." Dane mumbles sarcastically, "and on that note, I'm going to attempt to not have food nightmares."

"Good luck, kid." Mr. Logan chimes in. "I'm already having them and I'm not even asleep yet..."

"Oh, jeez. You guys are such wimps." Mom tries to defend herself. "Fine, I guess I won't tell you what's in the Meatloaf recipe then." She gets a big smile across her face as they both groan again. "I said I WON'T tell you...but here's a clue: There's no meat in it..." She bursts out laughing when their pleading for her to "STOP!" hits a high. "Alright, you guys, lights out! See you in the morning."

They both wish her and each other good night and Dane reaches up above his bed to turn off the lamp Mr. Logan had found in one of his boxes, leaving the electric candle on the kitchenette as the only light in the room. Mr. Logan and Mom shuffle to get comfortable in their proverbial beds and then close their eyes and lay silent. Dane also pulls himself down underneath his blanket and falls silent, but stares in thought towards the grey concrete ceiling. Thoughts swirl around his head like a tornado feeding his frustration of being trapped in this single-room bunker for 5 days with no outside contact and no knowledge what's happened to his friends above ground. Although, he thinks, there is one question that he can find the answer to now.

For 2 hours he lays silent until he is sure that his mom and Mr. Logan are into a deep sleep. He finally sits up slowly to avoid as much of the plastic squeaking made by the airbed as possible, spins so that his feet are on the floor and pushes his weight forward until he is off the bed in a standing position and stops. After a few seconds he hears nothing and decides to proceed. He kneels next to his bed and feels around on the cold floor until his hand finds his jeans. He reaches underneath his jeans and pulls out his phone. "Please, please be on vibrate" he prays in his head as he holds the phone in front of him. His finger finds its way to the power button and cautiously holds it down. The screen glows to life illuminating his face, which immediately shows concern as the start-up jingle blares forth into the silence.

"SHIT!" he whispers to himself as he pulls the phone against his chest and smothers it with his hands. It quickly goes quiet and he turns to see if he's woken up the other two. They hadn't stirred at all, so he slowly pulls the phone away from his chest. He points the screen down towards the floor and pushes the power button again to light up his path. He first moves away from the couch to go around the top of his airbed and, once he is on the other side, begins working his way back in the direction of his roommates taking very small steps in the light of the phone. He makes it to the end of the couch where Mom's feet poke out from the cover of her blanket. He can also see Mr. Logan who is wrapped up in blankets lying in the same direction on the floor a few feet in front of the couch. He angles the phone away so as not to wake them with the light and continues past until he reaches the cabinet. He hesitates, staring at the small metal handle on the left door. He looks back one last time to make sure that Mom and Mr. Logan haven't woken up, takes a deep breath in and lets it out slowly, then reaches forward and grabs the small knob on the door and pulls.

Locked.

"Dammit..." Dane mutters to himself as he looks around, unsure of what to do now. He clicks off the screen of the phone and contemplates his next move. He hadn't seen Mr. Logan with any keys, but it could be hidden in any of the kitchenette cabinets, or under a specific jar of food in the pantry, or a hundred other places in this small room. "What the hell is he hiding in there?" he thinks to himself.

Feeling defeated for the time being he turns the phone back on and quietly follows its light back to his bed. Kneeling next to it, he pulls his jeans over the phone to hide the glow and turns the screen on one more time. 11% left on the battery. He powers it down to reserve what's left and sets it on the floor next to his bed as he carefully lies down again. With thoughts and questions swirling in his head it's almost an hour before he's able to finally fall asleep.

The smell of coffee lifts Dane from his sleeping state. Mom is already in the kitchenette putting together God knows what type of bunker breakfast. He can hear water running behind him as Mr. Logan showers in the back corner behind a fully drawn curtain. All of the frustrating thoughts he was having last night before he fell asleep immediately fill his head again. He quickly decides that he's going to keep his distance from Mr. Logan while keeping a very close eye on his movements. Maybe he can pick up hints on how to get into the cabinet and see what he's hiding. Lying and staring at the concrete ceiling he tries to imagine what could possibly be in there. A secret food stash? More info about InCorps? Weapons?

"Well, you're up early today." Mom breaks into the flood of imaginary scenarios running through his head, snapping him back to reality. He looks at her with a groan and rubs his eyes. "You have some plans today, or something?" she jokes.

"Yeah, biiiiiiiig plans," he sarcastically jokes with her as he rolls off the slightly deflated air bed, takes his medicine and puts his jeans on. "Big date...with a radio...and a Twinkie...ugh..." he groans at the thought while mom laughs.

"No Twinkies yet!" she exclaims through her laughter, "First, a real breakfast."

The water turns off in the shower area and a voice startles them, "REAL breakfast. I like the sound of that!!" Mr. Logan exclaims spryly as he dries himself behind the curtain, then forcefully pushes it aside and emerges adjusting the collar of a polo shirt, only a towel wrapped around his waist. Dane and Mom focus back towards the kitchenette as to avoid seeing anything they shouldn't. "What're we having?" he digs into his ear with a finger in an attempt to drain the water from it.

"SPAMcakes!!" Mom says, clearly proud of her concoction. To her dismay, but not necessarily to her surprise, a huge groan comes from the men of the bunker. "...and apple cinnamon baby food oatmeal..." she says softly, preparing for another groan.

"Oh, that actually sounds ok!" Mr. Logan drops into a chair at the table and looks over at Dane to get agreement in the form of a smile and a nod. "Welp, let's eat!"

"Hey, hey, hey mister," Mom points a finger in his direction causing him to stop in his tracks. "Clothes first!" she orders.

"Yes, please." Dane agrees with her jokingly. "I'd like to actually keep my SPAMcakes down!"

Mr. Logan laughs as he heads back to the shower where his boxers and jeans hang just outside the curtain. "Kid, I don't know if that's possible, clothes or not!"

"Uggggggggggh………" Aside from the whistle of the wind blowing through the surrounding trees, a groan is nearly the only noise that has occurred in the clearing for almost 5 days. A body in a Hazmat suit shifts in the previously undisturbed blanket of ash, rolls onto its side and pushes itself onto its hands and knees. Moving slowly, as if painfully, it stands and reaches one gloved hand up to wipe off the frost that has accumulated on the helmet's plastic viewer. As the hand pulls away the doctor's face is revealed shivering intensely, white as the boundless snowy tundra that surrounds her, lips blue, the fear in her eyes imminent as they scan her surroundings erratically. Yellow bodies scatter across the clearing, the helicopter looms silently over the scene and the peak of the mountain is visible over the trees, still spewing smoke into the sky.

Suddenly, something stirs across from the helicopter and catches her attention. Her joints are frozen and stiff, her muscles weak from not being used in days, but she forces herself to move forward through the snow across the clearing. Ahead of her, another yellow-suited body slowly sits upright pushing the ash off of himself. She reaches the man and falls to her knees beside him and grabs his shoulder, startling him.

"Calm down Allen, it's me." she shakiy assures the man as she reaches out and scrapes the snow off his facemask with her glove revealing his terrified face underneath. "Are you ok?"

"What...what happened?" the man says through shuttering blue lips, ignoring her question. "They all...they just collapsed!"

"Hey, focus!" she snaps at him, grabbing his attention. She then looks around again as if the answer was somewhere in the clearing. "I...I don't know what happened. We just have to..." she trails off as her eyes fixate into the distance.

"What?" asks the man as he looks into her mask and sees fear overtake her face. "Doctor, what is..." he stops short as he follows her gaze to the ground a few feet away from him. Unable to pull their eyes away, they struggle to help each other stand and carry each other forward. After a few unsteady steps they stand at the edge of a five foot deep crater in the snow. In the bottom, a few inches of melted snow create a pool over the scorched rocky surface of the mountain. Their attention is diverted for a moment as they hear rustling around them and turn to see the other men begin to wake up slowly. Unconcerned, they turn back to the crater below them and peer in with wide eyes as a tattered and mangled stretcher bobs back and forth on the surface of the water.

Chapter 13

"Pizza!" Dane exclaims, drawing longing coos from Mr. Logan and his mom. "A cheeseburger!" he continues on with his list of the first things he's going to eat when they get out of the bunker. "….Ooo, ooo, a cheeseburger pizza!!"

"I dunno," Mr. Logan counters him confidently taking a swig from a frosty beer bottle, "I think SPAMcakes might be my new favorite."

Mom swats him playfully on the arm as she senses his sarcasm. "C'mon, they weren't THAT bad…were they?" She does not receive the answer she was looking for, or an answer at all as the two guys divert their attention away from the question. "Fine, whatever. You guys can cook dinner then!"

They both continue their silence as Mr. Logan digs through the box marked "Other Stuff" and Dane moves fairly quickly up and down the tuning dial of the radio, unfocused and mainly just doing it for show. He had been observing every move Mr. Logan had made that day while also looking around the bunker inconspicuously for the hiding spot of the key. Unfortunately, it did not bring any new developments and he was no closer to getting into the cabinet than he was the night before. He does his best to be patient and reminds himself that they could be down there for a really long time. Before long, Mr. Logan has to show him someth-

"FOUND IT!!" the man exclaims, interrupting Dane's thoughts, and shoves his hand up into the air emphatically. Startled by the sudden outburst, Dane and Mom both look over to see what has gotten Mr. Logan so excited. "I wasn't even sure if I had gotten a chance to pack it before the mountain went up." he brings the item down in front of him and peers at it in his open hand.

Without saying a word Dane and Mom implore Mr. Logan to include them. Their stares finally wear on him and he is snapped out of his moment as if he just remembered there are two other people in the room. "Sorry," he apologizes without an ounce of real apology, "something...kinda sentimental..."

This is the first time Dane and Mom have seen real emotion from Mr. Logan besides his anger outburst on their first day together. Mom walks over and kneels next to him putting her hand on his shoulder as Dane looks on from the couch, his attention completely removed from the radio in his hands. He sits tall on the edge of the cushion to get a better look and sees what has made Mr. Logan so reminiscent...a flash drive.

"I don't understand, John," Mom inquires softly, her hand still on his shoulder, "what is it?"

"Well...it's a flash drive." Mr. Logan's humor returns as if it had never left, then his face gets serious again and he continues quietly. "Remember how I told you they were watching me after the whole thing happened at InCorps? Well, one day, my whole computer just happened to wipe itself clean and crash while I was trying to save all of my personal stuff to this flash drive. Photos, home videos, everything. I don't know if any of it actually saved because my computer was fried, but if it did and the world actually did get destroyed, this would be the last thing I have left of my...my family."

Mom displays immediate confusion and quickly looks up to Dane who shares her thoughts. Mr. Logan had never had any family at his house the entire time he had lived across from them nor had he ever mentioned them. They realize in this moment that they actually know nothing of their neighbor's past.

"John," the words barely make it past her lips, "I'm so sorry. Are you still close with them?"

He wipes his tear-filled eyes with the back of his hand and sniffs to clear up his breathing. "Uh, yeah..." he pulls a smile to his face as looks at up to Mom, then over to Dane, "...we're still close." he mutters quietly then immediately clears his throat loudly to shake off and move past the rush of emotions. "I didn't even think until this morning that I might have thrown it in one of these boxes!"

He reaches back behind his head with his hands and the flash drive and pulls a chain out from underneath his shirt, looping the drive onto it like some sort of new-age locket.

Suddenly, Dane perks up. How had he not seen Mr. Logan's necklace before? He begins thinking back: Mr. Logan had always worn collared shirts until he went to bed each night and he had been drying himself off inside the shower when he takes them. Of course, THE KEY!! He tries to hide his excitement as they continue to console their friend. Mr. Logan seems mostly recovered from his moment of sadness and is repacking everything into the box that he had just pulled out, clearly trying to avoid the barrage of questions that would come if he stayed in his memories. Dane keeps a serious face, but can't help but plan his next move to get into that cabinet. All of the questions he had about its possible contents flood back into his mind and he knows it is going to be a really long day as he waits for his moment to act...

Down the mountain a little ways from the cleanup site, the shack sits quiet and dark. The smoke had stopped rolling out from the small chimney days ago and the windows have frosted over completely. Inside, the computer towers still lie silent and lifeless and the seismometer has run through its supply of paper, which now piles blank on the floor below, the needle lying next to it.

Suddenly, footsteps can be heard crunching through the snow outside as a shadow becomes visible under the door. With a quick turn of the handle Kurrt puts his full weight into the door and stumbles completely naked into the middle of the room he had been forced to call his home the last few weeks. He rushes to the far wall of towers, leans his full weight against it and slides down to sit on the floor. He wraps his arms around his knees and squeezes tightly for warmth against his uncontrollable shivering. His heart and lungs feel frozen over, his muscles ache in atrophy from the cold and his mind can't focus on anything else. His eyes stare lifelessly across the room. After a moment, his brain begins to refocus. "What had happened? Why was everyone in the clearing dead?" Thoughts and questions begin to build in his head. "Wait, is my heart rate rising?" His shivering slows down slightly, his breathing starts to normalize and just now creates vapor clouds in front of his face.

He suddenly doesn't feel so cold anymore. He stands, using the wall to keep him steady, and looks around the messy room. He feels something grow inside of him. His body begins to feel warmer, stronger. "Could my circulation be coming back so quickly? That's not possible," he thinks to himself. As he stumbles his way to the center of the room small green currents become visible streaming up from his feet and hands towards his body. He falls to his knees and feels himself losing control as nerves fire throughout his body sporadically, causing twitches in his muscles. They are soft and spread out at first, then grow much more violent and seizure-like. The currents continue in to his chest where they converge into his heart, causing him to fold over, resting his head on the wooden floor. His chest lights up like a flame inside a lantern outlining his other organs and ribcage and sending a soft green hue over the otherwise dark room. His teeth grit, his body tightens as it strengthens within him.

With a blood-curdling scream, the shack is filled with a blinding green light. The walls and tin roof rattle uncontrollably, sparks fly from the computer towers and other equipment, the windows hold for a moment, then explode outward into the wilderness.

Then, it's over.

The mountainside is quiet again. Ash continues to fall like a gentle snow around the clearing. Suddenly, from inside the shack, a deep, powerful laugh breaks the silence.

"Still nothing on that radio, huh?" Mom asks her son from the couch where she sits with Mr. Logan after filling themselves at the dinner table. Luckily, Mom hadn't felt too innovative tonight and went with a simple beef stew and salad that she found vacuum packed in the freezer.

"The usual..." Dane sighs with disappointment, but not surprise. He has found his way to his airbed and has sprawled out to relax while scanning.

"Keep at it kid," Mr. Logan encourages, "someone's gotta say something at some point. I mean, I don't know about you guys, but I've kinda enjoyed the media silence."

"Well, I guess the last thing we heard was that show with the two guys arguing, so..." Mom agrees with him without necessarily saying it.

"Yeah," Dane ponders quietly from the bed behind them, "I miss the noise though. I miss just being able to turn it on and shut my brain off."

"Oh, God forbid you have to use your brain for a change, huh?" Mom jokes with him as Mr. Logan laughs.

"You know what I mean..." he scoffs quietly as he tries to remember what it was like to have music, TV, phone apps, and other forms of entertainment at his disposal. He also thinks back to time he spent with his friends talking and laughing endlessly. His last couple times with Sherri on the mountain and at graduation. He had taken so many things for granted.

A small skip in the radio static catches everyone's attention and causes Dane to sit up straight with wide eyes. Mom and Mr. Logan look over the back of the couch in Dane's direction with surprise in their faces. The second he heard it his fingers had jumped off the tuning knob which now sits mere millimeters from a possible signal, maybe even a voice! The three exchange one last hopeful look and Dane's fingers find their way back to the knob as his eyes fixate on the dial.

He slowly works in a counter-clockwise direction, being as careful as he can not to miss anything. Mom and Mr. Logan look on with impatient excitement as Dane works with surgical precision, his anticipation growing with every number the orange dial passes over. After a few moments the disappointment begins to settle itself into the room's occupants. Dane had now gone well past where they had thought they had heard the skip. With frustration, he begins to work his way back up through the numbers.

"I think it was right around 102!" he exclaims, now having passed it twice and begins to work his way back down.

Mom sees his desperation. "Dane, it might have been nothing." she tries to calm him. "Just slow down sweetie."

"It had to be something!" Dane exclaims as he tunes back and forth from 100-104 impatiently. "We haven't heard anything in days, how could it be nothing!?"

"Sometimes there's skips in the airwaves, Dane" Mr. Logan comes to Mom's assistance and tries to settle him down. "It doesn't necessarily mean there's a signal."

"No, it had to be something..." Dane says to himself, having given up on trying to convince them. Mom and Mr. Logan exchange worried looks and let him continue scanning.

"The kid's got determination, there's no doubt about that." Mr. Logan whispers to Mom as he lays out her sheets and pillow on the couch. She has made her way over to where Dane's airbed lies on the floor. After hours of ardent scanning, he has fallen asleep in his jeans on top of the blankets.

"Yeah, that's never been a question with him." Mom agrees as she shimmies the blanket out from underneath his legs and lays it over top of him. He still holds the static-spewing radio tightly in his hand, so Mom turns the volume way down instead of risking waking him up by trying to take it from him. She gives her son a loving look and reaches up to turn off the lamp that shines above his head before making her way back to the couch-bed Mr. Logan has prepared for her. "We just always had to make sure it was aimed in the right direction..." her whisper trails off as she tucks herself in.

"Nothing wrong with that," Mr. Logan whispers back as he cozies up on the floor in front of the couch, "some of the best leaders in our history were not born that way...they just needed someone to believe in them."

Silence fills the dark bunker as the occupants drift off to sleep to end their 6th day in their isolated, concrete home. After a couple of hours a noise breaks through the silence. Nobody stirs. Then it comes again.

"............is it................-re we on? This.........broadcasting fro-..............been 5 days since the strangest natural dis-........the death of everyone in the world as far as we know and.....-ntinue to wake up. Stemming from the Mt. Rainier exp-........what caused this strange phenomenon and what will be the long-term effect-"

Suddenly, the little, red Power light goes black and silence once again fills the bunker.

Chapter 14

"Mom, did you hear that?" Dane asks from his airbed with surprise in his voice.

She sits up lethargically to peer over the back of the couch. "Hmm?" she manages to pull the response from her lungs as she squints confusedly around the dark room.

"Shhh, listen." Dane is now sitting upright with his head cocked to one side to allow his ear a better angle to where he believes the sound to be coming from.

They are quiet for a few seconds, then..."THHHHPT!" The thunderous noise from beneath Mr. Logan's blanket draws the same disgusted reaction from them both.

"UGGGGGHHH, GROSS!" Dane exclaims pulling the blanket over his head. "Dear lord, someone open a window!!"

"Haha, that's terrible..." Mom, now wide awake, makes her way quickly from the couch to the kitchenette. "I think some coffee smell should cover it up though!"

"I hope so! What the hell was in that beef stew?!" Dane mumbles from beneath his blanket. While underneath he sees the radio that he had accidentally slept with. He scoffs at the silent electronic, grabs it and sets it off the side of the bed. He is not in the mood to deal with it today after his deflated excitement from the night before. He throws the blanket off of himself, now realizing he slept in his jeans, and heads for the shower before Mr. Logan gets a chance to use it first.

Mr. Logan is the last to wake up as he rolls over on the floor with a groan. "Good morning, guys...hey, are those coffee grounds still ok? They smell kinda weird..."

Later in the day, a day filled with the same normal, boring routine, Dane has opted for a book Mr. Logan found in one of his boxes simply titled "Bunker Life" instead of scouring through the lonely, static-filled radio stations.

The excitement with the radio the night before had distracted him from his mission to figure out what is hidden behind the locked cabinet door, but his interest had been renewed in his current boredom. He peers over his book at Mr. Logan, who sits at the cabinet tuning the knob on the CB radio with the right door wide open. "Hello? Hello? Can anyone read me?" he repeats multiple times into the small microphone. He had done this periodically during their stay, but had gotten frustrated with not getting a response about as quickly as Dane did with his radio search.

"Apparently there's no other 'lunatics' who own an emergency radio in our neighborhood, huh?" he says mostly to himself, but briefly sends a disappointed smirk in Dane's direction. Dane simply raises his eyebrows, then returns his eyes to his book. He hadn't even read much of the book, and what he did read he wasn't comprehending. He is far too deep in thought about how he's going to get that key and investigate the cabinet. Could he do it while Mr. Logan is sleeping? Too risky. Will Mr. Logan take a shower later in the day giving him the opportunity? He had said something at lunch about conserving water, so probably not. What the hell is in there anyways!? He looks across the room to his mom, who is keeping herself busy going through the shelves of food, no doubt contemplating her next "Bunker Concoction". He needed to know that they could trust Mr. Logan. He had to figure this out for her. For her safety.

"Hey, kiddo," she looks down to her feet near his airbed to see the abandoned radio, "how come you haven't checked the radio at all today?"

"Ugggggh," Dane doesn't even attempt to hide his frustration with the box's constant disappointment, "I don't really feel like it today, Mom."

"Really? I had to tuck you in with it last night!" she gives him a quick smile, which is not returned by her son. "Just give it a quick scan. Remember Bunker Survival 101..."

Dane catches her hint, "...maintain contact..." he grumbles.

"You guys WERE listening to me!!" Mr. Logan excitedly joins the conversation. "Go on kid, give it a once over, for old time's...er...I guess for present time's sake."

"Ugggggh, fine." It seems to take every ounce of Dane's strength to pull his body off the couch and drag it over to the side of his airbed where he picks up the radio then shuffles his feet back to the couch and plops down heavily with a big sigh. His fingers find their way to the volume knob where he's expecting to click the power on with a small turn. To his surprise, there is no click and the knob turns smoothly back and forth as Mom had not turned it off the night before. Confused, he turns it all the way counter clockwise and, finally *click*. He turns it again to the right *click* and yet nothing happens.

"Jeez, did you kill the batteries already?!" Mr. Logan jokes from his spot on the floor in front of the cabinet. "Well done, kid!" He pulls open one of the lower drawers on the cabinet and digs for a moment, "Here," he tosses 2 double A batteries over to Dane, "I don't have a ton of these, so remember the word for the day: Conserve!"

"Thanks," Dane says as he pulls the battery cover off the back of the radio, "and got it." He ejects the two worn out batteries and puts the first new one in. He grabs the second and uses the flat end to push against the small spring and shoves the opposite end in. Immediately, the radio springs to life.

"-can't really describe what's happened just yet, but it's a very strange phenomenon. The biggest question is if it's natural, chemical, terrorist, or what...we currently have no idea."

"MOM, I got something!!" Dane's excitement overcomes him. He turns towards his mom, but she has already rushed over to the side of the couch with her hand over her mouth in disbelief. Mr. Logan sits a few feet away, mouth agape in a smile, eyes glowing with happiness. None of them have heard another voice in a week and, until this point, didn't even know if anyone was still alive.

Dane's wide eyes return to the radio as if he had just been handed that cheeseburger pizza he mentioned the day before and the group, overcome with a gamut of emotions like they have never felt before, goes entirely silent as they listen in.

"Once again, reports are coming in that a majority, if not the entire world population perished in the 2 days following the eruption at Mt. Rainier in Washington only to strangely reawaken around 3 days later, beginning yesterday in the local region and seemingly moving outward through the US and Canada and across the world." projects the man's voice through the radio. *"It's a very scary and concerning situation as some of the areas across the globe such as South Africa and Australia still have entire areas that still look like victims of mass murder or mass suicide."*

"And possibly the scariest part is that we aren't even sure those people will reanimate," a woman's voice joins the conversation, *"though the reports we have gotten show that they would have been the last ones affected by this phenomenon, so they may just be the last to come back to life."*

"It was personally just plain alarming to come to at the news station last night surrounded by confused coworkers who had also just woken up, or some who had still not come to." continued the man. *"We couldn't get our phones to work to call emergency services, but, luckily, one by one they all awoke just as we had."*

"Yes, then going outside to see if others in the city were experiencing the same type of thing, it was like a bunch of zombies roaming the streets trying to figure out what had happened." the woman adds. *"And to see it so dark and hazy*

outside due to the overcast of the smoke from the mountain..."

This catches the group by surprise and they look away from the radio to each other as if to validate their confusion...surely the mountain wasn't still smoking this many days later.

"It was definitely surprising to see the mountain still emitting smoke, seemingly just as arduously as it was the day of the blast!" added the man, confirming their concerns about the mountain as if he had read their minds. *"Right now there is absolutely no view of the sky above the Seattle area and we received word a little bit ago from some of our international correspondents that the cover has spread that far, essentially covering the entire continental US, some of Canada and into the Pacific and Atlantic Oceans."*

"This is amazing!" exclaims Mr. Logan drawing surprised looks from both of his bunker mates. "No, sorry, it's terrible...but it's AMAZING!!"

They don't disagree with him. Though scary, it is very good to hear that people are alive and that most everything seems to be normalizing up top. Dane is especially encouraged to hear that his friends are most likely just fine and that he won't have to be in this bunker any longer...

"Hopefully only another week or so down here and we'll be good to go back up!" Mr. Logan finds a way to immediately kill his inner excitement.

"ANOTHER WEEK!?!" Dane catches Mr. Logan and his mom off guard with his outburst. "They said they're fine, why the hell would we have to be down here for ANOTHER WEEK?!"

"They didn't say anything like that, kid." Mr. Logan argues softly, trying to avoid setting the young man off. "They also have no idea if they're fine. The radioactivity that could have come from the explosion, or could still be coming from the mountain could have an effect on all of these people that just hasn't exposed itself yet."

"BUT-" Dane starts, but is silenced by his mom's hand on his shoulder.

"He's right, sweetie." she says softly to his dismay. "We don't have any idea what happened yet, or will happen in the next few days now that people are coming back to life...which is a really weird thing to say, but I think it's smart to wait it out a little bit."

Dane lets out a huge sigh, defeated by the adults around him. "It just...sucks."

Mom moves around and sits down next to him on the couch, putting her arm around him. "I know, Dane," she consoles him, then injects a happy tone to her voice, "but just think about how exciting the next few days will be now that we have an outside connection. We'll be getting updates, making plans, and when we finally feel it's safe to head up everything should be completely back to normal!"

Dane sighs again, but knows they're both right. He focuses back in on the radio as mom heads off to get dinner prepared and Mr. Logan, keeping his spot on the floor, slides a box close enough to him to sort through as he also listens in with great interest. Dane turns it up loud enough for them all to hear. Much to his delight, silence would no longer be part of their bunker stay.

Chapter 15

Breaking news updates come through the radio on a constant basis. The bunker mates have not turned it off since first hearing the voice come through, which has now been 2 days. In that time they have learned that the eruption of Mt. Rainier seemed to cause an outward-moving wave of death that eventually spanned the entire globe. Everyone in the world remained dead for about 4 days in what the radio personalities had termed "The Blackout" and then begun to wake up in the same outward pattern from the mountain. Once the population had awoken, systems began to get back up and running, most of life had gone back to normal and nobody seemed to have any further effects once the occupants of the cities and areas around Mt. Rainier were tested. Ideas of terrorist attack and radioactivity were quickly deserted by the media and a testing had been scheduled by the GSA at the smoke-spewing peak of the mountain, which was now access-restricted and being heavily patrolled by the US military.

"Once again, reports are coming in from around the world that there are no immediate health effects as well as no signs of radiation in the aftermath of The Blackout. It seems that the world has returned to normal for the most part and cleanup efforts have progressed on many of the sites of accidents that occurred due to The Blackout, including vehicle accidents, plane and ship crashes and more. In sad news, the death toll due to those accidents has risen across the world to over 2,000 and hospitals continue to be swamped with more and more injured. Stories continue to stream into the news station about the heroes of The Blackout, such as the many pilots who were able to pilot their planes to safe landings without help from ground crews who had already succumbed to their death, or the elderly lady in Michigan who's dog was in the process of fending off a pack of wolves that had made its way into her house when she woke up, no doubt saving her life. It's amazing to hear of the

different experiences that happened in the hours leading up to The Blackout."

Repetition begins to get the best of Dane as they lay around before bed listening to the radio announcers talk in endless circles of the same information, gradually adding small updates to it. "UGGGGGGGHHHH, how much longer do we have to be down here!?" he whines in his mom's direction. "I don't think I can stand to hear them say 'The Blackout' one more time!" This draws a chuckle from Mr. Logan.

"Just be patient, sweetie," she encourages him, "we know most everything is fine, so I don't think there's anything to rush back up for. The longer we can wait the safer we'll be."

"Ugh, such a 'Mom' answer..." Dane continues his whining.

"She's right, kid," Mr. Logan joins in, "plus, they still haven't tested the peak of Rainey yet and we're pretty close to it. I'd rather not risk it, would you?"

"You're getting pretty good at the 'Mom' answers too." Dane grumbles and lets out a sigh as he tucks himself under the sheets of his all too familiar airbed, then reaches off to the side to take his pill and turn the radio down. "Goodnight..."

Mom sends a concerned look in his direction, frustrated that her efforts to protect her son are wearing on him. Suddenly, she feels a hand on her arm and looks over to see an empathetic look on Mr. Logan's face. "We're doing the right thing," he consoles her, "he'll see that someday."

She just smiles at him, then rolls over on the couch to drift off to sleep with Mr. Logan soon following her lead.

Inside the shack, the luggage bags remain looking as if they had exploded. Clothes and food wrappers spread across the cold, wooden floor and a cloud of steam pushes its way into the room from underneath the bathroom door as a running shower can be heard. The computer towers stand dark and silent as if nothing in the world had changed over the last week, though the computer tower next to the desk beeps incessantly. The lamp on the desk in the middle of the room shines bright in the darkness, the only other light coming from one small windowpane where the morning hue streams in, diminished considerably by the smoky overcast that now covers most of the earth.

The water shuts off in the bathroom and Kurrt emerges moments later, dripping wet with a towel around his waist. He pushes the wet hair back off his forehead and steps forward into the room causing a quick increase in the beeping of the tower next to the desk. With an inquisitive look, he makes his way over to the desk, wipes his hand on his towel and reaches forward to push the power button on the monitor, the beeping increasing with every inch he moves closer. With a slight touch of the button the screen shines to life displaying the map of the mountain with an incredible green brightness.

"Off the charts..." he mumbles quietly under his breath with a disappointed look on his face.

He turns away from the computer and makes his way over to the mess of clothes on the floor. Reaching out for a t-shirt he realizes he is still dripping wet and pulls back to look into the wet palm of his hand. Confusion takes over his face as he sees small green currents running from his fingertips down into the palm of his hand. He raises his other hand in front of him to see the same thing occurring and stumbles back a step as the brightness of the darting currents increases. Suddenly, a burst of light from his hands makes him turn his head to avert his eyes for a moment. As he slowly returns his gaze forward he is even more confused to see a green orb has appeared in each palm, rotating in mid-air about a half an inch off his skin and glowing bright. Studying the glowing phenomena before him he begins to feel small tingles all over his body. Now noticing that his hands are completely dry he looks away from them to his arms and torso to see water droplets moving across his body from his feet to his legs up past his stomach and chest, out of his hair and down his neck and finally down his arms into the floating masses in his palms, which glow slightly brighter with each droplet they absorb.

With so many questions swirling through his head, Kurrt just stares blindly into the light of the globules. What could they be? How did they pull all the water off his body? What will happen if he closes his han- "GAAHHH!!"

Before he can even finish the thought in his head he closes his fingers around the orbs, sending an intense glowing energy up his arms and into the center of his chest and is jolted as if receiving an electric shock in an emergency room. With his head back, chest pushed out and hands in tight fists stretched out at his sides he closes his eyes and begins to smile as he savors the overwhelming energy that now radiates through him.

"Ahhhh, YES!!" he cries out in joy, now bringing his head forward and opening his eyes, which glow forth bright green, emitting vapors as if they were on fire. "This is amazi-Wha...WHAT THE...?!" he cuts himself off as his eyes make their way down towards the floor and he realizes that he is no longer earthbound, but instead, hovers about 3 inches above the cold wooden floor he once stood on. "AHHHHHH HAHAHA!!!" he laughs wildly. Then, as if he subconsciously knows what to do, he opens his hands wide sending the green light shooting back out from his chest to his palms and recreating the floating globules in his palms and he slowly floats back down to the floor.

With equal confusion as excitement, he brings his hands back in front of himself and once again studies the mysterious orbs, noticing they are much smaller than they had been a few moments ago. In a matter of seconds they begin to spin faster and faster and, with a small burst of light from each, they disappear, taking with them the green currents that ran through his hands and arms and the glow from his eyes.

Astonished by what just occurred, Kurrt throws on a white t-shirt and some dark grey jog pants and sits at the desk in front of the bright green monitor and stares blankly into the machinery and blinking lights. "I think..." he starts, then raises his empty hands in front of him with a smile forming on his face, "...I think I'm a friggin' superhero."

"In even more news of the world returning to business as usual in day 4 after the Blackout, we are getting breaking news that the President of the United States has scheduled an official press conference for tomorrow at 3pm Eastern Standard time." the deep-voiced news anchor keeps a calm in his voice. *"President Michaels is still safeguarded in the PEOC at this time, but has released a statement that he will be coming above ground for the first time since the Mt. Rainier explosion."*

"This is very exciting news!" a female voice joins the conversation.

"Yes, it's extremely encouraging to everyone around the world!" the man continues his calm excitement.

"MOM!" Dane exclaims from the couch without looking away from the radio. "Did you hear that!?"

"Dane, we're in a one-room bunker..." Mom says jokingly from the kitchenette about 10 feet away.

"That's noon here tomorrow," the hope in Dane's voice is obvious, "do you think we can go up for it?"

"Sweetie, we've talked about this." she hates to dash his hopes.

"But it's the President! If he's going up, it HAS to be safe, right?!" he continues his push.

"Not necessarily, kid." Mr. Logan enters the conversation from the dark corner where he was taking readings on the generator and water levels. Dane had almost forgotten he was there in the excitement. "The government knows a whole lot of stuff that we don't. You have no idea what kind of information they have, what precautions they're taking that we don't have the luxury of...you couldn't even imagine."

Without a word, Dane looks back to his mom hoping that she'll finally join his side of the argument. With sympathy in her eyes, she gives him a forced smile and shrugs her shoulders. He's lost once again...

"God dammit." Dane mumbles under his breath and returns to the radio updates in his lap. He knows this is the time to act. It's not going to get any safer than it is now. He has to convince them somehow...or, if he can't convince them, maybe he could show them. But that would have to wait just a little while longer...

Chapter 16

The next morning, as the persistent voice of the radio announcer advertises the 8am hour, Dane sits up on his squeaky airbed and stares blankly around the dark bunker with squinty eyes. He had hardly slept all night, but this had also helped him make sure to be the first one awake. With an unenthusiastic groan, he rolls off the side of his bed and grabs his towel, turns the radio volume down low, and shakes a pill out of his pill bottle then quietly makes his way over to the kitchenette. He turns on a small stream of water, tosses the pill onto his tongue and takes a quick sip to swallow it down, then makes his way over to the shower to prepare for the day, the millions of thoughts and ideas that kept him awake all night still running through his head.

The morning progresses as usual: Mom and Mr. Logan wake up while Dane is in the shower, Mr. Logan makes coffee, Mom makes breakfast, they all sit together and eat while discussing various different topics of what's going on above ground, then they each find their own projects to keep them busy. Much to Dane's excitement, this is a day that Mr. Logan has decided to shower. This is his chance. He hides his anxiousness to the best of his ability by doing something he knows how to do very well at this point: Slump into the couch and tune through radio stations. He puts on his best bored face and lets the adults continue their morning around him.

"Welp, kiddies," Mr. Logan announces with a stretch, "time to get the bunker stink off!"

"I don't think that's from the bunker…" Dane jokes softly raising his eyes from the radio. Mr. Logan laughs loudly and shakes a finger at the boy in acknowledgement of a good joke, but it takes every ounce of Dane's energy to pull his lips into a smile. Mr. Logan grabs his towel and makes his way to the shower chuckling the whole way. Once the water sprays forth and he is hidden behind the curtain Dane perks up. He has only minutes.

"Mom, we're going up!" he stands and makes his way to the kitchenette where she sits reading another book they found in one of Mr. Logan's boxes.

"What!?" She's taken aback by his sudden excitement. "What are you talking about?"

"Shhh," he urges her shooting a glance over to the shower curtain that hides their companion. He has a happy excitement in his eyes that his mom hasn't seen in a very long time. "We're going up." Dane whispers again as if there's nothing else in the entire world to say.

"Dane..." Mom gives him a saddened look. She knows what her son is feeling and can't wait to get out of the bunker too, but feels helpless knowing that it could still be dangerous above ground. She remembers what Mr. Logan said a couple of nights ago, *"We're doing the right thing, he'll see that someday."*

"Mom, there's never going to be a better time." Dane prods through whispers as not to alert Mr. Logan just yet. "The President is going up today, they're sending people up to Rainier later today, it's safe! I know it is!" She continues her sympathetic look, drawing further frustration from him, "You've gotta BELIEVE me!"

With that one word, Mom snaps out of the empathy she feels for her son and one more phrase from Mr. Logan finds its way into her thoughts, *"Some of the best leaders in our history were not born that way...they just needed someone to believe in them."*

"Ok, Dane." She finally caves and a grin breaks through the side of her mouth. "But what about Mr. Logan? He'll never go now, or let us go."

"We have to go without him." Dane's excitement shows as he lays out the plan he had spent all night coming up with instead of sleeping. "If we go now we can close the latch as soon as we're out, then he can decide what he wants to do."

"Well, I'm leaving a note." Mom starts to scramble around, knowing they don't have much time before his shower is done. "He saved our lives, he deserves a 'thank you' at least." She finds some paper and a pen in one of the kitchenette drawers and begins to scribble her message.

John,

We literally owe you our lives. Going with our instincts on this one. Please let us know when you're above ground and we can properly repay you.

Thank you, more than words can say!

Your Bunker Mates!

Dane has rushed over to his airbed and grabbed up all of his belongings: his pills, his cell phone and the action figure stowaway. Mom sets the note in front of the coffee pot and pauses as she rereads what she has written.

"Mom, you ready?" Dane whispers hastily. She turns, tears in her eyes but a smile on her face, and nods her head. "C'mon!" Dane ushers her over to the ladder in the dark corner of the bunker. On his way past the shower he notices Mr. Logan's clothes lying on the floor outside of the curtain. On top lies his necklace with the USB and a key hanging off of it. Dane had completely abandoned his cabinet mission when the voices came through on the radio. It no longer mattered, they were leaving.

They find the metal ladder that leads up to the sealed lid that has separated them from the world above for over a week. Dane grabs the rung just above his head then turns to his mom to make sure she's still with him. He knows that they will have to do this quickly for Mr. Logan's safety if it's not as safe up above as he thinks.

"I'm going to release the lid then put my weight into it and get above as fast as possible," Dane outlines the final phase of his plan, "then I'll pull you up and we can shut it right away. Mr. Logan will hear us and see the light, so he can seal it back up if he wants to stay."

Mom is still without words and continues to force a smile through her nervousness, but manages to nod her head to her son. As scared as she is, she is proud of him for being so strong and driven. He begins to make his way up to the cover and she follows right behind him. When he's reached the top of the ladder, he pushes himself up against the lid to allow Mom to get as high as possible on the ladder. With his shoulder scrunched up against the metal he reaches out with one hand to grab the round handle that seals the bunker, then the other as he prepares himself to turn and push. He gives one last look down to his mom, the only loved one he knows to have left in the world.

"Ready?" he tries to drum up some confidence through his shaky voice.

"Ready." She echoes.

With her final vote of confidence he is empowered, ready to escape this cement prison. With a huge exertion of his strength he shifts the handle in a counter-clockwise motion emitting a huge metal clang and a hiss of hot air shoots down against them.

"What the hell was that?" a scream comes from the shower. "I almost slipped and broke my..." Mr. Logan's head pops out from behind the curtain, eyes wide with surprise and confusion. He looks around the living area quickly realizing that no one is there, then shifts his gaze to the dark corner, which now has streams of light falling down around the ladder. Finally, he spots them atop the ladder and fear over takes him, "NO!! WHAT ARE YOU DOING!?!"

Dane immediately extends his legs and throws his weight upward against the lid, sending it flying open. Light floods down causing all three of them to divert their eyes. Dane throws himself up through the hole and onto the grass of Mr. Logan's lawn. Still unable to see, he feels for the hole and reaches in to find his mom's arms and pulls her up forcefully.

"YOU CAN'T GO UP YET, IT'S NOT SAFE!!!" Mr. Logan screams after them, now running across the cement floor holding an untied towel around his waist. With mom on solid ground and his eyes still working to adjust, Dane makes his way behind the open lid, plants his feet and drives through it like a linebacker. "NO, DANE!! I'M SUPPOSED TO PROTECT Y-" he shouts from halfway up the ladder as the door is sent slamming shut above him.

Dane blinks his eyes rapidly, still waiting for them to accept the little bit of light that has fought its way through the overcast. He finds his way over to his mom who is still on her hands and knees, one hand over her eyes to block out the blinding light. He kneels down next to her and grabs her arm to help pull her upward to a standing position.

"Ah…I can't see." Mom groans in pain.

"I know," Dane still squints against the sun, but takes a look around him. Cars drive by on the street and children play on one side of Mr. Logan's yard. On the other, a man has stopped his lawn mower and looks at the two as if they were aliens just beamed down to earth. Straight ahead, their house stands tall, covered in ash. It's very clear that everyone else has had time to clean off their properties and Dane can see the work he will have ahead of him, but can only feel relief in this moment that this world is not like the one he had earlier dreamed of.

As Mom's eyes recover from the barrage of light, she too begins to look around and a smile comes to her face in realization that everything seems ok. They are both startled by a loud, metallic bang behind them and spin around to look at the bunker lid. Mr. Logan had locked it down again just as Dane figured he would. Not knowing when they'll see their neighbor again they turn back towards their house. Mom gives Dane a big smile and puts her arm around his shoulders, "Let's go home."

A black SUV squeals up quickly to a large, window-covered skyscraper in the heart of downtown Los Angeles. The back door is swung open by a large suited man and a woman exits hastily, her heels clicking all the way up to the front door, which the man rushes to open as well, and through the lobby. She keeps her eyes down, her dark hair pulled back tightly into a ponytail as she scans her badge at the security desk and boards an elevator headed upward. Turning to face the front of the elevator, she raises her head for the first time since exiting the vehicle, an intensely serious look carving out the doctor's face as the elevator doors close and she heads upward.

The digital number reaches 73 then continues for 3 unnumbered floors and dings, signaling their intended destination. The doors slide open and she prepares to step off, but stops mid-stride as she realizes there is someone standing directly in front of the elevator. A dark-skinned man in a black suit stands with his back to her, his hands folded behind his back as he turns a shiny, silver ring on his left hand. Though the entire thing caught the doctor off guard, the man still stands there strong and silent longer than she expects.

Finally, without turning around, he breaks the silence, "Come with me, Doctor." he utters in his deep voice just loud enough for her to hear and heads straight down the hallway, never looking back to make sure she follows. Hesitantly, the doctor exits the elevator and follows the man down the hallway where they enter a large curtained-off glass office facing out towards the rest of the city, the ocean and the Santa Monica Mountains. He walks around the large mahogany desk and sits down in a large chair facing the window and peers off into the scenery, still fiddling with the ring that now props up in front of him. She didn't think she could get more nervous, but with one word he makes that possible. "Sit." He says calmly, but firmly.

She makes her way to a black cushioned seat in front of the desk, "The Electric Chair" she had always called it in her head. She had never sat in it before and suddenly didn't find the nickname to be so humorous. Having a seat on the edge of the chair as if to touch as little of it as possible, she positions herself upright with as much poise and confidence as she can muster and awaits the man's next words. Once again, they do not come as quickly as she hopes...

"Is this going to be a problem, Dr. Wong?" he asks with a consistent calm as he still faces away from her.

"No, sir." she exudes confidence in her first words since exiting the SUV. "We have everything under control."

The chair spins around suddenly and the man's palms meet the desk with a large thud, "UNDER CONTROL!?!" the power in his voice catches her by surprise even more than the impact of his hands on the desk. "What the hell was he even doing up there?" His eyes pierce into her with anger.

"He's collateral damage, sir." she attempts to regain her composure. "Even if he's still alive, we'll find him and contain. Kurrt will not be an issue."

"He better not be, we have much bigger things to worry about than a sarcastic seismologist..." he trails off in thought as he resumes spinning the ring on his finger, then moves to the next topic, "...where's our boy? Is he safe? And how much does he know?"

"Due to The Blackout we're not exactly sure where he is, sir," she worries about his reaction so continues on quickly, "but we had a safe-house plan in place and, as far as we know, that plan has been carried out. We're still waiting on an update, but he should be safe, and he should only know what he needs to know to serve his purpose."

"Good, make sure of it." he orders her. "Despite what happened with Kurrt, I want you to take the lead on this. I've got enough on my plate explaining everything that's happened to try and save this company." He fixates his eyes on hers with a cold intensity, "Do what you have to do. Get Kurrt back here...and find the boy."

Her eyes locked on his, she simply nods her head, stands and exits the office down the hall and towards the elevator. Her head sits tall on her shoulders with a renewed sense of purpose as she steps aboard and turns towards the closing doors. Once they are closed, she allows her emotions to build within her. Her face holds strong, but tears begin to glaze over her eyes. Out of nowhere she grimaces and reaches up to rest her fingers on her temple as it begins to surge intermittently. As the elevator screams downward she reels with sudden pain. Preparing to release a scream from her lungs at the peak of the pain, it suddenly ceases. She feels an energy swirl from her head that moves down towards her shoulders.

She slowly raises her eyelids to reveal two brightly glowing blue eyes. They gaze down to see blue trails, like vapors of mist, running through her arms towards her hands. As the fear grows within her the trails begin to glow brighter as they converge in her palm and a flash causes her to avert her eyes. She turns back slowly to see a small blue globule that reminds her of liquids in space, floating in her palm. She studies it for a moment with confusion, then turns her hand over to see if any changes are visible on its backside. The orb shoots a surge of energy forward from her hand against the elevator doors in front of her, leaving a dent and a scorch mark in the metal as she's thrown violently against the back wall. She pulls her body upright again, the glow in her eyes quickly fading back to normal and she looks back at her open, empty palm again with even more confusion.

The ding of the elevator reaching the ground floor startles her. She quickly gathers herself as the doors slide open. Her heels click through the lobby at a slightly faster pace than when she arrived as she exits the building and climbs into the same SUV. The man in the suit closes the door behind her. "Drive!" she orders as the SUV speeds off.

Chapter 17

"As we await the address from President Michaels scheduled in about a half an hour we can't help but wonder what will be said in regards to the Mount Rainier events and The Blackout. Clearly, this turned into a global occurrence and there will have to be a meeting between world leaders to discuss the recovery from it, as well as preventative planning in case of future instances. Figuring out the source of the event, whether it is, in fact, Mount Rainier or something completely unrelated, will be a huge part of that."

"DANE!" Mom shouts over the newscaster's resonating voice. "What are you doing? The President is coming on soon."

"I'm just changing, I'll be right down." Dane's shout is muffled through the t-shirt he is pulling over his head...the first different shirt he's worn in 10 days. He surveys his room for a moment, remembering how much he appreciates his bed, his computer, even just having a window! His eyes settle onto the phone charger sticking out of the wall next to his bedside table. HIS PHONE! He hadn't even thought about it since they got back above ground. He scrambles into his pocket and pulls it out, shoving his thumb onto the power button and bringing it to life after a couple of seconds. The battery light glows forth a bright red and displays 9% battery left. He rushes over to the wall and grabs the charger then darts out of the room and down the stairs. The phone hasn't stopped vibrating since its startup with incoming text messages, emails and other notifications as he reaches the bottom of the stairs and makes his way into the living room. He finds an outlet next to the couch and plugs the charger into the wall, then the phone into the charger.

Mom moves around the living room, straightening things that had been jostled by the blast while the news station blares forth on the TV with similar stories to what they've heard on the radio the past few days. Pictures and shaky home videos show Mount

Rainier with the smoke spewing out of its top, which they saw when first coming back above ground, but the display of bodies lying all over the world in mass amounts during The Blackout, people coming back to life and the confusion and chaos that ensued in the days after draw her attention. Dane sits on the couch and, after straightening some books on a shelf and propping up the picture of the man in uniform next to the door, Mom moves to join him to look on the TV in bewilderment. Dane begins to flip through the barrage of notifications on his phone.

Incoming Text: Gavin - Bro, what the hell is going on?

Incoming Text: Gavin - It's Armageddoning all over my Summer O' Fun!

Incoming Text: Gavin - Dude, where are you? I just woke up a little bit ago, Tim said he hasn't heard from you either...

Incoming Text: Tim - Dude, that was crazy! Let me know you and your mom made it home. Are you gonna leave the city?

Incoming Text: Tim - You alright man? Everyone here went into a coma or something.

Incoming Text: Tim - I'm gonna come over

Incoming Text: Tim - Hey man, I hope you're alright. I just left your house and made sure everything was closed up, it's been getting a little crazy here. People looting abandoned houses and stuff.

Incoming Text: Tim - Where you at? Text me!

Dane looks away from his phone to his mom, "Tim locked everything up. He said people were looting abandoned houses and stuff." he updates her as if reading the text aloud.

"Thank god," she lets out a sigh without taking her eyes off the television in front of them, "our house sticks out like a sore thumb!"

Dane looks back down to his phone and still sees the text message notification in the corner. He clicks on it and it displays **1 new message: Sherri**. Butterflies build in his stomach as his shaky thumb moves over the phone screen and touches the message to open it...

Incoming Text: Sherri - Hey Dane, it's Sherri. I hope you and your mom are ok! Something happened, everyone died. I just woke up a few hours ago. Gavin and Tim said they haven't heard from you since we were at the school. Please be safe and let me know you're ok!

"Who's that one from?" Mom interjects herself into Dane's thoughts and he scrambles to close the message.

"Nobody...I mean Sherri." he stammers. "She just wanted to see if we were ok."

"That's sweet," Mom turns her attention back to the TV, "you should text her back, let her know we're fine."

"I know! I will!" Dane unintentionally gets defensive and tosses the phone onto the table next to the couch. After a few awkward moments staring at the newscast, he reaches back over and grabs the phone again and starts a text:

Outgoing Text - Hey Sherri, we're ok. Weirdly enough, our neighbor had an underground bunker and we just came up a little bit ago for the address. You and your family all ok?

As soon as the text goes off, he realizes how much shit he'll get from his friends if they realize that he texted Sherri first. He immediately begins a group text to Tim and Gavin.

Outgoing Text - Guess who's alive bitches!! Our neighbor had a bunker under his yard, no reception the whole time. Glad you guys are ok!

He sets his phone on the arm of the couch next to him and joins his mom's gaze into the newscast, which is showing a flurry of people in suits prepping the stage that holds an American Flag, a Presidential Flag and a wooden podium that bears the presidential seal. They bustle back and forth across the stage, stopping to check the microphones and their cords, adjust the flags and guide the media personnel to their seats. The whole time the voice of one male and one female newscaster talk through the possibilities of what will be discussed in the President's speech.

"What do you think he's going to say?" Dane's eyes don't leave the television, but the question draws his mom's towards him.

"I have no idea, sweetie." Mom's response is quiet, nervous. She looks down and takes a couple of seconds to think about it and her nervousness overtakes her. She has no words to answer her son's question or to help ease his angst. She sheepishly returns to watching the television.

They are both startled when Dane's phone jingles and vibrates the couch, then does it again, then again, and again and again.

"I think I'll put it on silent..." Dane says apologetically as he reaches over to check the messages from his friends. He clicks on the notification on the screen and it opens up the group text with Gavin and Tim.

<u>Incoming Text: Gavin</u> - He's back from the dead!!!!!!!

<u>Incoming Text: Gavin</u> - Just in time too, we were about to come over and start divvying up your shit!

<u>Incoming Text: Gavin</u> - I called dibs on your computer, so...

<u>Incoming Text: Tim</u> - Dude, welcome back to the world!! What was it like living in a bunker for almost 2 weeks!?

<u>Incoming Text: Tim</u> - Lol, nice Gavin. I get his car and porn stash!

Dane laughs to himself reading his friends' ridiculous razzing and types up his reply:

<u>Outgoing Text:</u> You guys suck...I mean I missed you guys SO much!

<u>Outgoing Text:</u> Haha The bunker wasn't the worst thing in the world, just boring. It's nice to have TV again And Tim, you'll never find my stash!

Just as he's about to hit "Send", the phone vibrates in his hand again, but a message doesn't appear in the group text. Momentarily confused, he sends off the text to his friends and clicks on the notification, which displays the same title that had put him in a nervous tizzy before: **<u>1 new message: Sherri</u>**. Immediately, the butterflies come back to his stomach as he hesitates clicking on it. Just as he's about to open it up mom grabs his forearm.

"Here he is," she exclaims pointing at the TV, "the President is coming on!"

Dane's eyes leave his phone to look into the television to see the leader of the US stride onto the stage raising his hand in a soft wave to the crowd before him. He confidently sets himself up behind the bouquet of microphones protruding from the podium with a very serious look on his face. Dane had always thought he looked a bit like Aaron Eckhart with a slight peppering of grey above the ears in his otherwise dark hair, which is parted and falls perfectly onto his forehead as if each strand has a pre-designated spot. He keeps his head down for just a moment, then raises it to face directly into the camera with his bright blue eyes.

"My fellow Americans, it is with great joy that I am able to join you today, but sadness that it is to discuss the topics that have affected our country, and the entire world, in the last week and a half. As you can imagine, 11 days in an underground safehouse can become very tedious and all I longed for was to join you all here, above ground to put forward my best effort to help in the recovery from the events that occurred."

Dane and Mom give each other a quick glance in confirmation of his bunker comments then immediately return to listening.

"Once my staff deemed that everything was safe, it was a quick decision for me to rejoin my fellow man and get started on the recovery process for our great country. Though there have been many speculations flying around about the possible cause or causes of the Mount Rainier explosion followed by the worldwide event that is being called 'The Blackout' I would like to urge Americans to have patience with our government officials who are doing everything possible to determine an exact origin. Please refrain from creating speculations and spreading rumors that may lead to civil unrest among our people and give our professionals the time they need to do their jobs."

As Dane and Mom stare on agonizingly waiting for any news the government might be ready to reveal the president clears his throat and adjusts his tie as if he just realized it's too tight. For the first time his eyes leave their direct gaze into the camera.

"Now," he continues, clearing his throat again and refocusing his eyes straight ahead. "what we do know is that the cleanup process has displayed a small, but not insignificant number of deaths from this occurrence when you consider that it was global. This comes as very good news from such an astounding and emotionally jarring event, though it is important to remember all of those who perished along with their families and loved ones. The American people have done a great job of..." he pauses for a second. His eyes suddenly seem shifty, unable to stay still on the camera. In one of the fastest seconds Dane has ever encountered, the President reaches his hand up to his forehead as he looks away and immediately crumbles to the ground out of frame. Mom jumps to her feet with her hand over her mouth as gasps and screams fill the conference room for just a moment before the feed cuts out to a default screen displaying the Presidential Symbol behind a piercing emergency tone.

Dane stares wide-eyed and mouth agape while mom stands next to him, her hand over her mouth in bewilderment. Tears begin to appear in her saddened eyes as she looks down at her son who can do nothing but look back with the same feelings of shock. "Oh my god..." are the only words she's able to push out of her lungs as she looks back to the TV hoping that it was all in her imagination, but is disheartened to still see the same emergency screen.

"Mom..." Dane finally finds his words, "is he...dead?"

She doesn't answer at first, hoping that she doesn't have to say Yes to his question. "I...I have no idea." she stammers through her astonishment. "I mean, he could just..." she trails off.

Dane looks up at her, expecting the rest of the sentence, but slowly her hand lazily finds its way back down to her side and her weight shifts. She seems to waver unsteadily for a moment so Dane quickly stands and reaches to put his hands on her shoulders. "Mom?" The moment he has ahold of them her head rolls back and her legs collapse from underneath her. Caught off guard, Dane does his best to guide her back onto the couch where she slumps away from him. With her in a safe, resting position, Dane swings around in front of her, brushing her dark hair off her face, "Mom, what's wrong!? Mom!? MOM, ANSWER ME!"

With a hiss and two mechanical beeps, the large metal doors with the InCorps logo brazen across them slide open to reveal the doctor in her usual pants suit, her dark hair pulled tightly behind her. She strides confidently through the doorway and makes her way down the hall until she reaches and joins the man from the office the day before, who stands in front of a window that peers into a laboratory, hands behind his back spinning the ring on his finger. They stand side-by-side without saying anything, only looking into the laboratory ahead of them as if each is waiting for the other to break the silence.

"I've set up a task force of my men to retrieve-" she begins, but the man's booming voice interrupts her.

"When you said that Kurrt was collateral damage," the man begins softly, but sternly, "was there anything that gave you reason to believe that to be true, Dr. Wong? Or was that just something that you hoped would put me at ease?"

The doctor can't help feeling like it's a trick question and that he has some further information that she doesn't. Her mind immediately flashes back to the moment she saw the large crater in the snow with Kurrt's mangled restraint gurney floating at the bottom. "Well, what I meant was that there's really no reason-"

"What you meant was for me to focus my efforts elsewhere while you attempted to clean up the situation...a situation that should have never happened." he interrupts her again with more forcefulness in his voice, though his eyes never leave the laboratory in front of them. "Well, the problem with that, Dr.

Wong, is that my efforts continue to get interrupted by your 'collateral damage'. Have you heard?"

She thinks for a moment about what he could be referring to, "About the President? That doesn't really have anything to do with-" she stops immediately when a door to the lab slides open and 8 men are wheeled in on standing stretchers, restrained from their foreheads down to their ankles and she immediately realizes he wasn't talking about the President. She knows these men. They were on the mountain with her that night and when they woke up 4 days later. These were the men she recruited the day before for her task force to investigate Kurrt's whereabouts and the condition of the mountain. "What is this?" she inquires, finally turning to look at the tall, statuesque man next to her.

"This..." the man pauses, then turns his head to look down on her for the first time, "is part of your ever-growing 'collateral damage'." His eyes immediately make their way back in front of them.

She continues to look at him with a wide-eyed confusion, recalling in her mind the strange occurrence in the elevator, then also turns her gaze back through the window as a group of men in hooded, white lab suits and gasmasks enter the room to study their subjects.

Chapter 18

The hums and beeping of medical equipment have lulled Dane off to sleep as he slumps uncomfortably in a partially cushioned chair in the empty Eatonville Hospital waiting room. The skin around his eyes show redness from crying and his body relaxes for the first time in hours since the paramedics rushed his mom from their house to the emergency room. He had never been so scared in his life, not even when the top of Mount Rainier blew during graduation.

Suddenly, a young doctor appears through a swinging door looking down at a clipboard in his hands and adjusts his dark-framed glasses, "Dane Denson?" As he looks up, he realizes that the sleeping boy is the only one in the waiting room and makes his way over to him quietly. He sets his hand on Dane's shoulder and shakes it softly, "Dane? Dane, wake up."

Dane jolts awake at the doctor's urging and his eyes dart around the room before finally settling on the man kneeling next to him. "Hey…uh…yeah. I'm Dane." he stammers sitting up in the chair rubbing his eyes to help them adjust.

"Dane," the doctor continues, "there's no easy way to let you know…your mom has passed."

The color drops out of Dane's face and tears immediately begin to form in his eyes. Seeing this, the doctor jumps at the chance to console him and hopefully deliver some good news.

"Hold on, there's more!" he grabs Dane's attention before he breaks down. "Ever since everyone woke up from The Blackout we've had to be very careful with any casualties. We're keeping any who are deceased from seemingly natural causes for five days to ensure that it's not just the same thing everyone experienced last week. Now, you said you were in an underground bunker during everything, right?"

Dane is still only moments away from breaking down, but the doctor's info has calmed him enough for the moment. "Yeah," he says shakily, "we went down right after the mountain blew and came back up earlier today."

"See?" the doctor pulls out a smile to help his case. "I don't want to make any promises or assumptions, but I think the best thing to do right now is to keep her for a few days and hope that she reanimates like everyone else did." His smile disappears and he puts a hand back on Dane's shoulder, "I do want you to be prepared if that doesn't happen, though. Sound ok?"

"I...uh..." Dane, overwhelmed by the whole situation, struggles to make sense of it all. "Yeah, I mean...is there any other option?"

"I think this is what's best. We can observe her and be prepared for whatever may happen, then update you." the doctor seems to succeed in calming Dane enough where he can hand him a clipboard for his information. "We'll give you updates on any changes that occur and, of course, you're more than welcome to come see her anytime during regular visitation hours."

Dane begins to fill out the information form in front of him with a look of hopelessness on his face. The doctor stays kneeling next to him for a moment drawing his eyes away from the clipboard. "Don't worry just yet, kid. If you want to see her before you go home just let Karen know at the desk and she'll tell you where to go." With his part done the doctor stands and leaves Dane to finish his paperwork. Dane sits and writes quietly for a few minutes then stands and makes his way towards the receptionist window to hand in the clipboard. She thanks him, then directs him to his mom's room. He slowly slinks back through seemingly endless white hallways before he reaches room #145. He takes a deep breath and pushes through the door and disappears into the poorly lit room.

Wind whips through the trees of Mount Rainier, which hold strong due to the buildup of snow on each branch. Black rocks expose themselves through the white expanse as far as the eye can see with small peaks of snow as if each were a small mountain of its own. Other than the slight swaying of the trees, the only motion comes from a curious little squirrel that finds its way down a tree and into a clearing in search of food. It sniffs as it darts around, every now and then stopping to dig into the snow if it thinks it's found something. Suddenly, as if sensing that it is no longer alone in the world, it perks up on its hind legs and looks around the clearing, sniffing the air around him.

BOOM!!!

The explosion echoes off into the distance and disappears into the seemingly endless wilderness. Where the squirrel once stood is now just a small crater of slowly melting snow that glistens a slight green glow around its edges. Across the clearing Kurrt kneels with a satisfied smile on his face, his eyes glowing bright and his right arm extended out, braced at the elbow by the left hand, with the green current-covered palm aiming directly at the crater. On each side of him are small holes in the snow where he had drawn his energy for the shot. The currents through his arms and the glow of his eyes slowly fade away, but the smile only grows larger as he stands.

"This is amazing..." he mutters to himself as he raises his palms in front of him to get a good look. "I'm absorbing water and using it as an energy pulse that...I mean, it had to go 1,000...maybe 2,000 miles per hour...Yes, it was definitely faster than a bullet."

Kurrt proceeds to laugh wildly into the wind. As his enjoyment of his newly tuned-in powers peaks, so does his curiosity. His laugh fades and he kneels again, palms open down into the snow below him. "Time to fly..." he whispers to himself. The currents reappear down his arms and up his neck, his eyes begin to glow as the snow below his hands begins to glow brightly, then is sucked into the now visible green orbs. He moves his hands around his feet absorbing extra snow then closes his hands into fists and stands tall. He drops his head, focusing his energy inward and causing the currents to glow brighter. He doesn't want to expend all of the energy in one shot this time, he has to curb it, control it. He breathes out through pursed lips as he slowly rolls his head back, raises his clenched fists out at his sides and prepares to levitate.

Suddenly, he shoots straight up into the air at an amazing speed. He immediately freaks out as he soars up at an amazing speed and begins screaming and flailing his arms and legs, which are now void of the green energy currents. As he begins to slow, he is able to recover from his fear enough to focus. He engages his body, reigniting the currents throughout, and angles his view down towards the mountain again. He is suddenly jolted in a downward angle towards the clearing, which is already hundreds of feet below him. Not wanting to impact at this speed, he angles his view slightly upward to the area where he had knelt and, just as he's about thirty feet off the ground, shoots in that direction.

His body tears into the snow surface and he tumbles across the clearing like a stone skipping across water, hitting every ten feet and slowing down a little more with each impact. Between impacts he notices a large black rock directly in his path. The scream that he attempts to pull from his lungs is knocked away when he finally hits and rolls through the snow out of control. At the last second he is able to put his hands up in front of him and he strikes the rock, catching himself just enough to prevent any damage.

He takes a few quick, panicked breaths and finally opens his eyes as if checking that he's still alive. "WHAT THE HELL!?" he shouts at himself. He looks at the rock in front of him, which both of his hands still grip tightly. He releases it with his right hand, which swings above his head. "Son of a b-"

As his hand swings back down to strike the rock in anger it is stopped just above the surface and the glow of green covers his face. The orb has reappeared between his palm and the surface of the rock, then the same occurs in his left hand. The orbs glow brighter and rotate quicker as they chip apart the rock and pull hundreds of small shards into them. After a few seconds Kurrt, kneeling in the snow with a large hole in front of him where the rock once stood, grips his hands into fists, pulling the energy into his body. He, once again, rolls his head back with his glowing eyes closed and extends his fists out to each side. This time he slowly lifts off his knees a few feet into the air. Steady above the snowy surface, he brings his head forward and opens his eyes, the smile returning to his face. "Now I gotcha." he says proudly as he brings his open hands to his sides, palms facing towards the ground and shoots up over the trees.

The next day Dane occupies one in a row of chairs that line the wall of a large hospital room. On the opposite wall, lined up perfectly, each with their own beeping monitors are three beds in slightly upward positions that serve as the resting places for recently deceased patients. Dane sits right at the end of Mom's bed, which is the furthest into the room. Next to her lies an elderly, grey haired man then a young, brown-haired girl who he figures can't be more than thirteen years old.

In the eleven hours since visiting hours had started Dane, along with the young girl's parents and older brother, had not left the room and the elderly man's wife and kids had come and gone. Gavin and Tim had visited earlier, greeting their grieving friend with huge hugs and stayed for a little while. After not being able to get Dane to leave the room for some lunch they left promising that they'd come back and see him the next day. The young girl's father, Gary, had also talked to Dane briefly after his friends left. His daughter, Alyssa, had had a seizure at their pool due to heat and dehydration, then succumbed to pneumonia at the hospital 3 days ago. Still unaware of the effects of The Blackout, the doctors had recommended the same thing to them that they had to Dane: That they wait a few days to see if she comes back to life. He was a religious man telling Dane they were putting all their faith in

God and leading a prayer with his family each hour. Not feeling quite up to socializing, Dane had kept to himself the entire day and avoided the father's invites to join them in their prayers.

The old man's family had spoken with the doctors during their visit. He was now on his 5th day in the hospital after passing and they would be discharging him at the end of the day if he had not come back to life by then. Dane had gotten a shot of pain to the pit of his stomach hearing this, hoping that he wouldn't have to have a similar conversation with the doctors in a few days.

The pain that resided in his stomach now was due to hunger, so he decides to find a snack machine to get him through the final hour. As he's about to stand up, the old man's family reappears in the hallway with a doctor. The old woman dabs her eyes with a handkerchief as her middle aged daughter and two sons console her. The doctor has a sympathetic look on his face as he speaks softly to her, continually referencing the clipboard in his hand. Dane, not wanting to witness the situation, grabs the backpack he had brought with him, throws it over his shoulder and heads for the door, giving Mom a loving look as he passes her bed.

"You outta here, son?" the young girl's father stands as Dane passes him and reaches out putting his hand on Dane's shoulder.

"Nah, not yet." Dane replies sheepishly, not wanting to get stuck in a conversation and also somewhat uncomfortable with this guy calling him "son". "Just grabbing some food."

Gary pulls his hand away, "Alright, son. We'll be here when you get back. Keep faith, Jesus will pull us through."

Dane gives him a quick look with a forced smile, then moves quickly towards the door. As soon as he pushes through, the somber group in the hallway heads towards him. He holds the door and gives them an empathetic smile and nod as they file into the room.

Happy to have avoided that situation he makes his way to the nurse's desk at the end of the hall.

"Excuse me," he speaks softly in the quiet hallway catching the attention of a heavy, older woman in nurse's scrubs, "is there a snack machine around here?"

"Yeah!" she exclaims with an overabundance of energy. "It's down this hallway to your right just before you hit the lobby!"

Dane thanks her and heads down the hallway, finding the machine easily. He puts in two dollars, pushes a few buttons and the machine drops down some pretzels and an energy bar, which he retrieves through the swinging door at the bottom. He chews and swallows the first pretzel, just now realizing how hungry he was. Not wanting to go back to the room while the old man's family gets the bad news, he wanders down a few hallways. Without even realizing it he flies through the pretzels and rips into the energy bar wrapper. As he bites into it, he is startled by a loud crash behind him. He spins around almost choking on the bar in his mouth and sees two large doors swing open wildly. A man in an EMT uniform and two nurses push a gurney quickly through the doors and down the hallway in the opposite direction towards a large red sign marked "EMERGENCY".

"We can't get a pulse and he's not breathing!" the EMT loudly informs the nurses.

"What happened to him?" shouts one of the nurses as she pumps a breathing mask over the patient's mouth.

Just as they blow through the doors to the emergency room Dane hears the EMT answer the nurse, "We don't know, we got an anonymous call and found him in an underground bunker."

For the second time in just a few seconds, Dane almost chokes on his energy bar as they disappear through the swinging doors and to the right down a hallway. Wide-eyed, wondering if it's possible, he rushes down the hallway after them and shoves his way through the heavy doors immediately turning right to see nothing. He quickly walks down the hallway looking into each room window as he passes, then stops abruptly. In the room before him he sees the gurney, but can't see the man's face as the emergency crew works erratically on both sides of him. They now have him hooked up to machines behind him that show no signs of life and, after a few minutes of CPR and shocks from an AED, Dane notices the pace of the nurses slow. They remove the equipment from their patient and begin to pack it away. He hadn't made it.

With defeated looks on their faces, they move from the sides of the bed and begin to clean up the area around their patient. Tears find their way to Dane's eyes again as one of the nurses approaches the bed and pulls the white sheet over Mr. Logan's face.

Chapter 19

With bloodshot eyes and drooped shoulders that struggle to hold his backpack, Dane slumps through the front doors of the hospital the next day at about 11am, three hours after visiting hours had begun. He quietly checks in with the receptionist who motions him in the direction of his mom's room, though he already knows his way very well by now. His feet slowly drag him down the hallway until the room comes into view. As he approaches the door he can see the little girl's family, now on day 4, and braces himself for an unwelcomed conversation.

Just as expected, when he pushes his way through the door Gary springs from his chair. "Hey, Dane!" Dane can't believe the positivity that rings in his voice, "You're late!" he jokes with a smile.

Dane sighs and pulls off as much of a smile as possible, "Yeah, I...didn't sleep much last night..." his voice trails off as he looks away to his mom's bed, but is distracted by something else. All three beds sit steady and quiet as they did the day before, but something is different. Next to mom, where the old man had been, is Mr. Logan. In his sleeplessness the night before Dane had wondered if they were going to keep him for observation, but he had completely forgotten about it on his way in this morning.

"Is everything alright, kid?" he draws Dane's attention by inadvertently using the nickname Mr. Logan had always called him. This sends Dane's head into a spin.

We killed Mr. Logan by opening the hatch when he didn't want us to.

Mom's dead too.

I have no idea if she'll come back.

It was all my idea.

Why am I still alive?

Why am I left here to go through this pain?

I was so selfish…

He remembers their escape, his mom falling to the couch and envisions what it must have been like for Mr. Logan to die in the bunker all by himself and a pain begins to radiate behind his forehead

"Dane!" Gary grabs Dane's shoulder when he sees his darting eyes well up with tears. "I know it's a lot, but we're in this together."

Dane tries to compose himself for a moment as the man wraps him up in a big, somewhat awkward hug. As he releases the boy from his grip he looks at him with loving eyes, "God will guide us through, I know it. Would you like to pray with us?"

Dane sheepishly thanks him and excuses himself from the room. As he makes his way down the hallway he looks down and notices his hands are shuddering violently. He had forgotten to take his medication this morning. He immediately whips his backpack around, digs into it for a few seconds and pulls out his orange bottle while making his way over to a water fountain. Tossing the pill back with a sip of water he closes his eyes to focus and begins to feel normal again. His hands steady and the throbbing in his head begins to subside.

"Yeah, he just stepped out for a moment." Gary's voice echoes down the hall. He looks up in the direction of his mom's room to meet two bright blue eyes and a familiar face that he had not seen in a long time. "Ah, there he is!" the man announces excitedly, pointing Sherri in his direction.

Inside the InCorps lab, Dr. Wong has not left her spot in front of the observing window for nearly an hour, enthralled as she watches the tests being run on her 8 colleagues. They exhibit almost the exact same symptoms she experienced in the elevator, but it seems that each person's is brought on by something different. A man named Cameron had yellow, spikey masses of energy appear in his palms when his body was exposed directly to UV light. Another, named Allen experienced orange flickering globes when he was exposed to fire. The only other one they had diagnosed to this point was a man named Charles, who reacted directly to carbon dioxide with white, vapor-like energy masses.

Each time one of the men reacts to an element it reminds her of her moment in the elevator, the pain she felt, the wonder at seeing the blue orb in the palm of her hand. If they are all experiencing this, she begins to worry about the abilities that Kurrt may have gained...if he were still alive.

Butterflies work themselves into her stomach as fear of what could happen overtakes her thoughts. She turns from the window and places a hand on her stomach to calm it. Her eyes are abruptly drawn downward by a sudden bright, blue glow which she quickly pin points to the hand on her stomach. As she pulls it away from her body she sees the blue energy amass itself in her palm again. She quickly closes her fist, harnessing the light inside of it, looks both ways to make sure there isn't anyone around and quickly makes her way to a bathroom down the empty hallway. She bursts through the door and locks it behind her, making her way over to a mirror. It is now that she is able to see her bright blue, glowing eyes for the first time. Not worried about them as much, she raises her closed hand up in front of her and slowly opens it, releasing the energy back into the small rotating mass. Remembering what happened last time when the energy expelled itself, she focuses on it intently, causing it to glow even brighter and rotate more quickly. She now notices that it seems to push against her hand much like two like-pole magnets pushing each other away. Bringing her other hand over top, she is able to feel it push in both directions, then, to her surprise, it splits as she pulls one hand away. With energy in both hands curiosity overtakes her. She brings both open hands down to her sides facing the floor and focuses on pushing the energy away from her palms.

She feels the energy radiate down the sides of her pants and, suddenly, she is floating a few inches off the ground.

She looks down in amazement and a huge smile grows on her face, then refocuses on her own bright blue eyes in the mirror ahead of her, "Time to get the boys together...we've got a friend to go see."

Meanwhile, inside the shack near the top of Mt. Rainier, Kurrt is busy at work. He had spent the entire previous day testing out his new abilities and working on harnessing them. He had learned that his "power globes", as he had been calling them, could absorb any sort of matter. The more dense the object, the more stable the energy they expelled, such as the snow versus the rock when he attempted to fly. He had also tested out the duration of the energy based on the objects absorbed. It didn't surprise him that more dense objects also lasted longer.

Now, though, he was working on a plan. His face illuminated by the computer in the center of the room, he was no longer tracking radiation and seismic activity. He had been scouring websites for hours, purchasing and ordering items for overnight delivery.

Outside of Mom's hospital room Dane sits next to Sherri, who listens intently as he talks a million miles per hour to tell her everything that has happened since he saw her at the school: Mr. Logan getting them into the bunker, a week and a half underground, escaping to see the President's speech, and what had happened to Mom. As usual Dane had been struck with nervousness when he first saw her, but her huge hug and consoling about his mother's condition had eased him a little. Telling her his story was the first time he had actually felt comfortable with her.

"That's so weird," she finally responds, "so your mom went down right after the President did? Seems too well-timed to be a coincidence."

"Yeah, I dunno." Dane shrugs his tired shoulders. "The doctors seem to think that being down in the bunker, like the President, basically just postponed The Blackout for us and that she'll come back...maybe."

"I hope they're right." Sherri says sullenly. "But it's weird that you're just fine...I mean...it's good, but...you know what I mean."

A big grin overcomes Dane's face, his first real smile in almost 3 days. "I know, thanks." he chuckles bringing some redness to her pale cheeks.

They are both startled by the door of the room opening suddenly behind Dane as Gary sticks his head out with wide eyes, "Did you guys hear what's going on? Something is happening up on Rainier, it just popped up on my phone."

"There's a TV in the lobby," Dane remembers noticing it a couple of nights ago while he was waiting there, "let's go!" The man goes back into the room for a moment to tell his family that he'd be right back, then emerges again as Dane and Sherri head down the hallway to the lobby.

A strange air hovers over the waiting room as the three enter hurriedly. Dane had never imagined that an emergency room waiting area could be so quiet. About 10 people waiting to be taken back are all staring at the small box TV mounted in the corner of the room, even the receptionist has slid open her glass window and is leaning into the room to see better.

Dane's eyes turn in the same direction as the others and fixate on the television. He begins to read the bulletin emblazoned across the bottom of the screen; **"BREAKING NEWS: Green dome appears covering top of Mt. Rainier in WA"** The video displaying above the bulletin is shaky footage that shows very clearly what looks like a large, round field of green energy encasing the top half of the mountain. As the video focuses in and out currents of energy can be seen running through the field like veins and smoke continues to spew from the top of the mountain and straight up through the field and into the sky.

"What the hell is that?" Sherri whispers softly to herself, catching Dane's distracted attention.

He looks over into her blue eyes with nervousness, "I have no idea," he shakes his head softly, then redirects his attention back to the TV, "but I doubt it's a good thing..."

"It kinda looks like a force field." Gary blurts out in the deathly silent room catching multiple people by surprise and drawing some irritated glances. "Sorry..." he backtracks his comment, then shrugs his shoulders in Dane and Sherri's direction, "it does, though." He looks back to the television while drawing a cross over his body with his hand.

The bulletin changes to read: **"BREAKING NEWS: Unexplained field covers previous volcanic site on Mt. Rainier. Incumbent President to address nation shortly."**

Dane stares in wonder and fear at the shaky video that continues looping on the TV. His stomach begins to turn as his mind races. He had been worrying about his mom for the past 3 days, then Mr. Logan since yesterday, now he was worried for everyone else, including himself. He needed to get ahold of Tim and Gavin. He needed to protect all of them and –

Suddenly, his thoughts are jarred back to the present moment as Sherri's hand finds his and squeezes it tightly.

Chapter 20

Down a long, dark hallway stands a lonely, metal door. A loud, inconsistent banging, the sound of saws and other power tools, and loud shouting resonate through the door and down the hallway. As the doctor approaches, the sign on the door can now be made out, "Ballistics Dept." below which an accompanying sign reads "No Admittance". She confidently strides up to the door and bangs on it loudly. Nothing. She bangs on it again and can hear the noises behind it die down. After a few seconds, she hears a small mechanical sound in the corner just above the door and sees a camera angle itself in her direction. As she stares into the camera intently, she hears the door unlock with a loud, metallic thud. It opens a few inches to reveal a short blonde-haired man covered in black oil and soot, peering through thick safety goggles that make his hazel eyes look much bigger than they are. She says nothing, only peers at him sternly through the protective glass layer of the goggles.

With a confused look on his face, the man looks out into the rest of the hallway to see if there was anyone else with her. "Ummm, yes?" his nasally voice offers as a silence-breaker to the awkward moment.

With an unfazed intensity in her glare she finally addresses the man in front of her, "Are you Simeon?"

The confusion on the man's face grows as he gives a quick look behind him to the men working, then back to the woman in front of him. "Listen, we're really busy and we've-"

"Simeon!" She interjects forcefully, catching the man off guard then continues calmly. "I need your help and, if you remember correctly, you owe the Doctor a favor."

The man's eyes go wide behind their protective goggles and he takes a step back. "The Doctor..." he stares at her in disbelief. Suddenly, he realizes she is no longer looking at him, rather past him over his right shoulder. He slowly turns to follow her gaze to a wall on the opposite side of the room where ten exoskeleton suits hang in a row, empty and lifeless.

He turns back to her with astonishment still in his eyes, "Yes ma'am," he nods his head softly, "anything you need."

Dane wasn't late the next day. After watching the breaking news the day before, Sherri had stayed with him and his mom for most of the visiting hours that were left, Tim and Gavin had come later in the day to support and, more importantly, give him a good razzing for getting to spend the day with his crush, then he had gone home and done some clean up in the yard so the house didn't look like a black sheep in a herd of white wool. He didn't know if his newfound positivity came from spending the day with Sherri or that the next day was Day Four and Mom should be waking up from her Blackout, but he slept great that night.

Striding into the hospital right at 8am, backpack on his shoulders for hopefully the last day, there is a bounce in his step. He makes his way down the hallway towards Mom's room, but as the door to the room comes into view he stops suddenly. Seeing Gary and his wife inside the door Dane quickly runs some math in his head and realizes that Alyssa is on her own Day Six. She would be discharged at the end of the day if she hadn't come back to life. Dane hadn't even thought about it until this moment. What may be a wonderful, happy day for him may turn out to be the worst day this family had ever seen. Reluctantly, he continues on his original path towards the room.

He pushes the door open slowly causing the couple to look up nervously. He gives them a sympathetic smile and catches Gary's eye for a moment before his head drops back down to the cross necklace he holds in his fingers. This is the first time he had seen Gary this way. He had always jumped up to greet Dane or anyone else who walked into the room. As Dane walks past them he reaches over and puts a hand on Gary's shoulder to console him. To his surprise, Gary launches out of his chair and wraps him in up in a hug. He slowly raises his hands from his sides to pat the man on the back in an uncomfortable embrace.

"Thank you, son." Gary speaks over Dane's shoulder. "This may not be an easy day for us."

As they release from each other Dane gives him another sympathetic smile while nodding his head and scrambles for something to say. "Just...keep faith." he stammers out, surprising even himself.

"We will. We will always have our faith," Gary reaches over and grabs his wife's hand, "but faith and hope are two very different things..."

Dane sees tears begin to appear in the man's eyes. "I'm here for you if you need me." Dane says as he reaches over and grabs Gary's shoulder hoping to get out of the situation as soon as possible.

"Thank you, son." Gary says shakily while fighting back the tears. "Same here."

Dane continues on his way to the seat at the foot of his mom's bed and settles in for the day, his positivity crushed. Not sure if it's more of a distraction from the sadness in the room or a habit since the green dome appeared over the mountain, he pulls out his phone to check the latest headlines. Speculation, opinions, conspiracy theories, a couple of articles about politics, entertainment, sports, but nothing too intriguing. Finally, one article posted in the "Local" section a few hours ago catches his eye.

Are we beginning to see the first side effects of Mt. Rainier explosion? - Citizens around base of Mt. Rainier reporting symptoms... – read more

Fully distracted and curiosity peaked, Dane clicks on the link opening a new page on his screen, adorned with a rotating loading symbol in the middle. Words begin to fill the screen from the top down as the article loads. Dane's eyes lock on the top of the screen and he begins to read when he is startled by a huge crash that rings into the room from the hallway. He stands cautiously and stuffs his phone in his pocket, then walks towards the doorway where Gary has his wife wrapped in his arms. Gary's head raises towards the hallway, then he looks back at Dane nervously. Dane steps slowly as if walking across a field of landmines, eyes fixated on the door. He catches Gary's fearful gaze as he passes them and sets a hand on his shoulder as if to say "Stay with your family, I'll check it out." Two more careful steps and Dane is able to lean out the door and look down the hallway. He looks both ways, but sees nothing out of the ordinary.

He looks back into the room at the huddled couple and shrugs, then turns back to the hallway, contemplating whether he should go investigate. Suddenly, he hears muffled screaming then another crash from down the hallway to the left, but still sees nobody. Slowly making his move into the hallway he is startled by a loud voice behind him. "Get back in your room!" shouts a male nurse running frantically in his direction. "Get back in there and close the door!"

"What the hell is going-" Dane starts as the nurse passes him, but is cut off immediately.

"Just get in there!" the nurse yells without slowing or turning around. Dane watches him run full speed down the hallway.

Against the nurse's request Dane takes a step out into the hallway, then looks back to Gary. He is startled as the hallway goes dark, bright lights begin to flash and a piercing alarm sounds throughout the hospital. "Close the door," he shouts back to Gary through the noise, who now cowers with his hands over his ears, "stay with your family and my mom. I'll be right back." Gary nods fearfully then jumps up and closes the door quickly, but continues looking out through the door's square window. Dane turns away and inches carefully down the hallway, staying up against the brick wall. He watches as the nurse slides to a stop in front of a door at the end of the hallway and reaches out to turn the door knob. Just as his fingers make contact with the handle an ear-piercing scream resonates throughout the hospital, completely drowning out the high-pitched alarm and causing Dane to drop to his knees and push his palms into his ears as forcefully as possible. Dane grimaces painfully as the scream seems to cut right through his hands and enter his head and then, just as quickly as it came, it's gone.

He slowly removes his hands from the sides of his head as he raises his gaze back down the hallway. Confused he slowly pulls himself back to his feet and resumes his path along the wall. He stops suddenly about ten feet short of the doorway when he sees a small girl in a white hospital gown nervously peek out of the room and into the hallway, her fuzzy hair messily covers her shoulders and curls out in all directions. She looks around frantically, her lip quivering, tears in her eyes. "What did I..." she mumbles softly to herself. "I didn't mean to..." She looks up and makes eye contact with Dane, who stands motionless pressed up against the white brick wall. They stare at each other with mutual fear and confusion. "I didn't mean to...I swear." she utters, immediately cupping her hands over her mouth and running down the hallway past Dane, sobbing the whole way until she turns a corner out of Dane's sight.

Dane continues gazing down the empty hallway for a few seconds, trying to make some sense of what is happening, then turns back to the room she came out of. He now notices that morning sunlight pours in from a hole in the wall opposite the doorway. Through the opening he can see a small grassy area and a rear parking lot, both with pieces of the brick wall strewn about them. As he inches up to the hole he can suddenly see the male nurse lying lifeless in the grass surrounded by pieces of white brick, the back of his head split wide open and the door lying over his body.

Dane quickly spins away from the gruesome scene and covers his mouth as his breakfast threatens a comeback. He closes his eyes and takes a few deep breaths to calm himself. As he slowly opens them again he now finds himself looking directly into the exam room the girl had just come out of. He forgets about his unsettled stomach and fear overcomes him as he drops his hand from his mouth and walks up to the doorway cautiously. In the middle of the room sits a lonely hospital bed, but as he reaches the doorway everything else in the room also comes into view. The destroyed and smoking machinery, shelving, chairs, two doctors and a nurse have been embedded into the brick walls of the room. As the sound of hospital staff rushing in his direction echoes from the hallway Dane begins to feel lightheaded. His knees buckle and his eyes roll back into his head as everything goes black.

A radiant, green hue from the dome shines into the shack from the busted out windows and casts a blanket over everything inside of it. The computer towers around the room are now dark and silent save for the one sitting next to the desk. Clothes remain strewn about from the open suitcases and food wrappers litter the floor, which has random scorch marks across it. Aside from the whir and beeping of the desktop the only sound is a constant electrical buzz that filters in from outside the shack, as if the dome is declaring its presence.

Outside the door a sudden rush of air can be heard, then a loud thud. After a few moments, the wooden door flies open and Kurrt enters with a large, plastic sack of boxes over his shoulder. He whips it around and holds it in front of him as if it were weightless. "Time to get to work..." he mutters to himself with a smirk, then drops the sack in the middle of the room with loud, metallic clanks coming from some of the boxes. He turns around and grabs the door to shut it, but stops and peers out into the wilderness, his eyes raising in the direction of the mountain peak. "Those assholes don't know what they've got comin'." He utters with a proud smile as he slams the door shut and disappears into the little shack.

Wind continues to rush down from the smoking top of the mountain, through the trees and past the shack as the sound of power tools and bright bursts of green light eminate from inside. A few hundred feet outside the shack's front door, at the edge of the clearing, stands a towering pile of rocks and trees. Sitting atop the pile is a gigantic power globe. Glowing currents run through it like electricity as it hovers, rotating in mid-air and slowly eating away at the pile of debris below it.

Chapter 21

With a groan, Dane turns his head to lay flat on the pillow. He grimaces as pain shoots through his entire body causing him to turn his head quickly to the right. "Ugggggggh..." he groans as he slowly sits up, his eyes squinting, having just seen their first light in hours. A blurry figure rushes towards his bedside, "Woah, easy there son," he immediately recognizes the voice. Gary's face comes into focus as he gets right above Dane and steadies his head on the pillow, "just lay back. Relax."

Dane's eyes continue to focus as he looks around the room drunkenly. "What hap-" he winces as pain shoots from the back of his head again. When his eyes open he sees Mom lying right alongside him and his thoughts become frantic, "Did I die? Was it The Blackout?"

A smile comes to Gary's face, "Nah, nothing like that." he chuckles, "The nurse said you took a little spill in the hallway, hit your head pretty good. They said you could have a concussion, so they set up a bed for you to recover."

The hallway! Suddenly, the memories come rushing back. He remembers the whole thing. The alarms, the scream, the little girl, the dead nurses and doctors. His eyes dart around the room and the beeping monitor behind him quickens causing Gary to take a step back. Dane tries to sit up again and it is only then that he realizes that his wrists and ankles are in restraints. He looks up at Gary with fear, "What the hell is this!? Why am I tied down!?" he exclaims as he tries to jerk his arms free.

"They said it was to keep you safe...that you might thrash around and hurt yourself while you were out..." Gary grasps for a way to calm the young man, "They said they were helping you...that they were going to help you..." he shouts with uncertainty in his voice. "I'm going to get a nurse!" He turns and runs out of the room.

"NO!! GARY, NO!" Dane tries to stop him, but he disappears into the hallway. "Shit!" he exclaims looking around the room for a way free. Mom, Mr. Logan and Alyssa lie motionless next to him. Gary's wife isn't in the room either, probably removed by the same people who restrained him. He stops struggling, suddenly feeling alone and hopeless and looks over at his mom. Why wasn't she awake yet? Was she really dead, not just blacked out? What had happened to him? Maybe he did have a concussion. Maybe they were actually going to help him. Just as he starts to tear up in the direction of his mom's lifeless body a figure appears in the background. He blinks rapidly to push back the tears.

"I hear someone took a little spill, huh?" a woman's voice breaks into his thoughts. He focuses past Mom on the doorway to see a woman in a black pants-suit, her dark hair pulled into a tight ponytail behind her. She strides up to the side of his bed with a confident sort of grace, her heels clicking the whole way, until she is looking down upon him. A comforting smirk finds its way to her mouth, "Hi Dane, I'm Dr. Wong."

"Bro, you said 3:30! What the shit?!" with his hands raised up at his sides in frustration, Gavin shouts in the direction of the red Jeep that screeches to a dusty halt halfway between two parking spots. He doesn't lower his arms awaiting a response as Tim climbs out of the driver's side in a white country club polo.

"Chill out 'bro'," he mocks his friend as he lifts the tailgate and hauls out a big, blue cooler, "some of us actually have to work summer jobs."

"Dude, all I know is that this stupid Blackout has basically cut more than a week out of my 'Summer O' Fun', so I'm beyond ready to get shitfaced!" Gavin exclaims with a pump of his fist as he heads in Tim's direction.

Assuming that he'll get some help with the cooler, Tim sets it down and closes the tailgate, then returns one hand back to the handle closest to him. With one swift move, Gavin grabs a beer can out of the cooler and shoots Tim a mischievous smile as he cracks it open and walks away with a big swig. "...such a dick..." Tim mutters just loud enough for his friend to hear him as he reluctantly grabs the other handle and heaves the cooler up by himself and follows Gavin down the trail.

"That's what you get for being late...'bro'." Gavin shoots back as they head down a trail through the trees. "I can't believe that force-field shit is going down on the mountain and we have to come out here to drink." He utters with frustration motioning to the encased mountain visible in the distance. After a few minutes of walking, the trees open up to a clearing in front of a lake where a bunch of other kids have grouped up by a small beach and at both ends of a bean bag toss game. Sherri, sitting with a group of girls next to a bonfire in the center of the park, throws her hand up into the air and waves when she sees them arrive.

Tim lugs the cooler over near the bonfire and drops it heavily in the dirt next to a few others, then grabs a beer out of it as if to reward himself. He says hi to Sherri and looks around the party and out over the lake as he drinks from the frothy can, then makes his way over to the bean bag boards where Gavin has begun weaseling his way into the next game. They socialize, play games, drink beer, goof around and have fun with their friends, getting progressively rowdier as a couple of hours pass. The glow of the sun behind the overcast of smoke gets lower in the sky, soon to surrender behind the mountain.

With the bag toss game losing its luster, Gavin decides to turn the fun up a notch. "Alright bitches," he proclaims with his hands up in the light of the fire, drawing eye rolls from a majority of his friends who have gathered around. "This is the Summer O' Fun..."

A reluctant roar emits from the crowd as Tim and Sherri roll their eyes, "He swears he's going to make that a thing." Tim whispers to her as they both share a mocking laugh.

"YES!" Gavin continues, "You juniors...and I hope there's nobody younger here," he draws a laugh from the audience, "you will try to top it next year, but you will fail...because this is THE one and only Summer O' Fun!" He turns and finds a large tree behind him that reaches out over the lake. "And I'm going to christen it right now!" he says as he makes his way up its wide trunk.

The crowd cheers at him as many of the kids raise their drinks up in the air as salute. They watch their friend climb up to the branch that he was looking for. He plants his feet steadily, turns back to the crowd, pulls a beer out of the back pocket of his shorts and raises it high, drawing a second cheer and salute from the group. He cracks the can open and chugs the beer down quickly, then tosses it into the crowd like a guitar pick at a concert. As he moves out along the branch he reaches up and grabs a smaller one for support.

Sherri suddenly finds herself woozy in the middle of the crowd and grabs Tim's arm for support, putting her other hand on her forehead.

"Hey, are you ok?" Tim puts an arm around to help her stay upright. "What's wrong?"

"I...I don't know." She stammers softly as the group around her chants "CANNONBALL! CANNONBALL!". Tim, assuming she has drank too much, leads her over to a log next to the bonfire to sit down and recover then continues watching Gavin from her side. Sitting with her eyes closed, breathing deeply Sherri begins feeling a bit better. She opens her eyes and attempts to stand, but feels resistance from her right hand as if someone were sitting on it. As she first looks down nothing seems out of the ordinary, but her face suddenly contorts in confusion as her eyes look upon her wrist and hand, which are suddenly made of wood and run into the log as if they were a branch extending from it. A startled scream leaves her lips as she quickly stands. She violently shakes the hand as if to shake away what she had just seen, then covers her face to cry.

Tim, surprised by her sudden outburst jumps up and puts a hand on each of her shoulders, "Hey, hey. What's wrong? What happened?" he consoles her. "No way, that's not possible. You must have just imagined it." He replies before she can answer him.

"I...I didn't say anything." Sherri looks up from her hands with tears in her eyes. "Why did you say that?"

"Didn't you just say your arm was made of wood?" Tim asks with confusion.

"No, I didn't. How did you know that?" she asks intensely. A burst from the crowd draws their attention up to Gavin, now at the end of the branch and ready to leap into the lake.

"Oh my god..." Tim utters under his breath. "What the hell was that?"

"What was what?" Sherri is now frustrated with her confusion. "What are you talking about? He didn't do anything yet!"

"He just..." Tim trails off looking around wildly. He immediately bends down and grabs part of the tarp that the coolers sit on. "We're gonna need this."

Sherri shoots him a weird look, then looks back up to Gavin, who peels off his shirt and tosses it onto the beach, riles up one more cheer from the crowd, then leaps from the limb. As he descends to the water he pulls his knees into his chest and wraps them up in his arms, then clenches his entire body t ghtly. As soon as he clenches he suddenly shoots downward at an amazing rate and crashes through the surface of the water, creating a huge wave in all directions. Tim immediately pulls the blue tarp up and over himself and Sherri as the wave floods up past the beach and over the crowd of people.

After a moment Tim pulls the tarp off of them and they stand and look over the clearing. As smoke rolls up from the soaked bonfire pit, all of the people begin to stand back up, including Gavin who now stands in the middle of a mostly dry crater directly below the branch. With a confused look on his face he turns to watch the wave continue in the opposite direction and into the trees on the other side of the lake, then turns back in the direction of the group. Tim and Sherri rush past the crowd, some soaked, others somehow dry as a whistle, and up to the edge of the crater.

"I don't know, man! Are you ok?!" Tim shouts, drawing another strange look from Sherri.

"Holy shit!!" Gavin exclaims with a laugh, throwing his hands above his head, "What the hell was that!?!" He steps up onto the shore as his friends gather with him to look down into the indent he has created in the lake bed.

Chapter 22

Dane lies in the hospital bed, restrained like a mental patient, and turns his head onto its right side so that he can look upon his mom lying in her bed, pale and lifeless, the garble in the background is drown out by his thoughts. He had expected her to wake up today if she followed The Blackout's 4-day pattern. Maybe there was something else that happened to her. Maybe she wasn't going to wake up. He thinks back to the day she collapsed...Wednesday. Yes, it was Wednesday. The day of the President's speech. Today was Saturday. He begins counting days in his head. Thursday, Friday, Saturday...Sunday! It was around noon on Wednesday, so Sunday at noon would be the 4 days! He had miscounted. There was still hope! A smile finds its way to the corner of his mouth as he looks upon her. Suddenly, the background noise intensifies and draws his attention to his left.

"Dane," Dr. Wong attempts to get his attention back, "are you with me? Do I need to repeat the question?"

"Yes, sorry doctor." Dane pushes his thoughts aside for the moment. Maybe it's the restraints, or her pantsuit in place of the normal doctor's garb, but he can't help but feel like this woman is not here to help.

"I just need to know what happened down the hall." She continues more calmly. "What did you see?"

"I...I didn't see anything really." Dane pulls out his best lying voice. "I heard an explosion, I ran down the hallway and I passed out and hit my head when I saw the nurse dead on the lawn."

"You saw a nurse? On the lawn outside?" Her face suddenly becomes twisted with confusion. "How did he die?"

"I mean, I assume he was crushed." Dane continues with the true part of his lie. "He went through a brick wall and had a big, heavy door on top of him." He finds it weird that she was confused by his comment.

"Can you describe what he looked like?" She attempts to get him to continue his recollection while he's talking, "Did you see anything else?"

"Can I ask you something?" Dane grabs hold of the interrogation for a moment, much to Dr. Wong's surprise.

"Uh...sure." She plays along.

"Why am I still restrained?" Dane motions to his wrists with his eyes. "Gary said it was to keep me from hurting myself while I was unconscious...I think we're well beyond that point, aren't we?"

She smiles and lets out a sigh as she reaches into her pocket. "You're completely right." She says as she pulls a ring of keys out of her pocket and begins to release his wrists, then moves down to his ankles. "I apologize. I was so focused on finding out what happened it slipped my mind." Dane can't help but feel like this is just a cover, but thanks her for releasing him as he rubs his wrists where the restraints had dug in. "Now," She continues while putting the keys back into her pocket, "can you tell me exactly what you saw? We're just trying to put the whole thing together to figure out exactly what happened and, as far as we know, you're the only one who saw anything." There is a sudden desperation in her voice that catches Dane off guard.

Dane decides to keep with his aloof story. "All I saw was the nurse on the lawn, then I passed out. I've never seen a dead body before." He returns his gaze to his right where his mom lies still. "I mean...dead from something like that."

Sympathy seems to find its way to Dr. Wong as her voice continues at a much quieter level. "Your mom?"

"Yeah..." he utters quietly.

"Well, from what I understand, there's still a chance for her." She continues with a confidence that seems to portray that Dane has a choice in the matter.

He turns his head back in her direction quickly, irritated. "What is that supposed to mean?!"

"I didn't mean anything by it, Dane." The sound of his name out of her mouth irritates him even more. "I just mean that the doctors informed me of her situation and that she could wake up tomorrow. They also mentioned that you haven't experienced any of the effects of The Blackout. Is that right?"

Dane doesn't oblige her with a reply as he turns his head back to look at his mom.

"Ok," she finally seems to break her solidity. "I'm glad you're feeling ok. Will you please let me know if there's anything further you'd like to share with me?" She reaches out a hand with a card clutched between her first two fingers.

Dane turns back in her direction, glad that the questioning is finally done. "Sure..." he agrees as he grabs the card from her and looks it over. A simple white card, it reads:

Dr. Maxine Wong
Head of Investigation
(555) 555-2552

CORPS

He has seen this symbol many times before on his medication bottles. All of the intuitive doubt he had before about the doctor immediately seemed to be confirmed and he was glad he didn't say anything about the little girl in the hallway.

As she stands to leave she stops at the end of mom's bed and leans forward onto the railing by her feet, which springs Dane to an upright, defensive position. "I really hope you'll be in contact with me Dane." She states with an intense, unblinking stare. "It could be a matter of life or death."

As Dane peers into the doctor's eyes, he notices a small, blue shimmer in their intensity. At first he feels pride at the fact that he has gotten to her, but suddenly, with a quick metallic hum, she smirks and nods at him then turns to stride out of the room as gracefully as she had entered, the sound of her clicking heels fading down the hallway with her. As Dane watches her exit, his eyebrows furrow in confusion as his eyes focus down onto the end of Mom's bed where there were suddenly two missing sections exactly where the doctor had placed her hands on the metal railing.

In the packed, noisy waiting room, Gary paces back and forth in between rows of chairs while his wife sits in the corner under the suspended TV, reading magazines. All non-patients were evacuated from their hallway once crews arrived to take care of the mess. This hardly concerns him, though, as he peers up above the reception desk to a white wall clock that reads 7:42. Visiting hours were almost over...and today was Alyssa's sixth day in the hospital. He is dying to get back to her bedside if this is her last night, but also doesn't want to alert them in case the explosion distracts the hospital staff enough to give her more time.

He anxiously rushes up to the receptionist window "Excuse me!" he exclaims louder than he had intended, startling the heavy-set woman behind it. "Sorry...it's just that visiting hours are almost over and we just wanted to see our daughter again tonight."

"I'm sorry sir," she begins unsympathetically then continues as if she's reading it from a script, "the wing your daughter is in is currently closed off to all non-patients. My guess is that we won't be letting anyone back there for the rest of the night, but, tomorrow being Sunday, we will be opening up patients' rooms to visiting hours an hour early, so you can return then."

"But we just want to say goodnight to her, then we can-" he is suddenly distracted when the door to Alyssa's hallway opens and a young man enters with a backpack slung over his shoulder. "Dane!!" he rushes over and sets his hand on Dane's shoulder. "Are you ok, son? What the hell happened in there?"

"I...I don't really want to talk about it." He say sullenly, barely looking up at Gary. "I tucked Alyssa in, you guys should go home and get some sleep." He rubs the back of his head where it aches.

"There was a woman that came and asked everyone questions." This finally catches Dane's full attention. "I think she was an agent or something. I didn't have much to tell her, but I mentioned that you were in the hallway when it happened."

"Well that explains the interrogation I just got..." Dane remarks with a huff of frustration.

"Sorry, son," Gary apologizes, "It just slipped out."

"Well, I didn't have anything to give her either." Dane sighs with tiredness. "I'm going to head home. I'll see you in the morning, Gary."

He hikes up his backpack and heads out the door. As Gary turns to join his wife his eyes drift up to the silent TV above her. *"BREAKING NEWS"* flashes across the bottom of the screen while live footage of a park in downtown Seattle streams above it. Gary squints and takes a couple of steps closer to see the small screen. His mouth drops open with astonishment as the cameraman follows someone who is flying around the park like Superman. As the person tries to land and tumbles to the ground the camera pans over to another man who is bent over a park bench. As he rises to an upright position the bench follows and he lifts it above his head with ease, turning to the camera with a huge smile on his face then releases one hand from the bench and balances it above himself with no effort. Suddenly, a blonde reporter steps into the view of the camera and begins speaking into a microphone as people behind her continue to display their strange new abilities.

"Oh my god..." Gary utters under his breath as he raises one hand to his forehead in disbelief. As soon as his fingers make contact with his skin his brain receives an instantaneous surge of information. Slight atherosclerosis in the right chest arteries. Worn down ACL in the right knee. Minor liver damage. Broken and repaired left Radius and Ulna. Weak tendons in both ankles. Two cavities. Hangnail on right index finger. He quickly pulls his hand away from his head and looks at it with confusion.

"Honey, are you alright?" His wife sees the look on his face and approaches him. The second she grabs his hand he receives a flash diagnosis of her as well.

Meanwhile, in the hallway where the incident occurred Dr. Wong pushes her way past curtains of plastic tarp until she is in full sight of the hospital room. She peers around the room examining the crumbling, body-shaped indents in the walls from the doorway as two men in hazmat suits guide the final nurse from out of the brick. The other perished medical staff lie in the center of the room, covered by sheets.

"Clear it and put it back to exactly how it was before." She barks out the order to the men as they guide the nurse down to the floor next to the others. "Then find her."

Behind her a fuzzy-haired little girl peeks in from the hole in the wall opposite the room breathing heavily with fear in her eyes. When the doctor turns toward the hallway she ducks her head back into hiding, then stealthily watches the woman disappear through the plastic. Fearful of what they will do if they catch her she pushes off the brick wall and streaks across the parking lot and into the night in her white hospital gown.

Dane pulls his car up to the front of their house, bouncing the tire on the curb slightly before coming to a halt. As he stands from the driver's seat, he peers over the top of the car and looks over the house. He has only had about an hour each night before it got dark, but he had been able to spray off most of the ash from the front of the house, the walkway and some of the yard with a hose. He would not be furthering that effort tonight, but, hopefully, this was the last night he had to come home alone.

He makes his way inside and up the stairs to his bedroom, tossing his backpack and phone on the bed with a huge sigh of exhaustion. He can feel his head throbbing now as he rips off his t-shirt and jeans and replaces them with a black hooded sweatshirt and plaid pajama pants. As he leaves the room he stops at the end of his bed, stuffs his phone in his pocket, then digs into his backpack. He finds his orange tube of pills and shakes one into his palm, giving the logo on the label a discerning look before he tosses it back onto the bed. He goes to the bathroom across the hallway, finds a Tylenol bottle in the cabinet and tosses one back with his pill then makes his way down the stairs.

After grabbing a bag of chips from the kitchen he finds the couch and throws himself onto it with another huge sigh, this time, though, in relief at the chance to relax. He unclips the bag and stuffs 3 chips in his mouth, not realizing this was a little bit too much at once. After a violent cough he immediately goes silent when he begins to hear an electrical hum, then the TV in front of him blares forth a rerun of Everybody Loves Raymond.

"What the…" Dane utters through a mouthful of chips as he sits still, unsure how the TV had turned on. After chewing the chips for a moment, he clears his throat so he can swallow and the TV instantaneously flashes to a college football game. He is startled by a loud ringtone that emits from his pocket and the vibration against his leg. Keeping his eyes locked on the mysteriously changing TV and nervous to make any sudden movements, he slowly leans to one side so he can get to his phone. He swallows the chips and clears his throat one last time, and the TV suddenly changes to a news report "WHAT IS GOING ON?!" he exclaims with frustration as he jumps up and looks around the room for an answer. His eyes finally settle onto the couch behind him and he notices the black remote buried in between the two cushions where he had been sitting.

"God dammit…" he utters to himself as he rolls his head back in frustration. With a laugh, he fishes the remote out of its hiding place and turns to sit back down. Once again, his phone starts dinging and vibrating with incoming text messages. He presses down the power button and looks at the notification: 4 new text messages: Tim + Gavin: Group

He swipes his finger to unlock the screen, then clicks the notification displaying the group feed, which is still coming in as he reads them.

<u>Incoming Text: Tim</u> - Someone got it on video!?!?!

<u>Incoming Text: Gavin</u> - Dude check out what I did tonight!! Click/openvid/vidplayer

<u>Incoming Text: Gavin</u> - How did you know that Tim? I just got it from someone a few minutes ago…

<u>Incoming Text: Tim</u> - I dunno, I've been having weird coincidences happen all night since I left

<u>Incoming Text: Gavin</u> - Weirdo…and puss for having to work in the morning. Hehe

Dane chuckles at his friends' arguing, then scrolls back up to the video link. He sets his thumb on it, turning the phone black as the video starts up, then shifts the phone sideways in his hand. He smiles watching his friend climb up the tree and rip his shirt off like a pro wrestler. As he continues watching, though, his smile fades to confusion. He uses his thumb to slide the video timer back a couple of times as he tries to figure out what he is watching. Finally, he closes the video player and goes back to the group text and begins typing.

Outgoing Text: What the hell was that!?!

Incoming Text: Gavin - Right!?!?!!?

Incoming Text: Gavin - ...and I have no idea.

Dane looks back and sees a bubble he hadn't read before he had sent his.

Incoming Text: Tim - That's what I said !

Outgoing Text: Gavin, god knows what's wrong with you...Tim, your text timing is off or something.

Thinking about it for a second, Dane realizes that Tim's texts are coming in BEFORE he and Gavin send theirs, so it's not a delay. But how could he be answering before they even type their responses...and what the hell did Gavin do in that video? As he thinks, he gazes up at the TV in front of him and stares in wonderment, completely disregarding the next incoming text message. He quickly looks back down to the phone and begins typing a message to his friends to turn on the news, but stops halfway through and glances at a new message that just came in.

Incoming Text: Tim - I know, I'm watching right now!! Gavin, check the news on your phone!

Without finishing his text, Dane gazes back up to the flashing screen in front of him and reads the bulletin over and over again, not believing it any more than the first time he read it.

BREAKING NEWS: SUPERHEROES EVERYWHERE!!

Chapter 23

After a long, mostly sleepless night watching the developments on the news Dane sluggishly pushes through the heavy door into the waiting room at 10am. It is much more vacant than when he had left the night before and he assumes they had cleaned up the scene in Mom's hallway during the night and let people return to their loved ones. He is relieved when the receptionist confirms this and allows him to head back after signing in. Dragging himself down the long hallway he suddenly realizes how happy he is to not be lugging his usual overstuffed backpack, then remembers why that is. Mom should be waking up today!

As he approaches her room he begins to hear jubilant talking and laughing coming from the doorway. He recognizes Gary's voice, but there is another, smaller voice he hasn't heard before. He slowly inches up to the doorway and leans forward to peer in curiously. As soon as he does, a loud greeting startles him, "DANE!!" Gary exclaims with excitement from just inside the door. "Come here, son," with a couple of steps he has made it to the doorway, grabbed Dane's shoulder and lead him into the room, partially against his will, "I want you to meet someone!"

Dane's confusion only grows as Gary guides him up to the side of the first bed in the room, where a young girl sits upright in a white gown, a big smile across her pale face. Dane looks away from her to Gary as if to confirm what he is seeing. Gary's eyes are glued on the girl, an even bigger smile on his face.

"Dane, this is my daughter Alyssa." Dane's unbelieving eyes return to the young girl as she extends her hand to him. He slowly meets her hand with his and shakes it softly. "Alyssa, this is Dane. His mom is in the bed over there and she's going to wake up today too, right Dane?" His hand plants a proud grip on Dane's shoulder as tears begin building in his eyes.

After a few seconds of silence while shaking her hand Dane senses the awkwardness growing and regathers himself, "It's so nice to meet you Alyssa." His hand releases from hers and he uses it, instead, to wipe the gathering tears from his eyes and forces a smile. "We've been waiting for you to wake up!"

"That's the crazy thing," Gary interjects excitedly, "she didn't just wake up. I think I, kinda..." he pauses realizing how ridiculous his next words sound, "I think I brought her back to life."

Confusion returns to Dane's face as he looks up at Gary and his huge, proud smile. Gary can't pull his eyes away from his daughter as she and her mom play with her hair and try to smooth out the kinks that have resulted from her lying in a bed for 6 days. Dane assumes it must be something to do with the strange powers that people are starting to exhibit, but could he really have the power to bring people back from the dead? As he gazes at the happy father, Gary's smile quickly fades and his eyes begin to dart around the room. Suddenly seeming unsteady on his own two legs, he reaches to grip the arm of a chair as Dane quickly throws an arm around his waist to stop him from falling.

"Daddy?!" Alyssa shouts with confusion as Dane struggles against the man's weight. He guides him to the floor as softly as he can, unsure of what to do next.

"Gary!? Honey!?" His wife comes rushing over with a pillow and places it on the floor under the back of his head so that Dane can set him down. Gary's wide eyes are fixed straight forward as his limbs and body twitch, seemingly in pain.

"Go get a nurse or a doctor!" Dane urges the woman through her shouts and Alyssa's crying. When she doesn't respond he reaches out and grabs her arm, "HEY!" he shouts, finally catching her attention, "Go get someone, ok?!"

As she looks back into his eyes Dane notices an intensity with her realization of what she must do. Deep inside her pupils he sees a small flicker of light. The moment she turns her head towards the door she instantaneously vanishes from in front of him. Instead a group of bright, jagged lightning bolts shoot from her spot out the door and Dane's hand receives a huge shock knocking him back against Alyssa's bed. Shaking his hand in pain he looks up to see the young girl peering over the edge of the bed with confusion, the ceiling lights flickering behind her. "Don't ask..." Dane shakes his head and makes his way back to Gary's side.

"So, what are you telling me, Miss Wong?" The booming voice nearly rattles the room as the man in the suit sits with his chair facing away from the Doctor. His right elbow propped up on the arm of the chair he spins the ring on his finger and looks out the window over the completely overcast Los Angeles skyline.

"Well, sir," she stands solid in front of his large desk though her voice has a slight shake to it, "it's not just in the Seattle area."

After a longer silence than she is comfortable with he responds, "And..."

"It's too early to make any completely conclusive reports, but what we're seeing is that it may possibly end up being global..." she trails off nervously, expecting an unpleasant response from the man. It does not come, so she continues, "The tests on our Rainier crew have been completed and the scientists believe that, during the Blackout, their immune systems were completely shut down for days. During that time, the radiation from the mountain slowly made its way in and activated and altered previously unused synapses in the brain and throughout their bodies. Those with stronger immune systems are seeing the changes slower than others, but it seems to be moving outward from the mountain."

Rather than go on and possibly say something that upsets him, she decides to wait for his response. After a long pause, he utters from behind his chair, "Anything else, Miss Wong?"

She thinks to herself for a moment. Was there anything else? She decided to avoid the topic of Kurrt for the moment since she had spent the last few days observing the tests on her men and cleaning up the scene at the hospital and didn't have much of an update. "There is one other thing…" she blurts, immediately wishing she hadn't. The man waits. She takes a breath and begins, "I did a check-in on Dane Denson earlier today. He is alive, well, not experiencing any effects of The Blackout or from the radiation."

To her surprise the man quickly twists his chair around and glares at her with an inquisitive look as he spins the ring on his finger. "This boy," he begins, then pauses, "he is completely unaffected?"

"Yes, he was in the hospital today with a simple concussion. He and his mother had been in an underground bunker and she went down about the same time as the President." She can see the wheels turning in the man's head, so she begins to backpedal, "It may be too early to deduce. Like I said, we can't tell if there are others who end up not experiencing any changes as well."

"Thank you, Miss Wong," she can tell that he is still in deep thought, "that'll be all for now."

She nods in his direction even though he has already started turning his chair back towards the window, then makes her way out of the room. He sits, brow furrowed in thought, staring out the window at the city incessantly spinning the ring on his finger. "I knew you were the key, boy." He whispers softly. He stops spinning his ring and looks down at his hand. Suddenly, his fingers elongate and his fingernails become long and sharp as his entire hand becomes very vascular and menacing. He grips his claw into a fist, then releases, turning it over as if studying it. "We shall see each other soon enough…Dane Denson."

Dane rushes to keep up with the medical staff and Gary's wife as they push him down the hallway on a stretcher. He continues to twitch and gasp for breath. Finally reaching an open room, one nurse hangs back and corrals their two followers, instructing them to stay outside, then disappears into the room with the rest of the staff. Dane looks down the hallway and realizes the room has an observation window. He quickly puts an arm around the crying woman next to him and guides her over in front of it where they can see the nurses and doctors working frantically on Gary.

"I can't watch this!" Gary's wife suddenly breaks down. She pulls away from Dane and rushes to a row of chairs about 15 feet down the hallway, immediately burying her face into her hands.

Dane's gaze returns to the scene through the window. As the white coats rush around him checking for blockage in his airway and hooking him up to the machines behind his bed he continues to struggle for life. Dane can see his right hand hovering inches above the bed, open but flexed tightly as if squeezing an invisible ball. "Is he having a seizure?" Dane whispers to himself. One of the nurses quickly makes his way across the room to a supply cart, opening up Dane's view to Gary's face. His eyes are wide and glassy, his mouth open, gasping. Suddenly, as his body begins to slow its involuntary jerking, his head begins to turn towards the window and his eyes fix on Dane's. Dane stares back into Gary's eyes, unable to break the gaze as he looks on in fear. He notices a single tear emerge from Gary's eye and stream down to the pillow, then his tightly contracted hand thrusts upward grabbing the hand of one of the nurses, who instantaneously crumples to the floor next to the bed.

Dane's hand covers his mouth, which hangs open in disbelief. As if in slow motion Dane watches the other staff rush to help their colleague, who lies lifeless on the floor with her eyes rolled back into her head. While they begin getting vitals and administering CPR, Gary slowly sits up on the bed and takes a few deep breaths while rubbing his forehead. He looks at the commotion happening below him, then up to the window and meets Dane's fearful gaze.

With a sadness in his eyes, he slowly rolls off the backside of the bed and sneaks past the medical crew and into the hallway.

"What…" Dane can't seem to find the words through his shock. "What was that?"

The man looks back at him shamefully. "GARY! HONEY!!" His wife, alerted to his presence in the hallway, rushes over and throws her arms around him before he is able to say anything. She pushes her lips onto his in intense relief and he is suddenly shocked, causing him to throw his head back.

"What the hell was that!?" he shouts looking at his wife in confusion as the lights flicker above them.

"Um, something weird happened to me earlier." She utters while wiping away her tears.

"I think there's a pretty good pattern of that lately," Dane scoffs, his eyes still fixed on Gary, "but what happened in there? What happened to that nurse?"

"Listen, son," he suddenly seems anxious, "I'm not sure, but we're getting out of here. We've gotta get Alyssa, ok honey?" he lays his hands on his wife's arms. Her tear-soaked face smiles back at him and nods in compliance and they immediately begin down the hallway towards Alyssa's room.

"But what happened in there?" Dane rushes to keep up with the couple. "Did you mean to do that?"

"I don't know, Dane." He responds with disinterest.

"But you have to have felt something! Didn't you?" Dane persists.

As they reach the doorway to their daughter's room Gary spins around quickly. "Listen!" Dane is surprised by an intensity he hasn't seen in this man before. Gary immediately pulls back and softens his voice, "All I know is, this morning, I did something that brought Alyssa back. In there," he points back down the hallway and pauses, unsure of his next words, "it's almost like something was inside me and I had to get it out…"

"What do you mean 'something'?" Dane inquires.

"I don't really know." He looks sadly at the door to the room then back to Dane nervously, "It's almost like...like I took the death from her...and..."

Dane's eyes widen in realization, "And you gave it to that nurse!"

"I didn't want to!" Gary exclaims as if he's on trial. "It was like it was...instinctual. I was dying. I had to get it out of me." He looks back to his wife with worry, "We have to go."

They quickly dart into the room to get their daughter. After a moment trying to process what he just heard, Dane rushes after them and stops abruptly in the doorway as if he had just run into a wall of bricks. In that moment he is unable to breath, unable to move. He gazes in wonderment across the room into two beautiful eyes that he hadn't seen in days and tries to find his voice. "Mom?!"

Through the shiny, silver hallways Simeon shuffles with haste, his loose-fitting, full-body mechanic's jumpsuit swishing across the smooth floor. He turns a corner and pauses, then slowly approaches the lone figure in the hallway from behind.

"They're ready." Simeon says quietly over the doctor's shoulder as she gazes into the holding cell in front of her.

"Good." She utters without turning around. "Time to get our boys ready too."

Simeon takes a step forward so that he is now beside the doctor and follows her gaze into the room where he sees eight men. A couple lay on beds on opposite sides of the room staring up at the ceiling, one reads a book at a small metal table in the middle of the room joined by two others who have a conversation with each other and the other three pace the floor tediously. As he looks over the scene he can't help but wonder why these men are in containment.

"Dr. Wong," he starts nervously, "if you don't mind me asking, what do you need from these-" he stops suddenly as one of the men at the table holds his hand up in front of him and breathes a deep breath into his palm igniting his bright, white power globe. To Simeon's surprise, none of the men seem phased by the display.

"These men and I..." she begins, then trails off as she raises one hand out in front of them. Pulling the anger from deep within herself, she directs it to her open palm and ignites her own blue globe, causing Simeon to take a step back and engage a rippling, yellow force field that encompasses his body and clothes perfectly. She looks back at him with glowing, blue eyes and an evil grin, "...we have a friend to visit."

Chapter 24

After an hour of excitedly filling her in on everything that has happened in the last 4 days, Dane and Mom are checked out of the hospital and head home. Dane can't help but feel like things will finally return mostly to normal in his life, aside from the fact that people are somehow getting superpowers, of course. They settle in at the house and catch up on the latest info the news can offer. Later that night it is revealed that the President and others that had joined him in his bunker had reawakened as well.

The next day, they see a taxi pull up across the street and Mr. Logan exits and strides into his house. They go greet their neighbor and get him up to speed with what they know over coffee and Capri Sun. Together they all learn that multiple attempts to investigate Mt. Rainier in the last couple of days have been unsuccessful. Amateur video shows crews trying to go through the field to be sent flying backwards as if coming into contact with a highly electrical fence.

Reports of people displaying special abilities stream in constantly over the next week as it spreads across the globe. The news correspondents discuss and debate their relation to the occurrences on Mt. Rainier and The Blackout while sharing stories from around the world of people and their abilities. Some of the stories are happy, showing people using their powers to help or protect others, but some show people abusing their abilities. Topics of creating new laws against using powers come about and rallies for the President and other leaders to step in gather around the world. As they continue to study people and their abilities, scientists began to put people into categories:

Ballista – Individuals able to shoot or fire

Shielders – Individuals who can shield themselves or change their body's makeup to protect themselves from harm

Metamorphs – Individuals who have the ability to change into other forms

Manipulators – Individuals able to control or alter the environment around them

Advanced – Individuals with normal, human abilities that have been advanced

Projectors – Individuals who can project themselves, their thoughts or their sights to others or their environment

Converters – Individuals able to change one thing to another, mostly temporarily

With the weekend approaching, Dane has grown sick of news reports and has reluctantly made plans with his friends to go to the lake. It will be his first time being out of the house since he brought his mom home from the hospital and all of his friends began gaining their abilities. He wakes up Saturday morning, already dreading the outing.

"Ugh..." he groans as he drags himself into the kitchen and to the counter where he plops down on a stool. He rubs his tired eyes intensely, then finally stops and opens them, blinking excessively. They finally focus in so he is able to see Mom standing in front of him, a critical look over her face.

"Ugggh, what!?" she urges. She chuckles at her overly-dramatic son and returns to prepping the food on the counter in front of her. "You know that being social is not the end of the world, right?" she mocks as she motions with one hand like she is sliding it under something, then flips it over, simultaneously causing the omelet in the pan to flip. She then pushes both hands in his direction causing a glass to slide in front of him followed by a carton of orange juice, which lifts and pours into the glass on its own, then returns itself to the counter.

Dane's eyebrow raises as he looks back at his mom's smiling face, "Says the mom who recently learned how to use "The Force" to her son who's probably the only powerless person left in the world..." he scoffs as he takes a drink of the juice.

"That's not true! There are still some people in China who haven't been affected..." she tries to make him better, then pauses to think, "Though, I did hear this morning that it's spreading quicker there than any other country." She notices the discern on his face and tries to rebound, "But I'm sure that's just because there's so many people there! You know, it's a numbers thing...Catch!" With just a quick motion of her hand the omelet flips out of the pan in Dane's direction.

He quickly grabs a plate off the table and thrusts it under the falling eggs. It hits the plate with a "Fwap" and part of it breaks off and falls over the side towards the floor. Before Dane can even react, it stops midair and makes its way back up to the plate where it sets down softly. He looks back up to his mom and her sympathetic smile as she releases her telekinetic hold on the eggs and turns back to the sink.

"Whatever..." Dane cannot hide his frustration as he takes his omelet back up to his room to get ready for the day.

The sounds of power tools and electrical pulses still radiate from inside the shack. Kurrt leans over the computer desk, which he has converted to a workstation for his project. During the week he had only left the cabin to collect more packages and food and had continually replenished the rocks and trees underneath his barrier globe. Being so close to the top of the mountain, he could feel himself getting stronger as the week went on and now he would have a way to harness it.

"Ahhhh, done!!" he steps back brushing his hands together as if knocking invisible dirt off of them, then holds them out to his sides in presentation as he looks over his finished product. Lying out on the desk in front of him he has created his own exoskeleton suit. Mostly black with green and silver piping running from the extremities to a dome in the middle of the chest. "OH, wait!" he exclaims spinning around quickly and digging his hands into an open box on the floor. "Almost forgot."

He spins back to the table and whips around a large piece of fabric that is green on one side and black on the other. He inserts the two corners of the fabric into a space on the neck of the suit and it automatically hisses and clamps down. "Yeahhhh," he coos in satisfaction as he looks over the suit one more time, "gotta have a cape!"

"Allllllright," he utters to himself as he sits in the desk chair and picks a newspaper up from the floor that he had brought back with him on his last trip, "time to test this guy out…" he thumbs through the newspaper looking over the headlines, then suddenly stops and sits upright in the chair, excitement in his eyes as he reads through an article. "Gotcha."

He quickly jumps up, grabs the suit and rushes into the bathroom, leaving the newspaper on the desk open to an article with the headline: ***GLOBAL LEADERS MEETING TO DISCUSS LAW ENFORCEMENT OF SUPERPOWERS***

With a cloud of dust and ash, Dane's Saturn skids to a stop next to his friends' vehicles at the opening of the trail. He reluctantly exits the vehicle, popping the trunk before closing his door, then makes his way around to the back of the car where he pulls out a case of beer and slams the trunk shut again. He looks down the trail with hesitation and lets out a huge sigh, forcing his feet to move.

After a few minutes the trail opens up to the clearing in front of the lake where Tim is setting up the bag toss along the tree line. He looks around and finally spots Gavin about two feet into the woods on the other side of the clearing with his back to them. He makes his way over to the coolers by the bonfire and sets down his case, also grabbing a pinecone off the ground. With a mischievous smile he stands and hurls it at Gavin, missing by about 10 feet.

Turning his head Gavin quickly spots his friend and smiles, "Heeeeeeey, there he is!"

Tim is alerted by the exclamation and looks up from the wooden game boards. "What's up, stranger!?"

"I see you didn't get the ability to hit a target." Gavin jokes as he turns and zips up his jeans, bending to grab a beer he had set in the dirt at the edge of the trees.

"Ha, hilarious." Dane sneers as he receives a forceful pat on the back from his friend. "Are you guys sure we should be hanging out so close to that thing?" he motions towards the giant, green dome over the mountain.

"Yeah, it should be fine." Tim approaches and gives him a hand shake with a half-hug.

"Yeah, I mean, we did it last week and the only thing that happened was everyone got superpowers, so…" Gavin jokes and trails off into a big guzzle of beer, drawing a chuckle and shared eye roll from his friends.

"So, you still haven't gotten anything yet?" Tim strikes a more serious tone.

"Nah," Dane tries to act like it's no big deal, "but you probably knew I was going to say that, right Miss Cleo?"

"Eh, I can only see one step ahead, and only things that happen to or around me." Tim grabs a beer from the cooler and takes a drink. "I try not to use it as much as possible. It kinda ruins the surprise of…well, everything."

It makes Dane feel a little better knowing that having powers may not be such a welcomed gift to all people. "So you can control it now?"

"Yeah, I've read a lot of stories of people who weren't able to control their powers when they first got them, but as it works its way into more of your system it becomes more stable." He motions over to their friend, who is throwing rocks at the edge of the lake. "Gavin said the same thing. He kept lurching forward uncontrollably and practically destroyed his room the first morning he had them. Now he knows how to harness it."

"Effin' right I do!" Gavin exclaims as he winds up side-armed. Suddenly, his arm streaks forward at an amazing speed sending a flat stone skipping across the lake. The friends watch as it shoots across the lake, hitting every ten feet or so then jumps off the water and explodes into a tree trunk on the other shore, sending chips of wood flying. A big smile covers Gavin's face as he turns to his friends for their reaction.

Unimpressed, Tim takes another drink of his beer. "He's been doing this shit all week..."

Dane's eyes show his surprise, then he tries to play it cool, "All I know," he smiles and points at Gavin, who still has a big, goofy smile, "is you're definitely not my bag toss partner!"

Later in the day, the friends are joined in the clearing by a bunch of people from their school and the party starts. As expected, everyone's superpowers are the topic of every conversation Dane joins into and most of them end with someone saying something like, "Dude, don't worry. You're lucky you don't have them," or "I don't even use mine that much." As much as he appreciates their effort, he can't help but feel like an outsider. He moves from group to group, joins in a couple games of bag toss, helps build the bonfire and does his best to hide his frustration while everyone else around him plays around with their powers. One girl creates a pink, viscous bubble around herself and guides it around the clearing at will, to which Gavin challenges her and sends her bouncing out into the middle of the lake with one good hip check. Tim shows off by calling shots in bag toss and predicting what people will say or do.

Around nine o'clock, what sun can creep its way through the smoky sky has mostly set behind the mountain. Dane sits near the bonfire listening to more of his classmates talk about what they're able to do and how cool it is, every now and then keeping himself included by interjecting with stories of what he saw happen at the hospital. As they continue on about their abilities, his eyes wander the clearing and finally settle on the trail opening. Standing anxiously looking around for her friends is Sherri, her curly blonde hair shining bright in the bonfire light. Dane withholds his urge to jump up and greet her and tries to continue focusing on the stories being told in front of him. Sherri spots a group of her friends and, with a big smile and wave, she makes her way across the clearing.

For the next few minutes Dane doesn't hear a single word from his friends. He can't think about anything else but when he and Sherri held hands in the hospital. He had sheepishly avoided her all week as all of the occurrences unfolded on the news. He finally reels his focus back in and excuses himself. "Be right back," he lies. He stands, takes a deep breath and heads across the clearing to the group of girls she has joined. The twenty feet seem to take hours to travel. Just as he makes it to the group where Sherri's back is to him, he raises a hand to touch her arm and get her attention...

"CRACK!!!"

A loud sound in the distance sends gasps of fear over the clearing, followed immediately by an eerie silence. When they all spin and look up in the direction of the mountain with fear they see a bright green light dart around inside the field like a pinball rattling around a machine. Suddenly, it stops and hovers, then shoots at tremendous speeds through the field, sending electrical currents scattering around the green globe and out into the sky as it streaks off into the distance. Within seconds the field seems to return to normal and the green trail left behind in the black sky fades.

As he turns back around Dane is startled to see, where Sherri should be standing, a swirling wind with grains of dirt and leaves. "Hey..." she slowly reforms with a small smile in one corner of her mouth and drops her gaze to the ground, unable to hide her embarrassment.

"I have no idea, but it can't be good." Tim utters as he and Gavin approach their friends, drawing simultaneous sighs from the group.

Chapter 25

"This is something that needs to be controlled!" The handsome, middle-aged man stands abruptly. His intensity shows through in his reddening face set beneath his dark, perfectly parted hair. "This is not one of our debatable cultural, racial or religious issues. This is global! We must come together to get a hold on this or there could be more, very real, very DANGEROUS consequences!" he slams a fist on the table in front of him to emphasize his point.

Across the large, leveled auditorium, translators begin speaking furiously to update the world leaders on what the US President had just said. Sitting behind desks with their country's nameplate and flag posted proudly, some nod their head in agreement, others sit sternly with concerned looks on their faces. The man's eyes dart intensely from leader to leader looking for someone to make the next move. Finally, from the front of the large room, a small, Asian man with grey hair and dark framed glasses behind a "China" nameplate uses his desk to pull himself up. His ill-fitting clothes hang off him, making him look even shorter than he actually is.

"President Michaels," he begins calmly, "though I do agree with you as to the need to have some sort of control on this phenomenon, I fear that it may not be that simple." He stops to clear his throat and take a drink of water, then walks out from behind his desk and ambles around the main floor, head down in thought. As the others, especially the President, watch on anxiously he finally stops and slowly raises his head. "It is an amazing thing...and yet maybe amazing is not the correct word. We have already seen some abuse of power in many countries. We have also seen peoples' abilities getting stronger as time passes."

"Exactly!" The President interjects sending an echo across the room. "Imagine the things that criminals and terrorists will do once their powers reach a peak...if they EVER reach a peak!"

The Chinese President smiles at him calmly, then resumes pacing the floor, "That is part of the reason we are all here President Michaels, but also for our citizens who may not know the proper use of their abilities...but do we restrict this at all if we can't restrict it completely?"

A sudden roar fills the room as all of the world leaders emphatically voice their opinions in their given languages to his question. Looking around the room quietly, the Chinese President finally raises his arms to signal their silence, and they slowly abide.

"We are all here today to find a solution. My nation's people were some of the last to be affected and most of what I have seen has been a fear to use their powers, aside from some rebellious citizens, who have been reprimanded." He looks around at the faces, all focused on him. "Tell me more. What have you seen?"

A man with a dark mustache stands behind his "Turkey" nameplate and adjusts his suit jacket. "It is true that some are afraid to use their powers. I had one of my officers tell me that someone able to walk through walls used their power to rob a bank, then they were blasted into a million pieces by a bystander who wanted to help. That bystander is now facing murder charges."

A woman stands on the other side of the room behind the desk displaying "Canada", "Our citizens were some of the first affected along with the US and Mexico." She speaks calmly, but with an intensity for change, "I've heard many stories about those fearing to use their abilities because there may always be someone with a power stronger than yours, or, as you mentioned," she motions to the Turkish President, "someone who doesn't know how to control their power, or even worse...someone that does..." she trails off looking down to her desk as the others in the room begin shouting their input.

"Thank you Mrs. Prime Minister," the Chinese President continues his calm tone, once again quieting the room. "We have definitely seen some abuse of power around the world, but I have also read and heard many stories of happiness and joy...miracles, some have called them."

"Yes," the South African President stands abruptly, "just the other day we had a small child fall into the tiger pit at a zoo and someone was able to materialize a hologram to distract the animal while another sent a bright red line out of his hand to lasso and pull the child up. It showed amazing use of abilities from those citizens, but, more importantly, a deep caring for their fellow man."

Another roar is drawn from the crowd as both positive and negative reactions to the stories turn into garble. Suddenly, from beneath the noise a voice booms out, "I don't know about you," it echoes across the room drawing silence from the world's leaders. Their eyes are drawn to the entryway between two of the levels as a figure enters the room out of the shadows, "but I don't think we should just sit back and hope that the good stories outweigh the bad." The man walks in confidently looking around the room at all of the eyes, hands behind his back twirling the ring on his left hand.

"And who are you?" the Chinese President makes his way towards the man, but stops before getting too close for safety. "Those doors were supposed to be locked and guarded."

"Oh, they were locked," he says with a smile as he turns away from the Chinese President and walks across in front of each level, "and I gave the guards the rest of the day off." He goes silent for a few moments as everyone watches him make his way across the room in front of President Michaels. "Mr. President." He extends his hand across the desk, causing the President to push back in his chair and look at it nervously. "Hm," the man huffs returning his hand behind his back, "such a reaction from someone who has funded my company and our research for so many years...and to think, I'm here to help!" he scoffs disappointedly.

"Ladies and Gentlemen," he nearly rattles the room with his booming voice as he turns away from the President, "I come to you from Los Angeles, California where my company, InCorps, is working on a solution to the problem you discuss today…and yes, it is a problem."

The sound of the InCorps name and the following statement causes the room to erupt. They yell and point fingers at the man, who stands firmly in the middle of the floor. Speculative news stories across the world have tied InCorps to The Blackout and the events afterwards and also accused them of not taking responsibility or offering their help to fix it. He holds his ground as the insults fly at him from all sides and in a plethora of languages. Finally, the Chinese President approaches him once again, causing the room to quiet significantly.

"Sir, this is a meeting of world leaders…" He talks sternly up to the looming man who doesn't return his gaze.

Before he is able to scold anymore, the man's voice cuts him off, "And you decided to have it in Hong Kong because the Chinese people were the last to get their powers and therefore are the least developed." He finally turns and gazes down into the Chinese President's eyes causing him to take a step back. "This made you feel safe didn't it?"

"I, sir," the Chinese President moves forward again and suddenly grows about four feet taller and much more muscular to the point where it seems his formerly ill-fitting clothes may burst at every seam, "was never worried about the safety of this council." He grumbles, heaving up and down with deep breaths through clenched teeth as he now looks down on the stern-faced man gazing up into his bloodshot eyes.

The man seems unfazed, bringing his hands in front of himself for a golf clap, "Very impressive Mr. President." He begins to look around the room with a smile raising his hands to the on-looking leaders, "And I can only imagine that the rest of your abilities are just as impressive…and this is the issue." He finally settles on one stern face, "President Michaels," he walks towards the President's desk once again, "did you get your flu shot?"

The President seems taken aback by the odd question, "Uh, yes, of course." He answers with confusion.

"To immunize you from the flu, of course." He turns and walks across the floor looking into the hundreds of faces that gaze down at him. "Now, what if there were a flu shot...for these powers?"

As his statement is translated the room erupts once again. Some leaders are angry, some confused, some doubtful, and still others seem hopeful. He lets them shout for a time, then raises his arms and projects his booming voice "Now!" he draws silence from the audience, "It will still take some time to develop, but I want to present my terms for you to discuss..."

Suddenly, the large, dome skylight in the center of the ceiling draws the attention of everyone in the room as it lights up a bright green and begins to shake until the glass shatters into a million pieces. Instinctually, the United Kingdom Prime Minister paints his open hands above himself leaving a blue protective layer, the Icelandic President waves her fingers around as they send bright sparks up into the air above her, the Kenyan President turns completely into stone and shields himself and his translator while others initiate their own protective abilities or prepare to fight. To all of their surprise, no glass rains down on the room as if it had been pulled in the other direction. They all begin to slowly turn their eyes upward to the hole in the ceiling. As they stare into the light, a figure begins to appear as it descends into the room, arms out at its sides and cape flowing violently behind it. As his feet touch the floor softly, Kurrt looks around the room into the nervous faces, "Sorry to interrupt," his chest-piece begins to swirl and glow as his eyes narrow and a smile finds the corners of his mouth, "but I have a few terms of my own..."

"Dude, there is no freaking way we are going up there!" Tim whispers to Gavin so that none of his other inebriated classmates hear him.

"Yeah, man," Dane chimes in quietly, "I'm with Tim on this one." He looks up at the green field surrounding the mountain top nervously.

"Oh, pfffft!" Gavin blurts out, clearly not worried about concealing their conversation "You're always 'with Tim on this one'!" he scoffs at Dane with some sarcastic finger quotes. "Seriously, we just saw whatever was up there leave, I can get us up there and past the military blockades quickly and we've got Timmy, who can tell the future! We'll be fine!"

"And what about Dane!" Tim shouts, then pulls back his intensity, "No offense at all man, but you don't have any superpowers to protect yourself with. What if that thing comes back while we're up there?"

"I can help..." a small voice comes from behind Dane causing them all to turn quickly. "I can disguise myself to help hide you behind me, and if I can't, Gavin can rush you away." Sherri enters the group sheepishly with an excited smile on her face. Dane catches her eye and mouths the word "NO!" while shaking his head slowly.

"It's decided!" Gavin says proudly and downs the rest of the beer in his can, crushes it and, in attempting to toss it into the cooler, accidentally hurls it like a fastball striking the cooler loudly. After the initial surprise, he throws his hands over his head, "YEAH BABY, SUMMER O' FUN!!" he draws a huge cheer from the entire party and some that are able to shoot things from their hands emit lasers, lightning bolts, balls of light and more up into the night sky.

The other three friends look at each other nervously, then over to the cooler where icy water flows out onto the beach from the can-sized hole in the side.

Chapter 26

The wind whips and swirls the snow and ash around into tiny twisters across the white ground and into the trees creating the only noise on the trail near the edge of the field. Stars have long become forgotten since the smoke from the mountain enshrouded the world and the only light, besides a small amount from the moon, comes from the glowing currents of the giant, green globe.

Out of nowhere, Gavin suddenly shoots down from the sky and impacts in the middle of the snowy trail. As he stands up, his two screaming friends fall at a more normal speed and land in a snow bank next to his crater with a THUD! Slowly, they stand up out of their imprints, disoriented from the fall.

"Dude, that's a rush!" Tim shouts shaking his head and brushing snow off his shirt.

"Haha, not bad, eh!?" Gavin walks out of his crater and offers a hand to each of them.

"Not a compliment, man." Dane graps his friend's hand and is pulled out onto more solid ground. "I'm just glad that was a snow bank and not a snow-covered rock!"

"You gotta learn to trust yer boy!" Gavin laughs at his shaken friends. "I had to toss you upward before I landed...unless you'd rather I hold onto you and break your legs when we hit!?"

"Snow bank is just fine..." Tim says with disdain.

"That's the spirit, Timmy! Alright, I'm gonna go get Sherri." He turns in the direction of the beach down the mountain and across the lake. "Be right back fellas!" He squats down and disappears into the air in an instant, leaving behind another large dent in the snow.

"So, we all know this is a terrible idea, right?" Dane brushes the snow off his shirt and pants, "Why the hell are we here?"

"I dunno, man." Tim has made his way up to the field and guides his hand around slowly about an inch away, studying the electrical currents that chase it. "At least it'll shut him up." His hand gets a little too close and is zapped when a current shoots out of the field, causing him to pull his hand back and shake it in pain. "You know, I'm not even sure we can get through this thing…"

Dane joins his friend up next to the green wall and slowly raises his hand up to it. As he waves his hand along it he notices that the currents don't react to him. Curious, he pulls his hand back, points his index finger and moves it towards the field. Just as he's about to touch it, THUD!! Gavin slams into the ground behind him with Sherri in his arms. "Goddammit, Gavin! You scared the shit out of me!" He exclaims throwing his hands up in the air in frustration.

"Dude, I told you I'd be right back!" Gavin says with a proud laugh that is interrupted by his friend.

"Wait! Dane!" Tim shouts and points at Dane's hand as Gavin climbs out of his indent and sets Sherri down on the ground. "Did you see that?"

"What?" Dane utters studying his hand nervously.

"When you threw your hand up," he exclaims excitedly, "it went through the field!"

"So what? What's the big deal?" Gavin inquires as he and Sherri join their friends near the bright green wall.

"It shocked me when I tried to touch it." Tim fills him in to what he missed. "You try it!" he urges his overly confident friend, then gets a look of realization on his face, "Wait, that's a bad idea."

"With pleasure!" Gavin ignores Tim's last remark.

"Ooook…" Tim takes a step back guiding his other two friends with him. "This won't be pretty."

Instead of just touching it Gavin takes a couple of steps back, winds up and propels himself forward. In the millisecond it takes him to reach the wall, hundreds of electrical currents extend to his entire body stopping him dead in his tracks, then send him tumbling backwards into one of his craters with a loud scream.

They rush over to the edge of the hole and peer down to see his smoking body slowly pushing itself onto his hands and knees. "Son of a bitch!" he bellows in pain as he sets his unsteady feet underneath him. They reach down and help pull him back up onto the flat ground where he eventually finds his balance.

"Is this little field trip over now?" Dane scolds him as he helps brush the snow and ash off his back.

"Wait, I have an idea!" Sherri can't hide her excitement. She walks away from the group off the trail and along the outside of the field, studying it as she goes. "There!" she exclaims after a few moments with the boys following her into the trees.

"That might work!" Tim matches her excitement while Dane helps Gavin along behind them.

"Mind sharing with those of us who can't tell the future?" Gavin quips sarcastically.

"The field goes right through this tree." She states and then pauses, hoping they will catch on to her idea without further explanation. Their blank stares draw a frustrated sigh from the young girl as she spins around and places her fingers on the tree, which immediately mimics the bark covered trunk and transforms up to her elbow before she looks back at them with a smile. They nervously look at each other, not sharing in her and Tim's excitement. "It's worth a shot!" She exclaims with a smile pulling her finger away from the tree and returning her hand to normal, "Dane and I can go explore a little, Tim can keep watch, and Gavin...help Tim and be ready to get us out of here."

"What!?" Gavin throws his hands up in frustration, "Now I'm the sidekick?!"

"UGGGHHH!" The group lets out a simultaneous groan as if they'd all planned it.

After a few minutes of arguing, they finally decide that Dane and Sherri will go in and make their way up the trail a little ways and Tim will use his powers to watch for anyone or anything coming. Gavin will alert them if they need to get out by pushing on the trunk of a tree that stands much taller than the rest in the area, sending the snow and ash into the air as a signal.

"I still don't know about this..." Dane utters as he walks up to the field next to Sherri's chosen tree.

"We'll be fine. I'll protect you!" Sherri assures him with a nervous smile as she puts her hand on the tree trunk and slowly becomes part of it from head to toe. She raises her free hand up, hesitates, then finally plunges it through the green field cleanly. With a wooden smile she steps forward through the green currents, guiding her bark covered hand around the tree until she is all the way through. "Ok Dane, your turn!"

Dane sends a scared look to his two friends, hoping that they'll bail him out and go back on the plan.

"Hey," Gavin shrugs his shoulders and smiles back at Dane, "she said you'll be fine and her nose didn't grow!"

As Gavin and Tim share a laugh Dane finds himself unable to smile as he turns back toward the green wall. With a deep breath, he closes his eyes and steps forward.

Loud explosions and other noises radiate into the shiny, metal hallway from behind the door marked "Ballistics Dept.". Inside, the men fly around a gigantic room that resembles an aircraft hangar in their exoskeleton suits while taking aim and shooting down designated targets with different colored energy strikes. The doctor watches from near the doorway with a proud smile on her face, having worked with them all week to hone their abilities.

From a small office on the other side of the hangar, Simeon emerges in his usual mechanics jumpsuit. "Doctor!" he shouts across the room as he scurries across the floor screaming and engaging his yellow protective layer every time an explosion happens near him. He finally makes it through the proverbial warzone and hurries up to the doctor. "Doctor Wong," he unsuccessfully tries to get her attention, "I think you should see this."

She finally takes her eyes off her flying team and looks down to the nervous man, who has extended his hand to her holding an iPad. She grabs it from him, annoyed by the interruption and clicks the screen on to display a breaking news report. Footage of Kurrt's entrance into the World Leaders Meeting in Hong Kong displays, followed by him focusing his energy globes on a large podium, which dissembles the wood and pulls it into him. "Now," he projects to the auditorium with a smile, "who's ready to help me out."

In that moment, the Chinese President, now 8 feet tall and extremely muscular, can be seen making his way across the floor towards Kurrt. "None of these men or women are going to help you!" he growls in a deep, powerful voice and winds up to strike the threat before him. As his fist flies forward, Kurrt calmly raises one hand in front of him and his eyes light up a bright green as he engages his energy globe just as the fist strikes.

Stopped in his tracks, green currents begin to cover the Chinese President's hand working up his arm and across his body as he looks on in confusion. "Hm, I've never taken in a person before...I'm down for an experiment if you are, Mr. President!" he utters menacingly as he focuses the energy, increasing the glow of the currents covering the gigantic man and then, in a bright flash, the hulking President is gone. The headline on the bottom reads *MAN ATTACKS WORLD LEADERS' CONFERENCE: CHINESE PRESIDENT, POSSIBILY OTHERS BELIEVED DEAD* as the feed cuts and the newscasters begin to talk about the attack at their desk with the red, white and blue background.

"DAMMIT!" Doctor Wong shouts and slams the iPad down onto the concrete ground, shattering it.

"That..." Simeon starts loudly, then pulls back his voice in dismay, "that was my...personal iPad..."

"Gentlemen!" the Doctor announces, ignoring Simeon's comment, "Our time has come!"

The eight men turn and fly or run in her direction landing and stopping in front of her and Simeon in a straight line, their eyes glowing all different colors. As they disengage their power globes and their eyes return to normal they are briefed on the news. "Kurrt has sent a message." Doctor Wong declares emphatically. "We still are not sure of his exact powers, but, much like you guys, he seems to derive his power from an energy source, except..." she trails off.

The men look at each other with confusion. Finally, Charles speaks up, "Except what, Dr.?"

"Except," the doctor pauses, "Charles, your power is created in the presence of CO_2, and Allen, yours comes from fire. These are supplied to you through your suits. Kurrt's powers..." she pauses again, "they seem to come from anything."

For a moment, the men look at each other trying to gauge each other's reactions.

"This doesn't change anything!" Doctor Wong regains their attention. "We're here to do a job," She feels the butterflies of nervousness and excitement hit her stomach and she closes her eyes to focus in on it. Suddenly, her hands fly open and her power globes blaze forth in her palms. She slowly opens her eyes revealing their blue glow, "now let's get to work."

The men follow her lead and engage their globes. Simeon shields his eyes and engages his protective field as he is illuminated with flashing lights and the air whips around him. Cautiously moving his arm away from his eyes he looks around to see that he is now alone in the hangar.

Chapter 27

The snow crunches under every step as Dane and Sherri make their way up the trail. Every time the wind whips across them Dane shutters and rubs his arms for warmth. He glances over at Sherri, whose blonde hair reflects the green hue the dome casts over everything underneath it. She walks steadily and seems unaffected by the cold, probably too excited to feel it, Dane figures. He wished he could be excited for an adventure. The last week had really worn on him and, as much as he felt like an outsider before with his medications, having no dad, being a mediocre student, athlete, and friend, there was no question about it. He was definitely an outsider now. A normal, run-of-the-mill kid in a world full of superheroes. Suddenly, Sherri looks over and catches his gaze bringing him back to reality. Realizing he had been looking at her the whole time, he quickly shifts his eyes down to the ground in front of him.

"You ok?" she asks comfortingly.

"Yeah, totally." He lies without lifting his gaze, then attempts to divert the conversation. "It was...it was just weird seeing you all made of wood like that."

"Yeah, it's...not exactly the coolest of powers to have." She laughs drawing a smile out of her friend. "But it got me here, so I guess it's not the worst either."

"Hey, at least you have them." Dane utters through chattering teeth.

"Yeah..." she immediately feels bad for complaining. "How are you doing with the whole thing?"

"Eh, you know, it's no big deal." He attempts to mask his frustrations, "I mean, my mom made me breakfast this morning without touching a single utensil or piece of food, so she's loving it." He pauses as he watches his feet in front of him. "I'm just happy she woke up."

"I know! I was so happy when I heard." She agrees with him excitedly as she looks at the beautiful, snow-covered trees around them. "So what do you think is going to happen with all of this, now that it's worldwide?"

After a moment of not receiving an answer, she looks back to her left, "Dane?" She realizes that he has stopped walking a few steps behind her. "Dane, what is it?"

Dane stares up the trail past the trees, a bright green reflecting in his eyes. As Sherri turns and follows his gaze her mouth drops. Underneath the cover of the trees a small shack sits illuminated by the bright green light of a gigantic, glowing ball sitting atop its pyramid of wood and rocks. Through the cover of the trees and distracted by their conversation, neither of them had heard the loud electric hum of the rotating ball, but it filled the air now that they had entered the clearing. He slowly begins walking forward until he is caught up with his friend.

"What the hell is that?" he utters, knowing full well that she also has no idea.

"Do you think that's creating the field?" she replies, unable to remove her eyes from the flickering currents.

"Maybe..." Dane trails off as he begins walking forward slowly, causing Sherri to follow. As he enters the small clearing where the shack sits, he glances up past everything to the mountain top, which spews black smoke. Studying it, he can begin to see a slight green glow coming from the edge of the opening, which suddenly goes in and out of focus. As he rubs his eyes he suddenly feels a sharp pain in his temple. "AHHHH!" he screams as he grabs his forehead and drops to his knees. The pain worsens and he suddenly can't breathe as visions flash through his mind.

"Dane!" Sherri kneels and puts an arm around him as he folds over in pain. "What's wrong?! Dane!"

Through his pain, Dane realizes he has felt this before. He remembers this. This pain. This feeling of being underwater. The visions of thrashing for life. He quickly reaches his hand down into his left pocket and pulls out his orange pill bottle. Bringing it in front of him, he now realizes that his hands are shaking violently. Sherri notices him struggling and grabs it out of his hand, pops the top off and shoves one of the small pills into his mouth. He throws his head back and feels it slide down his throat, then waits with his hands cradling his head. Slowly, the pain begins to recede and the shaking in his hands settles down until both are gone.

Down the hill, Tim is focusing on seeing as far ahead as possible while Gavin paces in the snow.

"I can't believe we're stuck out here!" Gavin shouts in frustration sending vapors into the cold air in front of him.

"Dude, chill. That's probably why nobody's investigated up here yet." Tim attempts to calm his friend. "At least Dane gets a little action. I feel bad for him."

"Yeah, me too. It can't be easy being the only person in the world without powers." Gavin agrees, then brings a smirk to his mouth, "Maybe Sherri feels bad too and will give him some 'other' action!"

Tim can't help but chuckle, "Did you see that kid going in there? He's probably too focused on not peeing his pants. He was scared shitless!" they laugh again, but suddenly Tim stops short. "Something's coming..." he closes his eyes to focus.

"Is it that green thing?" Gavin is suddenly serious and alert, "Should I signal them?"

"It's not the green thing..." Tim continues to focus with his eyes shut tightly. "Oh shit...DO IT! SIGNAL THEM!"

Without another question Gavin loads up and hurtles himself towards the enormous trunk of the tree. He hits with his hands extended out in front of him and sends it leaning to one side. He looks up, waiting for it to sway back towards him so that he can push it again, but it doesn't return to upright. His sight is drawn down by groans and cracks as the tree begins to uproot right under his feet. He can do nothing but jump back and watch the tree go over slowly taking other, smaller trees along with it until it crashes to the ground. He looks over his shoulder in Tim's direction, whose eyes are now wide in bewilderment. "Uh...I guess I don't know my own strength yet..." Gavin utters with a shrug.

"We have to get Dane and Sherri's attention somehow, they're coming!" Tim begins to look around frantically for a way to alert his friends.

"Wait..." Gavin grabs his arm stopping him, "did you say 'they'?"

Unable to respond, Tim just looks back at him with fear in his eyes.

In the clearing, Dane and Sherri have continued their investigation now that his episode had passed. Deciding to stay away from the giant, glowing ball they settle for the shack. Dane has climbed onto a wooden crate along the shack's wall and balances off the side to get a view into the shattered window.

"Do you see anything?" Sherri inquires anxiously from a few feet below him. "Is anyone inside?"

"I don't think so..." Dane groans he tries to angle himself off the crate with one foot, his hands gripping tightly to the frame of the window. "I can't really see." His foot finds a groove in the wood siding and he is able to push himself up a few inches, giving him a clear view into the lower window pane. Inside, dimly lit by the desk lamp, he sees empty boxes and clothes scattered across the floor surrounded by the walls of computer towers. The desk sits in the middle of the room empty except for a few tools, the lamp, and the monitor. Dane squints to see better, then his eyes go wide showing equal amounts of confusion and surprise. "I...I think we should go." He utters.

"What is it? What's wrong?" Sherri can't hide her concern.

Dane jumps down and grabs her arm, "Let's go." They turn and begin making their way down the trail hastily until Dane stops abruptly.

"What? Dane, what's going on?!" Sherri is now getting frustrated.

"The tree." Dane says under his breath. "The tree...it's gone!" he points down the trail where they had just come from.

"What!? Where is it?" Sherri shows her fear for the first time.

Before Dane can even consider responding they hear a low rumble, then a roar rushes above them like a fighter jet. They both turn their eyes up to see a blue streak shoot across the sky above the dome followed by other streaks of various colors. As they turn simultaneously like the Blue Angels and approach the area above them again, Dane feels himself pulled violently to the ground next to the trail and behind a black boulder. He looks over to Sherri, who emulates his worry then directs her gaze back up to the sky. Reaching the clearing, the lights stop and hover into a circular formation around the blue light, then begin to descend, passing right through the green field and setting down softly on the snow near the shack.

"Spread out! Find him!" a woman shouts sending men rushing towards the shack and the area around the giant globe. She stands firm, hands behind her back, and looks around the clearing until she faces the trail and Dane can finally make out the face of the Doctor from the hospital.

"We have to get out of here." he whispers to Sherri without taking his eyes off the Doctor. Hugging the rock next to her he doesn't get a response, but suddenly he feels her grab his hand tightly.

Suddenly, another low rumble comes from the distance catching the attention of everyone in the clearing. With a growing roar, a green flash shoots towards them from the distance, through the field and slams into the trail's opening to the clearing about ten feet away from Dane and Sherri sending debris up into the air. Instinctually, Sherri engages her powers as her entire body quickly becomes black rock. To both of their surprise, as her transformation reaches her hand it spreads to Dane and he is suddenly also camouflaged against the black rock, unable to move.

"Shhh," Sherri instructs him as if knowing he was about to freak out. He abides and they put their focus back on the settling cloud in front of them.

"Doctor! So nice to see you!" Kurrt shouts his facetious welcome across the clearing as he comes into view.

"Don't give me that shit, Kurrt." The Doctor's eyes now glow bright blue with anger as her crew gathers behind her. "I know where you just came from and what you did. This doesn't have to get any uglier, just let us help you and get you what you want. We're willing to listen"

"Listen!?" Kurrt belts out a laugh that echoes through the trees around him. "Now you're willing to LISTEN!?" his anger suddenly presents itself. "Were you 'listening' when I told you about the leaks?! You banished me to this goddamn mountain, then I tried to warn you about the radioactivity! Did you 'listen' then, Doctor?!" to Dane's dismay, he begins to stroll towards them until he reaches the boulder. He leans on it with one hand and gazes back to the Doctor with a smile. "You don't know how to listen...you never have. You and your dogs only know how to act."

Slowly growing, a glow of green lights up Dane's black, rocky face and he can see the rock begin to vaporize piece by piece in front of him and go into Kurrt's palm.

"So...LET'S ACT!!" Kurrt shouts as he quickly raises his other hand and shoots a continuous beam of energy towards the Doctor and her men. The Doctor quickly engages a blue shield in front of her that deflects the green energy up into the sky as her men scatter in all directions and into the air. As Kurrt tenses to increase the strength of the beam, he suddenly grows in size becoming about 4 feet taller and much more muscular. "Hm, well that's new." He grumbles to himself in a much deeper voice, then turns his focus back to the doctor who now struggles to hold her defense against his energy. The green glow eating away the rock continues to grow and advance. Dane's eyes widen in fear as it is just about to reach his rock-composed arm, but a sudden flash nearly blinds him as a glowing yellow ball with spikes impales itself into Kurrt's shoulder. Cameron hovers in front of them, squeezing his hand into a fist which simultaneously causes the yellow ball to explode, sending Kurrt flying back onto the ground. While on the ground groaning he slowly shrinks back down to his normal size. In the clearing ahead, the men regain formation around the Doctor and engage their energy globes with their exoskeleton suits.

"Alright, fellas. Let's have some fun." Kurrt utters under his breath as he slowly climbs to his feet. In a bright flash of green he shoots straight up leaving green currents glowing in the snow. The Doctor and her men immediately do the same and follow him into the air and through the field. As the rumble disappears into the distance Sherri releases her power, turning herself and Dane back to normal.

"What the hell was that!?!" she shouts with fear.

"I was going to ask you the same thing." Dane mumbles as he looks his normalized hand over with confusion.

Chapter 28

"DUDE!!! We thought you guys were toast for sure!" Gavin exclaims, throwing his arms around Dane once he has made his way through the field.

"Yeah, so did we…" Dane utters as he apathetically returns the hug. "What the hell happened to the signal?"

"Well, Mr. Sidekick here managed to, oh, I don't know, break the signal." Tim roasts him pointing to the gigantic tree and the opening in the woods it created when it fell. "I thought you guys would've heard it."

"It was probably the noise from the nucleus." Sherri adds her input as she guides her wooden figure around the tree trunk and through the field, releasing the tree and immediately returning back to normal. "That's why we didn't hear it."

"You gave it a name?" Dane chuckles, noticing his friends' confused looks. "We think it's what's powering the field…it's a long story. Can we get off this mountain and we'll tell you everything?"

"Yeah, I think that's a good idea." Tim agrees motioning to Gavin. "Let's go, you fake-ass Paul Revere."

"Ha ha, freaking hilarious!" Gavin mutters sarcastically as he grabs Tim and prepares his jump. "I think someone's getting tossed in the water when I land." They disappear up into the air towards the beach across the lake.

"Well that was crazy." Dane breathes a sigh of relief. "How did you even do that…you know, change me too?"

"I have no idea." Sherri shrugs her shoulders. "I've never been able to do that before. I can usually only change myself."

"Well, I'm glad you did." He utters. "It would've been a much shorter trip for me."

Gavin lands next to them with a loud THUD. "Alright, Danger Dane, you ready to go?" He grabs onto Dane, who looks into Sherri's bright blue eyes one more time.

"I told you I'd protect you." She says softly with an adorable smile. As he begins to smile back he is abruptly whisked up into the dark night air.

Dane slowly pushes open the door of the house and walks in with his eyes glued to his lit-up phone screen.

"Dane!?" Mom shouts anxiously as she jumps from the couch and rushes to see if it's him. "Oh my god, are you okay?" she shouts frantically as she comes into view and immediately wraps him in a huge hug. "I've been texting you like crazy!"

Smothered into her shoulder Dane can't help but think she's heard about what happened on the mountain. "Yeah, I'm fine." He attempts to comfort her, "All your texts just popped up when I was on my way home. There wasn't service at the beach."

"Jesus, I was so worried." She wraps him up in another big hug.

"Why? What's wrong?" Dane works to squirm his way out of her arms so he can figure out what she knows.

"Well, there's a huge..." she trails off as she points towards the living room, unsure how to explain it. "They're all...fighting! It's crazy!" She grabs his arm and pulls him into the room where the TV blares.

As it comes into view, Dane reads the bulletin at the bottom and listens to the anchor's words in disbelief.

SUPERHERO MAYHEM ERUPTS IN DOWNTOWN SEATTLE

Colored streaks fly in all directions through the buildings of the city avoiding green energy bursts from Kurrt, who is now encased in a mini, green force field. The doctor streaks around him in circles, wrapping him up in a blue energy rope as the men shoot various forms of rays and pulses, all deflected by his shield. He escapes her grasp and fires back at them with his hands and chest piece, picking them off seemingly with ease as civilians fly and run for safety or engage their protective abilities. One of the doctor's men is hit and falls like a ragdoll onto the top of a parked car, crushing it, as another is hurled through a tenth floor office window and out of sight. Another video shows him absorbing the corner pillar of a building like he had done to the rock Dane and Sherri had hid behind. He floats away in his field as the building crumbles to the ground behind him.

As the videos replay and the anchor encourages everyone to flee the city and not to intervene in the battle, Dane looks away to his mom with wide eyes, unable to speak. He knows he can't tell her about what happened on the mountain, but maybe what he saw could help stop this guy. His phone practically hasn't stopped vibrating in his pocket since he pulled up to the curb. He pulls it out and flips open the cover, to his dismay, seeing texts from all three of his friends. Without checking them, he closes it and turns back to the TV. "What should we do?"

"I don't know, sweetie." Mom utters as she reaches out and the remote comes floating over to her and softly sets down in her hand. She flips through the news channels, which have all focused on the chaos in the city.

As they watch, Dane is suddenly overtaken with emotions: Fear, anger, sadness, helplessness. Without a word he turns and heads upstairs, ignoring his mom's worried calls. He rushes into his room and frantically looks around, finally darting over to his dresser and rustling through the clothes that hang out of the open top drawer.

Mom appears in the doorway aggravated that he was ignoring her. "Dane! Didn't you hear me? I think we should leave!" She says sternly, still not getting a reaction from her son. "What the hell are you doing?"

 Not finding what he's looking for in the drawer, he spins and rushes over to his desk and pulls out his chair displaying a pair of jeans lying on the floor. He grabs them and shoves his hand into each pocket until he finally pulls out a white card, dropping the pants to the floor. He gazes at the card as he turns it over in his hand to display the Doctor's name and phone number alongside the InCorps logo, then looks at Mom's confused gaze from the doorway and smiles at her.

In the dark downtown, smoke rises from destroyed cars, collapsed buildings and charred holes in the street. The doctor leans against a pile of concrete where Kurrt had destroyed the road, her clothes tattered and dirty and her hair beginning to fall from its tight ponytail onto either side of her face.

"Allen, come in!" She orders through an intercom on the cuff of her sleeve. Not getting a response, she peeks around the concrete wall to see if Kurrt is still there. "Charles! Whoever's left, form on me, evacuating for regroup."

Suddenly, the concrete begins to crackle causing her to step back. A slight green glow forms in the center of the pile and becomes larger until the concrete begins to chip away and creates a hole large enough for Kurrt to come into view. As the final pieces of concrete are absorbed into his hands he moves forward through the hole towards her, causing her to engage her blue shield.

"Smart move, Doctor." He says confidently with glowing green eyes. "Can I ask, where do you get your powers from?"

"I don't know...I think...from my feelings. From my emotions." She utters nervously hiding behind her blue shield while still trying to seem strong and steady as always.

"Interesting." Kurrt continues to advance on her slowly, causing her to move backwards. "And your boys? From something delivered by their suits, I suppose? You see, doctor, that's where you're all at a disadvantage, because my suit is just a supplement, and my power," he holds his hand up in front of him and engages his energy globe, also lighting his eyes up bright green, "well, my power comes from anything and everything."

As the globe begins to light up brightly she focuses her energy into her shield causing it to glow brighter. Kurrt's face grimaces and his muscles tighten as he turns his palm in her direction preparing to fire and they both stop, suddenly distracted by a ringing. With an angrily confused look, Kurrt shouts, "Are you kidding me!? Are you really getting a phone call right now!? What, did your parents see you on the news or something!?"

He focuses in again and his palm and eyes glow brighter than before. Just as he's about to shoot he is hit by another yellow ball that immediately explodes, sending him back onto the ground. He looks up to see hundreds of white particles rain down on him, exploding in bright, white bursts as they hit him and the ground around him and then he is pelted by a series of orange fireballs. He recovers only long enough to engage his shield as he pushes himself off the pavement. A red electrical current and a purple ray deflect off the shield as he reaches his feet and sees five of the men gather alongside the doctor.

"Your boys are dwindling, Doctor." He says with a smile. "Why don't you guys regroup and come see me later for some more fun." He turns and begins to walk away from them. "And next time," he shouts with only a turn of his head as he raises his arms out to his sides, "could you knock, please?"

The Doctor's eyes burn bright blue with anger as they watch Kurrt float a few feet above the pavement, then streak off into the dark towards the mountain. As the glow recedes from her eyes, she looks at the guys around her and nods as if to silently say "Thank you" then looks back up at the green streak that slowly fades in the sky. "We're going to need some help." She mutters as she turns to walk away, pulling the phone out of her pocket to see who called.

Chapter 29

"The news is calling it 'The Battle of Seattle'." Mom chuckles as Dane sleepily drags into the kitchen the next morning. Toast pops out of the toaster and she motions with her hand, sending the bread floating to the counter in front of her where a knife magically spreads butter on the slices. Another motion and the pan flips the eggs that sizzle off to her side.

"How original." Dane mutters unenthusiastically. He sits at the counter where a plate immediately slides in front of him on its own. Buttered toast floats over and sets down softly, followed by eggs and a glass of orange juice. Normally, he would have been immediately annoyed, but not today. Today was different. He reaches into his pajama pants pocket and pulls out the Doctor's card and looks at it under conceal of the counter, then stuffs it back into his pocket and out of sight. "Your powers are getting stronger, Mom!"

"I don't know if they're stronger," she says without turning to him, "I think I'm just getting better the more I use them."

"Well that's good too!" He says through a mouthful of eggs and toast.

"You're in a good mood today!" She finally turns to him as if to check that it is in fact her son sitting at the counter. "What's the deal?"

"Nothing." Dane's chewing slows and he notices Mom is studying him. "I swear! Just...slept good, I guess."

"Ok," Mom's voice holds an element of doubt as she turns back around to orchestrate her cleanup. "So, what do you have planned for today?"

"I dunno," Dane now realizes he'll have to downplay everything to keep her suspicion at bay, "I might meet Tim and Gavin for lu-"

"You're not going anywhere near the city, right!?" Mom interrupts as she quickly spins around and glares intently at him.

"No! No, of course not!" Dane defends. "I'm not stupid!"

"Ok, good." Mom seals her warning with one final glare before turning back around and motioning to the small TV on the countertop. "Besides, it looks like they've got a good deal of it cleaned up already. I guess if anything good comes of it, people begin to figure out how to use their powers to work together and overcome the bad stuff that happens."

Dane chews his breakfast as his eyes fix on the small TV screen to see people cleaning up the city streets. People with various forms of super strength help move pieces of collapsed buildings, those who can create fire and pulses of heat melt the piles of concrete to fill in the holes in the streets and still others tend to people who were trapped in the rubble or injured during the destruction. A look of determination forms on his face and a glimmer appears in his eye. "I'm counting on it..." he mutters under his breath.

Inside the shack, the exoskeleton suit lies in an unorganized heap on the desk as Kurrt floats horizontally in the middle of the room with his arms crossed on his chest like a mummy, green electrical currents flashing like small lightning bolts between his body and the floor. Slowly, his eyes open into a blank stare at the ceiling of the shack. After blinking a few times a smile finds his lips as he recalls the events of the previous night. He reaches his arms out to either side and effortlessly floats into an upward position and sets down softly on the floor and begins gathering some clothes to put on.

As he pulls the shirt over his head and down to his chest he stops, "I wanna try something first..." he says to himself and pulls the shirt off, throwing it back to the floor. He strips off the jog pants he had put on and stands in the middle of the room in his underwear just as he had woke up. He clenches his fists and tightens his entire body as his face grimaces and he suddenly blows up into his goliath monster form. As astonished as he was the night before he studies his hands and arms and the rest of his gigantic, muscular form. "Thank you, Mr. Chinese President." He grumbles in a deep, gruff voice. He closes his eyes and takes a deep breath in, then lets it out and slowly deflates down to his normal size, once again looking over his changed hands, arms and body. "This changes everything!" he exclaims as he excitedly throws on some jeans and a dark grey zip-up hoodie, pulling the hood over his head and making his way across the floor. He throws open the rickety, wooden door and is met by a gust of cold wind and the morning light that creeps through the overcast cloud, causing him to squint to see the small town that lies in the distance. "Now to find the right candidates…"

The Doctor rushes through the shiny, metal hallways while Simeon scurries behind, trying to keep up with her long strides as he swipes through screens on an iPad.

"They're not perfected yet, but the concept, at the very least, should keep him from engaging his globes." He can't hide the shakiness in his voice as he squints through his goggles at the bright screen. "AH, here they are." He exclaims as he reaches the device up towards the doctor, who stops abruptly and turns to grab it from his shaky hand.

She looks over a 3D blueprint of oval-shaped encasements with a small compartment extended into the middle. "So, we can alter these to fit hands?" She inquires with an intensity that expects nothing other than a "Yes" from Simeon. "What does all of this mean?" She motions to the specs that surround the rotating blueprint on the screen.

"Oh, don't worry about that...science stuff." Simeon says candidly, then notices her glare and attacks the more important question, "Of course they can be altered. Easily. And, like I was saying, the concept of having the anti-matter in the center compartment will deter him from engaging his globes."

"How so?" the Doctor pushes.

"Well, from what you've told me, he absorbs matter." He pauses as if assuming this was enough of an answer. She looks away from the iPad once again with a glare. "Well, if the antimatter rests in his palm and he engages his globes, one of two things will happen..." he fades as he contemplates his next words.

After a moment of impatient waiting she ushers him along, "And those are!?"

Simeon begins slowly, "Well, I don't really know..." suddenly his pace quickens with excitement, "I mean, One, he could absorb the opposite of what gives him his powers, therefore taking away his power...or two, he will absorb antimatter, which is the opposite of the matter he is made of and..." he pauses, "well, the most likely scenario is it destroys him and creates the first dark matter humans have ever seen firsthand." He looks up to the doctor with worry in his eyes, "You could be looking right into the creation of a black hole on earth, or worse...I assume you've heard of the Big Bang?"

She looks into his fearful eyes for a second, then turns away handing him the iPad. "Get them ready." She orders sternly as she heads away from him down the hallway. He adjusts his glasses as he nervously looks over the blueprint on the screen and hurries in the opposite direction quickly.

The Doctor passes through a large, metal arch into a hallway with more normal décor and continues forward quickly as a door hisses and slides shut behind her with a loud BANG! Her heels click loudly on the marble floor as she turns a corner and makes her way up to clouded glass door. Her hand reaches for the handle, but stops abruptly clenching into a fist. She closes her eyes and takes a deep breath in, then lets it out slowly through pursed lips as her head drops. After a moment she lifts her head confidently and opens her eyes. She forces her hand to push down the handle and her feet to move forward into the office where the man looms large over his desk, the phone pressed to his ear.

"Yes, Mr. President, we are taking care of the situation by day's end." His voice maintains its loud intensity, even in defense. "No, sir, there will be no need for that course of action. We have a plan in place and will keep you updated...Absolutely, thank you sir." He reaches the headset over and sets it down on the receiver, "Tell me you have a plan, Miss Wong." He booms across the room without looking up at her.

"Yes. Yes, sir." She is immediately angry with herself for not sounding more confident.

The man waits a moment, then peers up across the room at her as she stands stable, her hands folded behind her back. "I can't help but hope that it's better than the plan you carried out last night in DOWNTOWN SEATTLE!" he screams slamming a fist against the desk and standing abruptly. As his hunching shoulders heave up and down with his deep breaths, the Doctor looks on nervously and notices his gritting sharp teeth and a yellow glimmer in his glaring eyes.

"Y-Yes, sir. We have someth-" she is interrupted by a ringing in her pocket. Equal amounts of embarrassment and fear boil up inside as she reaches down and squeezes it through the fabric of her pants, causing it to fall silent.

"Why don't you get that, Doctor," the man urges through clenched teeth as he still heaves with anger, "it may be important."

Reluctantly, she pulls the phone out of her pocket, not recognizing the number on the screen, slides the green ANSWER button and sets it on her ear. "Dr. Wong." She listens for a moment with a confused look on her face, "Wait, who is this?" Surprise suddenly takes over her face as she rotates the phone away from her mouth and looks over the desk into the man's glare, "Sir, I'll be right back." She doesn't wait for his response and quickly turns and rushes out the door into the hallway. She anxiously walks about twenty feet down the hallway and returns the phone over her cheek, "Ok, tell me what happened." She listens for a moment as she studies the sincerity of the voice on the other end. "How did you two even get up...you're positive? You're 100% sure that's what you saw?" She listens again in amazement, "Ok, we will meet you, but let us handle Kurrt. You're not getting involved." She pulls the phone away from her ear and swipes the red button across the screen.

After clicking and swiping a few times she puts the phone up to her ear and begins to hurry back down the hallway towards the office door. "Simeon, change of plans. I'll be there in five minutes." She orders, immediately hanging up the phone and stuffing it back into her pocket as she pushes through the office door again, this time only leaning in the doorway. "Sir, I have to go. I just received some information that will help us bring Kur-"

"Yes, of course Miss Wong." The man interrupts from his desk where he now sits twirling the ring on his finger. She turns to rush away, but is stopped abruptly by the man's booming voice, "By the way...how is our little friend, Dane Denson?"

"Dude, what is it with all you guys and being late all the time!" Gavin throws his hands up in frustration as he paces back and forth in the empty school parking lot. Tim and Sherri do their best to ignore his ridicule. "I'm serious, I waste so much time waiting on you guys!"

"What the hell else do you have to do right now?" Tim shoots back at his friend as he lies in the backside of his jeep playing on his phone. "What, are you going to start drinking at 11:30 in the morning?"

"Maybe!!" Gavin shouts, drawing chuckles from them.

"You really need a job..." Sherri mutters shaking her head from her seat next to Tim, "Hey, there he is!" she points over the recessed football field to the winding school driveway where Dane's rickety car kicks up dust as it approaches.

As it slides to a stop next to the other three cars, Dane throws the door open and stands from his seat, his phone pressed to his ear, "Yes, I promise you! It'll make it easier to take him down, but we'll have to get in there somehow, then you just have to keep him under and he's all yours. 7 o'clock we'll be where Kenneth Trail meets the field. We can be your decoys while you and your men handle him...no problem." He slides the red button ending the call as he walks around the back of his car towards his friends.

"Look at you, wheelin' and dealin'!" Gavin rags on him as he joins the group.

"Yeah, you know me..." Dane mutters shyly as Tim and Sherri jump up from the Jeep, anxious to hear what they're doing there.

"So, who was that?" Sherri urges him to start explaining.

"And what are we doing here?" Tim continues.

"And why the hell are you late!" Gavin interjects, drawing a punch in the arm from Tim and a sigh of frustration from Sherri.

"Sorry, that was someone I met before who can help us." He turns to Sherri, "The woman from the mountain, she's a doctor who works at InCorps. We're going to help her men stop that guy, Kurrt."

"We're WHAT!?" Gavin suddenly takes a more serious tone. "Us?! The four of us!?"

"Yeah, man," Tim adds, "you saw what he did in Seattle. What the hell are we supposed to do?"

As Dane starts to explain Sherri grabs his arm, "Dane, you don't even have any powers to protect you. That woman and eight men couldn't even stop him...you could get killed."

"We could ALL get killed!" Gavin continues pacing the lot with his hands on his head in disbelief.

"Listen, we can do this." Dane urges them. "Sherri and I are the only ones who can get up there besides the Doctor and her men. Once they've got him wrapped up, we can stop him."

"But you just told her we'd be her decoys." Sherri shows confusion in her face.

"That's what she's going to think." Dane says slyly. "I'm counting on them to take care of the nucleus, which should drop the shield, then I'll need your help."

"I don't like this, man." Gavin utters nervously. "Someone's going to get hurt and I'm pretty sure it's either going to be you, or us trying to save you."

"You guys have to trust me." He looks pleadingly around at his friends' worried faces. "Please. Be at the trail at 6:45. I'll meet you there, but I have to go find someone first."

Dane turns and jogs around his car and hops back in, slamming the door behind him. As he turns the key and starts the engine Sherri pokes her head in his window, an empathetic look on her face. "Dane, we don't have to do this. They can handle this without us."

"Maybe." Dane fixes his gaze ahead of him so he is not swayed by her bright blue pleading eyes. "But maybe they can't. Maybe they do need us."

"Dane..." she pleads, "what did you see up there...in the shack?"

This catches Dane off guard and finally draws him to look at her. He thought she had forgotten his surprise as he looked into the shack's window that night. He knows there's no way he can tell her, even though he wants to. Her look of desperation begins to wear on him, so he looks away again, grabbing his shifter. "I saw a way to beat him...but I can't do it without you." He looks at her one more time as he shifts into drive and speeds away across the parking lot.

Chapter 30

In the quiet Eatonville Hospital waiting room, people sit spread out in the rows of chairs reading magazines or looking at their phones. The receptionist is immersed in paperwork behind her plastic window as nurses and other staff move around behind her in their multicolored scrubs. With a hiss the automatic doors slide open, not quickly enough for Dane who squeezes his body through them and rushes across the room to the receptionist's window. His entrance had not even drawn her attention away from her work.

"Excuse me," Dane aims his soft words towards the opening at the bottom of the window, finally drawing an irritated look from the woman, "I'm looking for someone I met when my mom was here last week. His daughter was in the same room as her and I need to get in touch with him. It was room #145 and his name was Gary. His daughter was Alyssa."

She looks up at the young man apathetically for a moment, then returns to her work. "I'm not allowed to release the information of other patients or their families."

"I know, but I really need his help." Dane pushes forward, "Can't you jus-"

"Listen, if you or a loved one don't have an emergency I'll need to ask you to leave." She says sternly without looking at him. "As I said, I'm not allowed to give out the information of our patients or their families."

Frustrated and desperate, Dane hunches down to the crack in the window, "Can you please help me, just this once?" She raises one open hand in front of his face as he continues, "I really need him to help me-" She closes the fingers together on the raised hand and, though Dane's lips continue to move and he can feel his vocal cords vibrate in his throat, there is no voice coming from his mouth. He takes a step back, attempting to ask what she did to him, but nothing comes out.

The cantankerous woman raises her eyes to him with her fingertips still clenched, "I'll need to ask you to leave, or I can have you escorted out." She opens the hand and returns her gaze back down to her papers, "Have a great day."

"Dammit." Dane utters under his breath mostly from frustration, but also to make sure she had returned his voice. He turns and starts heading for the doorway catching glances from the concerned onlookers in their chairs as he contemplates how his plan will play out now.

"I know where Gary is." He is startled by a small voice in his path to the doorway and stops suddenly. Looking ahead he sees a small girl with a nervous smile on her face, her frizzy hair pulled into loosely braided pigtails that rest on the front of her shoulders. "I can help you find him."

Tim's Jeep pulls up abruptly to the curb in front of the Eatonville library and both doors fly open.

"Listen, I know Dane's got his whole plan and everything," Gavin exits the passenger side slamming the door behind him, "and that's fine. I just think we're going to need some help...like, a lot."

"I'm not disagreeing with you, he just said to trust that he's got it figured out with that doctor lady." Tim slams his driver's side door and rounds the front of the car to the sidewalk. "Maybe the less people there the better. You know...casualties."

"Well, that's a hopeful thought." Gavin adds sarcastically as they begin walking. "Like Sherri said, that woman and her eight guys couldn't even slow him down. Now you're going to add a human wrecking ball, a future teller, a girl who changes into a log and a kid with no powers at all and expect things to go any better?"

Tim has no response other than a shrug of the shoulders as he swings open the door of the coffee shop and walks through, followed by his friend.

"Well, I'm not seeing it." Gavin now talks quieter as he surveys the people around the room. "If you think we'll be fine grab a scone and a latte and I'll meet you outside, cuz I'm doing some recruiting." He turns and leaves his friend standing there and begins moving from person to person telling them about their plan.

Tim stands where Gavin left him, hesitant to talk to anyone. Finally, he decides to give in to Gavin's effort and begins talking to people on the other side of the room. Once they have informed all of the seated patrons Gavin approaches the line of people waiting to order. He puts his hands on a couple of guys' shoulders and leans in with a whisper, "Yo fellas, we're gonna take down that bastard that wrecked Seattle. Kenneth trail where it meets the force field at 6:45. We've got professional help, but we need as many as we can get to take this guy out. Be there! Thanks guys." He pats their shoulders and turns away. Seeing that Tim has already talked to the other people in line, he catches his eye and motions towards the door.

One of the men that Gavin had just talked to turns slowly and watches the boys exit through the double doors. Reaching the sidewalk Gavin points across the street to the town's grocery market and they rush out of the man's sight as a smile comes to his mouth and a glimmer of green flashes in his eyes from under the cover of his dark grey hood.

"I don't know, really," the young girl speaks softly from the passenger seat, "it's like my scream put some sort of a...like a tracker on the people at the hospital that day. That's how I knew you and that doctor had been up on the mountain the night the Seattle thing happened. I thought maybe you were planning something when you showed up at the hospital today and I wanted to help."

"Well, I'm happy you came." Dane says with a sense of relief in his voice. "I don't know how I would've found Gary otherwise."

The girl nods as she looks out the car window solemnly at the passing neighborhood.

"I'm Dane, by the way." Dane continues.

"Jaz." She replies without taking her eyes away from the window then goes silent for a few moments. "So, you actually trust these InCorps guys?"

"No, not really," Dane utters with his eyes focused on the road ahead, "but, trust or not, I need their help to get this guy." His car slowly rolls up to a stop light.

"Turn right." Jaz says with a point of her finger. He flips on his right turn blinker, checks to the left and turns as directed.

After a few more moments of silence and thinking, Dane suddenly perks up, "Wait, did you say you knew the Doctor was on the mountain that night?" he looks over to the young girl with confusion, "How did you kno-"

"That one! Right there!" She points at a light blue house on their right and Dane pulls the car up along the curb.

"You're sure? This is Gary's house?" he looks up at it through the windshield.

She squints her eyes in the direction of the house for a moment, "Yes, he's in there. So is his wife and daughter."

"Welp," Dane unbuckles himself and shuts off the car, "let's go get our boy!"

They throw open their doors and exit the car to make their way up the sidewalk. As they climb the cement step and approach the bright red door of the house, Dane looks over at the bouncing, fuzzy head of the young girl who walks beside him. He had been in such a rush since the hospital he hadn't even taken a second to consider whether he could trust her or not. He had initially thought it was a strange coincidence how she showed up at the hospital so quickly, then her comment about the Doctor struck him as weird, but it was too late to start questioning now. He absolutely needed Gary's help. She suddenly looks up to him with big, hazel eyes and a nervous smile and Dane's concerns immediately disappear. With a nod of his head he returns her smile, "Thank you for this."

"Whatever you've got planned," she pauses as Dane reaches his fist up and knocks on the door, "I hope it works."

Dane looks down nervously as they wait for a reply from inside the house, "Yeah. So do I..." Suddenly, his gaze is drawn back up as the curtain of the window alongside the door is pulled aside just enough for someone to peek out at them. The second he sees who it is, Gary's eye widens in surprise and they begin to hear the clicks of the door unlocking.

"Dane!" Gary whispers sliding the door open just enough to slip out onto the step with them, then shutting it behind him softly, "How are you, son?" he reaches out and pulls Dane into a very fatherly hug. Awkwardly, Dane gives in and wraps his arm around Gary and sees Jaz over the man's shoulder chuckling and smiling jocosely at his discomfort.

"Good. I'm good, thanks Gary." Dane replies.

"Well, to what on God's green earth do I owe the pleasure?" Gary finally separates himself from Dane and looks at his two nervous guests. "Is everything ok?"

Dane is suddenly at a loss for words. Until a few moments ago, he wasn't even sure this was really Gary's house. How is he supposed to explain everything that's happened and ask this man to risk his life? If he did, would Gary say yes? What would he do if he said no? What would happ-

"I'm Jaz!" the young girl snaps Dane back to reality as she sticks a hand out to Gary.

"Well, hello Jaz." Gary meets her small hand with his own. The second they touch his eyelids flutter for a moment, then he looks down to her and shakes her hand softly, "It's very nice to meet you. You have some very cool advancements in your lungs and vocal chords!"

Jaz looks over at Dane confusedly as Gary releases her hand. "Pretty cool, huh?" Dane brags with a smile. "That's actually how we found you, Gary. When Jaz screamed that night in the hospital she said it left some sort of an imprint or something that she could track on everyone who heard it."

"So that's what that is..." Gary utters out loud to himself as he looks back to Jaz with a smile. "As you can imagine, with my abilities, I check my family's health regularly." He begins explaining, "Well, ever since that night in the hospital there's been something in myself, my wife and my daughter that isn't in my son. It's almost like a reverberation trapped behind our ear drums." He looks back down to the little girl, "I think your sound wave is stuck in our ear canal and it's at a sound level that we can't hear, so we don't even know it's there. But maybe you can hear it...and track it!"

She looks up to Dane in astonishment, then back to Gary, "You think so?"

"I mean, I can't be 100% sure, but it kinda seems like anything is possible these days." He says with a shrug of his shoulders. "I'm sure you guys saw the Seattle thing?"

Dane perks back up as if he just remembered his plan, "That's actually why we're here."

"Wait, don't tell me you're getting involved in that stuff." His eyes fix intently on Dane, "Dane, please tell me you're not getting involved. Did you even develop any abilities after we left you?"

"There's a plan!" Dane starts his recruitment while avoiding the question, "We're meeting at Kenneth Trail in a few hours. We've got a way to stop him, but we need your-"

"Dane! Son," Gary cuts him off and sets his hands on Dane's shoulders, "this is not something for you kids to put yourselves in the middle of. You saw what he did in the city last night."

"But they didn't know how to stop him. I do," Dane argues hurriedly, "but I need your help. Please!"

"Dane..." Gary, still holding his shoulders tightly, shakes his head in contention but is suddenly distracted when the door behind him creaks open slowly.

Gary's wife sticks her head out cautiously with a nervous look, "Gary? Is everything ok?"

Before Gary can respond, Alyssa pushes herself into the opening in front of her mom to see what is happening outside. As Gary looks lovingly upon his family Dane realizes his defeat. He had just gotten his family back. Why would he want to risk his life? Why would he risk leaving his kids without a father?

"Everything's fine, honey." Gary says calmly turning his attention back to Dane. "It was great to see you, son. Jaz, it was great to meet you." He turns to follow his family back into the house, but stops just inside the door and turns back to them, "Let them handle this one, Dane. God will see the rest of us through. Please, don't try to be a hero."

As the door swings shut in front of them Dane hangs his head and sighs in frustration. Jaz looks up at him with her big, brown eyes, "So," she utters sadly, "what now?"

"Well," he says softly as they turn and step off the porch onto the sidewalk and make their way towards the car, "I guess I should probably go say goodbye to my mom..."

Chapter 31

"But I don't think you understand," Simeon once again scurries down the shiny, metal hallway in his oversized jumpsuit attempting to keep up with the Doctor's hurried pace, "you are all exhibiting an increase in your energy output since you returned from the mountain."

"Yes, I did understand that part, Simeon." the Doctor's frustration in his vagueness is obvious, "I just don't see why that's a problem if we're about to go back and take him on again."

"It's not...well, as far as I can tell it's not." Simeon looks down to the IPad in his hands and adjusts his goggles to reread his data from their morning examinations. As they reach the window to the laboratory the Doctor stops and looks in to see the five remaining men sleeping in glass rapid-healing chambers. Simeon skids to a stop next to her without looking up from his screen, "My only thought is-"

"It's ready, right Simeon?" she pushes him past the previous topic.

"Huh?" he finally turns his eyes up to see her glaring down at him, "Oh, yeah. It's ready."

"And their suits?" she urges.

"They're getting charged and reloaded as we speak, but-" he attempts to return to his original thought.

"Wake them in an hour and tell them to gear up. We're leaving at 6:45. Got it?" She immediately turns and makes her way down the hallway without waiting for a response. Suddenly, Kurrt's angry voice rings through her head, *"You don't know how to listen...you never have. You only know how to act."*

The clicking of her heels on the floor slows to a stop and she turns to see Simeon still standing at the window anxiously going through his data. "What is it, Simeon?" her voice ripples down the empty hallway, catching his attention.

"Excuse me?" Simeon looks at her as if she had just sprouted antlers.

"What's your thought?" She asks softly taking a few steps back towards him. "...on the increase in our energy?"

"Oh!" Simeon is unable to hide his surprise, "Well, I can't be 100% sure which caused it, but I think that being so close to either the opening in the mountain or Kurrt's energy nucleus enhanced your abilities more rapidly than if you're, say, here, hundreds of miles away in LA. So, that leads me to believe that one of those is also the main source of his powers and why he's so much more powerful than anyone else." he chatters away excitedly, "I was thinking that if you're able to somehow get the nucleus into the top of the mountain it may drown it. Then you could lead him away and it could weaken him, but..." he pauses, nervously looking down to his IPad screen again while he thinks.

"But what?" the Doctor attempts to keep her calmness present. "Go ahead, Simeon. Say it."

"Well," he continues, looking up into her eyes with fear, "you said that the nucleus seems to be deriving its power from the rocks and trees stacked up underneath it, which leads me to believe it absorbs all matter just like Kurrt does. So..."

"So, what!?" The Doctor's impatience suddenly presents itself again.

"Well, think about it!" Simeon's first display of intensity catches the Doctor off guard, "What is that mountain made of? Matter. What's the core of the earth? Matter. What is the whole earth and everything and everyone on it made of?"

The Doctor's eyes widen and begin to glow blue as the fear wells up in her stomach. After a moment, the glow fades and she gathers herself. She takes a couple of steps forward and sets a hand on Simeon's shoulder, "Thank you, Simeon. You're a very smart guy and I'm lucky to have you here." She turns and heads back down the hallway away from him, "One hour, get them ready." She orders back to him without turning around then walks through a door that slides closed behind her.

Simeon's cheeks puff as he lets out a deep breath through pursed lips. "That woman is going to destroy the whole damn world..." he mutters to himself as he turns to make his way back to the ballistics room.

"Dammit!" Dane curses under his breath.

"What's wrong?" the little girl in the passenger seat sits up abruptly and scans around the car to see if they're in danger.

He pulls the car up along the curb in front of his house and throws the shifter into park. "She's not home." He motions his head to the empty driveway, then slams the steering wheel in frustration, "Dammit."

"Your plans haven't really been working out very well so far." Jaz comments quietly and their eyes meet with a shared sense of worry. "I hate to ask again, but...what now?"

Without answering her question Dane throws off his seat belt and begins climbing out of the door of the car, "C'mon, I have to grab something."

Jaz follows his lead, unbuckling herself and climbing out the passenger side onto the walkway. As she stands from the low-riding car she surveys the quiet neighborhood and peers above the houses across the street to the mountain with its giant, green field looming in the distance. As Dane meets up with her and heads up the sidewalk she follows slowly, unable to take her eyes off the mountain. A flutter of nervousness grows in her stomach as she thinks about going up there soon. "Hey," she utters as her small finger taps Danes arm to get his attention while he fumbles with his keys, "are you sure we should go up there?"

Dane follows her eyes across the road and gets his own set of butterflies that cause him to look away quickly and back to the keys in his hands. "I dunno, Jaz," he says quietly, "probably not. But I'm not turning back now."

She finally pulls her eyes away and looks up at him with a nervous smile, "Me either."

With a return smile and a nod of his head Dane fits the house key into the knob, turns and swings the door open. "HELLOOOO!?" he shouts taking a couple of steps into the entryway. Getting no response, he turns back to the small girl standing just outside the door cautiously, "Come on in, I just have to run upstairs for a second."

Jaz takes a couple of steps inside as he hands her the door to close behind her and heads up the stairs in front of them. She walks in and surveys the kitchen, then moves across the entryway to the living room.

Upstairs, Dane throws the door of his messy room open and makes his way across the floor, avoiding dirty clothes the whole way. He grabs the orange bottle of pills off his computer desk and stuffs them in his jeans pocket, then looks around the room. Finally, his eyes lock onto what he was looking for and he rushes back across the room. Headed straight out the door he reaches over and grabs a black hoodie that sits on the end of his bed, but stops in the doorway when he hears a THUD behind him. With a confused look, he turns and looks down to see his superhero figure lying on the floor. He takes a couple of steps back into the room, bends down and softly picks it up. A sad smile comes to his mouth but he quickly regroups himself, heading back out of the room and towards the stairs.

Walking around, studying everything in the room Jaz slows at the entertainment center. She runs her fingers along the spines of some books, reading their titles, then picks up a picture of Dane and his mom on his graduation day. Tears begin to form in her eyes as she looks at Dane's awkward smile and the pride in his mom's eyes as she embraces him lovingly.

"That's my mom." Startled, she looks up to see Dane standing across the room at the bottom of the stairs, a sad look on his face.

"Yeah." Jaz sniffles as she wipes her eyes with the back of her hand, "Yeah, I figured."

"I'm just gonna go write her a note." Dane points and turns towards the kitchen, but stops short and turns back to the young girl, "Hey...are you ok?"

"Yeah!" her mouth forces a smile underneath her red eyes and nose and she quickly sets the picture back on the shelf, "I'm good. Go ahead."

"Ok..." Dane stammers as he turns back to the kitchen. He doesn't believe her, but doesn't want to press something she'd rather not talk about. He pulls out a drawer and begins digging through its contents. Finding a pen and a piece of paper he shuts the drawer and begins scribbling:

Mom,

Came home for my pills, but you weren't here. I'm going to be gone with the guys for a while tonight and didn't want you to freak out. We won't go anywhere near the city and I'll be careful. Please, don't worry. I promise I'm fine! I love you.

Dane

He sets the pen down and rereads it for a moment as Jaz walks into the room, her eyes mostly dry. "What's wrong?" she asks quietly as he sets the paper on the counter.

"I expected to say more," Dane speaks softly, unable to pull his eyes away from his note, "but I don't know what else to say. I mean...how do you say goodbye to your Mom?"

Jaz looks down and circles the toe of her shoe on the linoleum floor, "I...I dunno." She mutters shakily, "I couldn't really tell you."

Realizing he probably hit the same sensitive topic as he had in the living room, Dane regresses, "Sorry, I didn't mean to-"

"No, it's fine." She stops him short, "We should probably get going."

Dane pulls the phone out of his pocket and clicks the power button, lighting up the clock on the screen. 5:57. "Yeah, we should." He stuffs the phone back in his pocket and reaches over to the stool next to him, grabbing the action figure. Jaz looks on with confusion as he holds it delicately in his hand, running his thumb over the Z symbol on its chest.

"What's that?" She asks softly.

"Nothing..." Dane sets the figure on the table next to the note, grabs his sweatshirt and looks up at Jaz with a smile, "Ready?"

"I guess so." She replies hesitantly and they walk out of the kitchen towards the front door.

As they reach the front step, Dane pulls the door shut and locks it behind them. "My mom's got some of my old stuff in the garage. You're going to need a coat."

"Ok," she smiles up at him, "I'll meet you in the car."

A short time later, Tim and Gavin stand on the trail in the green glow of the gigantic field, shuttering in the cold wind that makes its way through the trees around them.

"I can't believe the one time you want to be early is when we have to stand in the freezing cold." Gavin criticizes his friend as he wraps his arms around himself for any extra warmth he can get, "And you know that Dane will be late, right?"

"We only have to wait eight more minutes, we'll be fine." Tim assures him.

"Oh yeah? What, did you look into the future already or something?" Gavin asks sarcastically with a glare in his friend's direction.

"Maybe I did!" Tim shouts back.

"Well, look again cuz one of us is not going to be fine!" he shoots back as he raises a clenched fist in between them.

Suddenly, Tim's eyes go wide, "Move left!" he shouts.

"Move left?" Gavin scoffs at him, "What kind of a comeback is-" he is stopped short as a green bolt of energy hits his right shoulder and sends him tumbling backwards down the trail.

Tim turns quickly towards the field and looks through the green currents that radiate across it. He quickly throws back his left shoulder as a green beam shoots through the field and misses him by only millimeters, then immediately ducks as another rushes just over his head.

"Very impressive!" a voice radiates from behind the green wall as Tim slowly stands and focuses his thoughts. Kurrt slowly becomes visible as he walks through the field, sending currents in all directions. "I'm K-"

"I know, skip the formalities." Tim shouts at the man, clad in his exo-suit, cape whipping in the wind behind him.

"Well, then, I guess you also know that this whole plan you kids have is useless, right?" Kurrt stops about fifteen feet from the nervous young man.

"I...I don't know. I can't see that far...only one step ahead." Tim utters with worry in his voice.

"That's ok," Kurrt raises one hand in front of him and ignites the energy globe in his palm, "that will still be useful to me."

With glowing green eyes, he begins walking forward causing Tim to backpedal slowly. After a few feet Tim suddenly stops, catching

Kurrt off guard for a moment, but he immediately continues his advance on the boy. "You know what's more useful than seeing the future?" he counters Kurrt's seriousness with a mischievous smile, "Having friends."

As confusion overtakes Kurrt's face, he is suddenly thrust backwards off his feet and hits a large tree on the side of the trail. Gavin, now standing where Kurrt had been, watches him crumple to the ground in front of the tree as he pairfully holds his charred right shoulder. "Take that, bitch." He mutters under his breath as he heaves in pain, then turns back to his friend, "Dude, let's get out of here."

"Ya think!?" Tim shouts, but before Gavin is able to reach his friend his eyes widen again, "Right!"

Without question this time, Gavin immediately plants his left foot and shoots himself a few feet to his right as Tim angles his body so that the green beam flies between them. Lying on his stomach in the snow, Kurrt aims again and shoots at Tim but misses again by inches. Tim shouts at Gavin to duck, which he does and Kurrt misses him as well. "Dammit!" Kurrt screams as he becomes irritated and pushes his way to his feet. Teeth clenched, his bright green eyes raise in Tim's direction and his chest-piece and energy globes begin to glow brighter. "AHHHHHHH!" He raises both hands in front of him and is about to shoot, when a cracking sound draws his attention upward and he is suddenly swallowed up by the needles and branches of a falling tree.

Relief on his face, Tim looks over to the broken trunk of the tree where Gavin stands, "Thanks, man."

Still clenching his shoulder with his left hand, Gavin begins walking in his direction, "Time to go..."

As Gavin reaches out to grab his friend and get them out of there, shock overcomes Tim's face as he realizes there isn't time and he thrusts his hands in Gavin's direction. A cracking sound in the tree draws Gavin's attention, but, by the time his eyes reach the location of the sound, Kurrt is already in his giant, muscular form and hurtling in his direction. Tim's hands impact against Gavin's chest sending him backwards into the snow and Kurrt's huge hand wraps around Tim. Gavin looks up from the ground in fear as his friend grimaces and struggles to get out of the man's clenched fist. Slowly he is engulfed by a growing green light and with one last, sad look and a bright flash he disappears into Kurrt's huge fist. Kurrt raises his head to the sky and hands to his sides as a bright green glow flows through his veins and into his chest-piece, lighting it up bright. A smile of triumph comes to his face as he lowers his head and opens his green eyes down towards Gavin, still lying on his back overtaken with fear.

In a quick effort to escape, Gavin throws his open palms back against the ground, sending him upright. As soon as his feet touch the snow he absorbs his weight and thrusts himself forward, his good shoulder striking Kurrt's oversized leg. Kurrt spins up into the air uncontrollably and shakes the ground around them as his huge body hits the trail violently and quickly shrinks back down to normal size. Gavin grimaces in pain from the impact, then immediately plants his feet and shoots upward at full speed in the direction of the beach.

As he watches the boy soar through the air from his place on the ground Kurrt focuses his thoughts, raises a hand and shoots a beam of energy. It strikes Gavin far off in the distance and sends him sprawling like a ragdoll into the lake with a huge splash.

"Yeah, I'm gonna like this one." Kurrt mutters to himself with satisfaction as he turns and floats back up the trail and through the field.

After a few moments with the wind as the only sound in the area, a whimpering comes from the trees beside the trail. Slowly, a protruding portion of a tree trunk transforms. Frantically looking around and trying to figure out what she can do, Sherri hurries down the trail away from the field with her hand over her mouth and tears streaming from her eyes.

Chapter 32

"Hmm, that's weird…" Mom utters to herself as she pulls her car into the driveway. She gets out and suspiciously looks down to the street one more time before pulling her groceries out of the backseat and heading for the house. As soon as she swings open the door, she can sense that nobody is in the house, but she takes a couple of steps in and looks into the kitchen, then across to the living room. "DANE!? ARE YOU HOME!?"

After a few seconds with no response she turns towards the kitchen and pushes the bags of groceries from her arms through the air to a soft resting spot next to the sink and reaches into her pocket to grab her phone. As she's about to pull it out she notices the note on the counter and stops worriedly. Hesitantly, she reaches out causing the paper to come floating over to her where it settles softly in her hand. She slowly lifts it up for her eyes to see and, after scanning over the words a couple of times, she looks over to the counter and worry overtakes her.

Moments later there is a loud rap at Mr. Logan's door. After no response the knocking gets louder.

"Ugggggghhhh…" Mr. Logan groans from his couch as he squirms uncomfortably. The knocking persists causing his bloodshot eyes to slowly open and dance around the room in confusion. "Ugggggghhh…" he pushes up on his elbow to sit up and spills the beer he had left balancing against himself when he passed out. He grabs it quickly before its entire contents spill on his couch and looks at it with irritation until the loud knocking causes him to wince in pain.

"Mr. Logan!? John, are you there!?" a muffled voice comes through the door before knocking again.

"Ugggghhh, coming!" he sets the half empty beer on the coffee table and stands shakily. "I'm coming, hold on." His first step is unsuccessful when his foot finds a collection of empty beer bottles and he almost trips back onto the couch. The knocking continues loudly. "I'm coming, dammit!" He impatiently pushes them out of his way with his foot and stumbles to the door rubbing his eyes. He pulls the door open just a crack and peers out. "What is it!?" he barks gruffly as his squinting eyes adjust to the sunlight.

"John, it's me." Mom says nervously, her hands fidgeting with the action figure in front of her. "I need your help...it's Dane."

"Sorry, honey," he grumbles through the crack in the door, "that's not my job anymore."

A look of confusion comes over Mom's face, "What is that supposed to mean, John?"

"I mean..." he starts angrily, then softens his gruff voice, "I mean, I failed...in more ways than you can know...that's all. I failed and it's all too far gone. Good luck, though." He begins to push the door closed, but it stops suddenly. Peering through the crack he sees one of Mom's hands has turned its palm towards him, holding the door in place. He chuckles as he looks down and shakes his head, "That's a very nice trick, Miss Denson, but I assure you I am of no help to you or Dane. Now, please leave."

"What happened, John?" Mom looks in at the disheveled man with empathy, "Tell me. Maybe I can help."

Hanging his head as much in tiredness as defeat he lets out a sigh then looks up to the young woman, "It's you who came to me for help, remember? Not the other way around." Taken aback by this statement Mom drops her hand, releasing the door. "I'm sorry Miss Denson...good luck." Mr. Logan says quietly through the crack as he pushes the door closed.

Knowing she still has to do something, Mom turns and makes her way to the car. Mr. Logan leans up against the other side of the door, resting his forehead against his arm and breathes a deep sigh. "Dammit!" he shouts as he slams his fist against the door, then makes his way over to his window. Pulling the curtain aside he looks up at the mountain, tall and intimidating with its shimmering field and trail of smoke that covers the sky. With another big sigh he closes the curtain and heads to the couch, grabbing an orange bottle off the table and shaking one small, white pill into his palm. He sits down on the couch, grabs the warm beer and throws back the pill. Staring straight ahead his mouth cocks to the side and he nods his head is soft frustration realizing he had just sat in beer.

Not far away, Mom drives erratically through the streets of downtown Eatonville looking for any sign of Dane, his car or his friends. She had been worried before, but after her calls went straight to voicemail and she didn't get a reply to any of her texts she was really freaking out. She had called the hospital and the police, but was now out of options. As she turns into downtown to make one more pass she suddenly hears a low rumbling. She reaches over and rolls her window down as she slows in front of a stop light. Straining to look up out the window, the rumbling grows louder and suddenly passes directly overhead, shaking the whole car. Out her windshield she sees a blue streak shoot between the buildings and out of town towards the mountain. Immediately, five multicolored streaks shoot through, one at a time, in the same direction. After a moment, the car behind her honks to push her through the now green light. Without even looking in the parking spaces or in business windows anymore, she fixes her eyes straight forward and makes her way through town, then floors it up the side streets towards the mountain trails.

As the wind shoots through the trees in random gusts Dane and Jaz wrap their arms around themselves for warmth and trudge through the snow and ash that covers the trail.

"All I'm saying is that nobody's going to want to see superhero movies or read comics anymore, you know?" Dane pushes home his point through chattering teeth. "I know I'm not."

"I dunno," Jaz replies keeping her eyes on the trail in front of her, "I never really cared about superheroes anyways. I always liked the Twilight movies more."

"Yeah, I could see that." Dane replies. "Too bad everyone in the world couldn't turn into vampires and werewolves, huh?"

"That'd be crazy!" a little excitement finally reveals itself in the young girl, "Everyone would be all pale and have red eyes...or sharp teeth and trying to eat the vampires heads off..." she trails off for a moment as she thinks. "I think I like it better with superheroes."

Dane laughs sending big vapor clouds into the air in front of him. "I was REALLY into superheroes when I was little. I always pretended like I was one, wearing capes and flying around our house in my underwear."

"EW!" Jaz spews her disgust at the thought.

"Yeah, I was a goofy kid." He chuckles as he reminisces, "But then I got put on these things." He pulls the orange bottle out of his hoodie pocket and rattles it in front of them.

"Why?" Jaz inquires.

"Attention deficit, I guess." He reminisces to a not-so-happy time, "They said it was hurting my grades, so my mom got rid of everything superhero-y in my life."

"Harsh..." Jaz mutters.

"What about you?" Dane suddenly realizes he knows almost nothing about his companion, "What's your story?"

"I dunno, nothing really." She struggles with the question, "I mean, I was told my mom died when I was born. My dad-"

"Wait! Shh!" Dane cuts her off as he abruptly stops walking and listens into the wind. "Do you hear that?"

"I don't know," she listens for another second then feels Dane grab the sleeve of her jacket and pull her behind a large tree on the side of the trail a few steps ahead where it angles to the left.

"Shh." He urges as he puts one arm across her and guides her behind him. Slowly, he leans out from behind the tree and up the trail towards the source of the noise and his eyes go wide. "SHERRI!" he shouts as he darts out from behind the tree, leaving Jaz behind. He rushes up the trail towards the sobbing girl and wraps his arms around her. "What's wrong? What happened?"

"It's Tim..." she sobs into the chest of his sweatshirt, "and Gavin...he got them!"

As she burst out into tears Dane stares straight up the trail at the green field with fear and grips his friend tightly for comfort. The thoughts begin to swirl in his head. Anger builds up inside him, blurring his vision. He feels like he's about to explode...

"So, uh, what now?" Jaz's words are so soft the wind almost carries them away, but they manage to catch Sherri and Dane's attention.

"Who's that?" Sherri says with surprise as her red eyes look up from being buried into Dane's shirt.

"That's Jaz." Dane informs her nonchalantly and turns towards the little girl with an annoyed look on his face. "You've really gotta stop asking me that."

"Well...actually...it's not a bad question." Sherri says as she takes a step back and wipes her eyes with the sleeve of her black, puffy coat. "I don't think you guys should go up there!"

"Wait, 'you guys'?" he turns back to Sherri, "What do you mean?"

"Well, I'm not going back up there!" She can see the disappointment in Dane's eyes, "Dane, he just sucked one of our friends into the palm of his hand, then he shot the other one out of the air! Just imagine what he'll do to you!"

"Dane, maybe she's right." Jaz approaches them slowly.

"No, not 'maybe'!" Dane shouts with frustration throwing his hands above his head. He turns and paces around the trail in thought. "She IS right!" his eyes lock on Jaz's, then turn to Sherri, "You're absolutely right. Just imagine what he'll do to me. But what does it matter!? Who cares!? News flash: The only kid in the world without superpowers gets fried! Would that be such a big surprise to anyone? Who would care?"

"I care." Sherri mutters softly.

"I care." Jaz follows her lead.

"Dane," Sherri reaches out and grabs his arm, "your mom cares."

Not sure if his eyes are glossy because of his fear, his anger, the loss of his two best friends, or the display of emotion before him, Dane hangs his head for a moment as Sherri rubs his arm comfortingly. Finally, he looks up into her blue, empathetic eyes, "I have to go up there. I completely understand if neither of you go, but I've gotta stop him. For Tim and Gavin...for everyone."

They watch helplessly as he turns and heads up the trail alone, then look at each other with a mutual fear in their eyes. As he turns and disappears out of sight, Jaz suddenly gets a confused look on her face.

"What's wrong?" Sherri asks, unsure of whether she really wants to hear the answer.

Jaz turns quickly and looks behind them, "Someone's coming!"

Chapter 33

Dane chatters in the cold as he approaches the field. About thirty feet away he stops and surveys his surroundings nervously. Snow and ash fall slowly, branches sway in the wind, but he sees no signs of Kurrt or anyone else. Suddenly, a squirrel darts out into the middle of the trail next to the field and looks at him intriguingly before darting off into the trees. Dane's eyes do not follow it as they lock on the middle of the trail where the squirrel had stopped. In the snow he sees scorch marks glimmering with green embers in front of a fallen tree that has been torn to pieces and he imagines the battle his friends had fought before their defeat.

He doesn't have time to get emotional before a rumbling causes him to spin around. As it begins to grow, he hurries off the trail and behind a large boulder. Slowly, the rumbling ceases and Dane nervously peeks out from behind the rock, not seeing anything. His ears suddenly perk up and he ducks his head a little lower as he hears footsteps. Before long, the Doctor and her men come into sight, walking up the trail cautiously.

"Dr. Wong!" Dane stands into view, triggering surprise in the already nervous group. They spring to defense and raise their hands in his direction, engaging their energy globes. He quickly ducks back down behind his rock, which he now worries may not be big enough to protect him, and covers his head in preparation for their shots.

"Hold fire!" he can hear the Doctor shout. He uncovers his head and slowly peeks out again to see her standing in front of the men, who have now lowered their weapons. "He's with us." She smiles in his direction and nods her head.

Dane slowly stands once more and looks over her team worriedly. Once he is sure he's safe, he takes a few steps around the boulder and approaches them. "Thank you for helping me."

"Well, if this works I think it will be me who is doing the thanking." She then looks around for a moment, "Are you by yourself? I thought you said others were coming with you to help?"

"Yeah, I...uh..." Dane is unsure how to tell her how badly his plans had gone so far and peers over to the wreckage that lies in front of the field.

The Doctor follows his gaze and begins to put part of the story together. She turns back to him and sets a hand on his arm, "I'm sorry, Dane. Do you still want to-"

"Yes!" Dane's voice finds him again quickly. "I'm ready. Let's go get this guy."

"Hold on there, cowboy." She ushers him down for a moment, "We need to discuss this plan since things have changed a little bit. One kid with no way of protecting himself is not going to be a decoy against the most powerful man in the world."

"Yeah, I guess you're right." Dane agrees as he hangs his head in thought then looks up at her with hopefulness, "but the rest of the plan can still stand. Get rid of the nucleus and I think it will weaken him. If not, then you'll just have to take him on again."

"Well, that doesn't sound reassuring." The Doctor's voice resonates dismay as she recalls the destruction that happened in Seattle the day before. "The only thing we've learned is that being close to the mountaintop seems to enhance everyone's powers, so maybe we should lure him away."

"I wouldn't suggest downtown Seattle again..." Dane utters sarcastically as if reading her mind, but earning him an irritated look from the stern woman.

"Wait, so we're busy luring him away from his power source," the Doctor looks at him inquisitively, "and what are you-"

"He's not alone!" a voice surprises them all from behind causing the men to engage for attack and the doctor's eyes to light up bright. Dane takes a small step behind the group for safety, but peers around them down the trail to see Sherri, Jaz and Mr. Logan walking towards them.

The Doctor drops her guard and steps aside so she can see Dane fully, "They're with you, I'm guessing?"

"Yeah," he says through a huge smile without taking his eyes off of them, "they're with me." Rushing in their direction his gaze locks onto Sherri, "It was a good line, only about 2 minutes late!" he laughs and embraces her and her puffy coat in a big hug, then reaches one arm over and pulls Jaz in against her will. As he releases them he looks up to his neighbor with a confused look, "What are you doing here, Mr. Logan? How did you know-"

"Don't you worry about it, kid." He smiles at Dane, then shifts his gaze past him to the Doctor, "I've got my resources. Hopefully, I can help in some way." As soon as the words leave his lips, Dane throws his arms around the man and squeezes.

"Thank you." He whispers as Mr. Logan pats him on the back softly.

Once he has released his neighbor from his grasp, Dane turns back to the Doctor, "We got this Dr. Wong."

"You're sure?" She looks the rag tag group over slowly. "These three showing up still doesn't do much to assure me of this plan."

"Don't worry Doc," he looks up at her with a new-found confidence, "we're good!"

She looks at Mr. Logan, the elder of the group, who simply shrugs his shoulders and smiles nervously. "Alright," she agrees hesitantly, "but he has to be stopped before he does something really terrible." She turns towards her team, where Allen reaches out a small device that resembles a metal headband. She takes it from him and walks towards the group, handing the device to Dane, "Take this. It's a Suspended State Preserver. Once he's out, put the nodes on his temples and he'll remain out."

"I can hold that until it's needed." Mr. Logan offers his services. Dane hands him the device and nods.

"This ends tonight." She turns and makes her way towards her team then stops and turns her head back to Dane, "Oh, and don't ever call me Doc."

He smiles as she turns back around and heads back up the trail away from them.

"Ok, gentlemen…" she instructs them loudly, "let's knock!"

At the bottom of the trail, Mom's car skids to a stop in the loose gravel. Relief and worry overwhelm her at the same time as she spots Dane's car, also recognizing Tim's jeep and Sherri's car. She jumps out and rushes up to Dane's silver Saturn, shading her eyes with her hand as she looks through the window.

"DAAAAAANE!!" She begins to look around for any sign of her son. Quickly realizing he is not in the area, she turns back to her car motioning with her hands to guide the keys out of the ignition and in her direction and slamming the door shut. She stuffs the keys in her pocket and turns towards the trail opening when she is alarmed by a sound behind her. She spins to see another car approaching, one she does not recognize. The car slows and guides to a stop across the parking area from her. She looks on nervously as the door opens and a man stands from the car, his eyes focused on her.

"Miss Denson?" the man shouts in her direction, then reaches back into his car grabbing a jacket off the passenger seat and slamming the door behind him, "Miss Denson! What are you doing here?!"

Confusion covers the woman's face as she studies him, trying to determine any sort of threat as he approaches her. "Do I know you?" she questions nervously.

"Yes!" his hands raise at his sides as if to display himself, but he slows for a moment, "Actually, I remember you well, but you only met me for a moment. I'm Gary, from the hospital. My daughter Alyssa was in the same room as you the whole time you were...blacked out."

"Oh, yes, I do remember." She immediately relaxes her tensed body and reaches her hand out to the man, who grabs it and shakes with his own. "What are you doing here?"

"Dane tracked me down and said he needed my help against that guy from Seattle. I told him not to get involved and to leave it up to someone else." Gary suddenly looks confused, "Are you here to help him with this plan of his?"

"No, of course not!" she says defensively then looks up the mountain trail nervously, "I wasn't even sure he was up here until now...he shouldn't be in the middle of something like this!"

"He's definitely an ambitious kid." Gary jokes following her eyes up the trail, but the smile leaves his face when he looks back at her and sees her worry. "Hey," he reaches out and sets a hand on her arm softly, "I'm with you...let's go get your kid before something happens."

She smiles at him with a silent "Thank you" and they make their way towards the trail opening. In the silence she tries to imagine what Dane is planning and why he feels like he needs to be involved, then tries to force the same thoughts from her mind for fear of what could happen...or could have already happened. After a few minutes they reach the opening to the beach and she ushers Gary to a stop momentarily to survey the area for Dane and his friends. "They hang out here sometimes." She informs Gary as she looks around the clearing. "DAAAANE!" she tries one more time, receiving no response, and turns with frustration to continue back up the trail.

"Miss Denson..." a voice comes through the trees and jars her to a halt. She backtracks to the opening, followed by Gary, and they look over the grounds again. "Miss Denson...I'm here..." the voice beckons agonizingly. She takes a few steps into the area cautiously and follows the sound in the direction of the beach. As the decline to the water becomes visible she sees a hand reach towards her from below, then collapse onto the sand. Her eyes go wide with surprise and she rushes towards the edge of the lake.

"He's out, but he's breathing!" she shouts as Gary catches up and kneels on the other side of the body.

"Don't worry, I've got this." Gary assures her as he reaches out and sets his hand on the boy's forehead.

A few moments after the Doctor and her men had exited, Dane has updated his group on the plan.

"I...I can't believe it." Sherri utters softly in response to the information she had just received. "All this time, he..."

"Just trust me guys, this will work." Dane pushes with confidence. "Yeah...it'll work." He utters to himself with a little less certainty as he gazes up the trail through the green shield then turns back to Sherri, "Ready?"

She nods her head despite the look of concern on her face and heads off the trail towards the same tree she had used the last time. As her hand makes contact her fingers, arms, and then the rest of her body mimic the bark and she guides her small frame around the trunk and through the field.

"That's cool..." Jaz mutters under her breath, drawing a smile from Dane as he pops open his orange bottle and swallows down a small, white pill.

"Alright, so you guys hang out here until the Doctor gets rid of the nucleus. That should drop the shield, then come up to the clearing," Dane instructs them as Sherri walks back onto the trail on the other side of the field, "but remember, always stay out of view. Without Gary, I may need your help, but hopefully not."

They nod their heads in agreement and Dane turns to head through the field. After two steps he is stopped suddenly as two small arms wrap around his waist. "Be careful..." Jaz whispers as she squeezes him tightly, then looks up to see him nod down to her. She lets go and takes a step back with Mr. Logan, who puts one hand on her shoulder. They watch as Dane passes through the field, joining Sherri on the other side, and the two continue up the trail, out of their sight.

__Chapter 34__

"Alright, guys, spread out!" the doctor orders as they approach the top of the field from the backside of the mountain. "Distract him and I'll get in there to take care of the nucleus."

The men immediately fan in all directions from their positions behind her as she reaches the top of the green sphere. She continues up above the field, stopping when she is a few hundred feet above the peak of the mountain and looks down as she floats in place. She closes her glowing, blue eyes and focuses her energy inward as multi-colored explosions occur around the outside of the field. After shooting their low-energy blasts, the men converge and float in a group on the front of the field to await Kurrt's reveal.

As the explosions slowly dissipate and the erratic, green currents subside a voice startles them from behind, "Quite a light show, boys!" They spin in midair as Kurrt throws one hand forward and shoots a beam that strikes Charles directly in the chest and sends him flailing backwards down through the field to the mountainside and crashing into the trees. The other men simultaneously scatter in all directions leaving trails of light as Kurrt continues to float in place. He closes his eyes and focuses inward to utilize Tim's powers, then raises his hand to target another of the men, "It's almost too easy…" his energy globe glows to life, but, before he is able to fire, he suddenly stops. He looks back towards the top of the field and smiles as he sees a blue light streak down through it and towards the clearing. As he watches her descend he quickly drops his right shoulder, avoiding a white pulse then immediately turns his body to the left as a yellow ball shoots past him, missing by mere millimeters. Keeping his eyes focused on the blue streak he throws his right hand up to the side and shoots high then low behind him, striking and sending Allen's orange streak and Cameron's yellow streak tumbling down through the field.

As the Doctor approaches the clearing from above, she zeros in on the nucleus. Her left hand whips at her side and engages a light blue streak, which she grips tightly. In a matter of seconds she is able to fly around the nucleus a dozen times, wrapping it in the blue energy rope then settles down onto the ground to get a good grip with both hands to haul it up to the mouth of the mountain.

Her eyes focus intensely on the wrapped up nucleus as she grips tightly with her left hand and reaches forward with her right hand. As she grabs the rope she is startled when Kurrt slams to the ground in front of her, "Well this is cute!" he walks towards her slowly hovering his hand less than an inch above the glowing rope, a blue current shooting from the rope to his finger every time it gets a little too close. "Kinda like Wonder Woman and her golden lasso, huh Doctor?"

Fear lights her blue eyes up brightly. She looks around to see where her team is then looks back at Kurrt as he continues to advance slowly. As quickly as she can, she releases the rope with her right hand and fires at him, then again, and again. To her dismay he easily dodges all three blue beams and continues towards her.

"I have a new talent I'm trying out, Doctor Wong." Kurrt brags snidely, "It allows me to see the future, such as what would happen if I grabbed this lasso of yours. I already know...do you want to guess?"

Before she is able to utter a word he engages the energy globe in his palm and wraps his fingers around the rope. Blue currents shoot from it erratically all the way down to the Doctor's hand and shock her into a paralyzed state. He smiles as he looks down and watches as the rope slowly turns green outward from his hand. Just as it's about to reach her, Charles' silver streak flies through the clearing and tackles her, disengaging her from her electrified condition. She tumbles through the snow and ash and comes to a rest in front of a rock at the opening of the trail.

"HAHA!" Kurrt laughs loudly, "Well done! That's the trick to this new talent," he points to his head, "I forgot to focus. It shuts off if I don't focus."

Lying in the snow and ash, the Doctor looks up at him shakily as his smiling face changes and becomes bigger on top of a much larger, muscular body. He turns his attention away from mocking her and focuses on the rope in his hand. With a huge grunt he heaves on it, sending the nucleus flying across the clearing in his direction. As it approaches him he screams out loudly and engages the energy globes in both of his enlarged hands. She watches in fear as it strikes him in his brightly glowing chest-piece and he immediately wraps his arms around the huge, green ball planting his energy globes on either side. Still screaming intensely as if in pain, he focuses his energy and pulls the gigantic field down into the nucleus and absorbs the entire thing into himself, sending a huge green flash shooting in all directions and for miles down the mountain. His eyes close, his arms fall to his side and he drops to his knees. Slowly shrinking back down to normal size, he works to harness the new abundance of energy within him.

Across the clearing, the Doctor recovers from her shock and scrambles to stand. As she reaches her knees she suddenly stops, her eyes looking up to meet a bright, green energy globe only inches from her face. Kurrt stands above her, his entire body now radiating a green energy. A smile once again crosses his face as he looks down with glowing green eyes. "Here come your boys!" Without looking he raises a hand behind him and shoots two beams that strike the remaining two guys the instant they touch down on the snow. The Doctor watches with fear as they crash backwards into the trees, then nervously moves her gaze back to the threat above her. "You won't have to worry about listening to anyone anymore because I'll be in charge of your powers now," he utters through his devious smile as the energy globe in the Doctor's face begins to glow brightly, causing her to lean backwards against the boulder, "and I don't need to look into the future to know...this is going to be good!"

Suddenly, a hand made of stone comes down from above and grabs onto Kurrt's forearm. He looks up above the Doctor's head with surprise to see two eyes looking at him from the stone's surface. "You should've looked anyways!" Sherri utters as they both look back down to Kurrt's arm and it slowly transforms to stone all the way down to his fingertips.

He screams in horror as the energy globe he still had engaged begins to chip away his hand and absorb it into itself. He struggles to pull away, but can't break their stone connection as the globe eats away to his wrist, then part way up his forearm. Just as it's about to reach Sherri's hand she disengages her powers completely, revealing herself and Dane on top of the rock. She releases her grip on Kurrt just in time, sending him backwards onto the ground. His screaming echoes through the clearing as the energy globe vanishes and he cradles what's left of his arm.

The Doctor stands slowly as Kurrt writhes in pain on the ground in front of her, then turns to the kids behind her, who look on with just as much surprise.

As he catches the Doctor's fearful gaze Dane suddenly snaps back to the moment and regathers himself. "GO!" he yells at the woman, "You've got to get him away from here!"

The fear instantly leaves the Doctor's face as she remembers the plan. Her eyes light up a bright blue and she takes off straight up with a blue streak.

"Ahhhhhhh, dammit!!" Kurrt groans in pain as he pushes himself to his knees and continues to hold his disintegrated arm against his body, "Stupid kids! Ahhhhhhh!"

"We've gotta get out of here, too!" Dane urges Sherri.

"No problem!" she grabs his hand and squeezes her eyes tight. As the wind swirls the snow and ash past them they gradually disappear into it and softly float off into the trees.

Kurrt continues to shout curses in pain as he pulls his unsteady feet underneath him and stands. He holds his arm in front of himself for a moment and studies it with an angry look on his face. "MOTHER F-" he is cut off as a blue pulse of energy strikes his shoulder and knocks him back a couple of steps. He angrily looks up towards the sky to see the Doctor floating above the clearing, a cocky smile on her face. She immediately shoots out of sight with a blue streak. Focusing all of her fear and anger inward, she is able to generate more energy than she had ever used before and is able to reach the Pacific Ocean in a matter of seconds. Knowing that Kurrt wouldn't be far behind her she continues to focus her emotions and push herself as far from land as possible.

Kurrt clenches his teeth, squeezes his eyes shut and grips his remaining hand in a fist in front of him. His green glow pulses for a moment as he summons all the energy of the nucleus. "AHHHHHHHH!" he shouts as his eyes shoot open with an intense green light and he is instantaneously gone from the clearing in pursuit of the blue streak, leaving a circle of green currents running through the snow where he had been standing.

Down the trail about a hundred feet, the only sound to be heard is the roar of Kurrt and his huge green streak flying overhead. Once the rumbling has traveled into the distance and his trail has dissipated from the sky, the mountain becomes quiet and the wind through the trees is once again the only sound.

"Ok, I think we're good." A voice materializes in the air over the trail. Suddenly, Dane and Sherri both become visible once again, their feet landing softly into the snow and ash. "That was so cool!" Dane exclaims looking at his solid hands and body, "Your powers are awesome!"

"You better say that," Sherri says with an air of cockiness in her voice, "they've saved your ass twice now!"

"Touché!" Dane agrees without a fight, then refocuses himself on the task at hand. "We've got to get to the shack before he comes back! This is probably our only chance."

Without another word they rush towards the clearing, slowing once they see the end of the trail open up. They step cautiously into the clearing looking in all directions for any sign of life.

"We're good, let's go!" Dane grabs Sherri's arm and begins to run across the clearing. They reach the rickety wooden door of the shack and Dane grabs the handle.

"Wait!" Sherri causes him to stop suddenly. "What are we going to do once we're in there...I mean, since we don't have Gary?"

Dane looks down to the ground nervously, " 'm not really sure," he then looks up into the girl's blue eyes with a sense of determination, "I guess we'll just have to play it by ear."

He turns the doorknob and throws open the door, which bangs loudly against the computer towers that line the wall behind it. As the wind blows snow and ash in along the floorboards, Dane takes a couple of steps in with Sherri right behind him.

Simultaneously, speeding over the Pacific Ocean, Kurrt harnesses as much of Tim's power as possible to see ahead to where he will end up finding the Doctor. His eyes quickly shoot open with a green flash as he gets a vision of her blue streak shooting underneath the ocean surface behind him, out of his sight. "She's keeping me busy." He utters to himself as he peeks over his shoulder with a smile and his vision is confirmed. "But why would-" he engages the globe in his remaining hand to attack her, but another vision causes him to stop short and his smile quickly fades. As his eyes look back up in the direction he had just come, worry, then immediate anger consume him.

To the Doctor's surprise, he stops, turns, and shoots off past her towards the mainland again. She surfaces from the water, watching as his green streak fades into the distance, then suddenly shoots forward in the same direction.

Once inside the doorway of the shack, Sherri can see the room fully. Surprise overtakes her as her eyes settle on the corner of the messy room where she spots the real source of Kurrt's powers. Huddled, shivering in his underwear with his knees pulled into his chest and his unblinking eyes staring forward as they oscillate rapidly, is Kurrt.

Chapter 35

"I...I don't understand." Sherri utters as she stares in bewilderment at the frail man huddled in the corner.

"I saw something on the news the other day that classified people by their powers," Dane explains as he makes his way into the room and begins to look around frantically, "and I think he's a 'Projector'. That's not really him out there." He points out the door as he digs through the papers and clothes that cover most of the floor, "It's his projection."

"It felt pretty real when I grabbed it." Sherri still stares at the frail man in disbelief, then finally looks away as Dane rummages through the room, "What are you doing?"

"Well, my original plan was for Gary to either take his consciousness away from him, if he could, or to transfer the unconsciousness from one of the Doctor's guys into him..." he stops for a moment feeling her confused eyes burning into him, "Yeah, he can do that. I've seen it." He continues to rummage through the room, moving Kurrt's mostly unpacked bags, "But without Gary, I think if we just knock him out it will stop him. I just need something...AHA!"

As he slides the last of the suitcases aside he finds Kurrt's putter lying behind it. He grabs the club displaying it for Sherri to see. "Are you sure that's going to work?" she questions.

"If he's not conscious he can't project, right." Dane says waveringly with a shrug of his shoulders as he approaches Kurrt, "It's worth a shot!"

Sherri takes a step back and prepares to shield her eyes as Dane raises the putter over his shoulder with both hands and targets the temple of Kurrt's head. He winds up and prepares to put all of his force into the blow when a loud "THUD" outside the shack causes him to stop. With the putter still raised he looks at Sherri nervously, then they both look over to the open door. For a moment, everything is silent.

Suddenly, with a huge crash, the ceiling and two of the walls and their computer towers are lifted from the foundation and shoot across the clearing and into the trees in one big piece. As Dane and Sherri slowly remove their arms from shielding their faces they see Kurrt's projection standing above them, bigger and more muscular than he had ever been. Pure anger on his hulking face, he heaves up and down with deep breaths through his clenched teeth.

Sherri slowly holds her hand out in Dane's direction and whispers through the side of her mouth, "Dane. Dane, grab my hand."

"OH, NO YOU DON'T!!" Kurrt's deep voice shakes the whole area as he throws down his hand in between the two kids, sending them stumbling backwards in opposite directions. Once separated, he shrinks back down to size and begins to walk towards Sherri holding his half-missing arm in front of him, "You and I have an issue to discuss, little lady."

The fear builds up inside of her as he advances. Once he's a few feet away a green light shines across the pale skin on her face as the energy globe ignites in his palm. With sadness in her eyes, she looks over to Dane and mouths the words "I'm sorry". Just as the energy globe is approaching her face she closes and squeezes her eyes tightly, suddenly disappearing, and is carried off in the wind.

"Son of a-" Kurrt shouts as he clenches his fist in front of him in frustration, then turns to Dane, who still stands against the wall where Kurrt's body sits shivering. "Well kid, I don't know what your superpowers are, but I think I'd rather just barbecue you." He immediately raises his hand, engages the energy globe and shoots a green beam of energy.

Dane can do nothing but hang his head in defeat and await impact from the beam, but, to his surprise, he only feels a small jolt and is able to watch as the beam flies past him and incinerates a hole through the wall of the shack.

"What the hell?" Kurrt utters as he grits his teeth and shoots another beam at the boy.

Dane feels a slight jerk again and watches as this one shoots past him on the other side and burns another hole through the wall. As he looks at the wall behind him he realizes he has moved and is now standing right in front of the hole made by the first beam. Confused, he looks back up across the floor to Kurrt.

"AHHHHH!!!!" Kurrt's anger reaching a peak, he screams as he throws his hand forward and fires multiple shots at the boy, which all miss him by inches as he is mysteriously yanked side to side. "STOP DOING THAT!!" he shouts across the wooden floor.

Suddenly, Dane's feet leave the floor and he begins to float. Unsure of how he's doing any of this stuff he looks wildly down towards the floor then around the clearing as he gradually gets higher. With his focus momentarily taken off Kurrt, he is just now able to notice his mom peering out from her cover behind the boulder at the opening of the clearing. Her hands are extended in his direction, guiding him into the air as Gary and Jaz peer out from behind trees close by. The moment he begins to put it all together Gavin streaks in behind the boulder, his part in protecting his friend being done, and Sherri reforms in the wind next to him.

Mom jerks her hand to the side, sending Dane a few feet to his left to dodge another of Kurrt's blasts as Jaz cups her hands around her mouth and screams, shooting forward a vibration of sound that leaves the man reeling in pain as he is only able to cover one of his ears.

"Why...why the hell can't I see ahead anymore?!" he screams to himself as he looks down at the energy globe in his palm in confusion.

With a blue streak and a loud THUD the Doctor rises from her superhero-style landing and begins walking towards him, "Your secret's out Kurrt. We all know this isn't really you, that is." she motions to the mostly naked man that sits shaking in what is left of the destroyed shack. "I have a feeling those guys are still in there," she points directly into his glowing chest piece as she continues to advance on him, "and I don't think they like you using their powers."

With Kurrt distracted for the moment, Mom guides Dane through the air and off to the side of the shack and behind the pile of logs and boulders where the nucleus once fed. Once his feet settle back on the ground and Mom releases her hold on him he peeks around the pile of debris and waves his hand to get Gavin's attention.

"That's ridiculous!" Kurrt screams at the Doctor, "These powers are mine now!"

He closes his eyes and clenches his fist at his side pulling all of his energy inward and he begins to grow bigger, stopping the Doctor in her tracks. After growing a couple of feet, his muscular arm begins to shrink back down, followed by one of his legs. He refocuses his energy and gets them to regrow, but they instantly deflate back down again, followed by his other extremities and torso. Reaching his normal size again he drops to his knees in exhaustion and defeat.

"You see, Kurrt?" she reaches out one hand with a blue globe in the palm, "It's over."

A gust of wind blows between them and catches the projection's attention. He immediately looks over to the shack, where Sherri suddenly stands, Gary kneeling next to her with his arm extending towards Kurrt's head.

"NOOOOOO!!!" In a moment that seems to slow down the entire world around them, Dane runs out from his protective barrier as Kurrt's projection reaches his hand up in their direction and activates his energy globe. Immediately, the Doctor fires a blue pulse into his shoulder setting his aim off-target, but he holds as steady on his knees as possible and refocuses on Gary. The Doctor extends one hand out towards the shack and, with the other hand, fires one more pulse that hits the projection in the other shoulder. Suddenly, Dane realizes someone else is near the shack. Mr. Logan has appeared from the backside of the wall and stepped in between them to sacrifice himse f. As the projected man falls backwards and Gary's hand approaches the forehead of the real Kurrt, he fires a bright green bolt with every bit of energy he has left inside him.

There is no time for Dane to react as, the second that Gary's hand comes into contact with Kurrt's forehead, the green beam hurtles towards Mr. Logan, ricochets off a blue shield in front of him, and shoots across the clearing.

As Kurrt screams in pain from his seat in the shack, his lifeless projection's eyes roll back in its head and green currents electrify erratically through its body. It strikes the ground, sending snow and ash up into the air around it and disappears as a huge green flash erupts and a pulse of energy shoots outwards, bending the trees in all directions.

Slowly, they all uncover their eyes and emerge from their hiding places. Smiles cover their faces as they see that Tim and the Chinese President have taken the place of Kurrt's projection in the middle of the clearing attempting to pick themselves up off the ground next to his dark, unlit chest-piece. Next to Gary, Kurrt's pale, weak body writhes in pain. The Doctor nods in Mr. Logan's direction in appreciation.

"WOOO BABY! We did it!" Gavin screams with his fists over his head in victory, "Fuck that guy!"

Looking around for some support his eyes settle on Mom and he sees the smile fade from her face and tears begin to glaze over her eyes as he looks past him. He looks at Sherri, Jaz, the Doctor, then down to Gary to see the same. Finally, turning to follow their gaze his smile also disappears and his hands drop to his sides.

After a moment they are all looking sadly upon Dane's body, lying lifeless against the pile of debris, green embers burning in the scorch mark in the middle of his chest.

Chapter 36

BEEEEEEEEEEEEEEEEEEEEEEEEEEEEEEEEEEEEEEEEEEEEEEEEEEEEEE
EEEEEEEEEEEEEEEEEEEEEEEEEEEEEEP! The sound of the machines
behind the hospital bed ring throughout the room and out into
the hallway as Mom, Gavin, Tim, Sherri and Jaz look down over
Dane's motionless body.

"See!? Wouldn't that have been sad!?" Dane suddenly springs to
life and looks around at the faces above him with a smile. "I
mean, if I were all hooked up and stuff."

"Dude, you weren't even dead!" Gavin scoffs as he turns away
and plops in a seat at the edge of the bed as the rest just roll their
eyes. "If anything, I was WAY more dead than you!"

"True, but I did get this cool battle wound." He pulls his hospital
gown down to show off the circular scorch mark on his chest. "It's
going to be a wicked scar!"

"Hey," Mom attempts to corral his enthusiasm, "you're just lucky
Gavin woke up on his own on the beach, otherwise Gary would
have already used that to knock Kurrt out and he wouldn't have
anywhere to transfer your unconsciousness!"

"Yeah," Gavin pipes up again, "he just gave that dude the wound
from the shot I took until he could bring you back. That
douchebag deserved to be in pain for a little bit before Gary KO'd
him. He did leave this one, though!" he excitedly pulls his sleeve
up over his shoulder to display his own scorch mark.

"Scar buddies!" Dane shouts with a laugh as he shoves Tim's
shoulder, "Where's your battle wound, Tim? Huh?"

"No battle wounds here...I guess I'm just that good!" Tim says
with a cocky smile.

"Yeah, good enough to get caught and end up helping the bad
guy, right?" Sherri adds her own dig to their friendly razzing,
drawing laughter from the group.

"Hey! He saved my life!" Gavin stands abruptly and quiets the laughter for a moment. "Then he helped almost kill the Doctor...and all those other dudes...and Sherri...and Dane...and Dane's neighbor...and me. Dammit, Tim, you really are just a huge, disappointing failure!"

Dane lies back in the hospital bed and can't hide his smile as he watches his friends joke around with each other. Sherri's smile draws him in and causes his stomach to flutter once again. Over the last couple of days he had been so preoccupied with everything going on that he hadn't been nervous around her. He missed this feeling. He liked it. His eyes are suddenly met by Mom's as she looks at him with a proud smile, but also a look of relief.

"Mr. Denson!" a voice from the doorway quiets the entire room and draws their attention. The Doctor walks into the room with her clicking heels and her black pant suit, her hair once again pulled back tightly. She flips through pages on a clipboard, "It looks like your results are back." She stops suddenly and looks up at the crowd before her, "Family only, please..."

Without questioning the stern woman, the friends immediately disperse from the bedside and out of the room. When she hears the door click behind her she continues forward and approaches the bedside opposite his anxious mom, still flipping through the papers. After a moment of staring at her, waiting for her to begin her diagnosis, Dane and Mom look at each other with frustration.

"Good news, I hope?" Mom attempts to guide the woman along.

"Well, that depends." The Doctor stops flipping and lets the pages settle on the clipboard as she looks over the top sheet. "It looks like your medication was, in fact, contaminated with small amounts of radioactivity all along. Clearly, that was missed during the recall examinations and you continued to take them, slowly building up your tolerance to the radioactivity that later came from the mountain."

"Wait," Mom interjects drawing the Doctor's eyes up from the diagnosis in front of her, "so you're saying that your company slowly poisoned my son over time and has now left him as the only normal human, defenseless in a world full of superpowered...freaks!?"

"Mom..." Dane tries to calm her.

"Miss Denson, let-" the Doctor begins before she is cut off again.

"You saw what happened up there!?" Mom's voice continues louder than before, "Do you see his chest!? He could be dead right now!"

"Mom!" Dane tries to bring her down once more.

"Miss Denson, I am well aware of the situation-" The Doctor attempts to continue.

"Yeah, you're just not going to do shit about it because you got your guy." Mom turns and paces in a small circle, pulling her anger back and succumbing to frustration as she finally awaits the rest of the woman's diagnoses.

"What we're prepared to do," she continues softly, "is, besides a great deal of monetary compensation, prepare you a long-term supply of your medication at no cost, monitor your vitals and do extensive regular checkups, at no cost, and..." she turns towards the door as it swings open and a large, square man in a suit and Ray Ban sunglasses walks in, folding his hands in front of him and settling like a statue just inside the door, "full-time protection."

Once the initial shock has worn off, Dane can't help but laugh, "You got me a bodyguard!?" He looks at the broad man, but suddenly his eyes are drawn past him and out the door. In the hallway his friends still joke around with each other. Gavin thrusts his fist at Tim's shoulder, who dodges him easily, then attempts to push Sherri as she laughs at him, but she disappears into the air current and reappears on the other side of him, while Jaz laughs along. "You know what, Doctor?" he smiles as he watches his friends, then turns his eyes to her, "I think I'm going to be just fine."

She turns and waves her hand at the man, who lumbers out immediately without a word.

"But, wait," Dane becomes serious once again, "did you say you're going to make me a long-term supply of my medicine? Like...the radioactive medicine?"

"Yes," the Doctor flips a page on the clipboard and begins to read again, "it says here that you had some side effects when you weren't on your medications...some visions, pain, shaking in your extremities?" she looks back up to him for a confirmation, receiving a confused nod from the boy, "The radioactivity in the atmosphere is too potent. Your body can't handle it without the changes allowed by a 'Blackout' and you were seeing the early signs of it malfunctioning. You'll die if you don't continue to take it...and we don't know if you'd wake back up like everyone else." She looks up to see worry on both of their faces and immediately returns to her findings on the paper, "So we're going to attempt to ween you off slowly and if, at any time, you experience any side effects, you can just continue taking your previous supply. Ok?"

Dane looks over to his mom, satisfied with the Doctor's presentation, and still sees worry in her face. Reaching over, he grabs her hand on the rail of the hospital bed and squeezes comfortingly.

"Ok." The Doctor nods and turns to head for the door.

"Hey, Doc! Just one more question." Dane shouts, stopping her a couple of steps from the door. She turns to him with a fake smile as she tries to hide her irritation with the nickname. "How much is a 'great deal of monetary compensation' exactly?"

A real smile finds its way to her lips and a mutual appreciation of one another is shared as their eyes meet. With only a nod, she turns and pushes through the door and out of sight.

The view of Mt. Rainier is different than it has been in the past week. The mountain still stands strong, a steady stream of smoke pouring from the top and into the sky, a blistering wind still blows down over the jutting, black rocks and through the snow and ash covered trees, but the absence of the green force field definitely leaves it seeming a little different. Naked, in a way.

Now, helicopters circle the mountain and utility vehicles make their way up and down the trails, "InCorps" proudly brazen across the sides of them. Stations equipped with an overabundance of armed guards stand defensively at every road leading to the mountain's many trails, campgrounds and parks.

In the clearing, the wind blows aggressively in sporadic gusts as InCorps personnel scatter the scene. Some run tests using handheld devices, others gather up the computer equipment, papers, and any other remnants from the shack. Through the commotion a man in a heavy, blue coat with the InCorps logo on the back and a walkie talkie in his hand makes his way swiftly to the center of the clearing where another man stands with his hands folded behind his back, surveying the scene around him and spinning the ring on his finger.

"Sir, I've received word that Kurrt has been successfully secured in our facility." He mutters quietly over the man's shoulder. Getting no reaction, he continues on with his report, "Also, Dr. Wong just sent word. She has all the samples she needed to get from the Denson boy and is going to release him from the hospital. She said she would report her findings and a plan of action to you when you return to Los Angeles."

"Very good." The man grumbles into the wind, more to himself than to his employee. As the messenger rushes back across the clearing and hops into a Hummer, the man continues to watch the workers scurry around the clearing to gather their data and clean up the scene. His eyes work their way up to the peak of the mountain, where a slight shimmer of green reflects from beneath the smoke. Simultaneously, the ring he continues to spin on his finger behind him begins to emit a soft energy-like hum and a tiny, green glow while a maniacal, pointy-toothed smile finds its way to his mouth.

**Chapter 37**

In the hospital waiting room the group all waits with boredom. Mr. Logan has fallen asleep seated upright in a chair with his head folded down to his chest. Gavin, Tim, Sherri and Jaz had just recently been ushered out of the back hallway and sit quietly in a corner looking at cell phones. Gary's eyes stare mindlessly into the muted television on the opposite wall as reports about the occurrence on Mt. Rainier flash across the screen and talking heads debate the issues silently. Every time the door from the hallway clicks and swings open Gary's eyes divert from the TV for a moment and the kids glance up from their phones to see who enters. There's something about hospital waiting rooms, or more about the nature of hospitals themselves, that makes the time there seem much longer than it really is, and, after such a harrowing, adrenaline-pumping event, that was definitely true in this case.

Finally, with a click, the door swings open and their nonchalant gazes find Dane and Mom entering the room from the white hallway. He turns and talks to the receptionist for a moment as his friends jump up and approach them. On her way past him, Jaz grabs and shakes Mr. Logan's arm, startling him out of his slumber.

"Well, that's all good to hear!" Tim foretells Dane's news immediately as he approaches.

"Jesus, Tim. Don't ruin it!" Sherri smacks his arm with the back of her hand, then turns back to Dane, "So, what'd she say?"

Dane slowly turns away from the plastic receptionist window and looks around at all of their caring faces. He had always had his mom and his friends, but, for some reason he couldn't figure out, he felt like something had been missing. He now had it. In that moment, he didn't feel like an outcast. A powerless weirdo in a sea of superheroes. This was a family...his family.

A smile comes to his lips as he looks into their anxiously awaiting eyes, "I love you guys. Thank you for being there for me."

One by one they work their way in and wrap their arms around the young man. Gavin reaches out and puts one arm around him with a confused look on his face. "That's a really weird thing for her to say to you..." he utters, earning him more harassment from the group as they all turn and make their way towards the front doors.

"Hey mom?" he turns to her and holds her back from the group, "When we get home, is it ok if I just relax for a couple of days?"

She lets out a laugh and puts an arm around his shoulders, "That's fine, sweetie." She leans in and kisses the side of his head, "I think you've earned a little time off."

As they step forward with their arms around each other the first set of glass doors slide open and they reach the entryway, where his friends have gathered on both sides of the doors that lead outside. Surprised, Dane and Mom stop and look up at them nervously.

"Prepare yourself..." Tim urges in Dane's direction.

Jaz approaches the other side of him and reaches up, setting her small hand in his. He grips it and looks down upon her fuzzy head. "We're with you." She looks up with her big brown eyes and smiles.

Dane's eyes look straight forward intensely. Though he's not really sure what he's preparing himself for he knows he can take on anything with this family of his. They take a step forward onto the entryway mat and the foggy glass doors automatically slide in either direction.

As they cautiously step out onto the hospital entrance they are bombarded by a rumble of shouting voices and small explosions of light that cause them to shield their eyes. They huddle together as a team as their would-be-attackers are held back by hospital security, shoving cameras, tape recorders and microphones in front of Dane and screaming their questions over one another.

Dane's eyes look around wildly, unsure of what to do. He gazes up to Mom, who, unfortunately, has the same look on her face. He looks over to the rest of the group, who stands back nervously, with the exception of Gavin who waves into the crowd with a big smile as if he'd just won the Super Bowl. Finally, after a few moments, the shouting begins to die down and one reporter is able to be heard clearly.

"Dane," she shouts as she pushes her tape recorder as close to him as she can get it, "how, exactly, were you able to take down the man on the mountain? Can you tell us?"

"Dane!" a man shouts before Dane can get a word out of his mouth, "Who are all these people with you?"

"Mr. Denson!" his attention is pulled in another direction as a woman pushes a microphone towards him, "We're told you don't have superpowers. What's it like to be the only person in the world without superpowers?"

"It's…uh," Dane begins, but fades off, unsure of how to answer the question. He turns and looks at his mom, who smiles down to him, then over to Jaz, Sherri, Mr. Logan, Gary and, finally, Gavin and Tim. "It's…"

"Dude, no." Tim utters to him across the group with his head shaking disapprovingly, "Please don't say that."

Dane smiles at him, then turns back to the microphone in front of him, looking into the reflective camera lenses that point in his direction, "It's pretty super!"

Dane will return in...
Plain Dane: The Hero Within

<u>Extra Chapter</u>

Hundreds of miles away, but only a few miles outside of a small town under guard of snowy mountain ranges, through layered concrete walls and behind heavy steel doors, two men in white jumpsuits, yellow gloves and boots and futuristic breathing hoods rush down a long, shiny hallway. Their hands push along a glass chamber sitting atop a mechanical gurney that floats mere inches off the ground. They turn a corner and approach two doors with threatening red and yellow "WARNING" stickers posted across them. This does not slow their pace as they ram the containment into the doors, sending them swinging open into a gigantic facility with more people bustling about. Some drive strange vehicles that whir as they pull other glass chambers around the room and insert them into holding cells. Others stand at long metal tables that look like they're set up for a college cadaver class. A large viewing deck surrounded by glass looms above them, empty and silent, but ever watchful.

The men guide their chamber across the busy floor and towards another set of doors, which stand behind two armored guards. They slow to a stop a few inches from the doors and walk around their delivery to display the badges that hang off the chest of their jumpsuits. The sentries immediately take a few steps to each side, the one on the left guiding his hand inside a small indent on the wall and placing it on a pixeled screen. The two men make their way back around behind the chamber as a blue light scans the guard's hand and, with a couple of beeps and a loud hiss, the doors slide open and they move forward into complete blackness.

As soon as they are past the doors a light clicks on above them. They continue forward and another light clicks on, then another, and another every few feet they travel. A few moments later they push the chamber to a stop underneath one of the lights and into an input panel against the wall, which hisses as it accepts the new pod. Once it has settled into place, the chamber lights up with a green glow and the men turn and make their way under the trail of lights that had led them there, each light turning off behind them once they've passed, and out the doors that hiss and bang to a close behind them.

The glow from the pod shoots out into the dark room as the screen on its side displays the adjusting interior atmosphere where Kurrt lies in solace, Simeon's antimatter gloves surrounding his hands like glass shackles and the headpiece planted firmly onto his temples with blue bolts of electricity shooting steadily into different areas across his forehead. The light from his pod refracts through another chamber next to him, this one upright and containing a man suspended in water. A breathing tube and other lines and wires snake from various parts of his body and into the base of the tank. On the front of his containment, a digital screen, darkened from the lack of recent use, displays his vitals underneath the title "J. Denson".

Suddenly, Kurrt's chamber lets out a series of beeps displaying "100% atmospheric conditions" and then, with one final beep, the entire room instantly goes pitch black once again.

About the Author

Growing up in the small Northern Michigan town of Onaway David learned to read before entering kindergarten and later developed a strong affinity for writing as well, whether it was short stories about the Looney Tunes or school reports and speeches. Paired with his love for all things "superhero" a story developed in his mind.

David moved from Michigan to Southern California in 2012 with everything that would fit into his small Saturn sport coupe and began writing in his free time. After multiple failed attempts at a snarky health and fitness book and a comedy TV script his original idea was the only one to stick to the page. Plain Dane was born.

4 years later, at the age of 31, a nearly exhausted bank account, an unexpected stint into unemployment and a bad living situation lead him to make a desperate move back in with his parents in snowy Onaway. There he completed his first novel Plain Dane: Dawn of Power

Besides writing David also loves playing and watching sports, cooking, everything Ninja Turtles, 90's Alt music, trying new IPAs and finding the best pizza anywhere he goes. Now living with his rescue pup Griffey in sunny San Diego he continues to write short stories and has begun working on the second book in the Plain Dane series.

Follow my journey on Facebook and Instagram
@plaindanenovel

Website: www.DavidLSchlaufman.com

If you enjoyed this book please leave a review with your favorite
retailer. Thank you for your support! - David

EDITORIAL REVIEWS for FINAL ACT

"Van Fleisher has created another intriguing and high-octane thriller novel in the wake of Final Notice, taking those eerily realistic science fiction concepts from book one and delivering on their repercussions big time in this follow-up roller-coaster of thrills ... The characters are once more armed with slick dialogue and realistic reactions to the chaos of the VT2, with a surprising amount of humor laced into what is essentially a dangerous and dark plot-line. There are genuine twists in the story which are difficult to predict but fit perfectly into the storyline overall, and this combined with the smooth narrative style leaves readers feeling like they're in the hands of a confident and accomplished storyteller. I would highly recommend Final Act to thriller fans seeking an intelligent, playful, and layered read." **K.C. Finn for Readers' Favorite**

***

"Author Van Fleisher continues his near-future saga with Final Act, the second installment of his Final Series. Well-penned vignettes from victims and wearers alike swirl around the main core of the plot. Fleisher isn't afraid to tackle some of the most controversial topics of the day, notably the American obsession with firearms and the tragically common trend of gun violence plaguing the country. Broken political systems, illogical bureaucracy, and dark distortions of the American dream make this timely thriller hit hard, while also posing existential questions that every reader will be forced to ask themselves. **Peppered with ordinary characters forced into extraordinary situations, this book may initially seem like escapist sci-fi, but in a world where a darkening future rarely feels far away, Final Act is a chilling, page-turning reflection of modern life. Final Act is a chilling, page-turning reflection of modern life."** **Self-Publishing Review.**

"Final Act by Van Fleisher is a skillfully written thriller with strong hints of science fiction and a compelling premise. It is packed with action and twists that are hard to predict. The beautiful prose coupled with the author's terrific descriptions infuse the story with an astounding sense of realism. *Final Act is an engrossing, suspenseful story that puts readers on the edge of their seats. Cunningly plotted and deftly written."* **Ruffina Oserio for Readers' Favorite**

***

" ... a vivid romp through relationships, politics, and technology that builds a complex, compelling interrelationship between all three. Readers will be on the edge of their seats as the cast of characters navigates the uncertain waters of political clashes and special interests over a technology and political process gone awry. *... a riveting story that is impossible to put down for political thriller fans seeking something different."* **D. Donovan, Senior Reviewer, Midwest Book Review**

***

"The ingenuity behind the premise of this book can't go unnoticed. The author blends political intrigue with revolutionary technology to create a recipe that will blow the minds of thriller fans. *... characters are exceptionally written and a plot that is unpredictable. An entertaining story from a master of the craft."* **Christian Sia for Readers' Favorite**

***

"... a political thriller and the sequel to the well-received predecessor, Final Notice. The premise is original and interesting, and Fleisher delivers a unique narrative with characters that can be comfortably read as a stand-alone. The exploration of the good and bad sides of technology is exceptionally displayed and the action sequences and tension are on point. *I recommend this book to readers who enjoy straightforward thrillers with a toe dipped into the realm of science fiction.* **Jamie Michele for Readers' Favorite**

FINAL ACT
A Novel by
VAN FLEISHER

FINAL ACT, A Novel

VAN FLEISHER

"The characters and events in this book are fictitious. Any similarity to real persons, living or dead, is unfortunate."

ISBN (Print Edition): 978-1-7320833-1-8

ISBN (eBook Edition): 978-1-7320833-2-5

TABLE OF CONTENTS

PROLOGUE

Two years earlier. Vijay Patel had invented the VT2, a fitness watch with extremely advanced capabilities that could analyze blood properties in real time, actually and accurately predicting the wearers' deaths to a precise date. While the concept was conceived to allow users time to get their affairs in order, talk with family and friends, or perhaps address a long thought-about bucket-list item, some receivers of their Final Notice decided to use their remaining time to right a perceived wrong or settle a grudge ... with complete impunity.

Given the easy access to guns, and the NRA's ongoing promotion of fear, America's love affair with guns continued to grow, fueling even more senseless murders by Final Notice recipients. Patel, stunned by the havoc his invention had brought about, worked in cooperation with Zoe Brouet of the FBI to stem the violence associated with the VT2 – violence that affected everyone from U.S. Senators to store clerks, from senior citizens to scientists.

The invention of the VT2 prompted millions to consider the question, "What would you do if you knew you had 10, 20, or 30 days to live?" FINAL ACT asks that question as well, but adds, "What might others do if they knew that you'd received your Final Notice?"

***

CHARACTERS

FINAL ACT contains two types of characters, which I'll call "Transient" and "Core." The Transient characters will typically appear for only one chapter and are used to flesh out the wider story, while the Core characters have a more important role and generally appear more than once.

Core Characters – In order of appearance

Vijay Patel
Zoe Brouet
Eric Hawke
Demi Magray
Alek Belikov
Vik Vasin
Jennifer Andrews Patel
Mike Kalin
J. Edward Konig
Bill & Nicole Andrews
Yuri Chernyshevsky
Ninad Banerjee
Moki Joe Hunter
Tocho Tom Hunter

***

CHAPTER 1 – WHEN IN ROME …

Rome, Georgia. The beautiful, crisp, autumn Saturday that greeted Mildred Pierce as she opened her front door and stepped out onto Broad Street masked what lay ahead. The sky was bright blue with only a few puffy clouds floating by, in sharp contrast to the thunderstorm of just a few hours ago. The storm had kept most folks indoors, and the empty streets suggested that few were ready to venture out.

Mildred was looking forward to having lunch with her best friend, Esther, who'd been away for a few weeks visiting her family in California. She had chosen her brand-new fall pantsuit for the occasion – a smart, two-tone grey outfit that complimented her lithe frame.

Mildred was nearing eighty, but with her tall, almost military-like bearing, and energetic, confident stride, she could have passed for sixty. She wore her silver hair in a medium bobbed fashion that attractively framed her wide grey eyes, upturned nose, and mouth that defaulted to a warm smile. She appeared self-assured and upbeat, completely belying her inner feelings.

It had been a rough few weeks without Esther's warmth and love, and she knew it would feel good to be back in the glow that her friend radiated. But a part of her also dreaded the meeting.

FINAL ACT

It was just a short walk to Sweet Pickles, a favorite restaurant of theirs. She loved the chicken salad, accompanied by the famous sweet pickles that Penny made, and she and Esther often shared a piece of Penny's delicious chocolate cake, as well. But when she reached Fourth Avenue, only a short distance from the restaurant, a black pickup truck purposely swerved toward the curb, sending a tsunami of muddy water from the morning rain that literally covered Mildred's fresh new pantsuit. She gasped from the splash and heard laughter and shouting from the passenger looking back from the open window. Shocked, she looked back as the truck sped away, its Confederate flag curtaining the rear window.

Mildred surveyed the damage and knew that she couldn't meet Esther looking like this. Her spirits momentarily dashed, she turned around and headed back to her apartment. Esther was always late, so even with this unexpected wrinkle, it would be OK. As she made her way quickly back to her home, she couldn't help but wonder why someone would do that to her. She knew it was intentional, and the hooting and laughter from the truck confirmed it, conjuring up the dark thoughts from the past that she had been wrestling with since she'd received her Final Notice.

Traffic was now at a standstill on Broad Street, and she could hear sirens and see flashing red and blue lights up near Second Avenue. She continued on her way, deciding which clothes to change into when she saw the Confederate flag in the rear window a few steps away from her. She stopped for a moment, the loud music blaring from the open windows, assaulting her ears. She also heard something else – laughter from long ago as the dark, unbidden thoughts raced through her head. She glanced down at her watch and made her decision. Unzipping her purse, she purposefully strode up to the truck, pulled out her silenced Glock 26, and put a bullet through the temple of the passenger, whose head jerked back, giving her a clear shot as she pumped another round into the driver's forehead while he stared at her, frozen, wide-eyed with surprise and fear. Calmly putting the gun back in her purse, Mildred didn't hear the sound of an alarm coming from the driver's watch. Muffled by the loud music and approaching sirens and obscured by the flag in the rear window, no one else heard the shots or noticed Mildred's act, and she simply continued her walk home to change clothes. Everyone else on Broad Street was trapped in traffic, texting, talking on their phones, or chatting with each other.

The sirens muffling the shots and the flag hiding the splattering of blood may have obscured Mildred's crime from everyone in Rome, but 1,085 miles to the north, just outside of Boston, Massachusetts, Vijay Patel was watching.

***

The dead bodies remained undiscovered when Mildred passed by again, now dressed in a clean blue pantsuit. As she walked past the motionless pickup, with its equally motionless driver and passenger sandwiched in the gridlocked traffic, she briefly glanced over. *Why did they do that? Because she was old? Because she was a woman? Because they were assholes? Or maybe all of the above?*

Mildred had never forgotten the many assholes she'd encountered over the years. The men who thought they were God's gift to women. The men who tried to grope her as though she owed them a piece of her body for a drink or dinner. And the men who used their positions and gender to try to intimidate her at work, some with promises of promotions and others with threats of losing her job. She stole another glance at the two dead men in the pickup, recalling their laughter, and, as though it were yesterday, she heard the laughter from an event of over sixty years ago.

***

FINAL ACT

Smyrna, Georgia. Mildred had just finished her basic training at Parris Island, South Carolina, and was home on a week's leave before shipping out to the Marine Corps Air Station at Kaneohe Bay, Hawaii. She was a Southern girl from Smyrna, and going to Hawaii would be the most exciting thing she had ever done, other than enlisting in the Marine Corps. She'd seen most of her friends since coming home, partying hard every night, but tonight, she had decided to stay home, watch TV, drink a couple of beers, and have an early night.

Mildred was staying at her older sister's apartment. Her mom was still with her sleazy boyfriend, and Mildred wanted no part of him. She hadn't forgotten his lewd and aggressive advances. Her sister was out for the evening and told her that she probably wouldn't be back until morning … late morning.

She had just started watching *The Twilight Zone* on TV, and she jumped at loud knocking, actually banging on her front door. She looked out the window and saw Jake Jackson, another guy, and a girl, all with beers in hand. Mildred had gone out with Jake a couple of times in the past, but there was never any chemistry, and she knew that. She'd also heard that Jake had recently completed his basic training and was shipping out to the Marine base in Okinawa soon.

Jake shouted, "Millie, one for the road! We're shipping out in the morning!"

She liked the nickname Millie, and it made her smile as she quickly debated whether to ignore them or answer the door. She decided to open it, and they all stumbled in. Jake introduced the guy with him as Travis, a buddy from basic training, but he had forgotten the girl's name. Travis introduced her as Tracey.

Millie had only drunk a beer and a half and estimated that

she was at least a six-pack behind them. She knew that the two guys had just been through a grueling basic training program, much harder than her own, so there was a strong sense of camaraderie and understanding.

Travis and Tracey sat on the couch and began to make out and pretty much do as much as they could with clothes on. Jake put his arms around Millie, pulled her to him, and tried to kiss her. She pushed away and tried to verbally deflect the move. "You're in good form tonight, Private First-Class Jackson."

Jake grinned briefly and twisted her around, pinning her arm behind her back. He pushed her into the bedroom and onto the bed. She cried out, and Jake pushed her face down into a pillow to muffle her scream. He called for Travis, who picked up a roll of tape from the top of a nearby box that Millie had been packing and sliced a piece free.

Jake kept his knee pushed into her back, grabbed her hair, and roughly pulled her head up just enough so Travis could place the tape over her mouth. Now, she could at least breathe, but the two men tied her hands to the headboard. She felt her shorts and panties being pulled and then ripped off. Then her legs were tied to the foot-board. As she laid there, spread-eagle on the bed, she could hear the two men breathing heavily, the rapid sound of zippers unzipping, and The Twilight Zone on TV in the background.

She lost track of time, and occasionally consciousness, as Jake and Travis took turns with her, cheering each other on to do it harder, longer. And that should have been the worst part, but it was the horrific and demeaning insults and profanities that they grunted, taunted, and whispered in her ears, that she was never able to forget. That and their laughter. She could just see the TV screen, with Tracey's reflection. The young woman drank a beer and intently watched the show, with neither awareness of nor interest in the brutal scene playing out less than ten feet away.

When they finished with her, they untied one hand and left, unhurried. Mildred considered calling the police or her commanding officer, despite Jake's threat that they would kill her if she did so, but she was pretty sure that her word against two male Marines and a civilian woman wouldn't carry any weight. It might even screw up her chance to go to Hawaii. So, she took a very long shower, kept quiet, went to Hawaii, and used the memory of that night to focus on her hand-to-hand combat training and marksmanship. No man would ever do that to her again. And like carrying an umbrella to ensure it won't rain, Mildred never needed to use her unique skills ... until today.

As Mildred's thoughts returned to the present, another thought occurred to her. *Why did I do that?* She shrugged her shoulders and wistfully answered to herself, "*Perhaps it was my #MeToo moment.*" And then she realized that today was probably the last time that she and Esther would share a piece of that delicious chocolate cake they ordered after lunch. She wouldn't burden her friend with her crime, nor the awful memories that prompted it. It would be difficult enough to break the news about her health.

***

Esther had been devastated when her best friend told her she had just days to live. And so, when she couldn't reach Mildred, she went to her apartment. Using the key Mildred had given her, she found the lifeless body, looking very peaceful, eyes closed, and the apartment spotless. Esther sat there for a few minutes, sobbing, and then called 911.

VAN FLEISHER

When the police conducted a routine inspection of the apartment, they found Mildred's gun and took it away for analysis. Rome being a very small town, the two police officers were aware of the murders a couple of days ago, right down the street from where they were at the moment. They saw that the magazine was two rounds short of being full – the same number of shots that killed the two men in the pickup. But how would a seventy-nine-year-old woman be involved with a double homicide?

***

CHAPTER 2 – HOPE VS. REALITY

Chestnut Hill, Massachusetts. Dr. Vijay Patel was in his home office, freshly showered after his routine fifteen-mile run. He tried to contain his excitement about talking with Zoe Brouet at the FBI, but it was still only 7 a.m.

A little more than two years ago, Vijay and his company, VitalTech, had introduced a watch, the VT2, which could alert wearers that they had ten, twenty, or thirty days to live – their Final Notice. The intent was to help wearers get their affairs in order, say their good-byes, or even cram in a bucket-list trip, and most people did these things. More than a few, however, had turned to revenge and murder. Those acts still haunted Vijay, and he was trying to minimize the damage.

On Saturday, his computer had pinged with two different alerts from VT2 users in Rome, Georgia, both listed as having guns. One of the users was a Final Notice recipient whose blood analysis data from her VT2 revealed a unique signature pattern – based on an algorithm that considered pulse rate, blood pressure, adrenalin, cortisol, and serotonin levels. The pattern was consistent with Final Notice recipients who had killed in the past.

The other alert signaled the death of a VT2 user who died instantly without having been under a Final Notice warning.

His blood analysis indicated a brief but extreme cortisol pattern indicating fear, at the same time as the Final Notice recipient experienced her raised levels. Vijay mused, both in Rome. Both exhibit unusual blood hormone readings at precisely the same time. Coincidence?

***

Washington, D.C. FBI Supervisory Special Agent Zoe Brouet was in her office early on Monday morning, too. She was short in height, high in energy, an athletic, honey-colored young woman, devoted to her job. Her phone rang, and she was pleased that it was Vijay and not a report of a mass murder somewhere. They exchanged pleasantries, but Vijay sounded excited, so she asked, "What's up?"

Vijay gave her the short version, "This could be a breakthrough! On Saturday, our system picked up two simultaneous alerts from two VT2 wearers in Rome, Georgia. One was Mildred Pierce, a Final Notice recipient and gun owner who displayed blood readings and hormonal changes that we believe are consistent with anger and revenge. And as an update, she died on Sunday of natural causes, consistent with her Final Notice prediction.

"The other person is Harlan Snell, a VT2 wearer, and also a gun owner. Snell had not received a Final Notice, but he died suddenly, and there was an extreme hormonal spike – at the exact time of death – that would indicate fear. The time of his death coincided with a short spike in Pierce's analysis that we believe shows happiness or satisfaction."

Zoe was writing down details as she took in the information. "Seems like more than a coincidence, doesn't it? Any thoughts?"

FINAL ACT

Vijay confessed, "I'll have to admit to playing detective over the weekend so, what about this? Pierce knows she will die very soon, and something, perhaps an encounter with Snell, angers her, and she kills him. Snell is surprised by the encounter; his cortisol spikes, and he recoils in fear as Pierce shoots him."

Zoe smiled despite the grave nature of the conversation. "Very plausible. You're hired."

Vijay laughed, "Check it out and let me know."

Zoe's interest picked up. "OK, I will, but are you saying that you can determine the likelihood that someone might kill by these hormonal changes?"

Vijay replied cautiously, "That's the track we've been following, based on historical and current findings. We've been able to pull out some old data from earlier incidents, and, along with these current ones, I'm feeling more confident that we can make that prediction. Still early stages and we have a long way to go with the lead times. This event in Rome wasn't captured until seconds before it occurred, so we have to look back historically to see if there's an earlier pattern we can pick up sooner."

Zoe fought against being too hopeful. "Hmm. You're right. Very short notices like that won't help us unless we happen to be standing next to a potential shooter."

Vijay remained upbeat. "Let's see where this leads us. At least I'm fairly confident that we've identified the right markers, and the device is capturing them."

"OK, but you know the pressure I'm under."

"I do, and I'm under pressure from myself, and that can be crushing. Let me know about Rome and if I still have that job offer."

Zoe laughed, "OK. Keep running those numbers."

She hung up, looked up the number for the Rome, Georgia police, asked for the ranking detective on duty, and was placed on hold. As she waited, she reflected that although it seemed like only yesterday, it was two years ago that the VT2 watch had hit the market. Vijay's invention had brought an unintended consequence along with its technology, with fatal implications for a number of people. Sales had soared to over ten million, and 65-70% of those VT2 purchasers had a gun. The number of incidents was growing at a rate that significantly exceeded the FBI's expectations, based on the earlier test period, and Zoe attributed this increase to two factors: Increased gun ownership (gun ownership had grown from 60% to 72% in the past two years) and significant publicity surrounding several high-profile VT2-related murders. These now-infamous murders had spawned copycat acts by users of the "Death Watch," as some of the more incendiary publications called it.

Zoe was interrupted from her thoughts when Detective Taylor came on the line. Zoe explained the situation to her carefully, given her desire to keep the level of cooperation between the FBI and VitalTech below the radar. She started with, "Have there been any shootings in Rome over the weekend?"

Zoe detected a few seconds of silence before Taylor answered in a pleasant, very Southern drawl, "Why yes, there have been? Why are you asking?"

Zoe picked up on the plural response, "Have been, as in more than one?"

FINAL ACT

Taylor replied, "Yes. Two men were shot and killed on Saturday morning."

"Was one of them Harlan Snell?"

"How did you know that? Yes. He and another local lowlife were gunned down in their truck. We think it was drug-related. What do you know?"

Ignoring the question, Zoe continued, "Are you familiar with Mildred Pierce?"

"Agent Brouet, Rome's a small town, but that doesn't mean we know everyone. Or at least, I don't. What's this all about?"

"I'm sorry, Detective. I can't give you any specifics, but we have reason to believe that a Mildred Pierce of Rome may have been the person who shot Snell or at least was involved with his and the other person's murders. We also believe that Pierce is now deceased. Can you please have someone investigate and get back to me?"

Zoe hung up without waiting for an answer and stared at the 'VT2 Watch List' on her screen. The report from VitalTech provided her department with the updated names and addresses of VT2 wearers, who had advised their doctors that they owned guns. The list also included all Final Notice recipients. Unfortunately, the information had been only marginally helpful for several reasons: First, gun ownership information was not comprehensively available and varied from state to state. The VT2 wearer's doctors were the primary sources of the information. When the Affordable Care Act and its required mandate were phased out, the number of people who had a regular doctor had significantly decreased. Some states even prohibited doctors from asking about gun access. Also, illegally or unofficially acquired guns were often not listed. Not surprisingly, at least so far, none of this information had helped Zoe and her team pro-actively stop Final Notice recipients from killing.

In the early stages of the device's roll-out, many incidents were a result of older wearers taking revenge for real or perceived age-ism slights. Then, several politicians had been gunned down by people who had received their Final Notice. Now, with an election looming, politicians were among her top concerns.

Another trending category of incidents was the result of spousal abuse, sometimes involving women using their husbands' guns to get retribution before their own 'Notice' period was up.

Recently, too, CEOs and other senior or supervisory employees of companies, both large and small, had become prime targets, including a recent, high profile murder of a major airline's CEO. The CEO had been credited with steering his company through bankruptcy, in part by dumping their existing pension plan off to the Pension Benefit Guaranty Corporation, an independent agen-cy of the federal government. As a result, many employees saw their pensions cut in half, while the CEO got a multi-million-dollar bonus. A ramp service agent of the airline, who had received his Final Notice, shot and killed the CEO at a company gathering that had been called to quell strike action. Newspapers from around the country carried comments from fellow employees expressing their sorrow for missing the opportunity to do it themselves.

As she thought about this incident, Zoe realized that even without the advance warning that Vijay was working on, this was one they could have stopped, by merely having access to one more piece of information – employment details: company, position, location. They needed to think outside the box to protect likely, high-profile targets, as defined by her boss. She made a note to ask Vijay if employment information was available and brainstorm with him to see if there was any other information he could provide. In the airline case, if they had been collecting information about potential triggers such as bankruptcies, layoffs, and strike actions, they could have matched Final Notice recipients against their list. The Final Notice shooter at the airline would have matched against the high-profile target CEO.

Less straightforward were the political and judicial targets. After a number of Republican politicians were killed during the VT2 test period, including three by a fellow GOP senator, the next wave gunned down were Democrats killed by white supremacists and neo-Nazis. In response to this, the Antifada, on the left, decided that retaliation was required. Senators and Representatives from local, state, and federal levels, already avoiding confrontations with their constituents at town hall meetings, had begun to hold streamed television feed meetings from secure locations. Despite their precautions, a few congressmen at the state level fell victim to left-wing killings.

Judges, too, often highly politicized, were at risk. Two judges, one at the federal level and another at the state level, had been gunned down by Notice recipients.

The vast majority of Notice killings were more mundane, although sometimes more tragic, often involving recent or long-standing neighbor disputes, employee-employer issues, or perceived service industry slights and rudeness. Family disputes, too, saw their VT2 incident numbers rise, although these were, in some cases, a result of arguments that got out of hand, but within reach of a gun.

Zoe was moved by all the tragedies she'd seen; in fact, she lived in constant fear of the next big one, especially after a tense meeting she'd had with her boss, Eric Hawke.

***

It was early on a Monday morning a little more than a month ago that Zoe had arrived at her office, and jumped with surprise to find Eric Hawke, the Executive Assistant Director, sitting in *her* chair at her desk. He was a serious, all-business, stickler for following rules, career bureaucrat, with his eye always on the next rung of the ladder. So far, during the current administration in the White House, that ladder seemed quite rickety and rife with both opportunities and pitfalls. The only thing that gave away his age was his short-trimmed greying hair that provided a sophisticated contrast to his black skin. While Hawke appreciated the effort that Zoe had made in trying to control the Final Notice killings - he had promoted her and expanded her department - he was under extreme pressure to rein them in. He was also pretty sure that the current 'after-the-fact' system would not help in the newly evolving scenario.

Curiously, Hawke remained in her chair, so Zoe sat in a visitor's chair. He wasted no time with formalities. She listened to his somber words as he said, "Our country is more divided than ever and polarized in ways we have never experienced – politically and culturally. The result is that we have factions on both the far right and left that will do whatever is necessary to achieve their aims. Plus, hate crimes against Latinos, African Americans, Muslims, and Jews are on the rise. That means guns and bloodshed. And that's on top of the credible belief that the Russians hacked into the last election cycle and plan to do it again. Even worse, other countries may join them."

The seriousness of Hawke's opening words weighed on her as she asked if there were any specific threats.

Hawke admitted that, at the moment, there weren't any. However, with a Presidential election looming, there was an increasing concern, both with respect to intimidation as well as actual attacks on candidates. There were concerns about

FINAL ACT

the Russians, Chinese, Turks, and Iranians, even the North Koreans and Saudis. But one that also concerned Hawke and Zoe was the increased likelihood and chilling willingness of Final Notice recipients to kill with impunity.

Zoe's mind was racing as she took in the implications and the new urgency that Hawke presented, when he asked, "Are you still in communication with VitalTech?"

"Yes, sir. We're still in the loop regarding VT2 users with guns …"

Hawke interrupted, "How big is that list now?"

"About six million."

"Jesus! Six million with guns? Have they been able to give us any help, other than names and addresses?"

Zoe had been very non-committal, "Vijay Patel is working on various possibilities."

"I thought he sold the business."

"He did, but he's doing this on his own." And when she saw the puzzled look on Hawke's face, she added, "The killings have always bothered him. I don't think he would have ever invented the watch had he known."

Sarcastically Hawke asked, "So now he's trying to atone?"

"Something like that."

He had looked at her incredulously but then stated, "I want you to develop a plan that deals with the situation as we know it today, taking into account the added threat of the political circus that we'll be dealing with, leading up to and during the elections. I need to understand our resource and capability requirements, lead times, and plans to deal with three threat levels, in reverse order of priority: Non-Political ... High-Level Non-Political including business leaders, religious leaders, and any other celebrity level threats ... and finally, Political and Judiciary."

Zoe's phone rang, bringing her back to the present. It was Detective Taylor. She confirmed that Mildred Pierce had died of natural causes and that a gun was found in her apartment. An analysis of the gun confirmed that it was the weapon used to kill the two men.

***

CHAPTER 3 - TOUCHING

Washington, D.C. Zoe called Vijay with the news from Rome and telling him that the job offer was still open. She added, however, "But the pay sucks and the working conditions are awful."

Vijay passed on the job but said, "Looking at Pierce's hormonal readings leading up to when she probably killed the men, it looks like something triggered an immediate spike, and she went from very calm, and even happy, to a state of rage and then an immediate return to normal. Not long after that, her anger returned for a short while, although it was on a very different level than earlier, returning to normal from then on."

Zoe asked if he had any explanation.

"I have no idea what happened when she killed the guys, other than saying it was sudden. Perhaps the killing gave her peace, and then she thought about it again later, and it agitated her once more. Something stirred her up twenty-seven minutes after the big spike."

Zoe commented, "I guess we'll never know."

Then she asked about adding employment details for VT2 wearers to the information he was sending her.

Vijay was uncomfortable with her request. "I'll have to think about how to handle that. I don't have direct control over VitalTech operations, and I'm not exactly close with their new CEO."

"That's too bad. Let me know if you can find a way."

She hung up and looked at a note her assistant had put on her desk. It was a note from Hawke with four names and phone numbers.

The note read, "Reach out to the U.S. Capitol Police, U.S. Marshal's office, CIA and Secret Service. They will all be expecting your call."

Hawke had told her that the FBI would be coordinating with the other four agencies charged with protecting the high-profile targets, as he had defined them, and Zoe would be the point person. The four names were her contact points.

She made the calls to the U.S. Capitol Police and U.S. Marshal's office. Zoe had a good working relationship with the USCP, who protect U.S. Congressional members while in the Capital. She was also familiar with the contact at the U.S. Marshal's office, which was attached to the Department of Justice, and protected the judiciary. Both contacts were aware of the threat that Final Notice recipients posed, as members of Congress and the Judicial branch had already fallen prey to these acts.

The CIA contact seemed smug, and even a bit condescending, and it struck her that the rivalry between the CIA and FBI was alive and well. Zoe had explained that she was running point for the Bureau. The agent made a comment along the lines that they would continue to deal with the bad guys in Russia, China, and elsewhere while she tracked down her "very dangerous geriatric Final Notice killers hobbling away with their walkers."

After that, she didn't know what to expect from the Secret Service, and she got the unexpected.

Secret Service Agent Demi Magray was cordial, interested, and sympathetic to Zoe's situation. The Service's Protection Division was used to defending against assassins and civilian crackpots, and their take on the world was more closely aligned with the FBI's. As she had with the other three agencies, Zoe gave Demi a high-level overview of the FBI's concerns, but Demi's positive demeanor encouraged Zoe to hint that she may be able to provide better information shortly. Demi was more interested than the others and suggested they meet to discuss the situation in more detail and to start building a strong working relationship. Zoe agreed.

***

They met at the popular Dirty Habit on F Street. Demi arrived first, and Zoe was impressed that she was seated in a prime, out of the way corner in the bustling and happening bar. Zoe thought she must have some pull. Demi was Zoe's blonde alter-ego: on the shortish side, athletic, blonde bob cut and blue eyes to Zoe's almost black hair, honey-hued skin, and dark eyes. They both shared the same subdued dark-colored clothing, sensible shoes, bright smiles, and handguns hidden away from view.

They were both serious professionals in roles that could be quite dangerous, but they were also gregarious and approachable. So, it was not surprising that they hit it off almost immediately.

The two law enforcement agents ordered non-alcoholic drinks and began the process of understanding each other's careers and lives: How long with the agencies – four years for Zoe and five for Demi; where they were from – Zoe from Lansing, Michigan, and Demi from Wallingford, Pennsylvania; where they went to school – Michigan State, Criminal Justice and University of New Mexico, Law for Zoe and University of Pennsylvania, Political Science and Columbia, MS in Sociology, for Demi.

Demi was fascinated by Zoe's French-Tunisian heritage and being raised by immigrants. Zoe laughed and explained that her parents were paranoid about obeying the law, so her career choice was pretty predictable. Demi came from a military background – both parents, so her choice was perhaps even more obvious.

Zoe explained her prime objective: trying to prevent Final Notice recipients from gunning people down, especially with an election year looming. Demi knew a little about the VT2 murders but was surprised and concerned about the potential size of the threat.

Time seemed to fly, and Zoe, reminded by a churning stomach, remembered that she'd missed lunch. She suggested they get something to eat, and Demi agreed, putting her hand on Zoe's forearm as she made some menu suggestions. Zoe didn't hear any of Demi's suggestions, as the electricity generated by Demi's touch took her back ten years to the first time.

***

Zoe had just scored two goals in her high school's State Championship match, breaking a tie in the last minute. It was the first time ever that the girls' soccer team had won in her Division, and she was flying high. After their short bus ride back to the school to shower, they were all going to a sleepover at a Southern Colonial mansion with a pool and six bedrooms, rented by the parents of one of their teammates, Annika.

At the school, they showered and celebrated, shouting, screaming, laughing, and even crying. Zoe was enjoying the strong shower spray when Annika said, "Want me to wash your back?"

"Sure." And that was the first time it happened.

Zoe was cute, athletic, and brainy, a combination that challenged a lot of guys. She also had an overly protective father. She wasn't allowed to date until she was sixteen, and even then, she had an earlier than normal curfew. On top of that, anyone wanting to ask her out was required to have an interview with her father before the day of the date. One of the few guys who submitted to the interview told her later that it was more like a series of warnings about what her father would do to him if he tried anything too physical. As a result, Zoe didn't date much; but for some reason, it never bothered her.

At the sleepover, still tingling from Annika's touch on her bare skin, she sat down next to her teammate, who was sipping a glass of wine. Surreptitiously, Annika took hold of Zoe's hand, down near the cushion, unseen from anyone. They talked about nothing and everything, and when most of the others were at the pool or passed out, Annika got up, towing Zoe behind her, and they disappeared into one of the six bedrooms that Annika had claimed as her own.

Door locked, Annika stayed in charge, kissing Zoe as she'd never been kissed before, while the tingling spread throughout her body. This was all new for Zoe, but Annika knew what she was doing, much to her inexperienced partner's delight. Zoe entered that bedroom as a virgin, but by morning, she knew she was gay. She thought of her father's concerns about her and boys and almost laughed, except that she wasn't sure if he'd rather her be the school slut or a lesbian. And she didn't want to find out. So, she stayed in the closet until she felt she could talk with him about it, but he died before that happened.

Once she began her path to law enforcement, she continued to keep her personal life private, enjoying an occasional night or weekend with Annika, who was also attending State.

***

Zoe was rattled by her reaction to Demi's touch, and she looked into Demi's eyes for any signs that the electricity flowed both ways. She had to be careful. Careers were at stake. So, they mostly talked shop, and when they left the Dirty Habit and said their good-byes, Demi took Zoe's hand in a polite shake. Zoe wondered if Demi had held her hand a few seconds longer than "just friends."

***

CHAPTER 4 – ONE DRINK AT A TIME

Quincy, Massachusetts. Alek Belikov sat at the bar in Sully's on Chestnut Street, nursing a glass of vodka. He enjoyed the solitude and space to unwind from the intensity at work and avoid the loneliness at home. He knew that if he drank at home, with a bottle at his disposal, he wouldn't stop until it was empty. Here, at least, he could exercise a bit of control, paying for each round as it was served and knowing that he still needed to drive home.

A slim, intellectual man with chiseled features and a sad look behind wire-rimmed glasses, Alek was employed at VitalTech and was part of the original team that developed the VT2. As a result, he had gotten to know Vijay well, held him in high esteem, and missed their more frequent interactions. He also missed the less formal culture that existed before the sale of the business to a private equity firm. He still enjoyed the mental demands of his job, as they kept his mind away from the grief that now quickly engulfed him when he wasn't working. He was also able to work long hours, helping to keep the demons at bay, but some nights those extra hours led to painful reminders. Tonight had been one of those, which is why he was at Sully's.

A long-time acquaintance and fellow Russian immigrant, Vik Vasin, plopped down on the empty stool next to him. Alek and Vik had lived next door to each other in nearby Allston, as children growing up together. As they progressed through high school, Alek focused on school while Vik hung out with a rougher crowd. During that time, they had grown apart but remained friendly with each other. Alek went off to MIT, and they had lost touch. Then, when Alek got a job at VitalTech in Quincy, they bumped into each other on occasion.

Perched on their barstools, side by side, their physical contrasts were as stark as their educational ones. Alek was of medium height, with a full head of dark hair, while Vik was shorter, much more muscular, with a shaved head.

Vik ordered a vodka for himself and another one for Alek. He felt for Alek. Although Vik wasn't married and didn't have kids, he still recoiled at the thought of losing a wife and child as Alek had. It had happened just over three months ago, and even Vik, who was no stranger to violence, was sincerely compassionate when he spoke with his childhood friend.

"Ya work late tonight?" asked Vik, avoiding the 'how are you doing' question. He knew the answer to that anyway.

"Yeah. I wanted to finish something I was working on. Easier than trying to pick up where I left off tomorrow morning. How you doing?"

"So-so. Win a few, lose a few."

It occurred to Alek that he never really understood what Vik did. "Sorry, but my head hasn't been fully in the game lately. What're you doing these days?"

"Kinda a combination of import-export and financial services."

"Big firm?"

FINAL ACT

"Big enough," Vik replied, somewhat aggressively.

"Hey, sorry. I'm a scientist, so I'm curious," Alek said. His effort to smile was palpable.

Vik tried to roll back his sharp tone, "OK. It's a small company, privately owned. The people we work for like to stay … in the background. No big deal. How're things at the Death Watch company?"

Alek grimaced at the nickname. "OK. We're expanding the watch's capability, so it does more than just tell people when they're going to die … and tell time," smiling more easily this time.

They downed their shots, and Vik ordered another round. Alek asked, for no particular reason, "If you knew you would die in ten days, would you kill someone?"

"Someone? Hell, I'd take out as many as I could before I went or got caught. I'd even take care of that motherfucker in Braintree for ya."

Vik realized that he'd crossed a line, and the conversation died as they both downed their shots.

Alek broke the silence as he waved to the bartender for another round. "I wish I could do it. But I'd be their number one suspect, and then I'd spend the rest of my life in an even worse hell. Plus, he's in jail, and even if I could get in, I'm not sure I could do it. Maybe someone working in the jail will get their Final Notice, and I could bribe them to do it."

Vik laughed. "That would be a cool coincidence. Has that happened? Someone paying a dying guy to bump someone off?"

Alek thought for a moment and replied, "I don't think so, but if they're dying, what would they gain?"

"I dunno. Money for their family, kids ..."

They sat quietly, nursing their shots.

This time, Vik broke the silence, "What if he gets off?"

Alek's assessment of that possibility as less than zero helped him to stay calm as he asked, "What? You kill your wife, someone else's wife, and two kids, and you get off?"

"I'm just sayin' ... a crooked judge, a jury member who don't go along, a hot-shit lawyer who finds that the cops screwed somethin' up. Hey, I've seen some weird things."

Alek was trying to stay controlled. "The only thing keeping me halfway sane is that the motherfucker will go to jail forever, and the inmates won't like that he killed two women and two kids."

Another silence descended before Vik asked, "How many people use the death ... uh, Final Notice ... to bump someone off?"

"More than we'd like. There are millions of gun owners wearing our watches right now, and that was a real concern when we were doing the initial tests with only hundreds of users. But even the FBI said the watch did what a doctor does – gives a prognosis – so it's up to the people what they do with their remaining time."

"That makes sense, even coming from the FBI. I gotta go. I'll take care of these," nodding at the glasses. "Take care of y'self, I'll see ya around."

FINAL ACT

Alek sat there thinking about their conversation, and especially Vik's reaction when Alek asked about his work.

***

Six months earlier, in The Boston Globe:

4 Dead in Tragic Domestic Violence Shooting

Braintree, Massachusetts. A tragic shooting last night destroyed two families in an apparent act of domestic violence that is still being investigated. The information available at press time is that a Braintree resident shot and killed his wife and 12-year-old son in their home after what neighbors described as a horrific shouting and screaming match between the man and his wife. Another woman, who is thought to have been a friend of the deceased, was also killed along with another boy, believed to be her son.

According to a friend of one of the slain boys, the other boy had been visiting his friend and his mother had come to pick him up. The suspect has been arrested and taken into custody.

The following day, the paper carried a story with additional details.

Thomas Sheehan killed his wife, Mary Sheehan, their 12-year old son, Shawn, Mrs. Anna Belikov, and her 12-year-old son, Luka, in a tragic shooting in Braintree. According to neighbors, arguments between the Sheehans were not unusual and were often heated. The altercation last night followed a typical pattern until the four shots were fired. Neighbors added that the police had been to the house many times in the past to quell the rows.

Mrs. Belikov, the wife of Dr. Alek Belikov of Quincy, had just arrived to pick up her son and had tried to calm Mr. Sheehan, even as he brandished a gun. Sheehan responded by killing all four of them.

***

Chestnut Hill, Massachusetts. Vijay had been devastated when he heard the news about Alek's wife and son. Before he and his wife, Jennifer, attended the funerals, Vijay went to see Alek. Having worked closely with him for a long time, he wasn't entirely surprised to find him in control of his emotions. At least, it appeared that way.

The two had met at MIT, and when Vijay started up VitalTech, he offered Alek a position. Vijay had also co-opted Alek onto his current team, developing additional health monitoring capabilities for the VT2. They worked from different locations, but they spoke regularly, and Vijay thought that Alek was doing OK, apart from being sad.

Jennifer knew Alek and his wife, too, and this senseless act of violence powerfully moved her. She and Vijay had initially established a foundation to promote gun safety and responsible gun ownership, but this tragedy was the catalyst that moved Jennifer to realize that their foundation had too narrow a focus. Vijay agreed, and Jennifer threw herself into working with local and national groups addressing domestic violence as well as gun safety groups.

***

CHAPTER 5 - SQUEEZE PLAY

Washington, D.C. It was late Friday afternoon, and Zoe got a text from Demi. "Having a few friends over this evening at 8. Hope u can make it. 900 7th St SW #14. D"

Zoe read it over and over again, looking for anything that would give her a signal. So, at 8:15, fashionably late or on-time, she arrived. The building was new and impressive, and she rang the bell at apartment 14. Demi opened the door and invited Zoe into a very spacious and tastefully furnished living room. She wondered how she could ever reciprocate, given her own very small and spartanly furnished flat.

She looked around to take it all in, and Demi awkwardly explained that her friends canceled last minute, but that she was looking forward to getting to know Zoe better. Zoe preferred to think that her friends hadn't been invited, but she feigned disappointment at not meeting them.

They sat on the couch, glasses of wine in their hands, and continued where they left off at the Dirty Habit. As the wine flowed, Demi wanted to hear more about Zoe's VT2 project. That was solid ground for Zoe, especially as Demi was also in Federal law enforcement and understood the business.

Demi expressed surprise that VitalTech was supplying information about the VT2 users. "Did you get a warrant to pry that from them?"

Zoe explained Vijay's remorse that his invention was causing people to kill, to which Demi replied, "Most companies would do their own killing for profits. Hell, some of the pharma and agri-chem businesses are already doing it."

Demi was moved by Vijay's integrity when Zoe added that he was in the process of supplying even more data. To Demi's question of what kind of data, Zoe held back and said, "That's all I know. He's still working on it." And then she let out a big sigh, explaining and exposing her frustration at not being able to get ahead of the killers, especially with the escalated threats. Demi took her hand in sympathy.

Zoe's internal monitoring system kicked back in with the physical contact, but she wasn't sure if it meant anything, so she asked, "Are you seeing anyone?" and held her breath.

Demi casually replied, "Nothing serious. How about you?"

As Zoe replied, "No," her desire, emotions, and possibly the wine, autonomously squeezed Demi's hand and softly pulled her closer.

They leaned in, and their lips met softly at first; and when they finally disengaged, a good while later, they were out of breath and laughing hysterically ... out of joy, happiness, and because they had both been playing a not-so-subtle game of 'Are you, or aren't you?'

***

Zoe woke the next morning with a smile on her face and reached out for Demi, but found only sheets and a pillow. She checked her watch and was shocked that it was after 9:00 a.m. She realized it was Saturday, but her phone pinged 24/7. Where was it? She put on her shirt and walked out to the living room, which was flooded with morning sunlight pouring through the floor-to-ceiling windows, causing her to squint. Her olfactory senses finally came to life as she smelled coffee and something else good.

She rounded the corner to the kitchen area, and there was Demi, preparing an omelet alongside a plate of croissants and cantaloupe. Zoe thought she might be dreaming. Demi looked up and with a big smile said, "Well, good morning, sleepy head. So, I guess all the talk about the lazy FBI is true!"

"I can't believe I slept this late! My phone usually gets me up."

"It got me up, so I brought it out with me so you could sleep."

If there were any important calls, they were destined to wait. Breakfast and then some more bedtime came first.

***

Quincy, Massachusetts. Two days after running into Vik at Sully's, Alek came home to his empty house, and just like every night for the past three months, 'empty' carried a huge emotional weight that he was barely able to lift. He knew he had to move, and move on, but just the thought of even going into Luka's room was more than he could bear. It was hard enough to have Anna's things in what was now his bedroom.

Among the day's mail was an envelope that looked different than the annoying advertising that seemed to be all he received anymore. It was from a law office in Boston, and inside was a check, payable to Alek Belikov for one hundred thousand dollars. The check stub details included:
Insured: Anna Belikov
Beneficiary: Alek Belikov
Amount: $100,000.00

Alek was puzzled. He didn't have a policy for his wife's death, and he couldn't figure out how she would have one either without him knowing about it. There was no phone number on the check, and it was late, but he'd call tomorrow to find out what it was all about.

***

As soon as Alek reached his office, he looked up and called the number of the law firm that had sent the check. He was quickly put through to Peter Annikov, the attorney in charge of insurance and wills. Mr. Annikov was immediately familiar with the situation, offered condolences, and explained that Anna's job as a teacher carried with it a basic life insurance policy. He assured Alek that the claim had been validated and approved.

Alek thought that maybe this was a sign that it's time to sell the house and move on, at least a little. The money would allow him to make a down payment on a condo without having to rush with the dreaded clean-up job at home.

He stopped by his bank to deposit the check, had a regular 9-5 day at work, and then met a real estate agent to look at a few condos. Alek was highly motivated to move, so after seeing the second condo, he asked the agent to make an offer. It was in a new building and wouldn't be ready for a few months. That was fine with him, and he told the agent that he would make a $100,000 down payment if his offer was accepted. He stopped at a diner for dinner, and even before he'd finished his dessert, the agent called with news that his offer had been accepted. Alek returned home, went to bed, and had the best night's sleep he'd had in months.

***

He was awakened from his sleep by the sound of his doorbell and urgent banging on the front door. He pulled on a robe and still half asleep, carefully descended the stairs. He opened the door to see two men in suits holding up badges, demanding to know if he was Alek Belikov. Right then, it was possibly the only question he could have answered, and he let them in. What came next shocked him into a full, wide awake mode.

Thomas Sheehan had been found dead in his cell.

The detectives asked the usual questions repeatedly, but in different ways, testing him for consistency. Where was he yesterday, last night? Did he know anything about it? What kind of scientist was he? Did he know anyone who'd want to harm Sheehan? Alek thought that was a stupid question as they must know he would. Only after the police finished with their rapid-fire questions was Alek able to ask one of his own.

"How did he die?"

The detectives were vague but stated that it appeared he was poisoned. He asked if they knew who had done it, but then quickly realized that they thought *that* was a stupid question. That's why they were questioning him.

The men gave him their cards and told him to call if he thought of anything that might help. They also told him not to leave the State.

Alek showered, dressed, and went to work, although he spent most of his day thinking about Sheehan – happy he was dead and that Vik's examples of how he might have gotten off were laid to rest. On the other hand, he felt cheated out of seeing him found guilty, even though capital punishment was not an option in Massachusetts.

He wound up working late so he could accomplish something before making his way over to Sully's to self-medicate, his mood a whole lot different than the previous night's.

Vik Vasin was at the bar, and Alek pulled up a stool alongside him. Vik greeted him, ordered a round, and asked, "Did you hear 'bout Sheehan? It was just on the news," pointing up at the TV on the wall. "Didn't say how it happened, just that it's under investigation."

Alek thought that perhaps coming to Sully's wasn't such a good idea. "Yeah, I heard."

Vik looked at him seriously, "You didn't do it, did ya?"

Alek blurted out, "No. Of course not!"

Vik laughed, "Just joking. But that should take a load off your mind."

"I guess. Would've liked to see him take a beating in court and put away for life."

"Yeah, but like I said the other night, there are no guarantees. Now it's done. Did the cops talk to you?"

Alek expressed surprise, "How did you know that?"

"Just guessing. You'd have to be pretty high on their list." Vik waved for another round.

"Yeah. They knew I'm a scientist and wondered what kind. The cops think he was poisoned."

"That so?" And then he turned and looked Alek straight in the eyes and said, "Well, it seems like someone did you a favor."

Alek shivered and knew he had just received a message, but he wasn't sure what it was. He reached into his pocket to pay and leave, but Vik put his hand firmly on Alek's shoulder and said, "Don't go. I wanna ask you somethin'," as he waved for another round.

Alek repositioned himself on the stool, creating a little more distance between the two of them.

"OK."

"The other night we was talking about the 'Notice' guys. You know, the ones that the watch tells them they're gonna die."

Alek nodded and mumbled, "Yeah."

Vik turned to look directly at Alek again and asked, "How hard would it be to get the names of some people who get the notice?"

Alek was taken aback by the question. "You mean for anyone to get it? That's very private and sensitive information. People wouldn't like to have that made public."

"But you could get it?"

"Well, sure. But why would anyone want information like that?"

"Maybe so they could help, you know, wit' hospital costs, house payments, kids ..."

Alek was both on high alert and moved by the notion that someone would do that. "Who would do that?"

Vik returned to his full-on direct eye-to-eye position. "Ya'd be surprised, but I know a guy that has made so much money that he wants to, how you say it ... 'give back' ... to people not so lucky as him. Could you help him do that, as ... a ... favor?" Alek squirmed on his stool and tried to look away from Vik's stare as he stammered, "I couldn't just do it on my own. I'd have to get an OK from someone."

Vik demanded, "Who?"

Alek scrambled around in his mind, questioning whether he would actually go to anyone with this request and, if so, who? Vik's direct and increasingly menacing stare didn't help, and he blurted out, "Vijay Patel."

"Who's that? You have to ask an Indian guy?"

Alek explained that Vijay was the inventor of the watch.

"OK. Ask the Indian and let me know." He handed Alek a napkin with a phone number written on it, adding, "Soon." Vik descended from his stool without another word and left.

***

Alek woke up the next morning and wished he hadn't. Although he'd decided, last night, to lie to Vik, the intensity of Vik's stare was etched firmly in his mind. On the other hand, he knew the answer would be "No," regardless of whom he asked or if he asked. He'd never do something like this on his own. So, he waited until mid-morning and called the number on the napkin.

Vik answered, at least he assumed it was Vik, "Yeah."

Alek had rehearsed what he would say. "I spoke with Vijay, and he said, 'No.' He felt that it was an invasion of privacy and would hurt sales." He started to apologize, but the dial tone told him how well Vik had received the news.

Alek thought about possible consequences coming from his refusal to help Vik. He thought about the hundred thousand dollars, and he was pretty sure Vik was involved, or maybe that guy who wanted to 'give back.' He'd used it to make a down payment on the condo, but he thought he could get it back. Could it be from an insurance policy? He tried to call the lawyer, Annikov, but when he did, he was told that Annikov didn't work there any longer and that they hadn't hired his replacement yet. Nobody else knew anything about it.

He decided that the condo was a huge opportunity for him to begin the process of moving on, and he reasoned that if anything ever happened to the insurance money, he could use the proceeds from the sale of his house to cover the loss.

He also decided to give Sully's a permanent miss. All in all, he felt OK — which, for Alek, translated to pretty good. He hadn't done anything wrong, and he was finally ready for the next chapter of his life.

***

CHAPTER 6 – JENNIFER

Chestnut Hill, Massachusetts. Marriage, motherhood, and money made for a very satisfying life, although to be fair, Jennifer could have done with a lot less of the latter if she had to. Still, it did make life a lot easier. Unlimited nanny services for Karima, decorating and furnishing their new home, and helping to support various local and national progressive organizations were all products of the significant money that Vijay had made with his sale of VitalTech.

The young couple loved their beautiful home in Chestnut Hill, outside of Boston. The custom, red brick, colonial-style house had been remodeled to provide lots of natural light, spacious rooms, a Japanese-style spa, which included a large soaking tub, and shoji screens separating a meditation/exercise room. But their favorite place was a real chef's kitchen, where Vijay and Jennifer took turns as head chef and sous chef – Vijay specializing in Indian cuisine while Jennifer cooked up everything else – typically adding a healthy Californian touch. They had made a number of friends and enjoyed entertaining in their sunny formal dining room or on the large deck beyond the French doors, dining alfresco, as often as the weather permitted.

Their daughter, Karima, had come into their lives almost two years ago. She represented pure joy for both of them, despite the sleep deprivation and dirty diaper duty that came with the package. Karima had Vijay's jet-black hair, light honey-toned skin, and Jennifer's grey eyes, due, no doubt, to some hushed-up British ancestry in Vijay's family in the distant past.

As important as all of that was, what she cherished most was her relationship with Vijay.

For most of her life – until she met this brilliant, exotic man – she felt perceived as the 'pretty blond,' and treated like a brainless 'Barbie Doll.' It didn't matter that she excelled in school. Most of the boys couldn't get past her beauty. And if they did, her brains intimidated them.

Even more painful, many of the other girls were jealous and aloof. Her response had been to turn inward and push herself even harder academically. But this only served to make her appear to be a snob. So, often alone and filled with conflicting emotions, she took comfort in the solitary sport of running and became an exceptional distance runner at Stanford.

After graduation, she continued to run marathons and other distance races. That was how she met Vijay and somehow, despite their diverse backgrounds – or maybe because of the differences – he really 'got' her. He knew she was intelligent as well as pragmatic. He knew she was compassionate, despite her privileged upbringing. He loved her wry sense of humor and independent view of the world. And he loved how she loved him and how they just … fit.

It all seemed idyllic to most outsiders, but Jennifer and Vijay both "pushed the envelope" insofar as their interests and activities were concerned, causing both of them to continually question and re-evaluate their priorities. Neither one of them could get enough time with Karima, and Jennifer could not get enough time with Vijay, either. As with many geniuses, Vijay was laser-focused and driven. He spent long hours working on ways to mitigate the Final Notice recipient murders – in his home office, at the VitalTech offices, and recently, in D.C., to consult with Zoe Brouet. He was also VitalTech's representative to the FDA and Department of Health and Human Services.

For her part, Jennifer worked tirelessly, putting in as much time as she could and funding many local initiatives with organizations such as REACH, The Brady Campaign, EveryTown for Gun Safety, Newtown Action Alliance, and Moms Demand Action. She even served as a type of loan officer, assisting women to become more economically independent through micro-loans that she and Vijay funded.

As if all of those activities couldn't keep them busy enough, their workout schedules, alone, were enough to exhaust most people. Vijay was up before the light of day and covered ten to fifteen miles in an hour to an hour and a half. He also worked out three to four days a week on his home gym machines. Jennifer covered the same distance in almost the same time after the nanny arrived, had three advanced MMA (mixed martial arts) sessions a week, and an occasional shooting range session and discussion group with the Boston Police.

The shooting range activity began with her outreach to the police concerning guns and domestic violence. A lieutenant on the force asked her if she'd ever shot a gun. She hadn't and expressed an interest in knowing more about guns and the fascination that so many people seemed to have with them. She was invited to a target practice session, and from that, informal discussion groups evolved, with the various participating officers at the practice sessions. Jennifer learned a lot about guns and also heard a lot of stories from the officers, who had collectively seen more than anyone should.

Vijay had gone to D.C. earlier in the day, planning to return the following afternoon. The nanny had left, and Jennifer had fed, bathed, and put Karima to bed, hopefully for the night. Sleeping through the night had become a more and more common occurrence, and she and Vijay were happily getting used to it. She sat down at her computer in the office she shared with Vijay, to deal with new mail while she munched on yesterday's leftover tandoori chicken and vegetables, compliments of Vijay. A glass of California chardonnay rounded out one of her favorite meals.

The doorbell chimed, and as she made her way toward the front door – still preoccupied with her emails – she realized that the house had become fairly dark in the late autumn evening, so she switched on some lights along the way. The slight delay made the caller impatient, and the doorbell chimed again, causing her to open the door hurriedly. The caller was a well-dressed man in his late twenties-early thirties wearing a suit, white shirt, and tie.

He spoke first. "Good evening, Mrs. Patel?"

Immediately after Jennifer replied, "yes," he surprised her by aggressively stepping toward her, causing her to step back into the house. At the same time, he produced a gun and coldly, almost robotically, stated, "Keep your mouth shut and don't make me use this." He thrust the gun towards her making her step back further into the house, and he shut and locked the door.

His next words were even more chilling, "I will follow you to your bedroom."

They ascended the stairs as Jennifer led him to her and Vijay's bedroom. He told her to sit on the bed and remove her clothes. Jennifer's mind raced with thoughts about what she could do, but with a gun pointed at her and Karima just next door, her first goal was to stay alive. She removed her pullover and slowly unbuttoned her blouse. Her slow-motion routine drew a "hurry up" from the looming figure standing before her, whose eyes never wavered.

Blouse off, she hesitated, but that just earned a jerking of his weapon as he growled, "Everything."

She continued removing her clothes and now, completely naked, with fear rising fast, her tormentor, sweating and with a strained voice, told her to lie back. Jennifer noticed a telltale bulge in his trousers. She processed this, and her state of anxiety rose a couple more notches. As she followed his command, he took a step closer. With his dark robotic voice, although now a bit more constricted, he said, "You tell your husband that we want Final Notice names or next time, this won't just be a strip show."

Jennifer was a Stanford grad with a Harvard MBA, but she wasn't just book smart. Despite the horrific position she had found herself in, she had been continually assessing and processing all aspects of her situation: the gunman's motives (which were now more clear) ... the type of weapon and whether or not the safety was on (She knew from her police shooting range experience that it was a Ruger LCR 357, a deadly weapon that did not have a safety switch.) ... and most importantly, the safety of Karima, and whether there was anything she could do to neutralize the intruder.

Suddenly, Karima cried out from her room, adjacent to where Jennifer was lying, naked on her back, feet almost touching the floor, with a gun pointed at her less than three feet away. The gunman instinctively turned toward the sound, and as he did so, the gun muzzle moved slightly away from Jennifer. That gave her an opening, and she was ready. She brought her right leg up, as she had been trained to do in MMA and landed a powerful and perfectly aimed strike to the bulging crotch of the gunman, who doubled over in pain. Instantly, Jennifer was on her feet and slammed the guy's face down onto her rising knee. The man and the weapon crashed to the floor. She grabbed the gun, took a few steps to her chest of drawers, and traded the gun for two pairs of pantyhose.

She used the pantyhose to tie the gunman's wrists behind him, and then his ankles, with knots she'd long since forgotten about from her Girl Scout days. She then quickly re-dressed as she called 911, only a little bit concerned that the beige carpeting would probably have to be replaced because the gunman's flattened nose was bleeding profusely. Then she retrieved the gun, checked in on Karima, who remained sound asleep, and went downstairs to wait for the police.

The police arrived, got a full report from Jennifer, and half-dragged the still mostly unconscious gunman down the stairs and into their car. She was pretty sure there was a look of admiration on the face of one of the officers as she described the scene when she took the guy down, but maybe he was just picturing the scene a little too vividly. The police asked about the 'Final Notice' comment, which she briefly explained, although she didn't understand the context of the demand.

Jennifer poured herself another glass of wine and called Vijay. Hearing about her ordeal, he wanted to come back immediately, but she reassured him that a police car was parked outside and would remain until the next morning. Vijay was also puzzled by the gunman's demand, but for the moment, the fact that his wife and daughter were OK was enough. He was immensely proud of Jennifer's bravery and skills, but he did ask her to promise him that she wouldn't open the door without checking first. She readily promised, upset with herself for her carelessness; then, she finished her wine, put on her pajamas, and went to sleep. Karima even cooperated and slept through until morning.

***

Vijay arrived home just before noon. He hadn't been able to sleep well that night following Jennifer's phone call, which was both extremely worrying and puzzling. *What did the guy with the gun mean by "Final Notice names?" On a simplistic level, it could mean the names of people who have received their 'Final Notice.' But why would they want those names, and why was it so important that a brutal threat was made?*

He and Jennifer discussed the situation, but for him, the first order of business was to have a sophisticated alarm system installed. Jennifer agreed, primarily for the safety of Karima.

Vijay got the number of the police from the card they had left and called. He was transferred to the detective handling the case, who told him that the guy they were holding was a small-time crook, who had been arrested a few times for theft and battery charges, both in New York and Boston. The police were pretty confident that he was acting for someone else, but so far, all they knew was that he'd been instructed by someone to intimidate Vijay's wife and issue the threat. He had no idea what it meant, and the detective asked Vijay if he knew any more about the context of the 'Final Notice' mention. Vijay explained that he was puzzled as well.

The detective continued, saying that a lawyer had not appeared to defend the attacker, which meant that he probably had little or no connection to a larger organization, or that they wanted to keep well below the radar. At some point, a public defender would be appointed, and then they might have more leverage to negotiate, in exchange for more information.

Vijay thanked him, but before they hung up, the detective laughed and said, "By the way, your wife really did a number on his nose." And then, still chuckling, "We'll let you know if we learn any more, and if you figure it out, please let me know."

***

CHAPTER 7 – THE ACCENT

Quincy, Massachusetts. Alek buried himself in his work and knew that this would be one of his late days, capped off with vodka, but not at Sully's. He did not want to run into Vik.

Early in the evening, the security guard came to Alek's workstation desk and told him that there were two FBI agents out front who wanted to see him. Alek froze for a moment, took a deep breath, and said, "OK, send them back."

The two men, one in his thirties and the other younger, perhaps mid-twenties, came in and showed their badges and a search warrant. They explained that they were investigating the Thomas Sheehan murder and had some questions. The older one said that they would need to check his computer or, if they had to, take it away for a detailed examination. He suggested that to make things easier and faster, his colleague could check the computer while he asked some questions. He also asked if Alek was currently logged in. Alek explained that he was automatically logged out within sixty seconds if he was not interacting with the machine, so, "No."

The agent explained that to ensure Alek didn't carry out any actions to delete data, he wanted Alek to give his colleague his password, let him sign in with it to search for various items like e-mails and financial transactions and then, assuming they didn't find anything incriminating, sign out. Alek could then reset his password in private.

Alek was uncomfortable with that, and although he understood the logic, he balked at the suggestion. The agent then discarded his friendly nature and flatly announced, "We are investigating the murder of the man who killed your wife and son. You have just deposited a check for a hundred thousand dollars, and last night the wife of an associate of yours was threatened at gunpoint. You will either answer my questions and allow my colleague to access your computer, or both you and your machine will come with us."

Alek was rocked back by the change in demeanor, the mention of the check, and a threat to a colleague. "Who was threatened?"

"We are not at liberty to reveal that. Do we do this here or at our office?"

Alek felt guilty, although he didn't know why, and he decided to please them, "OK, here is my password."

The younger agent went to work clicking away while the other one began his questions. He started with questions similar to those the police asked the other morning. No, he didn't poison Sheehan or have someone else do it. He didn't know anything about it other than what he had read or seen on TV.

"What about the hundred-thousand-dollar deposit?"

Alek explained about receiving the check and calling the lawyer. The agent asked him for the lawyer's name, and number and Alek looked at his cell phone for the number of Mr. Annikov and read it off.

Finally, the agent asked Alek if he knew why anyone would threaten a VitalTech employee. Alek squirmed in his seat, and it seemed like the oxygen had left the room. He asked for more details, and when the agent refused to provide any, Alek told him that he didn't know.

The younger agent pushed away from the computer and announced that it was clean and that he hadn't found anything. They asked Alek to sign in and reset his password to confirm there was no problem with the machine. He did, and there wasn't.

The older agent announced they were finished for the time being and thanked him for his cooperation. After they left, Alek did some random searches and operations with his computer, but it seemed fine. What he really wanted to know was, *Who was threatened? Could Vik be involved? How could he find out without someone knowing that he knew something? But there was something else. Did the agent checking his computer say, "There vus nothing?"* And then he realized that they didn't leave their cards or ask him to call them if he had further information, things that the other police did. They had put him on the defensive, and he became compliant.

He went to the lobby and asked the guard if the police or FBI had been out to the VitalTech offices today or yesterday to see anyone else? The guard hadn't heard of anything. Alek asked if the agents had shown him their IDs, and the guard said they had and that he'd gotten a good look at the older guy's but not as good a look at the other's – "the younger one with the accent." When Alek asked about the accent, the guard said that he'd heard them talking when he went back to let them in, but he hadn't thought anything of it.

***

Chestnut Hill, Massachusetts. That same evening, Vijay was alone in his office, mulling over the attack and the message. He felt that an alarm system would help keep Jennifer and Karima safe, but he didn't understand how the aggressive attack on Jennifer related to VitalTech and the Final Notice names? *What was the link? Unless the police could get the attacker to talk, it would remain a mystery. Should he ask Mike Kalin?*

Following the IPO and sale to the private equity firm of Konig, Konig & Litt (KKL), Vijay was given a seat on the VitalTech Board and a new CEO, Mike Kalin, was appointed. Initially, Vijay had been impressed with him. Kalin was self-deprecating and passed along any credit for his accomplishments to his great teams. He wanted to play down the announcement of his appointment and keep it minimal. No lengthy articles, pictures, etc. He felt that VitalTech was doing so well that any news of a changing of the guard could only hurt. Everyone seemed happy, except Jennifer. She didn't like him at all, although she couldn't explain why, just that It was "something about him."

It had all started well, but then stories began to surface about Kalin's management style and personal stability, particularly regarding sexual harassment and business ethics. Several of Vijay's original team began to leave, and as the stories mounted and defections continued, Vijay became concerned. In his straightforward, sometimes unfiltered way, he raised the problem at a Board meeting and asked Kalin, point blank, to comment on the accusations. Kalin tried to gloss over them and called them empty and false, but to Vijay, this was personal, so he persisted, demanding better explanations. That's when Vijay realized that many on the Board wanted to turn a blind eye. Business was good, don't rock the boat. Even J. Edward Konig, the Chairman of both KKL and VitalTech, tried to steer Vijay to calmer waters.

FINAL ACT

Vijay had backed down, but his concerns were even greater and real, for now, he knew that he'd made a powerful enemy. After the meeting, Kalin had called Vijay and threatened to remove him from the Board if he ever tried to make a move on him again. Vijay held back his anger and told him that he would not bring up the matter again without concrete facts. Kalin wasn't placated and sneeringly told Vijay that he was looking to move the VT2 production from India to China. Vijay started to erupt, but held back and asked Kalin why?

Kalin taunted him, "Are you concerned about your little brother losing his cushy job?"

Vijay's brother, Sanjay, was the Production Manager at the Pune factory in India, and Vijay knew that Sanjay had done a super job setting up, ramping up and managing the VT2 production line. Wade Thomas, VitalTech's COO, had nothing but praise for Sanjay and the Indian operation, but Wade, too, was being replaced. The Indian production unit had achieved, and in some cases exceeded, their output, quality, and cost goals. Vijay understood that the real reason for Kalin's threat was personal.

Vijay kept his cool and replied, "You can look into whatever you want, Kalin, but I've invested too much into this to let someone tear it down for spite. See you at the Board table."

In addition to his Board position, Vijay had another reason to fear Kalin. Vijay, along with his small team of scientists, continued to push the capabilities of the VT2 to provide additional health benefits. They couldn't afford not to. Apple had picked up the scent of the potential market and was adding health capabilities to its watch. His team's efforts had been rewarded with significant advances, including a diabetes monitoring feature, advanced blood analysis for recovering cancer patients, and arrhythmia detection. These were laudable accomplishments, but of lesser importance to Vijay. He managed the team, setting its direction and goals, to develop new healthcare capabilities, but he alone was working on a single, "off the books" issue: finding a consistently accurate set of markers that would identify, in advance, those Final Notice recipients who were emotionally pre-disposed to kill before they died.

So far, each ray of hope had been dashed when anomalies appeared, and as scientists, they hated anomalies. For example, the data and readings from one incident puzzled Vijay and the team – Senator John McAdam. He had killed three fellow senators without displaying what was emerging as a signature combination of cortisol-serotonin imbalances. McAdam's VT2 data was so diametrically opposite to that of a killer that Vijay and his colleagues questioned the evidence related to the murders.

Still, Vijay was convinced that he would find a reliable set of markers. He was less confident, however, that the patterns would be detectable early enough to help the FBI stop crimes. To succeed, he needed time, and he needed access to VitalTech's data.

Zoe Brouet had shared with him the highlights of a meeting with her boss and his serious concerns about more high-profile murders by Final Notice recipients. She had also asked him about getting employer information for VT2 users. VitalTech had that information from most of their users, and Vijay understood that those details could be useful to the FBI, but he was hesitant to expand the report right now.

When VitalTech originally agreed to offer the FBI information about users who had access to guns, Vijay owned the business. Now that VitalTech was owned by KKL, and given his less than rosy relationship with Kalin, he was pretty sure that if he asked Kalin, the answer would be, "No." Even worse, if he asked and Kalin didn't know about the cooperation, Kalin might pull the plug on the FBI information entirely. *Could J. Edward help?* Vijay didn't think that he would say "Yes" without running it by Kalin, and as he'd witnessed at the Board meetings, Kalin was golden.

Vijay said to himself, *"Just a few more days,"* as he looked at his own VT2 and was pleased that his pulse rate was normal.

After Kalin's threat about moving the VT2 production out of India, Vijay called his brother Sanjay. He was undecided about sharing the potentially bad news, but Kalin's mention of his brother made Vijay realize that it had been a while since they had spoken. And that fed his guilt. Despite his generosity – he had purchased houses for his parents and his brother, allowing them to move from their slum community – when Vijay compared his lifestyle to theirs, it made him feel awful. The reality was that it was not a fair comparison. Their lives were simpler but, at least, as fulfilling. Intellectually, Vijay knew that, but it didn't help assuage his guilt.

Sanjay updated Vijay on their mother and father. They were in good health and were happy enough. He related that now that their father had retired, he visited the bank every day, to check on Sanjay's account. "It makes him happy, and it gives him a sense of purpose, I guess."

That was a gut-punch to Vijay, but he forced a laugh and asked, "Fathers are still doing that in India? I'm glad he can't see my bank account, although I could always tell him it was in rupees."

That got a laugh from Sanjay, and Vijay decided to keep the Kalin threat to himself.

They chatted a bit more, and Sanjay told him that he was seeing a girl, but it was still early days. Vijay was happy for him and kidded, asking if he needed any advice from his big brother. After the call, Vijay was overcome with conflicted emotions. While it had been good to talk with Sanjay, Vijay was now under even more pressure to avoid ruffling Kalin's feathers.

He began to think about the upcoming trip that he and Jennifer had agreed upon, following her recent ordeal. They would all go to California to visit Jennifer's parents in Mountain View, and Vijay would make a detour while they were there. That was something he'd wanted to do for a long time, and it boosted his mood considerably.

***

CHAPTER 8 – LONDON, KENTUCKY

Lexington, Kentucky. Marianne Abbott had felt strangely calm as she drove south on I-75 from Lexington. She'd flown into Blue Grass Airport the day before, rented a car, and did her required shopping. Then she booked into a local hotel, had a bite to eat in the restaurant, and retired to her room for an early night, partly because she was tired but also because she wanted to be on the road very early.

Before going to bed, however, Marianne prepared the items she'd purchased, carefully loading one of the three ten round magazines with the 9mm rounds. She didn't think she'd need the other two magazines that came with the gun. She briefly thought about how easy it was to buy a lethal weapon as she snapped the magazine into the cold, black Glock 19, and reviewed the instruction leaflet. Then again, this was Kentucky.

At 4:00 a.m., her bedside alarm rang, so she quickly showered, made herself a cup of coffee for the road, and took her purse and small overnight bag to the car. The drive to London, Kentucky, would take her an hour and twenty minutes, and during the trip, all she could think about was her mission.

It had been twenty-four years since Marianne and her mother had escaped from London, leaving behind her father and older brother, to go into hiding where her father couldn't find them again. They had escaped once before, but within a week, her father and brother had tracked them down and dragged them home. Her father beat her mother until she was close to death while her brother held Marianne down by sitting on her, grinding himself sensually into her butt as she helplessly writhed in horror as her mother was beaten.

Afterward, her father locked her mother in the bedroom, and he and her brother took Marianne to the motel to earn their beer money, just as they'd been doing since she was twelve. There was a week's backlog of clients, so Marianne's night of horror was even worse than usual. Her brother made it even more disgusting by capping off the night with his aggressive, cruel style of brutalizing sex.

A few months later, she and her mom snuck out again, and, with the help of a friend, they flew out of Lexington to Chicago, where they stayed with her friend's parents. That was a long time ago, but Marianne would never forget the terror, pain, and shame of London.

When her mom passed away a few years ago, Marianne lost the only person who knew the terrible story that haunted them both.

She left I-75 and continued south, down London's Main Street with all the familiar fast-food outlets. London hadn't changed much – high crime rate, school drop-out rate, and unemployment. It was still early, and there were few cars on the road. The town was as lifeless as Marianne hoped the remainder of her family would soon be, and she was counting on the early hour to ensure that her brother and father would still be sleeping when she arrived.

She turned onto Old Whitley Road and then into the trailer park. Her mom's friend, who had helped them escape twenty-four years ago, had stayed in touch and told Marianne where her father and brother were living. She spotted the lot number and pulled in next to a battered old pickup. She took the Glock from her purse, and as the leaflet explained, she 'racked-the-slide,' which chambered the first round. Gun in hand, she banged on the flimsy door. Her bleary-eyed brother opened it with one hand while he rubbed his eyes with the other. Now with both eyes very widely open, he was staring at the barrel of Marianne's gun.

Marianne motioned and said, "Inside," as her brother backed into the trailer. It was fairly dark inside, so she ordered her brother to turn on a light. The trailer looked as she'd imagined it – filthy and cluttered, the kitchen area overflowing with beer cans, partially empty snack bags, pornographic magazines, cups and ashtrays filled with cigarette butts, and other debris. But it was the stench that overwhelmed her ... stale beer, filthy clothes, and cigarette smoke embedded in any absorbable material available. Her nose immediately stuffed up to protect her, and her eyes watered against the onslaught of foul odors. She could see that her brother had been sleeping on the couch. Beyond the closed door at the back must be a small bedroom ... and her main objective.

Her brother was now more awake, with his eyes focused on the gun. "Call your dad out here," Marianne ordered.

Her brother took a few steps, banged on the closed door, and shouted, "Pa, come out here ... now!"

Slowly the door opened, and her grizzled father came out in his underwear, rubbing his eyes, much the same as his son. As he focused his vision, however, he jolted to a wide-awake state of fear very quickly, "Shit, it's Marianne."
Her brother's eyes slowly shifted up from the gun and looked at Marianne, any color from the warmth of his bed draining from his face.

Marianne's father tried to establish some authority and regain his composure by sneering, "What the fuck do you want?"

Marianne replied, "To paraphrase Johnny Cash, just to watch you die," as she quickly squeezed off two shots, hitting them both in the stomach. The two bodies thumped to the floor, bleeding profusely, mouths agape with pain, and disbelief. Marianne watched for a few seconds, long enough to look each of them in the eye. Then she put an extra round into each of their heads.

Desperate for fresh air, she left the trailer and went to her car. The trailer park was still quiet and dark. *Perhaps gunshots were pretty normal around here*, she thought.

She retraced her route back through town to the I-75, stopping at a mailbox to deposit her gun. During her drive to Blue Grass Airport, for her return flight to Chicago, she dredged up her memories from the past; going back to that day, her father announced he was taking her to the park.

She was twelve years old, and she was thrilled that her father even took notice of her. They stopped at a motel, and her father asked her to come with him as he needed to see someone for just a minute. Inside the dingy motel room, the 'someone' was the first of possibly hundreds of tricks she would be forced into before escaping. That first time her father held her down, slapping her face until she lay there quietly, sobbing, as one after another beer-breathed men were let in by her father, as he clutched their money in his hand.

And it didn't stop there. Once, instead of another older man, it was her brother who joined in, and after that, she was fair game for him, any time, any place, if her mother wasn't around. When Marianne told her mother about her day 'at the park' with her father, her mother angrily accosted him, only to be brutally beaten, with threats of even worse if she or Marianne ever told anyone.

Marianne tried to remember everything from those years in hell, driving carefully while wiping away her tears, in the hope that the fears, thoughts and even the double execution she had just carried out, could be wiped away as well. As she waited for her flight, she glanced at her watch, and with sad recognition, she knew that this was one thing that wouldn't go away – alternating with the time on her watch was the message, "This is your FINAL NOTICE." Marianne had removed the source of her personal hell, but she had less than a week to live.

Her crime, if you could call it that, might have gone undiscovered had it not been for the Final Notice recipient list that Vijay was sending Zoe. Marianne's gun was discovered in a mailbox and given to the London Police. It was traced to the store where she had bought it, using her father's address. There was no urgency, and so, a week later, when an officer went to the trailer park, he found the two very dead bodies, who had been killed with the gun the officer had with him.

When the London Police reported the crime so that Marianne Abbott could be contacted, the FBI found her name on the Final Notice list. Her flights to and from Lexington and the rental car details confirmed her as the prime suspect, but by that time, just as her VT2 had predicted, Marianne had passed away. Before dying, however, she wrote a long and detailed letter to her mother's friend, thanking her for her help, both recently and twenty-four years ago. Marianne provided details of the motel and her father's operation and asked her friend to share it with the police. She had ensured that her father and brother would not be able to harm anyone, ever again, but sadly, she also knew that she wasn't the only girl in the world to go through that particular hell on earth.

***

Chestnut Hill, Massachusetts. Although it seemed apparent that Marianne had killed the two Abbotts, Zoe sent a note to Vijay to see if there was anything else that he could see that might lend more credibility. What he saw did indeed indicate, by her emotional stages, that she could be capable of murder. But there was one other piece of information that Vijay possessed that assured him of her guilt.

He was excited by the similarities to Mildred Pierce's behavior. Both had gone through the same range of emotions, but while Pierce's emotions were confined to minutes, Abbott's took place over many days. The difference in elapsed time was probably caused by geographic realities, as Vijay could see by the GPS tracking of the VT2. Marianne's VT2 had been tracked from her home in Chicago to the trailer in London, and then back again. Mildred Pierce had experienced all of her emotional changes within a single mile.

The GPS functionality proved that Marianne had been at the crime scene. It also made Vijay realize the full power of a system that could detect emotions as well as pinpoint where the person was. At least, in theory, law enforcement could have known about Marianne's potential to kill, and they could have intercepted her at any point along the way from Chicago to London.

***

CHAPTER 9 – MEET MILES

Pasadena, California. There was one particular anomaly that Vijay couldn't let go of, and that was a VT2 user in the earlier beta test who received his Final Notice but survived. The VT2 team had learned that the user had contracted rabies, but the disease seemed to reverse itself, and the Notice was automatically rescinded. Vijay had given in to his inquisitive nature to make a side trip to Pasadena, during his, Jennifer and Karima's visit with Jennifer's parents' in Mountain View. He wanted to meet the rabies survivor, Vince Fuller, and – for an altogether different reason – his wife, Trudi.

An attractive woman of a "certain age" with auburn hair, sparkling green eyes, and an infectious smile answered the door of a comfortable-looking home in Pasadena's Highlands area.

"Trudi?" Vijay asked.

"Yes, and you must be Vijay."

"And I'm Vince," interjected a fit-looking older man as he came around the door. Vince had been excited about meeting the man who invented the watch. As they welcomed him in, Vijay almost tripped over their dog, who looked like a fair-sized dog when viewed from above but stood only about four to five inches from the ground on impossibly short legs. The dog looked way up at the very tall Vijay and appeared to be smiling, as confirmed by his little stub of a tail wagging to and fro.

Vince said, or rather announced, "Vijay, meet Miles."

Vijay squatted down comfortably and scratched Miles' head between his large pointy ears. "What kind of dog are you, Mr. Miles?"

Trudi answered for Miles, in her own voice, "He's a Pembroke Welsh Corgi. And believe it or not, he was bred for herding sheep, although he's had to make do with herding us around for most of his life."

"Ahh. I've seen little guys like you with the Queen." Miles seemed to like that, and his tail wagged even faster. Vijay had seen Queen Elizabeth of the UK on TV with short-legged dogs like this, but didn't know what they were called.

"Please come in," Trudi exhorted as she led Vijay inside, Miles at his heels. When Vijay was comfortably seated, Miles came over and rested his chin on Vijay's shoe earning him another head scratch from the long-armed visitor, who hardly needed to lean over to reach the stretched-out corgi.

Over teas and a coffee for Vince, the three humans launched into an animated conversation ranging from Vijay's questions about Vince's bout with rabies to the Fullers' interest in Vijay's heritage and India in general.

Vince explained his ordeal with rabies, and he credited his VT2 for saving his life. Without the Final Notice warning, he wouldn't have gotten the treatment in time.

The Fullers were fascinated by Vijay's story about his life in

India and how he matter-of-factly described his family as living in a slum. His literal rags to riches story was impressive and heart-warming. Vince's management consultant side came forth when Vijay described the VT2's manufacturing process under his brother's management in India.

Vijay expressed his appreciation of Trudi's popular song, "Crazy Eddie Got A Gun," which had been adopted by several progressive organizations promoting better gun control. That segued into some of the things that he and Jennifer had been doing with their foundation in support of gun safety and control, particularly concerning domestic violence.

Vijay asked if there was anything specific that sparked the idea for the song, and Trudi surprised him by explaining that she had attended the now-infamous NRA event where a number of people were killed. He tried to get into more detail about her experience, but she seemed to shut down and said she'd rather not talk about it.

As Vijay awkwardly shifted his attention to Vince, he noticed that Vince wasn't wearing his VT2 and asked about it.

"I decided that I didn't really want to know," explained Vince, with a sheepish grin. "Getting one Final Notice was enough, even though it saved me."

Trudi held her arm up and shook her sleeve down, revealing a VT2. "So, I'm wearing it now; not for the Final Notice – I think I'm with Vince on that – but I've recently finished treatment for cancer, and the new improvements you've made with detailed blood analysis have helped save me time. I've shared the reporting aspect with my doctor, so I don't have to go in, and she's told me what to look for to spot any problems. It's pretty impressive that I can load updates to my watch while it's charging.

Glancing down at his own VT2, Vijay was shocked when he noticed that two hours had already slipped by, so he didn't mention that Tesla could add horsepower or improved fuel consumption via internet downloads, a feat he thought was much more impressive. He needed to catch his flight back to San Jose.

It had been an enjoyable time, and as he reluctantly rose and gave Miles another head scratch, he realized how warm and genuine Vince and Trudi were, with Miles being the icing on the cake. They exchanged goodbyes and unanimously agreed it would be nice to stay in touch, and the Fullers hoped that next time they could meet Jennifer and Karima, as well.

***

Mountain View, California. Jennifer met Vijay at the San Jose Airport after his hour and fifteen-minute flight from Bob Hope Airport in Burbank. Nicole and Bill Andrews, Jennifer's parents, were delighted to be on their own with Karima. Vijay asked if she was worried that her parents could irreversibly spoil Karima in the hour that she was away? She wasn't worried but chuckled that they would certainly do their best.

Vijay told her about his visit with Vince and Trudi, and especially about their dog, Miles. He was obviously taken with him. He related Vince's explanation of his bout with rabies and that Vince had credited the VT2 with saving his life, and that Trudi was using the watch now to help monitor her post-cancer condition.

He explained, too, that he'd asked about the genesis of Trudi's song, "Crazy Eddie Got a Gun." Vijay smiled and said, "And I was surprised by her answer. She had attended that NRA session in D.C., where the top NRA guy was killed. Others, too. But when I asked for more details, she refused to talk about it. She just shut down."

"Hmm," she muttered as she pulled into the Andrews' driveway.

Her "Hmm," alerted Vijay to the fact that Jennifer hadn't said a word since leaving the airport. He looked at her and sensed that something was wrong. "What's wrong, Jen?"

"Nothing."

And then he *knew* that something was wrong, and he put his hand on her shoulder as she parked and turned off the car. "Tell me."

"It's really nothing. It's stupid."

"What's stupid?"

Jennifer sniffled. "Ever since Kari was born, I've been trying to get back into shape."

Vijay interrupted. "You're in great shape! What are you talking about?"

"I told you it's stupid. I tried to wear some of my old jeans that I'd left here, but I couldn't get into them."

Vijay tried to humor her. "Maybe your mom washed them, and they shrank."

"You know that's not what happened."

"OK, maybe not, but you look amazing, and I love you." He undid his seat belt, leaned over, and kissed her.

She smiled, sniffled again and wiped the ripening tears from the corners of her eyes. "I love you, too, Vijay." Then she took a deep breath and said, with a smile, "Let's go see if Karima has survived!"

***

Vijay had an uneasy relationship with Jennifer's parents. Her father, Bill, had worked in financial services for almost fifty years and was retired now. Vijay could never get past the first time they'd met; there was no mistaking the disappointment on Bill's face as he took in his daughter's dark-skinned fiancé. Possibly even worse was that Bill smoked, and whenever he needed a cigarette, he'd ask Vijay to come outside with him. Vijay was uneasy saying "No," so he found himself outdoors, continually adjusting his position to be upwind of the smell.

Nicole was a very well-connected interior designer, mostly retired, except for a unique client now and then. She was always nicely dressed, and it seemed as though she was always drinking. As Nicole's drinking progressed, her voice got louder, and she grew more affectionate. Fortunately, she was much shorter than Vijay and needed his cooperation to plant a kiss.

Jennifer watched Vijay's efforts to get along with her parents with some embarrassment, humor, and a great deal of appreciation for his ability to carry it off.

Both Nicole and Bill had been horrified by the attack on their daughter, and they were very proud of how she handled it. It had become a favorite story of Bill's, and as he retold it over and over to his friends, the description of the damage Jennifer inflicted grew in severity. Still, they were very concerned about Jennifer's and Karima's safety. Vijay and Jennifer did their best to assure them, but their normal parental fears were not easily mollified.

FINAL ACT

The two couples had been discussing the White House attack on California's agreement with car manufacturers, which led to a more general discussion about the divisiveness in politics across the country. Through his connection with Zoe, Vijay was a witness to how deadly that divisiveness could be, both in a political sense as well as the rising tally of hate crimes, especially against people of color. He was looking forward to voting in a U.S. presidential election for the first time, now that he was a full U.S. citizen, and he asked Bill and Nicole for their views on the upcoming elections.

Bill took the lead and launched into a much too detailed description of the current situation and how the country came to be where it was. He had vastly overestimated Vijay's fundamental understanding of the process, prompting Vijay to expose his political naivety. "What would you say are the fundamental differences between the Democrats and Republicans?"

The question generated some laughs with Jennifer chiming in, "Like black and white, night and day, and some might say, good and bad."

"Now, now," Bill countered. "It's not that bad. I've been a registered Republican all my life. Still am, although that's not how I necessarily vote these days."

Nicole added, a little louder than necessary, "Thank goodness! I jumped ship before he did. When Obama ran, I just felt it was the right thing to do, especially after W. Bush's second term. And I felt the same way when Hillary ran – it was time for a woman."

Jennifer looked surprised when her father didn't comment and asked, "Dad, didn't you vote for Hillary, too?"

Bill didn't look at her or anyone else when he answered. "No. I thought having someone from outside the inner machinations of government would be a good thing."

Jennifer shot back, "And how is that going?"

Vijay inadvertently saved Bill further discomfort by returning to his question about the differences between the two parties.

Bill explained that the Republicans had always stood for fiscal responsibility, small government and states' rights, strong military, tough on crime and supporting free enterprise.

Vijay looked puzzled and said, "But the national debt is now the largest ever, the federal government is interfering with states' rights, as we were discussing earlier, and we seem to be abandoning our historical allies, making ourselves vulnerable. Worse yet, the government seems to be committing most of the crimes."

That drew laughs from everyone, even Bill, and Nicole commented to her daughter, "You married a smart one, alright!"

Thinking about his recent conversation with Trudi and the NRA, Vijay raised the subject that always made him uncomfortable, because of the unfortunate connection with his invention, the VT2: "Why are guns so important to the Republicans? I know it's related to the Second Amendment, but in the 1700s, no one could have ever conceived of the weapons we have today."

Bill shrugged and offered, "Actually, guns aren't an issue with the Party, but they are to the NRA and a good chunk of the GOP's constituency. It's a political issue."

FINAL ACT

That confirmed Vijay's feeling that he'd never understand the motivation behind most of the prevailing political arguments: *Why did it appear that some people wanted to suppress votes, not provide healthcare and worst of all, ignore the science of climate change and environmental damage?*

And then he heard, "Come on, Vijay. Keep me company outside while I have a cigarette."

***

Boston, Massachusetts. Vik Vasin shook Charlie Tomkins' hand and wished him luck. He had just spent almost two hours going over plans, photos, and maps, plus handling instructions for the Glock 26. The gun was easy to use, and with ten 9mm rounds, it should get the job done. And Vik was confident that Tomkins would get the job done. He loved his children too much not to.

***

Lexington, Massachusetts. Tony Longo walked Anna Petrov only partway up the path to her rambling home. He knew that her father hated him, and if he heard them at the door, there would be a scene. They embraced and enjoyed a long goodnight kiss in the moonlight and said their goodbyes. Tony wasn't sure that Anna's father didn't have surveillance cameras, so the kiss was as far as it went. Besides, they had just spent two of her allotted three "date" hours in bed.

He returned to his car, and closing the door as quietly as possible, slowly turned around and drove down the long drive to the main road. A vehicle was parked at the intersection, facing out, with the trunk open. An older man seemed to be struggling with a spare tire. Tony stopped his car, got out, and went to see if he could help, in part, because there was no room for him to get around the stopped car. As he approached the man, he asked, "Need any help?"

Those turned out to be his last words as the man turned, pointed a gun at him, and pumped two rounds into his head. Tomkins looked to be sure that Tony was dead, closed his trunk, and drove off.

Another car crept up the road from a short distance away with its lights off. Engine still running, Vik Vasin got out, looked at Tony's body, returned to his car, and drove off. Charlie had passed the test, but Vik knew that not everyone would, and that could prove to be a weakness.

***

The following morning, Charlie Tomkins retrieved an envelope from his mailbox. Enclosed was a cashier's check for $50,000. He drove to his nearby bank branch, asked to speak with a manager, and deposited the check equally into the two savings accounts of his children. Three days later, Charlie passed away, just as his VT2 had told him he would. When a gun was discovered at his home, the police matched it to the execution of Tony Longo, son of a high-ranking Mafia Don. There didn't appear to be a connection or motive, and a routine check of his finances didn't raise any flags. Nobody thought about looking at his children's accounts.

Anna Petrov was distraught, perhaps even more than one might expect, if they were unaware of her early pregnancy. Her father didn't seem at all concerned about Tony's death, but then he didn't know about his daughter's condition.

The Longos, however, were on a war footing, despite the conclusive evidence that Charlie Tomkins, an insurance salesman with no relationship to the Russians or any other gang, had committed the crime. They were convinced it was the Russian mafia, known as 'Bratva,' that had done it, but there was nothing for the Mafia to justify an attack.

Charlie Tomkins hadn't been on the FBI's radar because he wasn't on the Final Notice list as having a gun. And he didn't attract Vijay's attention because his hormonal activity didn't include anger or aggression when he carried out the assassination ... just a spike of anxiety.

***

CHAPTER 10 – DECISIONS

Quincy, Massachusetts. Although Vik Vasin was a number of levels down the food chain in the Russian Bratva, he received word (along with a thick envelope) that a certain high-level Bratva Captain appreciated his handling of a sensitive family situation.

Vik continued to frequent Sully's but he hadn't seen Alek lately. That was fine with him, as long as he kept his mouth shut. So far, so good. Vik's phone pinged with a message that Nick had arrived. He paid up, exited the bar, and scanned the parking lot until he saw a pair of headlights flash on and off. Getting in the car, Nick handed him a cloth bag containing a gun and ammunition.

Vik looked at the bag and asked, "What is it?"

Nick shrugged. "G26, same as before."

"How much?"

"Two Gs, same as before."

Vik protested, "How come so much? I can get one of these for six hundred at Bass and half that on the street."

Nick smirked and replied sarcastically, "Yeah, but this one ain't traceable. Guaranteed. You want to save money? Go ahead. Buy it wid your own name at Bass."

"Don't be a wise ass."

"Just sayin'."

"Yeah, yeah," Vik replied grumpily, "I need two more. When can I get 'em?"

Nick raised an eyebrow and asked, "You hiring an army?"

"Yeah. Somethin' like that. When?"

"Tomorrow. Same time, same price." Nick held his hand out. "You owe me two Gs."

"Yeah, OK." Vik pulled an envelope from his jacket, removed two banded packs of bills, and handed it to Nick. "Tomorrow. Same time."

***

Chestnut Hill, Massachusetts. Vijay was trying to spend more time at home following the attack on Jennifer. The police hadn't been able to obtain any additional information from the recovering assailant, and they truly felt it was because he had none to give. So, the puzzling threat relating to the 'Final Notice names' remained just that – puzzling.

Vijay had just finalized the formatting for the new report that would be sent to Zoe, once he was satisfied with the accuracy and consistency. Depressing as it was, the Marianne Abbott case had given him new insights and hope. When he plotted her emotional and hormonal reactions, he could see a build-up of a few days, from normal to peak anger and aggression, and then back to normal. He needed to run this new behavioral signature pattern across all known Final Notice killers, but so far, it was looking good.

The report included the potential psychological, behavioral markers, employment details, and GPS tracking ID. GPS would be a surprise for Zoe, and he was still kicking himself for not thinking of it earlier. The function had been built into the device from the outset as an aide to emergency responders, but he and the management team had suppressed it until it could be thoroughly tested, to avoid false alarms. After the IPO and Vijay's departure, it stayed on the back burner, obscured, no doubt, by the high number of senior management changes taking place.

Overall, he was happy and confident. Finally, he could do something to counter-balance the Final Notice inspired deaths.

He would have been even happier with this accomplishment if he wasn't conflicted over the legality and ethics – both from an eavesdropping, surveillance standpoint, as well as his clandestine use of VitalTech's data. He could rationalize that the surveillance of VT2 wearers would only be used if someone was about to commit a crime, but he hadn't found a good argument that justified his unauthorized use of VitalTech's system. The very public revelations about social media's sharing of personal information with tech companies rang loud and clear in his mind.

What bothered him even more deeply was that he hadn't shared it with Jennifer, either. On the one hand, he knew that her moral compass was closely aligned with his own, but he was certain that she would have misgivings. Each time he had the moral argument with himself, in the end, he would come full circle and accept that if the dangers that Zoe had described were real, the FBI needed all the help they could get. Still, he needed to have that talk – actually, two talks.

After dinner that night, once Karima was asleep, he tackled the second talk first. It was about getting a dog. He had been enthralled by the short-legged smiling pooch, Miles, although he couldn't picture him as a deterrent to a determined and armed intruder. Something bigger and scarier looking was required.

He shocked Jennifer at first when he said, "What do you think about getting a cuddly little companion for Kari to grow up with ... and protect you as well?"

Jennifer smiled and replied coquettishly, "I thought that's what we've been doing most nights and even some mornings ... but I'm not sure how much protection a baby can offer."

Vijay laughed at his miscommunication faux pas. "And I think we should continue to try, but I was talking about a puppy."

Now Jennifer laughed, "Ahh, the protective part! Are you still thinking about the corgi? They're cute but not very scary."

"I agree. Miles planted the idea, but when it comes to protecting you and Kari, I was thinking more along the lines of a rottweiler or a German shepherd. But perhaps something a bit more cuddly for her to grow up with."

Jennifer was all in, "How about a mix? They have these doodle dogs that are a combination of a poodle and another breed?"

"Like Karima?

She laughed, "Exactly."

Always the action man, Vijay reached over to his tablet and

searched for doodles. The results had them gushing over the dozens of doodle crossbreed puppies for almost an hour, as they researched breed characteristics and breeders. Looking at the characteristics, it didn't take long for them to agree on a shepa-doodle, a cross between a German shepherd and a standard poodle – smart, loyal, great with kids and protective of family. And there were a couple of breeders in the Boston area.

Jennifer, with a big grin on her face, said, "OK, we've got the cuddly protective one checked off. How about the other cuddly addition?"

But Vijay reluctantly put that activity temporarily on hold. He wanted to clear his mind of his ethical dilemma. "I'm always ready for that, but first, I need to discuss something with you, and I want your candid opinion."

Jennifer was disappointed, but she knew that this must be very important, so she put her other desires on hold and an arm around Vijay's shoulder to focus on what he wanted to say. "Sure, 'V,' what is it?"

Vijay took a deep breath and explained, in more detail than ever before, the problems that the Final Notices were causing and what the FBI was up against. Jennifer realized just how badly the Final Notice deaths had affected him. She had been aware of the historical information-sharing agreement with the FBI, but it seemed as though the situation had become much more dangerous and volatile. Memories of the recent attack swept over her, and she asked Vijay, "Would you like some more wine?" He declined, but she poured another glass for herself.

Vijay said, "If VitalTech was still my company, I would have no qualms about helping the FBI as much as possible to stop the murders. But it's not mine, and there's no one I can approach to get approval. Kalin and I are not exactly great friends, as you know, and J. Edward is smitten with him, as are most of the Board."

Jennifer retorted, "That's because you created an amazing product that people want, and they're buying it. Plus, you and your team are making it even better."

"Jen, that's part of what I wanted to talk about. The team is driving healthcare advancements. But I'm focusing on something else. I'm working on extracting data that can help the FBI stop attacks before they happen."

Jennifer was surprised and curious. "How long has that been the case?"

"Truthfully, since the very first murder, but there was so much going on back then – with the beta tests and the IPO – that most of my efforts were in my head. Trying to come up with a workable application has been elusive."

"And have you found a solution?"

"I have, and I'm close to trialling a prototype."

Jennifer asked, "What kind of data are you looking at?" And then, smiling, she added, "Keep it simple and high level."

"Hormonal readings like cortisol, serotonin, adrenalin."

Jennifer interrupted, "Good, you haven't lost me yet. So, are you saying that these readings, when applied to a Final Notice recipient, will indicate that they will commit murder?"

Vijay chuckled, appreciating his wife's quick mind. "Yes,

although it's not quite that straightforward or definitive. It indicates that they are angry and agitated at levels similar to other recipients who have carried out shootings. Therefore, they should be considered a threat."

"That sounds pretty 1984ish on several levels. But do you really think Kalin will approve enhanced intel to the FBI?"

"I'm not even sure he knows about the current level of info-sharing, and I don't know how much time I have before they throw me off the Board and the team, which would end any hope of helping the FBI. And given the potential threats that Zoe has shared with me, more murders could include some very high-level people."

"Kick you off the Board? Why do you think that would happen?"

"Kalin and I have had words, and it wouldn't take much for him to convince J. Edward."

"So, what can you do?"

Vijay finally got to his point. "Build a 'back door' into the VitalTech monitoring system so that I can continue to have access and provide Zoe and the FBI with valuable data, even if I'm kicked out."

Jennifer was alarmed. "That would be illegal."

"Probably, but I was going to ask Zoe to see if she could give me immunity."

Jennifer had worked for J. Edward Konig at KKL, and it was she who brought VitalTech into play for the high-flying private equity firm. "What if I ask J. Edward? VitalTech is his company now."

Vijay had hoped Jennifer would cheer him on, but he wasn't surprised by her pragmatic recommendation for caution. "I don't think that's a good idea. He'll ask Kalin, and then this show's over."

Jennifer was concerned, but she understood how important this was to Vijay, and she didn't want to stand in his way. "Will you talk with Zoe first?"

"I will. Thanks, Jen. I love you."

"I love you, too."

They headed for bed, but neither of them was entirely present. He was modeling "what if" scenarios in case it all went south and trying to decide what to do; she lay there worrying about the legality of what Vijay was considering and the threat of another attack.

***

Quincy, Massachusetts. Vik Vasin had just briefed Louie Vinzano on a plan to take out a high-level Italian mafioso. Vik smiled inwardly as he imagined the mob's confusion about another hit on one of their people, this time from another Italian. But Louie was different than Charlie. For starters, he had twenty days left on his Final Notice. Too much time … time that he might talk. Secondly, he was more emotional than Charlie, and Vik was unsure if he could shoot someone. But this was a big hit, making it even more critical to confuse the motive and keep the other side uncertain about who did it.

Vik had compiled the habits of Frank DiVinci, a high-ranking Capo in the mob. He knew that on Wednesdays, Frank would say good night to his wife and kids and go out for his weekly evening shift at "work." Actually, it was his night to use a buddy's house for a visit from a prostitute. Frank would arrive between 9:00-10:00 p.m., and a hooker would arrive at 10:00

p.m. Vik's plan was for Louie to intercept the hooker, pay her off and then ring the bell at 10:00 and kill Frank.

Vik had Louie drive to the address, and then join him in Vik's car, parked nearby. They watched as a taxi cruised down the block, and Vik gave Louie the go-ahead. Louie met the cab, stopped the hooker as she was getting out, and explained that plans had changed; then, he gave her enough money to make her and the taxi driver smile.

When the taxi drove off, Louie approached the house. He rang the bell, and when Frank opened the door in his plaid boxer shorts, white, wife-beater t-shirt, and black socks, Louie froze.

Frank shouted, "What the f," before Vik, who was shadowing Louie, put two silenced shots in Frank's chest, pushed Louie inside, and closed the door. Louie was still in shock.

Vik took the gun from Louie and pressed the one he'd just used into Louie's hand. He thought for a moment, saw Frank's gun on the coffee table, and with his still gloved hand, picked it up and fired a single shot into Louie's forehead. He then placed Frank's gun in its dead owner's hand and quietly left, congratulating himself for his foresight, quick thinking, and thoroughness, as well as having saved S50,000.

***

CHAPTER 11 – UNWELCOME NEWS

Chestnut Hill, Massachusetts. The morning after Vijay and Jennifer's talk about the FBI info-sharing plan, Vijay got a call from J. Edward.

"Good morning, Vijay," J. Edward boomed from his office speakerphone. "Have I caught you at a good time?"

Vijay was concerned to get a call from J. Edward, given all that was happening, but he tried to stay positive, "It's always a good time to speak with you, J. Edward. How can I help you today?"

J. Edward got straight to the point, "Are we still cooperating with the FBI and sending them the names of Final Notice recipients with guns?"

Vijay was on high alert, but answered honestly, "Yes. Same as we all agreed initially."

"So, we're not giving them additional information?"

Vijay's heart was racing, but he replied honestly, "Nothing has changed."

"OK, Good. That's what I thought." And before Vijay could ask why, J. Edward said, "Say hello to that beautiful wife of yours for me. Ciao."

Vijay knew that J. Edward was only asking because Kalin had asked him. But why was Kalin asking questions about their cooperation with the FBI now? And why the question about giving them more information?

Vijay was still pondering those questions when the phone rang again. It was VitalTech's in-house counsel, someone new, who told him that he was to cease and desist all further development concerning VitalTech immediately and that an extraordinary Board meeting was being called for this afternoon to remove him. The lawyer added that as a current Board member, at least for the moment, Vijay was free to attend and that he would shortly receive an e-mail reiterating their call and details of the meeting.

The burning question in Vijay's mind was what prompted Kalin to ask J. Edward about it? Cautiously, Vijay asked Jennifer if she'd spoken with J. Edward recently.

She said, "No," and asked why he was asking.

He summarized his call from J. Edward and the second one from VitalTech regarding the Board meeting.

She replied, "You're not going, are you?"

"I'm not sure. On the one hand, I expect Kalin already has his votes lined up, so it's a done deal. On the other hand, this cooperation has been going on for almost two years, and J. Edward sanctioned it. And I prefer to face my accusers."

"To what end?"

Vijay smiled at his wife's practical wisdom. He knew it would be a tough meeting, and he knew it would be hard for him to maintain his composure. He said, "Good question. Let me think about it for a bit."

FINAL ACT

Jennifer had a bad feeling.

The e-mail from VitalTech had arrived, confirming that he had been removed from the VitalTech Healthcare Enhancement Team. And sure enough, when Vijay tried to log in, his access was denied. But then he tried again, using a newly established alternative entry point, and he was in.

At MIT, Vijay was friends with a couple of brilliant fellow-Indian students. They were currently making pretty good money from the Federal Government to test-drive software and look for vulnerabilities. They had never been stumped. One of the terms they used for back door software strategy was "whack-a-mole." Vijay hadn't understood the phrase until they showed him the game where you hit a plastic mole on the head as it popped up from its hole, only to see another mole pop up from another hole. They explained that once you hacked into a system, be sure to create additional entry points in case you get whacked.

Vijay's phone rang again, and it was Alek. He'd just heard the news that Vijay was off the team. Vijay hadn't spoken with Alek for a while, and it was nice to hear his voice. Alek told him that the team was still making good progress and a number of them, knowing that Alek and Vijay were friends, said to say hello and that they would miss his input and guidance.

Alek asked if Vijay could share the reason for his removal and Vijay told him it was mainly because of his poor relationship with Kalin, but also because of a disagreement regarding VitalTech's cooperation with the FBI.

At the mention of the FBI and Final Notice names, Alek felt the floor give way. He wondered if Vijay was threatened and, if he had, was it because he'd thrown out Vijay's name to Vik. Alek thought he could trust Vijay, but he couldn't bring himself to reveal what he knew, so he offered his sorrow for Vijay leaving the team and said it would be good to get together some time. Vijay agreed and began to make some notes for the Board meeting.

***

Boston, Massachusetts. The Boston police were pretty sure they understood the mechanics of the Louis Vinzano-Frank DiVinci murders, but they couldn't figure out the motive. Vinzano's death was immediate, and DiVinci could have lived for a few seconds after being shot, enough time for him to get off one great shot that killed Vinzano. But Vinzano had no police record, and there was nothing to link him to DiVinci or any mob members. What the police did know, however, was that one more mob member was out of the picture. That was the bottom line, and the case was closed for the police – but not for the Mafia. They knew that the guy who killed Frank DiVinci didn't do it for himself.

***

Quincy, Massachusetts. Vijay arrived at VitalTech's new HQ. Following the IPO and sale to KKL, VitalTech moved to a new commercial building and hired what seemed like hundreds of people. There were indeed a couple of hundred cars in the parking lot. What did they all do, he wondered? Gone was the raw start-up infrastructure – ground floor offices and metal circular stairs built with a sense of urgency and economy. Now there was a mostly empty ground floor with a couple of security guards and a bank of elevators.

He announced himself and was asked to produce ID and sign in.

"Who are you here to see?"

"I'm here for a Board meeting."

FINAL ACT

"Who is your point of contact?"

"Mike Kalin."

The security guard called a number and said, "There's a Mister Vijay Patel to see Mr. Kalin."

"I'm here to attend the Board meeting," Vijay added while thinking, *I'm not here to see Mr. Kalin.*

The guard listened, hung up, and said, "His secretary said to have a seat. They'll send for you when they're ready to start."

Vijay smiled and thought, *Let the games begin.*

When he was finally called up and entered the Boardroom, everyone else was there except for J. Edward. And very few made eye contact. He had been tried and found guilty. Kalin was smiling and said, "J. Edward is on the speaker from New York."

That was J. Edward's cue, "Afternoon, Vijay. Can you hear me?"

"Loud and clear," replied Vijay truthfully.

J. Edward's booming voice continued, "I've called this meeting as a result of learning that you've been sharing customer information with the FBI. Mike and I spoke earlier, and we have already decided, as you know, to remove you from your role with the Healthcare Enhancement Team, with immediate effect. This meeting is to decide if you should be removed from the Board, as well. The rest of the Board are aware of our concerns, and they'd like to hear your side of the story."

Vijay began, "It's pretty straightforward." Then, with emphasis and a bit of sarcasm, "As you will no doubt recall, during the VT2 test phase, a number of shootings occurred as a result of the Final Notice, and the FBI became involved. They asked to be advised of any Final Notice recipients who had access to a gun. We discussed it internally, both among the VitalTech senior management team, as well as with you and your IPO lawyers, and we decided to quietly provide the information, rather than have the FBI get a subpoena and possibly turn off prospective customers ... or worse, reduce enthusiasm for the IPO. Following that decision, the information was automatically sent out to them, certainly until the change of ownership. I don't know what happened to the feed or policy after that."

It was clear that more than a couple of Board members had just heard a different story than they'd been told, and one asked, "Is that true, J. Edward? This cooperation started before the change of ownership and with full knowledge by you and all the senior management?"

J. Edward mumbled and said, "Maybe not all senior management."

Kalin jumped in, "Well, it was kept from me, and I consider that concealing vital information."

Vijay responded, "I wasn't the person that hired you. However, if I recall, I did make myself available to you for as long as you wanted me around to answer any questions. You decided to discontinue our session in under an hour."

Kalin charged back, not realizing that the landscape had dramatically changed, "You've kept this from me, from us, and I move that you are removed from this Board with immediate effect. Do I have a second?"

FINAL ACT

After a complete and lengthy silence, Vijay offered, "I'm happy to answer any questions, either now, or whenever. The VT2 was borne out of my imagination and the collective skills of many people who put their hearts into it. It's the leader in the marketplace. Let's keep it there."

J. Edward's voice boomed from the speaker, "Well, it looks like the motion fails."

Kalin's face was beet red, and he lashed out, "Well, as CEO, I'm removing you from the HET."

Calmly, Vijay replied, "That's your call, and I accept that. There are some excellent people there, doing excellent work. They don't need me. Thanks, have a nice day and see you at the next board meeting."

Vijay left and knew that he had won the battle but not the war. Of even more concern was what triggered this witch hunt.

***

CHAPTER 12 – A WHOLE LOTTA RUSSIANS

Chestnut Hill, Massachusetts. Jennifer was happy for Vijay that the Board meeting went well, but she was puzzled by Vijay's indifference to being removed from the HET.

Vijay explained that he wanted to distance himself from the team and the VitalTech database so he could work behind the scenes.

That didn't sit well with Jennifer. "Has Zoe given you a 'get-out-of-jail-free' card?"

Vijay felt a pang of guilt. He hadn't asked Zoe, so he honestly said, "Not yet."

Jennifer understood his thinking, but as they discussed earlier, previously, he had been authorized to access the database. Now he was hacking into it and planning to send the FBI even more info. In addition to it being illegal, another part of her misgiving was that she didn't entirely trust the FBI or government. "What's to prevent the FBI from using or sharing the information for purposes beyond Final Notices?"

Vijay countered that he was in control and that he could always pull the plug and stop the info flow. To further support his case, he pointed out that recently, two additional Final Notice recipients had carried out murders.

FINAL ACT

That quieted Jennifer for a moment, but she didn't accept that Vijay would be able to rein in the FBI if they veered out of line. She was heading out to a meeting, though, so for the moment, they agreed to disagree.

***

Quincy, Massachusetts. Vik Vasin's Final Notice army was in a constant state of growth and shrinkage. Growth through recruitment and losses through natural causes, as predicted by their VT2s, or unnatural causes, if Vik decided to expedite the Recipient's death. Regardless of how it ended for the Recipient, the army was doing its job, taking out turf enemies without revealing who or why someone was doing it. They were, in a sense, invisible. Vik called them his "Zombies." Some required more work and creativity than others, and not all his plans were successes, but neither did any of them give away who was behind the murders. Vik made sure of that. There was always plenty of suspicion, but no proof and the cops just completed their paperwork while Vik's Zombies took out the bad guys. Some of the cops were even grateful.

Vik's work was recognized at the local Bratva level, but that was about to change. His boss invited him to dinner to meet an all-together different type of animal. This guy wasn't from Boston or even New York. He got his orders from 4,500 miles away, and Vik had a feeling that he wasn't interested in bumping off some local hoods.

Vik was introduced to him at a nice club in Boston. They shook hands, but his name wasn't mentioned. Vik asked, "What's your name?"

"Call me, Yuri." With a strong Russian accent, he asked how Vik's process worked, where he found his "Zombies," and how he controlled them.

With great pride, Vik took Yuri through his recognition of the power that the Zombies represented: How he first tried to get the names through standard intimidation methods. They even laughed together about Vik's man getting the shit kicked out of him by a woman. And finally, Vik's deceptive FBI gambit on a conditioned target to gain access to the VitalTech system and how that system revealed that VitalTech was sharing the data with the real FBI.

Yuri asked questions about VitalTech's database, and Vik fed him statistics, including the fact that there were ten million users and over six million with guns. Yes, we have their e-mail addresses, locations, and whether they have a gun or not – and we also have many doctors' names and contacts. Yes, meeting the Final Notice Zombie is difficult, but we have a guy that can track them using localized blue-tooth beacons, so we can go to the same stores, even the same aisles as they do. Vik was only interested in the Boston area, but Yuri was thinking well beyond that.

Vik was asked about Zombie management and admitted that it was much less scientific than the rest of the process. Their motivation was always the same – enough money to help their families. And surprisingly, even though they needed the money, only about two out of ten would kill someone for it.

Sometimes the Zombie needed support, even if that meant delivering on their Final Notice ahead of schedule. The goal was to take out an enemy without leaving a motive or connection to the Bratva. Vik admitted – or was it bragged – that sometimes if they screwed up or were killed in the process, he could stiff them or their family for whatever money he'd promised.

That last comment wasn't received with quite the admiration or gratitude Vik expected. It was, in fact, quite the opposite.

FINAL ACT

Yuri looked at him with his cold blue eyes and said, "That is not very smart. And if we work together, that will not happen." Nonetheless, he thanked Vik for the information and said someone would be in touch.

***

Chestnut Hill, Massachusetts. Vijay felt he had finally cracked it! The data checked out with a degree of accuracy that would give Zoe up to a 24-hour lead time for high probability shooters. He sent her an e-mail to arrange a detailed conference call and suggested that she bring in a senior IT person so they could discuss and create a functional interface between the data that the VitalTech system would send, and the end-user system that the FBI would deploy. He also hinted at a game-changing enhancement, but wouldn't say what it was.

Ten minutes later, Zoe called, and Vijay assumed it was about his e-mail, which in a way it was.

"We've stopped getting the Final Notice feeds. Not sure when it happened, as I've been away, but our last report was yesterday at 11:35 p.m., EST. Did you need to take it down to work on the enhancements?"

Vijay was puzzled, and he tried to log in to his original back door. Blocked! He tried another door, and the whack-a-mole strategy paid off. He told Zoe he'd get back with her and called Alek on his cell phone.

Vijay had to be careful with what he could share with Alek, although Alek was aware of the original FBI cooperation, so he asked, "Have there been any changes with the agreement to supply the FBI with Final Notice names?"

Alek sounded tentative and cautious, "Not sure about that, but there have been ... there are ... changes are going on right now."

"Like what?"

"I've been let go along with most of the team."

"What?"

Alek answered as though there was someone eavesdropping. "A new IT Director was appointed, and he's cleaning house. Can we meet somewhere?"

Vijay replied, "Of course. Why don't you come here? We can talk, have dinner, and you can meet our daughter, Karima."

"Sounds good. What time?"

"Just call me when you're on your way."

***

Alek hadn't been to Chestnut Hill before, and he was impressed with the area and the Patels' tastefully decorated home. Jennifer and Karima were out when he arrived, so he and Vijay sat down to talk. Vijay wanted to know what happened to the team and the FBI report. He was about to get more than that.

Alek explained, "There have been rumors all week that the IT department was about to get a shake-up. We'd heard that Kalin was livid about the FBI cooperation and that he'd instituted a witch hunt to find anybody who'd been associated with it."

FINAL ACT

Vijay interrupted, "How did Kalin find out in the first place if J. Edward didn't tell him?"

"I don't know. There were a few people in IT who admitted that they'd known about the cooperation. They were fired on the spot. Then a new IT director was appointed, Dimitri Pavlova. He came down to our area, asked what we knew about the FBI program, and then read off four names – and mine was one of them – and told us we had thirty-minutes to clean out our personal stuff. Our system access had been canceled by the time we returned to our desks."

A wave of guilt swept over Vijay as he questioned whether he was the one who had created this problem for Alek and his colleagues. It was his decision, initially, to share the information, but he also knew it was the right thing to do and that Kalin's retribution was dead wrong.

"I'm sorry, Alek. I feel responsible for what's happened, but they shouldn't have taken it out on you. Besides, taking the info away from the FBI could be disastrous."

Alek asked, "What's so important about the Final Notice names? At best, it's helped the FBI a little bit in wrapping up cases. It's never stopped a crime, has it?"

Vijay agreed, "No, it hasn't. Just knowing who received their Final Notice isn't that much of a help." Vijay was weighing options as he asked, "What are you going to do now?"

"I haven't even thought about it."

Vijay made his decision. "Perhaps there is something we can do together, but it must stay very confidential."

Alek said, "I'd love to work with you again, but before we take that next step, there is something I need to tell you."

Alek told Vijay about his conversations with Vik Vasin, the murder of his wife and son's killer, Vik's questions about getting Final Notice names so that a generous benefactor could help them out, the insurance check, and Alek's discomfort when Vik pressed him for the information. He was even more uncomfortable telling Vijay that he had used his name as the approval step and that he lied about Vijay rejecting the request.

Vijay became more and more animated as Alek confessed. "So that's what the hired gun meant by 'We want the Final Notice names.'"

Alek was lost, "Hired gun?"

Vijay explained Jennifer's ordeal, and it was Alek's turn for feeling guilty, as he recalled the FBI agent's comment that a threat that'd been made. "Oh my God, I'm so sorry. I had no idea who I was dealing with," and he told Vijay the whole story about the money and the – probably fake – FBI agents.

Vijay was trying to piece it all together. "So, you think this guy, Vik, wanted names of Final Notice recipients so he could pass them along to a generous benefactor? And when he thought I refused, he sent someone to intimidate me? And when that didn't work, he infiltrated the VitalTech system posing as the FBI?"

Hearing Vijay put everything together embarrassed Alek. Sheepishly, he said, "Knowing the whole story, I think Vik wanted the names, but not for a generous benefactor. But threatening Jennifer with a gun and impersonating the FBI means that for whatever reason he wanted the names, it's extremely important to him. And given who he is, it's not for a good cause."

FINAL ACT

Vijay's mind was churning, "Seems like we're running into a whole lotta Russians. Sorry, maybe it's because they're friends ... acquaintances of yours, which is natural; but Vik, his benefactor friend, the life insurance lawyer, the possible FBI imposters and now, Dimitri Pavlova."

Vijay glanced at his watch, "Let me call Zoe, my FBI contact. She told me that their info flow from VitalTech just stopped. Do you have any theories about that, or what suddenly pointed Kalin to the VitalTech-FBI cooperation?"

Alek shrugged, "Nothing more than my comment about Kalin and his anger about feeding info to the FBI."

Vijay wondered, "Could the FBI imposters, upon discovering the real FBI feed, have told Kalin? Is there a connection?"

Zoe picked up, interrupting that thought. Vijay apologized for not getting back with her sooner. He explained the VitalTech shakeup and terminations and that the CEO was unhappy about the cooperation with the FBI. That was probably the reason the info stopped. Vijay also asked her to check if FBI agents had recently visited the Quincy VitalTech offices and specifically Alek Belikov. Finally, he offered his suspicions about the large number of Russians entering the frame.

Zoe asked why Vijay wanted to know if the FBI had visited Belikov, and Vijay detailed the purported FBI visit to Alek at VitalTech. He omitted Alek's account of his meeting with Vik Vasin to protect Alek. Zoe explained that she was on her way to a meeting, but she'd find out about the visit and get back with him. Right now, the critical question for her was, how did all this affect the progress that Vijay had made on the behavior forecasting?

Vijay hadn't sounded out Alek yet about helping him with the enhanced information flow to the FBI, so he remained cautious in front of Alek, but he said, "Don't worry. Our conference call is still on."

Vijay hung up with Zoe and began explaining about the new threats the FBI was up against and his own work on developing an enhanced behavioral report. He admitted that his original VitalTech access had been shut down, as well as a second access point, but that he had set up other doors, too.

Alek laughed out loud, "Whack-a-mole!"

Vijay laughed too, but added, seriously, "I can't pay you what you're currently making."

That made Alek laugh again, "I don't have a job, so currently, I'm not making anything."

The real truth was that, right now, they needed each other. Alek needed Vijay's friendship and support more than money. He also sensed an opportunity to work against Kalin and possibly help the FBI. And there was something else. All of the Russians that Vijay had referred to were not good examples of his countrymen. They were examples of the worst of his countrymen and most of the ruling class.

Vijay knew that Alek's wizardry with data systems and security would be invaluable to his efforts going forward. Alek also had an extremely imaginative vision, and he once prophesied, well before it became a reality, that most peripherals – such as watches, health monitors, and phones – would become obsolete and that communication and data transmission would be handled by wearables. Alek even predicted another stage in telephony; implants, a chip implanted close to the brain that would allow conversations and data exchange

FINAL ACT

without devices, confessing that the idea came from a 1967 movie starring James Coburn. That inspired him to design a microchip that he had embedded in his head by a veterinarian friend. It never worked, of course, but Alek used to kid Vijay about the day when Vijay would get a call with the caller ID reading, "Alek's head." Vijay smiled – it felt good to be working with Alek again.

They were both laughing and regaling old times when Jennifer and Karima came home.

***

CHAPTER 13 – FAMILY LIFE

Chestnut Hill, Massachusetts. Jennifer had been surprised but happy to see Alek. Vijay explained Alek's situation, and Jennifer was sympathetic and genuinely pleased that he and Vijay would be working together again, although she was very uncomfortable with their project. Hearing that VitalTech pulled the plug on their cooperation with the FBI increased her concerns and raised alarms. There was a lot to digest, and it would take a while to think it all through, but Jennifer could feel her anxiety increase.

Fortunately, Karima's antics had become the center of everyone's attention, and Jennifer joined in. Karima was busily flashing coquettish smiles at Alek, then giggling and turning away. Alek was smitten by the little toddler with jet-black hair and light eyes. He had insulated himself from being around anyone with a family for a long time. But now, as his defenses melted away, he began to melt too. His eyes welled up, and he excused himself to use the bathroom.

That evening, over one of Vijay's delicious Indian vegetarian meals of gobi aloo, baijan, rice, naans, and a couple of chutneys, Alek was re-introduced to normal family life, if you could call a multi-millionaire's life, "normal." Driving home and later, as he lay in bed before falling asleep, Alek reflected on the day's events and felt that a new and meaningful chapter in his life was about to begin.

FINAL ACT

After Alek left, and Karima was in bed, and the dishes washed and stacked in the dishwasher, Vijay and Jennifer brewed a couple of teas and discussed the evening ... and Alek. Jennifer was pleased that Alek seemed to be in a good mental state, and she was happy for Vijay that they'd be working together. Given her concern about Vijay's project, however, she asked what prompted VitalTech's decision to stop the FBI cooperation.

Vijay confessed that he didn't know, and that it was still just an assumption that VitalTech had stopped it.

Surprised by his comment, she asked, "Well, if neither you nor VitalTech stopped it, who else could have?"

Vijay decided to come clean with the whole story. So, he explained about Vik Vasin leveraging Alek to get the Final Notice names, as well as the fake FBI visit and Kalin's knowledge of the cooperation.

Jennifer lost her relaxed demeanor and stiffened, immediately transported, once again, back to the evening of the attack. Her concerns were now at a red or orange alert level, and in a very agitated way, she stated, "Vijay, this guy Vasin and whoever visited Alek, posing as the FBI, are criminals, and your hacking is clearly against their interests. That poses a real danger to you, me, and Karima! That's what brought that scumbag to our home, asking for the names. Now they have access, and if you try to stop them, or re-instate the data feed to the FBI, do you not think they'll try again? And they won't make the same mistake they made last time."

Vijay was caught between Jennifer's concerns for all of them – especially Karima's safety – and his desire to end the violence created by his invention. But he couldn't do both with 100% certainty. He took Jennifer's hand and said, "I'll call J.

Edward tomorrow and see if he can get Kalin to re-instate the data if VitalTech is withholding it."

***

Washington, DC. Zoe had attended a meeting where she was shown some recent police reports covering Final Notice recipient shootings. The reports detailed murders of Italian mob members by Final Notice recipients in the Boston area. They were unusual for several reasons: First, the victims were Italian mob members and family, shot by Final Notice recipients who did not appear to have criminal connections or a motive. Secondly, with one exception, the shooters were all killed immediately following their act, either by what the NRA would call a 'good-guy,' suicide, or another shooter. And last, when she had mentioned these to Vijay, he told her that none of them displayed the typical hormonal signatures of any of the killers he had seen so far. He marked all of the Boston Final Notice killers Zoe had mentioned so that he and Alek could look at their hormonal signatures in more depth.

As for the FBI and police, priorities being what they were, these particular crimes were treated with a lower sense of urgency than shootings involving non-criminals, so there was not a lot of follow-up and detail. The Bureau would deny it, but they seemed to adopt the attitude that if the warring mobs wanted to kill each other off, have at it. Besides, Zoe had her priorities, and these weren't high on her list, either.

Still, she needed to understand how and why these seemingly unconnected Final Notice recipients were becoming involved. Zoe called a colleague in the Boston office to see what additional information she could get. The agent confirmed what Zoe already knew about the Italian mob victims, and that the shooters had no criminal backgrounds or motives. But then, he dropped a bombshell by stating that the victims were very likely all targets of the Russian mob, aka 'Bratva.' He added that after the third murder, the Italians had retaliated by gunning down a number of Bratva members.

Zoe asked about the 'good-guys' involved with the Italian shootings, and the agent shared that one was an off-duty police officer and the other a private citizen. Zoe asked for names and was told that the police officer was Terry Sullivan and the civilian, Lev Panova. The agent added that Panova had a license to carry, witnessed the shooting, and acted on his own to protect others.

Before hanging up, Zoe asked about agents being sent to VitalTech – possibly to see Alek Belikov, within the past thirty days. It took the agent a moment, and he said, "No. No visits to VitalTech. I do see a link to Belikov regarding a police visit to his home."

Zoe asked why Belikov was interviewed. Reading the report, the agent explained that it concerned the death of Thomas Sheehan – his wife and son's murderer. The agent added that Belikov was cleared when they found the murderer. "Who was it?" Zoe asked.

The reply added one more Russian to the growing list. "Serge Chernov."

Zoe hung up, pulled out her tablet, and ran searches on Sullivan and Panova.

There was nothing out of the ordinary with Sullivan, and his 'good-guy' label seemed plausible, although this was the first time an armed 'good-guy' had delivered what the NRA had touted as a fringe benefit of armed citizens. Lev Panova was a different story: a naturalized US citizen who arrived from Russia with his parents when he was six years old. No occupation listed, but there were a couple of arrests for theft and drugs a few years back.

Zoe stared at her screen, not seeing it but thinking: Five Italian mob members who would be likely Russian mob targets … shot by Final Notice recipients who did not appear to be connected to them … who, in turn, were immediately killed or committed suicide. The Italians responded in a straightforward way, not carried out by Final Notice shooters. Had the Russians hacked the VitalTech system after their fake FBI visit, figured out who had received Final Notices, and then convinced them to kill? Or were the murders just made to look like they did it? And Vijay was right; there are Russians coming out of the woodwork!

Her phone pinged, jolting her back to the present. It was a text from Demi: "Pasta ok tonight? xo" She texted back, "Sounds great! Xoxo"

Zoe and Demi had quickly settled into a routine with Zoe staying with Demi three to four days a week. She had taken Demi to her flat, and they both agreed that Demi's was preferable. Zoe was content with what was the closest family life she'd had since she went away to college. Demi was an upbeat, high energy, and fun-to-be-around partner. She was a bit secretive, although that was a big part of her job, and very inquisitive, peppering Zoe with questions about work and other friends. The last part was easy. Outside of work buddies, some acquaintances and now Demi, Zoe didn't have any real friends in Washington. Demi was all Zoe had and all that she wanted.

***

Chestnut Hill, Massachusetts. As promised, Vijay called J. Edward Konig, who seemed to be in a good mood, blabbing about a huge acquisition he was close to completing. His mood changed abruptly when Vijay asked about the FBI data feed, "Are you aware that VitalTech has stopped the information flow to the FBI?"

J. Edward answered, "Mike and I discussed it, and I told him it was his call."

Vijay, trying to maintain his composure, shot back, "J. Edward, you know why we initiated it and how important it was with a hundred users. There are ten million users now, and the FBI is concerned that, given the political divisiveness in the country, especially with elections coming up, the VT2 Final Notices harbor the potential to wreak havoc."

J. Edward replied, "Vijay, you know as well as I do that the information we gave the FBI never helped them stop a shooting. Hell, if it is critical to our national safety, they would subpoena the information, but they haven't done that yet because they know it won't help."

Vijay cautiously replied, "But what if the data could be enhanced to help them be proactive?"

"How would that happen? As smart as that watch is, it can't read minds."

Vijay was getting his hopes up, "You're right, it can't read minds, but it can read blood."

"Huh? Read blood?"

Vijay was getting into full stride, but he knew he had to keep it simple for J. Edward. "The VT2 works by reading blood, and so far, we've only been reading health vital signs. But the watch can detect behavioral aspects that, when modeled against other users who have killed, can identify new Final

Notice killers. In short, it can pinpoint Final Notice recipients who display similar readings to past killers. Does that make sense?"

"Sure it does, but that's all theoretical."

"Actually, it isn't," confessed Vijay.

"How and when did that happen?" blurted J. Edward.

"I've been tinkering with it ever since the killings took place during the test phase. Now, I think I've nailed it," Vijay proudly, but cautiously replied.

"Does the FBI know about this?" asked J. Edward.

An alarm went off for Vijay, but he answered truthfully, "I've hinted to Zoe, my FBI contact, that I'm working on something that might help, but that's all she knows so far."

"Damn, Vijay. With all the news about government eavesdropping and surveillance, if this gets out, it could be a huge turnoff for sales. Let me think about it."

"J. Edward, what do you think will happen to sales or VitalTech if Final Notice recipients start killing politicians and judges?"

"McAdam killed three senators, and nobody blinked," J. Edward countered. "I'm uncomfortable with it. I'll talk with Mike."

Vijay knew it was over, "He won't like it. He killed it in its present state. Why would he like a new, improved version?"

"I'm not going to take sides in this fight between you and Mike. He's been charged with running the business, and that's his number one priority. If the FBI wants to establish a "Big Brother" society, they need to force the issue. I have to go, Vijay. Leave it alone."

***

That evening, Vijay, Jennifer, and Karima had finished their dinner. It was Vijay's turn to bathe Kari. He always looked forward to the happy, giggling, 'splash party,' as Jennifer called it. At least that's what it sounded like to her. Tonight was no different, and having put Karima in her bed, Vijay changed out of his wet clothes, brought about by some very exuberant splashing, and joined Jennifer in the family room.

Their relationship had been somewhat strained lately, and the previous evening's discussion highlighted Jennifer's very plausible concern for their family's safety. Vijay was very down after his call from J. Edward, and he really didn't want to discuss it with Jennifer right now, but he wanted to get their relationship back on track, and he knew she'd ask if he'd made the call.

In as upbeat a way as he could muster, Vijay volunteered that he'd spoken with J. Edward and explained about the enhancements and that J. Edward was interested and wanted to think about it.

Jennifer asked if Vijay thought there was a chance, and he said, he was hopeful, and then changed the subject to a much happier discussion, their new shepa-doodle.

His ploy worked, at least it appeared to because Jennifer was excited about getting their puppy in just two days. They had already named him: Fritz. Her enthusiasm brought Vijay's mood up as well, and, at least for a while, they returned to happier times.

They had been telling Karima about her new fuzzy 'brother,' showing her pictures and the cuddly toy dog they had already bought for her. Her pronunciation of Fritz was more like Fwitz and would remain that way for some time. Like good 'dog parents,' they already had his bed, a small fence-like cage to keep him contained, a water-proof – rather, a urine-proof – rug, and enough toys to start their own pet shop. Vijay, of course, had picked up a FitBark as well, to monitor the pup's exercise and sleeping data.

Jennifer had an earlier than usual start to her next day, so she excused herself, and Vijay returned to his office.

Vijay had never fully considered scrapping the enhanced information he shared with Zoe. When he found out about the Boston murders and saw that their signatures or profiles were very different than the Final Notice killers they had investigated in the past, he could have made a case for delaying the launch. Instead, he and Alek had worked even harder, spending the entire day incorporating these new emotional profile variants into the system.

Vijay was reviewing the new system in anticipation of their call with Zoe the following day when an alert beeped, re-directing Vijay's attention to it. His pulse quickened, and he quickly grabbed his phone and speed-dialed Zoe, despite the late hour.

Zoe answered immediately, "Hi Vijay," and noting the unusual time asked, "Is everything OK?"

Vijay tried to stay calm and focused as he quickly explained that a Final Notice recipient, Mitchell Connelly, was exhibiting acute signs consistent with anger, rage, and retribution. "He is listed as having a gun and is currently on East Capitol Street between 5th and 6th Streets heading in the direction of Lincoln Park. He's a retired government employee. That's all I know."

***

Zoe, and Demi were, in fact, on their way home from a restaurant and were still functioning in an upbeat, happy, two glasses of wine way. "So, you're saying that this guy is not just out for a late-night stroll?"

Vijay replied, much more seriously, "His markers are through the roof!"

Zoe shifted behavioral gears. "OK. I'm on it! Thanks."

***

Washington, D.C. The two law enforcers were not far from Connelly's location. Demi's phone had rung just after Zoe's, so when Zoe turned to her, Demi spoke into her phone, "I can't talk now," and hung up when Zoe shouted, "Come on, let's go get a bad guy!" and started running.

Demi began to follow, but after only a few yards, she stopped and screamed out, "Damn, I twisted my ankle. Go ahead, and I'll catch up."

Zoe picked up the pace, and with her earbuds in, she reconnected to Vijay, as she ran in the direction of Lincoln Park.

Vijay gave her the current coordinates, and after a while, Zoe said, "OK, I think I see him just ahead. There's no one else around. Talk with you later."

She was closing the gap, and as she approached the lone male, she shouted out, "FBI. Turn around with your hands raised high."

At that same moment, a dark figure stepped out from behind a tree. Zoe saw him out of the corner of her eye and tried to react, but he was able to land a sharp blow to the back of her head, sending her sprawling onto the sidewalk.

Vik Vasin calmly stepped over Zoe, never taking his eye off Connelly as he turned right to complete his job. Vasin watched as Connelly walked right up to his target and put one 9mm round in the middle of his forehead. Seconds later, just as planned, Jack Meacham, ex-Army, with a permit to carry a weapon and about to become the newest 'good-guy,' happened onto the scene and killed Connelly.

Vik watched and drew a little closer as police and people gathered. Meacham was questioned, and he explained that he saw this white guy shoot this black guy, so he did his duty and took out the shooter. It was a good story, and it would be corroborated by the cameras they knew were surveilling the area. Vik smiled and thought to himself, "Yuri, or whatever his real name was, would be pleased. We got a very big fish tonight, and it was a hell of a lot easier than the minnow in Boston. He even had his own gun."

Demi had caught up with Zoe, just as she was coming to, still groggy and with an aching head.

Breathing hard, Demi helped her up and asked, "What the hell happened?"

Zoe was still half out of it and muttered, "Someone whacked me."

They walked slowly to the crime scene, Zoe, with her head spinning and Demi limping, and they decided that since they had nothing to add, they really weren't in a condition to talk with law enforcement to get the whole story. Nor did Zoe want to get into explanations about the details of why she was there. She did, however, find out about the victim – he was one of her Number One Priorities, a Supreme Court Justice.

***

Demi called an Uber to take the two of them to her flat. She made an icepack for Zoe's huge bump and got her to bed, but Zoe didn't sleep well. The combination of pain when she moved her head, the many questions swirling around in her addled brain, and the fact that she had failed to stop a top-priority murder, made sleep impossible.

She was up early, swallowed three aspirin, and winced when she touched her new bump. The ice had helped, and the blow didn't break the skin, so the damage was not visually noticeable. But that didn't make it feel any better. Demi was up even earlier, had made coffee, and she handed Zoe a steaming cup.

"How was Vijay involved with whoever we, or actually, you, were chasing?"

"Vijay is testing an enhancement to the report he sends me."

Demi interrupted, "I thought that stopped."

"It did," but Zoe caught herself. "I don't know where this lead came from. I haven't spoken with him since we took off running. I'm sorry, I forgot to ask how your ankle is?"

"Oh, it was fine this morning. Must have just buckled, trying to start up too fast to keep up. So, who whacked you? Did you see him?"

"I think I caught a brief glance, but now I have zero recollection. Not sure I would even recognize him."

Zoe noticed her laptop open on the coffee table with Demi's cup alongside it. "Is that my laptop?"

"Yeah. I tiptoed out of the bedroom to let you sleep, put on some coffee, and realized that my laptop was still in the bedroom. I didn't want to wake you, so I thought I'd find out on the news what happened last night."

Demi retrieved the open laptop and brought it back to the kitchen counter. There was a news feed site on the screen, and Zoe saw the headlines.

"Supreme Court Judge Murdered!"

The stories from all the news sources covered the same points – that Supreme Court Justice Jefferson Darrow had been shot to death as he walked from the Supreme Court to his home in Washington, D.C. Darrow had been on the bench for over fifteen years and was considered to be the Court's most conservative justice, as well as only the second African-American to be appointed. He was now the first Supreme Court Justice to be assassinated.

The suspect, Mitchell Connelly, had been a federal government employee who was ultimately let go for incompetence. He made the news occasionally, ranting about getting even, although he was mostly dismissed as a nutcase. Connelly was very left-wing.

The GOP and the right were having a field day with the damnations of the left's resistance to the President's agenda and the anger over the various machinations of the Supreme Court appointees. The murder became a focal point in portraying the left as without principles. They further ridiculed Connelly for his senseless act, as the President still had time to appoint another politically aligned justice.

FINAL ACT

Demi asked, "So who were you chasing? The killer?"

"I think so, although I don't know for sure who I was approaching or who whacked my head."

"Do you think it could be related to your Final Notice watch?"

Zoe's head jerked up from the screen. "The murder or me getting whacked on the head?"

Demi replied, "The murder," and she pulled the laptop toward her and scrolled to the very bottom. She pointed to an article from The Boston Globe. "Given the raised tension between the Left and Right wings, extreme violence from either side should come as no surprise. However, there is an additional perspective that perhaps Connelly's action was triggered by receiving a Final Notice alert on his VT2 watch."

And then Zoe remembered the call from Vijay.

***

CHAPTER 14 – ONLY IN HORSESHOES ...

Washington, D.C. She'd been looking forward to the upcoming call with Vijay, but right now, Zoe was having a hard time feeling positive. There were so many open questions from so many areas: Was there a Russian connection with this latest shooting? Will there be reprisals as a result of the Justice murder? Will Vijay's help be effective? Hopefully, she'd be able to answer the last question soon, when her IT guru joined her for the call with Vijay. But first, she needed to talk with Vijay privately.

Vijay picked up and said, "You're early, and what happened last night? You never called back, and then this morning, I read all about who Connelly was stalking. What happened?"

Zoe sighed and apologized. "I'm sorry. Someone knocked me on the head as I was running after the suspect, who I assume was Connelly. I'm OK, but I missed the chance. But how did you know where he was?"

Vijay replied proudly (so focused on his new system that he never asked about Zoe's attack), "That's the other piece of information I mentioned the other day. The VT2 is GPS enabled, so when I saw the markers spiking, I was able to track him, as will you. I'm just so sorry I called you too late. We were so close."

FINAL ACT

Zoe recalled one of her father's favorite expressions, possibly because it was so American, and her father was French. She seemed to remember it was attributed to a baseball player: "Close only counts in horseshoes and hand grenades." And she added, "By the way, the FBI did not visit the VitalTech offices. They did visit Alek Belikov at his home, but that related to the death of his wife's killer. They subsequently found the killer, and guess what his name was?"

Vijay didn't have a clue what his name might be, but he knew where she was going with this. "Vladimir Putin?"

"You're close – same nationality. And there was another one that played the role of a 'good-guy' in one of the Boston Italian murders. We need to figure this out very soon, especially given what we know the Russians can do with elections. Can we put the call back thirty-minutes so I can break the GPS news to Ninad Banerjee, our IT guy? He had put together something pretty slick, but with GPS, I think it's about to get even slicker!"

"Sure. I'll have Alek with me. And Zoe, no one other than you and Ninad, can know the source of this info. If it doesn't prove valuable, we can shut it down, but if it does help, I'm willing to take the risk. And in that vein, is there any precedent for the FBI to protect and grant immunity to hackers who help you?"

"Actually, I could be in more trouble than you," she said, without answering his question.

Disappointedly, Vijay asked, "I take that as a no?"

"Yes."

***

Zoe had enlisted the aid of Ninad, one of their top IT guys, to develop an application that would capture and integrate data from various sources, including the critical data from VitalTech. In an amazingly short space of time, Ninad had developed something that Zoe could only imagine in science fiction terms. She gave him a quick call with the GPS update, half thinking he'd throw a fit after all the work he'd put in. Instead, he almost screamed with joy! "That's fantastic! See you in 30 minutes."

***

Chestnut Hill, Massachusetts. Vijay called Alek to alert him of the short delay to allow Zoe's IT guy to consider the effect of the GPS addition. They discussed some of the report details, and Alek assured Vijay that nobody would be able to spot the data outputs that they had engineered. Then, they made the call to Zoe and Ninad.

Zoe and Vijay introduced their colleagues, and Vijay projected a live report prototype, showing Final Notice recipients with threat levels color-coded from green to red. These levels were based on Vijay's detailed modeling of past Final Notice killers. Zoe's team could click on any of them for their names, addresses, employer, date of death prediction, gun owner or not, photo - if available - and live GPS location. Their doctor and next of kin notification details were also available.

Vijay added something else. "In addition to receiving data on all Final Notice recipients, the new report will include all VT2 wearers, including those who have not received their Final Notice, as soon as they migrate out of the green zone behavioral threshold. They will be identifiable as non-Final Notice recipients. You can import this or not. It's your call, but the idea is to track the real, bad guys."

Zoe asked Ninad if that could be integrated.

FINAL ACT

Ninad replied, "Yes. No problem, and we can always filter it out if we need to." He was very upbeat. "This is exactly what we need. I have put together a two-dimensional app. I call it the 'Final App,'" he said with a smile that only Zoe could see. (And only Ninad could see Zoe's eye-roll.)

"Can you give me screen control so I can show you what I've done?"

Vijay handed over the conference call screen control, and he and Alek were about to be blown away by Ninad's work.

Ninad opened the app, and a map of Washington, D.C. appeared with a large number of dots ranging from green to yellow to orange to red. The orange and red dots were blinking and moving on the map in real-time.

Ninad explained, "This is a simulation-based on the little information that Supervisory Agent Brouet has shared with me, but we will quickly be able to go live as soon as we begin receiving your live feed. The dots represent your Final Notice people. As they exhibit more aggressive readings, the dots change color and begin to blink at the orange and red levels; and when they reach those levels, they are pushed out to local law enforcement in the vicinity."

He clicked on a dot, and a box appeared. "Clicking on a dot will bring up this detail box, displaying whatever information you provide, plus information that we hold. That includes our facial recognition files and a lot of federal, state, and local government data. We'll be able to push this app out across the country to all levels of law enforcement."

Vijay chimed in, "Very impressive, but how did you get this far so fast, and why did you assume that we could provide GPS info?"

"I was talking to my cousin, Ganesh, who used to work with you, and he told me about the watch's capability, including its GPS functionality. So, I built the app with the ability to use a broad range of data, in case you gave it to us."

Vijay asked Ninad to pass along his regards to Ganesh, and Zoe broke in, "Ninad, please show them the other dimension."

"OK. This app, so far, will tell us the hot spots insofar as all Final Notice people are concerned; but we need to stay focused on protecting our priority targets, and the danger increases as a Final Notice person gets closer to one of our priorities. This is especially true for those Final Notice recipients similar to the ones in the Boston area, who may display a different reading from a traditional revenge seeker. So, Supervisory Agent Brouet is requesting that as soon as possible, and until the elections are complete, all priority targets are given a tracking device of some kind."

"You can buy them all VT2's," intervened Vijay, half-joking.

"That's certainly an option," chuckled Ninad as he regained control. He switched to a new screen which, in addition to the Final Notice dots, showed blue dots in a few different sizes. They were also moving about the map. "The blue dots represent our priority targets – judges, senators, etc. – and they will also show photos and details when the dots are hovered over or clicked. When orange or red dots move closer to them, alerts will be pushed out to local and federal law enforcement. The program will also be able to discern the directness of an orange or red dot's path toward the blue dot, injecting another level of urgency. Any questions?"

Zoe jumped in and stated the obvious. "We believe this is just the tool we need, but it's dependent on getting info from you and getting the priority target's acceptance of carrying a tracking device."

Vijay asked, "Since this is for their protection, why wouldn't they accept it?"

Zoe laughed. "Some of our politicians would rather not want others to know where they are from time to time. But more importantly, what degree of certainty do we have that you can continue to provide this information from now through the elections?"

Vijay answered, "Alek and I are pretty sure we can continue to provide the information, unless VitalTech somehow uses a legal method to stop us, based on a leak, or some proof or strong evidence that we have invaded or hacked their system. How are you going to answer the inevitable question about where this information is coming from?"

Zoe answered, "As Ninad mentioned, a lot of the information we've covered today is already at our disposal. You've told me that you don't have comprehensive user photos or employment details, but we have immediate access to over ten-million facial recognition files and tens of millions more from local and state government systems. We have access to tax records, mobile phones, and internet tracking, social media monitoring, and countless security cameras around the country. I'd be surprised if anyone would question where the intel is coming from, but you're right about a leak. If we're asked in a legal forum, we'd have to tell the truth. But we've been receiving data from VitalTech for two years, up to a couple of days ago. And we still don't know if it was VitalTech or someone else that has stopped the data feed, so it's a pretty muddled situation. And hopefully, if we have to, we can ask or possibly force VitalTech for the data by declaring a national emergency. Seems like more of an emergency than a wall."

Vijay was impressed and excited. "We're willing to take the risk but do me a favor. Change the name of your app so that it doesn't immediately create a connection to the VT2. And Ninad, can you stay on the line with Alek to make sure we have the correct interface details?"

Ninad chirped, "Will do."

Vijay signed off. "OK. Thanks, Zoe, and congratulations, Ninad, on some very cool programming. Alek, please give me a call when you finish up with Ninad. Bye, all."

Vijay sat back in his chair and took a very deep breath. He'd just taken a step to the other side of the law, but he rationalized, *It shouldn't be this way. This cooperation is vital, and as long as the data is not abused, it's in every law-abiding person's interest.* He sincerely believed that, but would Jennifer?

He needed to find out. Jennifer had just put Karima down for her nap, so he asked if she had a minute, and she did. He began with the Supreme Court justice murder and how the new system that he and Alek had been working on identified a Final Notice recipient in an elevated emotional state, consistent with previous killings. "It was in D.C., so I immediately called Zoe to give her his coordinates."

He skipped the part about Zoe being attacked, "I lost touch with her after that, and then this morning I learned, along with the rest of the world, that a Supreme Court Justice had been murdered by a Final Notice recipient. Our system was so close to stopping it, and if the FBI had been receiving our data directly, they would have had the time to stop it."

Jennifer was impressed with what Vijay and Alek had created, but it was still illegal. "Is Zoe able to get you immunity?"

"No. But she's also risking her job by accepting the data."

"That's fine, but that doesn't keep you out of jail, nor does it make the Russians or whoever the bad guys are more tolerant of your actions. Vijay, I was able to handle the situation with a single goon, but they won't use that simplistic approach next time. Please, think of your family."

Vijay's gut twisted as he absorbed Jennifer's plea, but he couldn't bail out on Zoe either. He inaccurately described a notion of Zoe's: "Jen, the FBI is trying to get VitalTech to give them the information, either voluntarily or via a court order. If that happens, I won't have to provide it." He left out the details about how the emotional indicators would be supplied.

Jennifer looked at him coldly, turned around, and left the room.

***

Washington, D.C. Zoe was thrilled with the new system that Ninad had developed; however, she still had major concerns. The biggest was that she was collaborating with someone who was breaking the law. How could she handle that with the Bureau? She was also concerned about the vulnerability of Vijay's information flow being disrupted. Knowing someone's behavioral state and their location was critical if they hoped to stop a killing. Could the Bureau formally request the information from VitalTech? If VitalTech said no, the Bureau's situation would be far worse. Could they demand it? Zoe was meeting with Hawke shortly, and somehow, she would need to discuss it with him. He won't be happy about the Jefferson Darrow murder, but at least now, we'll have a better chance once Vijay's data starts to flow.

And then there was Demi. Zoe understood the expression, "Love is blind." *Was that happening to her?* Several little things had begun to add up: Demi taking her phone from the room ... looking at her laptop ... questions. And then the incident the other night: Getting a phone call just before Zoe started the chase, twisting her ankle which recovered very quickly, and then getting ambushed by a guy who seemed to know she was coming. Zoe knew that she'd have to figure these out on her own.

***

CHAPTER 15 – YOU'VE BEEN HACKED

Washington, D.C. Zoe was ushered into Eric Hawke's office, and she felt a sense of déjà vu, reminding her of when, as a child, she'd done something bad, and her father was waiting for her. The Executive Assistant Director was utterly focused on a document, and Zoe wasn't sure if he even knew she was there. She stood there for what felt like a long time until he finally looked up, handed her the document and asked, in a very downbeat way, "Did we have any chance of stopping this? Are we kidding ourselves that we can?"

Zoe looked at the dossier detailing the Darrow murder, organized her thoughts and replied. "If it happened a week from now, we'd have an excellent chance."

She recounted the close miss last night and then took him through the developments of the morning with Vijay and Ninad. To Zoe's surprise, Hawke was impressed with the system, and Zoe pressed on with the point of getting high priority targets to accept a tracking device.

Hawke reflected, "From what you've said, if Darrow had been carrying a tracker last night, Vijay would have seen him as the target, and preemptive protection might have saved him. I don't think we can force some of these people to carry one, but then they're even dumber than many people think.

"I don't see any way other than this system to stop further problems," he continued. "Give me some options and costs on the best tracking devices. I think we can get pretty broad acceptance."

Zoe was encouraged by Hawke's realization that without the system, they had no chance, so she addressed her biggest concern. "Yes, sir. I'll get some options, and speaking of options; we have a problem. If I felt there was another way to limit our Final Notice exposure, I would, but VitalTech has the proprietary information that we need."

Hawke interrupted, "And they're giving it to us. So, what's the problem?"

"They're not giving it to us. Vijay is, and he's hacked into their system to get it for us. VitalTech cut us off the other day."

"Why?"

"We don't know. It all happened very quickly. Their new CEO found out about the cooperation and stopped it. Then he tried to remove Vijay from the Board and his work on additional medical enhancements. Vijay was finalizing the new system outputs, and he decided to take the risk to help us."

"Is this Vijay a saint or something? Why would he risk so much to help the FBI?"

"Strange as it may seem in today's world, he's just a really, good guy." Ignoring Hawke's eye roll, she asked, "Can we grant Vijay immunity, and if not, what are the chances of getting an emergency injunction, at least temporarily?"

"Definite 'No' regarding immunity. The emergency injunction is a possibility, especially given last night's disaster. There's concern that gun-happy 'patriots' on both sides will begin to play tit-for-tat. We're even discussing implementing Secret Service protection for all presidential candidates and Supreme Court Justices. So, anything we can do will help. Let me get some opinions. Anything else?"

"This may be just a heads-up if it doesn't spread – and some of it is still just conjecture – but there have been a number of unusual murders in the Boston area. They appear to be gang against gang, possibly Russians against Italians."

Hawke snapped back, "I hope you're not wasting your time with those! We should be cheering them on."

"I've just been following them because they are Final Notice related." Zoe explained the motiveless crimes, 'good-guy' appearances, and a lot of Russians. She also drew a comparison with last night's shooting. "Although there weren't any Russians involved in last night's shooting, that we're aware of, there are similarities to the Boston killings. A Final Notice recipient kills someone, and a 'good-guy' is on the scene to take out the killer. And although Connelly might have had a loose, deranged motive, he was backed up by someone who stopped me from getting there, and Connelly doesn't seem like someone who would have a partner."

"You're saying Final Notice people are being managed? And that we're pretty certain it's Russians doing the managing in Boston?"

"Yes, sir."

"Let me know immediately if any of your suspicions turn concrete. Anything else?"

"No, Sir. That's all. I'll keep you posted."

Hawke's gaze told Zoe that he was now somewhere else, and the meeting was over.

***

As Zoe headed back to her office, she felt that the meeting with Hawke had gone better than she expected. He could have arrested her and Vijay for conspiracy to commit a crime, and a cyber-crime. But now she had another of her concerns to deal with; Demi.

Zoe had planned to spend the night at Demi's, and it was Zoe's turn to either cook or bring home carry out food. That was a no-brainer for Zoe. Ten out of ten nights, she opted for carry-out, and tonight was not an exception. She decided on Indian food and stopped by RASA, a hip Indian restaurant in southwest D.C., that was one of their favorites. They both loved their salad, called "Sexy and I Know It," and the equally quirky "Tikka Chance On Me" chicken tikka. But Zoe's enthusiasm for the food was tempered by her need and fear of a confrontation with Demi.

***

Quincy, Massachusetts. Alek and Ninad had wrapped up the data streaming details, and Alek was tweaking a couple of things when something within the VitalTech system caught his attention. He called Ninad back and asked him to verify that the original data feed was still not being received. Ninad checked and confirmed that was the case.

Alek's next call was to Vijay. "Vijay, everything's good to go with Ninad, and the new data feed is now live, but I spotted something that puzzled me." Vijay waited for what came next. "I found another live outbound data feed, almost identical in content to what was previously being sent to the FBI. It was very cleverly masked by the disabled FBI link. That's why I missed it earlier. The destination of the new live feed is obscured."

Vijay asked, "Could it be that the FBI link was restored?"

"No. I called Ninad back, and he confirmed that their link remains dead."

"What's your take? Could it be an internal link to a VitalTech department or person?" Vijay was trolling through possibilities.

"I don't think so. It seems to be set up to exit the VitalTech system. I'll keep digging."

"You said 'almost identical in content'?"

"Yes. The newer feed includes GPS coordinates."

***

Washington, D.C. Zoe opened the door to Demi's flat. The flat seemed darker than usual, and the sensual aroma wafting from a dozen candles won the contest with the savory Indian food. She looked up as she returned the key to her purse and noticed a lot of flickering candles and a big bouquet. Demi heard her enter and, with a big smile, announced, "Happy one-month anniversary!" Zoe put the bag of food on the counter and accepted an inviting kiss. They embraced, and two hours later, ate their room temperature meal.

Just before they returned to bed for the night, Zoe's phone rang. It was Vijay, and Zoe answered in her very good mood voice, "Hi!"

Vijay asked, "Are you alone?"

"I can be." She went into the bedroom and closed the door. "OK. I'm alone."

Vijay explained that Alek had found what appeared to be a second outbound data feed, but so far, he didn't know where it went. "You mentioned the Russian-Italian shootings, and maybe this is how they're finding their killers. The fake FBI agents might have hacked into the system."

Zoe was puzzled about why Vijay thought that a hack had occurred then, and he explained, "They threatened to take Alek's computer away unless he allowed them to have a look while they were there."

Zoe's mind was spinning. "I agree. I think you've been hacked, or actually, VitalTech has. Finding one, or even two Final Notice recipients might be lucky, but five?"

Vijay added flatly, "The new feed contains GPS coordinates."

"Damn! I met with Hawke today, and I had to come clean about our cooperation. He understands and is checking out whether we may be able to demand the data from VitalTech in the interest of national security. The murder the other night will add weight to the request, and he also bought the idea of GPS trackers for the potential targets."

Vijay interjected, "Getting the data directly from VitalTech will help, but we'll have a wrinkle with supplying the behavioral info. VitalTech doesn't know anything about that."

Zoe thought about that for a few seconds and replied, "OK. Let's see where it goes first and keep me posted regarding the unknown data feed. Your new data feed is coming through, and Ninad already has it up and fully integrated. We'll start pushing it out tomorrow to a couple of test groups within the

FINAL ACT

Bureau for feedback before we roll it out wider. Thank you very much, Vijay. This is a game-changer for us."

"You're welcome, Zoe. Maybe you can bring me Indian takeaway when I'm in prison."

She laughed but explained, "Sorry. We just had Indian tonight. But let's try to keep you on the streets, and let's talk tomorrow."

Zoe quickly opened the door, and both she and Demi jumped.

Demi exclaimed, "Oh, I was just coming in. Who were you talking with?"

***

Chestnut Hill, Massachusetts. Jennifer was still awake when Vijay finished his call with Zoe. "What's the latest with the FBI cooperation?" she asked, rather coolly.

"They're thrilled with the new data feed and are confident that this will slow down or even stop killings."

"Have they asked VitalTech yet about supplying the data?"

"No. Not yet."

The only sound was the rustling of the comforter as Jennifer rolled over, away from Vijay.

***

CHAPTER 16 – ALL HELL BREAKS LOOSE

Washington, D.C. Zoe arrived at her office with one thing on her mind - What is going on with Demi? Five minutes later, it was possibly the last thing on her mind.

Two judges and a state senator had been shot, one of the judges fatally. Zoe took small consolation that none of them were Final Notice shooters, so she didn't have to get involved. There was a message from legal that they needed to speak with her, and there was a memo that all presidential candidates and Supreme Court justices were to receive protection. The Secret Service would protect the candidates, and the Supreme Court Police would guard the justices.

Protection for presidential candidates usually doesn't begin until much later in the nomination process. President Obama received his protection eighteen months before the election, the earliest ever, based on threats, and Hillary Clinton, as a former First Lady, already had protection when she ran. Now, over twenty candidates would be eligible to receive protection, but they could choose to refuse it. John McCain had refused, believing that the security would act as a barrier between himself and the electorate. But even that short while ago, the nation was less divided.

She looked at Ninad's new App and almost panicked at the number of orange and red dots crawling all over the D.C.

map until she realized it was filtered to all VT2 users. So, she held her breath and filtered for Final Notice recipients only. Although that significantly reduced the crawling dots, there were still twenty or more, and then she laughed. It was still rush hour. No wonder there were so many angry people out there.

Ninad had programmed a number of automatic alarms so the system self-monitored, signaling when there was a potential incident. He had already imported the Secret Service agents into the GPS tracking system so that they would be visible. She could see a number of them around, mostly near the White House, but soon there'd be many more, jetting all over the country as the candidates pressed the flesh and tried to connect with voters. Assuming the Supreme Court Police and Justices get trackers, it would start to get pretty busy.

Her desk phone rang. It was Legal and Sue Parks, a senior attorney was her way to Zoe's office.

Zoe hadn't interacted with many people from Legal, and she didn't know Sue, who was probably a little older than herself and was all business. Sue asked, "How long have we been receiving information from VitalTech?"

Zoe looked it up and printed the original letter of agreement dated two-and-a-half years ago.

Sue looked at it and asked, "And when you stopped receiving the information the other day, what did you do?"

Zoe stated that she called Vijay Patel, and Sue asked what his explanation was.

Zoe explained that Vijay had sold the business, was on the Board of VitalTech, but was not in an executive position. She also covered the fact that VitalTech's new CEO was unhappy when he learned of the information sharing and that he had probably pulled the plug.

"But you haven't spoken with VitalTech's CEO or anyone else at VitalTech to confirm that, correct?" Sue asked.

Zoe realized that in dealing with V jay, that step was not as apparent as Sue just made it. She explained that from the outset, all of her VitalTech dealings had been with Vijay. The VitalTech data that the FBI had been receiving was a continuation of what Vijay had set up when he was CEO. Vijay was also collecting that data as part of an ongoing product improvement project he was coordinating for VitalTech. Vijay's project involvement ceased, and both Vijay and the FBI's data feed stopped at the same time.

Sue continued, "Eric mentioned that you are now getting a new report directly from Vijay Patel, but not in his capacity with VitalTech?"

Zoe confirmed. "That's correct."

Sue expressed her concern. "That puts us in a very vulnerable position if it gets out that we are conspiring with someone who does not have legal access."

"And that's why I advised Assistant Director Hawke. I was concerned about the legal issues, but of even more importance to me was the potential loss of the information. Without it, we have no line of defense to protect our judges, politicians, or anyone else from people who may kill because they have nothing to lose."

Zoe explained the incident with the Supreme Court justice and how using this system, even before it was fully functional, almost saved his life.

Sue asked, "My understanding is that the new system that Vijay Patel has developed is significantly better than the one you received in the past. If a request is made to VitalTech and they grant our request to resume the original report, how will you deal with the gap in quality?"

Zoe was starting to realize that there was no easy way out of this and that she just had to hope that Vijay wasn't found out. So, she decided to withdraw her request to ask VitalTech to restore the information feed formally, and she apologized to Sue for wasting their time.

But Sue wasn't done. "While we appreciate the importance of the report, we cannot allow you to utilize stolen or pirated property. I'll be drafting a cease and desist order that will be with you before the day is out. I'm sorry."

***

Zoe called Vijay and explained the disaster that her legal people had delivered. Zoe and Vijay agreed that there was nothing more they could do to ensure that Vijay's system would continue, but they also decided to risk the consequences and keep the information flowing as long as they could, at least until the elections were over.

Vijay gave Zoe an update on the mysterious information feed. Alek had found the access point created by the fake FBI visit. It was relatively crude and had already been deactivated, possibly by VitalTech system security. It would have been sufficient, however, to deliver names of Final Notice recipients from a defined geographic area, for example, Boston.

The new mystery feed, however, did include everything in

the original report, plus the GPS tracking feature. It was created five days before the Supreme Court justice was shot, which was possibly enough time to help someone identify an appropriate Recipient. The one they chose would have been straightforward to enlist, given his high level of militancy.

Zoe suggested that perhaps the two system breaches were independent of each other. They were using the same idea, so maybe the genesis was related, but the Supreme Court target was in a different league than the gang killings. She also raised another point. "The guy who whacked me over the head seemed to be waiting for someone. Could he have tracked me by my VT2?"

Vijay thought about that. "Yes, but if that's the case, the report coming out of VitalTech either contains some extra sophistication built-in, along the lines of what Ninad developed to identify routes, speeds, convergence on targets, etc., or they were tracking you."

Zoe shuddered at that thought and added, "That would also indicate that whoever is behind the effort has an agenda that we need to stop ASAP."

And at precisely that moment, Zoe's computer sounded one of those piercing urgent alerts that Ninad had incorporated into the new system.

***

Zoe opened the alert. It was from Des Moines, Iowa. A Final Notice recipient was headed in the direction of a town hall meeting, where a Democratic presidential candidate was holding an informal meeting. Iowa had been pretty busy with candidate visits for the past month. Zoe called the Des Moines FBI office and spoke with the Special Agent in Charge, who was en route to the venue. He advised that, based on the alert pushed out by Ninad's App, the presidential candidate was safe and had been locked down, apparently against her will, and that the local police were also responding. He patched Zoe through so she could track what was happening in real-time.

Zoe listened in as the FBI and police neared the venue to intercept the suspected Recipient. She reminded the agent to try to capture the suspect alive, just as a burst of shouting erupted. "What's going on?"

The agent replied that the police had been diverted to a shooting a short way from the venue. After what seemed to be a much longer time than it was, the agent advised that the suspect had been shot.

Zoe almost screamed with anger, "How? Why?"

The agent said he would try to get her connected to the scene and the bodycam of the local police officer in charge. A few seconds later, Zoe was viewing the scene and talking with the officer. The officer explained that they were two blocks from the targeted venue and that shortly after arriving, a call came in from a witness that a man had been shot.

Zoe asked for details of the shooting. The officer confirmed that the witness saw a man walking toward the venue, when a car coming from the direction of the venue, stopped in the middle of the street near the man on foot. The driver quickly exited the vehicle, approached the man on foot, and fired two shots. He then hurried back to his car and drove off. Police were looking for the shooter, but the shooter's car description was vague.

Zoe asked for confirmation that the victim was the Final Notice Recipient, and the officer confirmed.

Zoe tried to make sense of what had just happened. She knew it wasn't a coincidence. Was there a handler who saw the police activity and, rather than abort, decided to silence the Recipient?

***

Des Moines, IA. Vik Vasin was pissed off. He'd had to spend a week in Des Moines to train his Zombie, and then somehow, the police had been tipped off. That meant that their knowledge about the D.C. judge job wasn't a one-off. He called the number he'd been given, using his single-use, prepaid, throw-away, burner phone, and explained what happened. The voice said to wait for further instructions. Vik grimaced at the thought of how long he would have to wait – in Des Moines – for further instructions. An hour later, a much happier Vik Vasin received a call to fly to Las Vegas ASAP to assist with a "business deal" in process. He wiped his gun and casually dropped it into the Des Moines River before heading to the airport.

***

Washington, D.C. Zoe was disappointed that they didn't have a suspect to question, but Vijay's system had probably prevented a presidential candidate's execution. She called Hawke and gave him an update. He shared her disappointment but then dropped a bomb – a warrant had been issued for Vijay's arrest.

Zoe erupted, "How the hell did that happen?"

"Legal was concerned about our exposure and contacted

the CEO of VitalTech to see if there was any wiggle room for us to use the data that Vijay was supplying. The answer was 'No' and Mike Kalin, VitalTech's CEO, apparently was livid, threatening to expose the FBI's illegal surveillance. He immediately filed a formal complaint, and charges were filed. Agents will be bringing Vijay in later today. You can advise him if you want."

Zoe was incensed and incredulous. "His system prevented an assassination today, and as a reward, we arrest him!?" But before she fully vented on Hawke and the system, she got a hold of herself and gave in, "I'll call him now."

"Thanks, let me know when you've done it,"

***

"Vijay, I can't begin to tell you how sorry I am, but I have some very disturbing news." She paused and drew in a deep breath, bracing herself to deliver the injustice. "I have just been advised that a warrant for your arrest has been issued for a number of cyber-crimes. I expect that FBI agents will be with you soon to search your home and bring you in for questioning and to appear before a magistrate. I have spoken with the Boston field office and explained the situation, but all they can do is make the process as easy as possible."

Vijay sat in total disbelief. All he could say was, "Seriously?"

"I'm afraid so. Our legal department was looking for a way around the legality of the information feed, and they decided to ask Mike Kalin. I guess it slipped out that you were already providing the information, and Kalin erupted and filed charges.

Zoe continued, "I explained to Hawke that your system prevented an assassination attempt, but there's nothing he can do, and I appreciate that you will now want to stop the data feed."

Vijay found his voice, "That's great. I helped stop a crime, so I get arrested?"

There wasn't much that Zoe could say to make everything right, "I know. That's what I told Hawke. Look, Vijay, I think that whoever is doing this spotted the police as we closed in on the Recipient and killed him so as not to leave loose ends. If Alek can find where the mystery feed is going, we have a chance to stop them."

Vijay's head was reeling with various emotions and fears. "I apologize for any lack of enthusiasm, but cheering you on from jail doesn't make me feel any better. I'll remind Alek how important finding the destination of the data is, but I'll also warn him that his help may garner him the same reward that I received."

"I'm sorry, Vijay," Zoe added lamely. And she was. "But you don't have much time. I can't say too much, but they will come with a warrant to search your office, computer, phone, and home. Call your lawyer and don't answer any questions until you have your lawyer with you."

A resigned Vijay sighed. "I thought you said they'd make it easy."

"As easy as possible. I'm sorry, Vijay."

***

CHAPTER 17 – RELATIONSHIP ISSUES

Chestnut Hill, Massachusetts. Vijay struggled with whether or not to kill the FBI feed. Part of him wanted to do it for what he perceived as a moronic lack of gratitude, but part of him knew how important it was to stop the killings. He called his lawyer, filled her in on the impending arrest and the background, and asked her about shutting down the data feed that prompted the warrant. Her advice was unequivocal – shut it down immediately.

He called Alek and summarized his call from Zoe, along with her belief that finding the destination of the mystery feed was critical. He told him that in light of his impending arrest and advice from his lawyer, he had shut down the data feed. He also told him that the system had helped stop an assassination in Des Moines, but that he would leave any decision about continuing to help the FBI up to Alek, adding that continuing to access the VitalTech system might also land him in jail.

With the easy conversation out of the way, he found Jennifer in Karima's room, playing joyfully with Kari, Fritz, and Ceci, the nanny. It pained him to take her away from that happy scene, to hear what he was about to tell her.

Jennifer was beyond angry, but she controlled her voice with icy calm and asked a few questions: "Who filed the charges?"

Head down, Vijay replied, "Kalin."

"Are you going to continue providing the data?"

"I've already stopped it."

"When will the FBI be here?"

"Soon, and they may want to search my office."

"How long do you think they'll hold you?"

"Jen, I'm so sorry. I don't know. When they take me in, please call my lawyer. She's expecting your call."

Jennifer was mainly outraged by the injustice of the charge in the face of all the help Vijay was providing, but her anger also stung because she had known he was making a mistake – and told him so – but he wouldn't listen. It was a shock, and the sheer number of unknowns was overwhelming. Still, she put on a brave face and made sure she knew exactly what she needed to do.

And so, when the doorbell rang, they were both the composed, prepared, professional couple that was actually pretty easy for them. The agents were very polite and almost apologetic. They managed to only partially fill one small box with papers, as there weren't very many in the office. Vijay kept everything on his very backed-up computer, which the agents took as well.

Jennifer called their lawyer as soon as Vijay and the agents left, reading off the list of crimes that Vijay was accused of, including: Intent to defraud, Hacking, Intellectual property theft and piracy, and Illegal access to communication. And then she called her parents in California.

***

FINAL ACT

Washington, D.C. Zoe wasn't a drinker, but a part of her was urging her to change. Vijay had always acted in the best interests of justice. Now, despite his efforts to help Zoe defend the potential targets, he'd been charged with a crime. Hopefully, she thought, *Real justice will prevail, and Vijay will be acquitted;* but in the meantime, it will be too late for those killed as a result of not having the best information.

She called Hawke to tell him that she'd advised Vijay. Hawke asked to see her.

***

Hawke was calm and even somewhat apologetic as he explained to Zoe that he was temporarily suspending her, pending a full investigation. Quietly, almost trance-like, Zoe handed over her ID and badge. She returned to her office, her mind swirling in a hundred different directions. When she left, it took a few moment's thought to decide to go to her place or Demi's. And that thought brought her full circle to her pressing concern of the morning, which seemed like days, rather than hours, ago.

She decided that she needed to confront Demi with her concerns about snooping, so she picked up two bottles of wine to help satisfy the urge that had hit her earlier, and which had now increased tremendously.

***

When Zoe arrived, Demi was home. She gave Zoe a hug and a peck on the cheek and said, "I'm so glad you're here. I just got a call assigning me to Protection as part of the presidential candidate protection program. I'm flying out tonight – in two-and-a-half hours, actually – to Manchester, New Hampshire, and I have no idea of how long, what the rotations are, or anything else, so I'll call you as soon as I know something.

"It was a real surprise," she continued. "I've been asking for a shot at Protection for a long time but was told that I wasn't ready or qualified. I guess with all the presidential candidates getting protection; they had to scrape the bottom of the barrel. But I'm sorry, how was your day? Why are you home so early?"

Zoe wasn't sure if she should laugh or cry, but this wasn't a good time for a talk. She didn't want to intrude on Demi's good news, "The usual. I just needed some down-time."

"OK, but you look down … or tired."

Zoe tried to smile, and she hugged Demi. "Hmm, tired, for sure. But with you gone, I can catch up on my sleep."

Demi noticed the two bottles of wine and asked, "You're not planning on partying without me, are you?"

Zoe got out a small laugh, "No. Just stocking up."

"OK! But I better finish packing. My rice will be here soon. Please stay here for a while. It would make me feel much better."

And so, sadly, Zoe watched the one person she cared for, and loved, (if she were honest), pack her bag and head off, for who knew how long.

Zoe unenthusiastically ordered a Margherita pizza with arugula and uncorked one of her wine purchases, a chardonnay. Her pizza arrived, but Zoe's mind was racing. She was sure that there was a connection between the Boston area gang killings and the political ones – the justice murder and the attempted assassination of the presidential candidate. She knew where the Recipient information was coming from and vaguely how it was being received, but not who was receiving it.

The Boston office was convinced that the gang shootings were carried out by the local Russian mob. If this was true, did the Russian mobsters share their ideas with another, more powerful group? How and when did they coordinate this ... and with whom did they communicate? Perhaps the one 'good-guy' in Boston, Lev Panova, could be squeezed to see what he knew. And then there was the guy in D.C. who clubbed her. Who was he? Could she ID him from photos? She made a mental note to pass Panova's photo to the Des Moines office to see if the person who witnessed the shooting could recognize him.

All of these questions were posed in the context of the obvious question: could this be a Russian government operation? And all of these questions were posed within easy reach of her wine glass, but a stretch, literally, for her pizza.

She dozed off and then woke up an hour later, staring at her untouched pizza, and almost empty wine bottle. Fifteen minutes later, she had finished both and had established a new drinking record for herself by a mile ... or at least two glasses. She numbly stumbled into bed.

***

Zoe was awakened from her chardonnay-induced slumber by her ringing phone. It was the FBI's dispatch office telling her that there'd been a shooting in Nevada and giving her the Special Agent-in-Charge's name and number. She called the SAC at the scene, who gave Zoe a quick summary. It was another execution out of the same playbook. A presidential candidate had been killed by a Final Notice Recipient, who was killed by a 'good-guy' who just happened to be there. Nevada had some of the least restrictive gun laws in the nation, so it was not out of the question.

Zoe asked why the candidate didn't have Secret Service protection, and she was told that the candidate had refused it.

She asked for and received details of the shooter. He was a Nevada resident and a Final Notice recipient.

Zoe jotted down the details and realized how blind she was without any advance warnings, compared with the Des Moines incident earlier in the day. And that triggered a sensation similar to a hard slap in the face or a bucket of ice water over her head; she had automatically gone from sleep to an active FBI agent despite being suspended.

She called dispatch to let them know that she was not the contact point, and the dispatcher apologized for the earlier call. Sadly, she'd been reminded of her situation and realized she was of no use to anyone … and she was alone.

***

Chapel Hill, North Carolina. The AA session had just adjourned, and Professor Judith Smith approached fellow member Brian Wilcox to ask a favor. This Chapel Hill chapter of AA was known as the 'Democrats' AA' and was another indication of the division facing the country. A couple of years ago, the members decided that the last thing recovering alcoholics needed were arguments about politics, which were literally driving people to drink.

Professor Smith headed up the Middle Eastern Studies Department at the University of North Carolina, which had just been criticized by the US Department of Education for failing to portray Christianity and Judaism in a sufficiently positive light. Vera DeVoyd, US Secretary of Education, was essentially stating that if schools didn't follow the Administration's line on

Israel or compare Christianity favorably to the Muslim faith, the Department would pull their funding. DeVoyd maintained this position, even though she had moved to allow religious groups to provide taxpayer-funded services for private schools, such as training or interim teaching roles.

DeVoyd had been criticized and ridiculed since she was appointed, and questions were fairly asked about her qualifications. Perhaps if the requirements for the position of Secretary of Education had been: wealthy Republican donor, extreme right-wing Christian, complete ignorance of the First Amendment, no relevant experience as an educator, and did not attend or send her children to public school, she would be superbly qualified; but at least – until her appointment – those weren't the qualifications.

But back to Professor Smith and Brian Wilcox. Wilcox was a gun enthusiast, and Professor Smith knew that he had a small arsenal at his home, which was a half a block from where she lived. Brian and her late husband, Gary, had been good friends for a long time.

"Hey, Brian, enjoy the session?"

"Eh, better than sitting in a bar, I guess," he joked, lamely. "How 'bout you?"

"It was OK. I was mostly lost in thought, thinking about getting a gun for protection. Ever since Gary died, my son has been after me to get a gun to protect myself. He's a gun nut ... sorry, he shares your passion for guns."

Brian laughed, "No problem."

"I don't want a gun in the house, but I told him I was getting one, so, could I borrow a gun for tomorrow?"

Brian turned serious, "Having a gun in the house could be a good idea if you have proper security for it and training, but it's a major responsibility and comes with some dangers."

Nervously, Judith replied, "I don't think I'c be a good fit with a gun, except for tomorrow. Can you help me out?"

"OK. I get it that you want to appease your son. And it's not like you're goin' to kill someone."

They both laughed, but Brian's was genuine.

"Sure, I've got one that any gun nut would approve of," he said with a smile. "Better give you a clip full of ammo, so he knows you're safe."

Relieved, Judith thanked him, "Thanks, Brian. You don't know how much this means to me."

Professor Smith had a private meeting with Secretary DeVoyd first thing the next morning.

***

CHAPTER 18 – CRIMINAL JUSTICE

Boston, Massachusetts. Anthony "Tony" Vinzano entered the one building he never wanted to enter and hoped he never needed to: the Boston Police District E-18 headquarters in the Hyde Park area of South Boston. Tony's grandfather had been stationed in Italy near the end of World War II. He met and fell in love with a young Italian girl, who, at nineteen, was considered "beyond her prime" by her parents and villagers. She was smart, funny, beautiful, and due to some Italian colonization misadventure in Africa, she was very dark-skinned. Both Tony's grandfather and his love survived the war, and the young woman became his future grandmother.

They had one son, Louie, who looked, well, Italian. Louie's son Tony, however, carried his grandmother's African genes, and when little Tony started getting bullied, Louie moved his family to the more diverse area of Hyde Park. Things there were better for Tony, both at school and with friends, but then, after a long illness, his mom died when he was twelve.

The price of medical care and the loss of Tony's mother took its toll on both Tony and his father – mentally as well as financially. Because of his wife's medical bills, Tony's father had to sell their house, and they moved into a small rented apartment, not far from where they'd lived for almost ten years. His dad's job in a small local factory allowed them to make ends meet, but that was all.

Five years later, Louie lost his job when the factory closed, and over the next few months, the small savings he'd squirreled away disappeared, and he started going into debt. As if that wasn't enough, Louie found out that he had twenty days to live, based on the VT2 watch he received when the factory closed.

Louie was devastated that he wouldn't live to see his son grow up, and also that he was leaving him nothing for the future except some debts. When Vik Vasin first approached him, Vik's offer sounded too good to be real, even though to do the deal, he'd have to kill someone. Still, Louie would be dead in less than twenty days, and leaving fifty grand to Tony was a pretty convincing argument. He'd killed a few people in Nam, so what was one more? It wasn't a woman or a kid, and Vik said it was a bad guy. Of course, Vik wasn't such a good guy either, so Louie was cautious. But finally, the lure of the money outweighed the crime, and he said yes.

Tony was scared to death because the cops had always treated him a little bit differently than his white schoolmates. Not as bad as the extremes he saw on TV, but enough to make him wary and nervous when they were around, knowing what they could do. Now, he was about to enter their house and go deep into uncharted waters.

The desk sergeant on duty, a burly African American with thinning short gray hair, was an old hand, and as he sized Tony up, he saw a frightened teenager. He also knew there were many sub-sets to that category, including those with reasons like: 'about to do something bad' ... or 'had done something bad' ... or simply, those scared of the police. So, the sergeant asked how he could help. Tony told him that he wanted to report a murder, and the old sergeant asked Tony to have a seat while he made a call.

FINAL ACT

A few minutes later, a younger, well-built white guy came out and invited Tony to follow him through the door marked "Authorized Personnel Only" to a small interview room. He introduced himself as Sean Lombardi, a homicide detective. He asked Tony's name, and upon hearing it, he smiled and said, "Ahh, a fellow Italian. That's rare around here. Most everyone else is Irish. I think I got this job because my mom is Irish, and she gave me my first name. So, Tony Vinzano, I understand you want to report a murder. What's the story?"

Tony began to tell Sean the story of a guy offering his father, Louie Vinzano, $50,000 to kill Frank DiVinci. He showed him the photo his father had secretly taken of the "guy" and then given to Tony.

Sean asked how Tony knew this, and Tony explained that about a month ago, his father took him aside and told him that he was dying and that it would happen soon. He'd asked his father how he knew that, and he'd pointed to his watch, the one they call the "Death Watch." Tony was wearing it now.

His father told him that he was going to have to do something bad to make sure that Tony could finish high school and find a job. He wouldn't say what, but he said that $50,000 would be deposited in Tony's savings account and that if it wasn't, by the time he died, to go to the police with this photo and tell them the story.

Sean tapped on his keyboard, and the files of the DiVinci-Vinzano shooting came up. Sean asked, "So you didn't know your father was going to kill someone or who it was until it happened?"

Tony had been more comfortable telling the story, but now, answering questions, he became more nervous and mumbled, "That's right."

Sean asked another question that sent Tony's fear factor, soaring, "Why didn't you tell the police about this right after it happened?"

Tony stammered, "I was scared. Scared of the police because my father had killed someone, scared that the friends of the guy my dad killed would come after me, and scared of the guy in the photo."

"So why tell me now?"

"Because I promised my father, I would. My father did an awful thing for me, and it wasn't easy. My father was a good guy. He was so sad when my mom died. Of course, so was I, but they were so happy together. He would have a bad day, and my mom would put her arms around him, and his bad day would go away. As my mom got sicker, I could see how much pain she was in, but when Dad got home, she lit up to make him happier. It was so hard for him, and then he does this thing for me that is so far from who he is, was ...,' Tony teared up and took a few deep breaths, "I couldn't let him down."

Sean was moved and said, "Thanks, Tony. What you've done by coming here today took guts." He asked Tony if he'd like some water or a soft drink while he got something prepared for Tony to sign. He stood up, put his hand on Tony's shoulder, and told him he'd be right back.

When he returned with some papers to sign, he asked Tony if he was still living at the same address, and Tony told him, "Yes."

Sean looked at him and said, "What you've told me today will upset the people involved with these murders. I live a few blocks away from you, and I'd feel a whole lot better if you stayed with my wife and me for a couple of weeks until it's resolved. My son is off at college so you can use his room. You'd be doing me a huge favor if you say yes."

***

Sean and a couple of his colleagues huddled together after Tony left, poring over the DiVinci-Vinzano murder files. The scenario that they had initially pieced together – of Vinzano shooting DiVinci and then DiVinci getting the last gasp lucky shot – seemed much less credible now. They were able to ID Vik Vasin from the photo, and it was like turning on the light as one by one, they began to recall the other murders by unrelated, motiveless perpetrators who had also received their Final Notices. They noted, too, the interest of the FBI. So, they contacted the Boston field office to give them the latest update.

When Sean apologized to his fellow officers for leaving early, because he was picking up Tony Vinzano, who would be staying with him for a while, there wasn't even one good-natured put-down or eye-roll.

***

Quincy, Massachusetts. Alek didn't need a long time to think about whether to continue helping the FBI before taking the system back online. Vijay could now honestly say that he stopped the feed, and he didn't need to know that Alek would switch it back on. Vijay's arrest hit Alek hard, and he redoubled his efforts to find the feed destination.

He called Ninad to explain why the system had shut down and why it was back up. He also emphasized the need to keep it all low key. Then they discussed the mysterious data feed. Alek explained that the feed's destination address was associated with a virtual private network, making the location impossible for him to identify. He asked Ninad if the FBI had tools to crack it, but Ninad told Alek about Zoe and the growing urgency to stop the killings. They didn't have the time.

Alek had a thought. He posed a question: "Why don't I just kill the mystery feed and see what happens? Maybe it will rile the beast and prod it into the open."

Ninad agreed. "Great idea! Give it a try."

So, Alek killed the mystery feed and began the wait.

***

Not that far from the Boston Police, District E-18 headquarters, the Boston FBI had done their best to make Vijay's arrest as easy as possible for him. They had treated him with respect and even ordered whatever food he wanted for dinner. He ordered a Thai green curry.

At 8:00 a.m. the next morning, his lawyer met with him and guided him through his statement to the FBI. Shortly afterward, he appeared before a judge where he pleaded not guilty, and his lawyer convinced the court, based on his service to the area as a respected business founder, as well as his cooperation with the FBI, to release him on his own recognizance. Vijay was back home before noon, and he could be forgiven if he thought that the U.S. criminal justice system was entirely fair and non-prejudicial.

Vijay's joy of being home was quickly dashed as he read the note from Jennifer on the kitchen island.

"Vijay: Kari and I have gone to visit my parents in California. I admire your desire to do good by helping the FBI. However, it's clear that their level of loyalty lags far behind yours.

FINAL ACT

I'm concerned about our family's safety, and until I can be convinced otherwise, Kari and I will stay with my parents.

Fritz is at the kennel where we got him. You can pick him up whenever you want.

I'm sorry.

I love you, Jen"

Vijay dried his eyes, changed into his running gear, and ran twenty miles. He was calmer when he returned but sadder, too, as the full force of Jennifer and Kari's absence hit him hard. Adding to this weight was the complete uncertainty of his legal fate.

***

CHAPTER 19 – DOWN & ALONE

Chestnut Hill, Massachusetts. Vijay called Alek to tell him he was out of jail and to catch up with whatever was going on. He did not tell him about Jennifer.

Alek had decided not to tell Vijay about re-connecting the FBI data-feed, but he did tell him about Zoe's suspension and turning off the mystery feed. Vijay was shaken by Zoe's suspension, especially in light of the national news of the presidential candidate being killed. He felt responsible for both events.

Dejectedly, Vijay said he agreed with Alek's decision. "Given the circumstances, that was a good call. And we can only hope that it will level the playing field, with the FBI and whomever the mystery feed recipients are, both off-line and without Zoe. It may even cause the other side to react and make a mistake."

Alek didn't correct Vijay's understanding of the situation in that Alek had restored the data feed to the FBI, but he felt very guilty. "I'm watching the system to see if it gets restored, but so far nothing. I'll keep you posted. And welcome home."

Vijay called Zoe on her cell phone and felt even worse when a very sad-voiced Zoe answered. He thanked her for her efforts to make his arrest easier and complimented the Boston agents. Then he asked, "How are you doing? I heard about your suspension, and obviously, I read about the Las Vegas and Chapel Hill shootings. I'm really sorry, Zoe, but I had to turn off the Final Notice data feed."

Zoe had been off-line since hearing about Las Vegas. "Chapel Hill?"

"You didn't know? The US Secretary of Education, DeVoyd, was killed by a Recipient. It seems the killer was a Democrat and a Professor at UNC, and the government was giving them grief over their Middle Eastern Studies program and wanted a different religious tone. The Professor got her Final Notice and had nothing to lose."

Zoe expressed surprise, "The Recipient was a her? That's two now, isn't it?"

"No, three. The woman in Rome, Georgia."

Zoe was slightly out of synch since being suspended, "Hmm. So, no one knew about this one because we can't use your system." She was right in a sense. The incident took place in the time between Vijay shutting it down and Alek reinstating it, but at the moment, she, too, was unaware that Alek had recently restored the feed.

"Yeah."

Zoe tried to assure Vijay that it wasn't his fault and that he'd done everything he could to help.

Both Zoe and Vijay were down and alone, but Vijay's mood was buoyed somewhat by retrieving Fritz. It even gave him enough optimism to call Jennifer. She was happy to hear from him and glad that his ordeal wasn't too bad, but she wasn't ready to return until more was known about who the enemy was and if they were contained.

***

Washington, D.C. Zoe had just finished her call from Vijay when her phone rang again. It was Demi, and while on one level, Zoe was excited to hear from her; on another, she wasn't looking forward to discussing her current situation.

Demi was very upbeat and excited about her protection assignment. She was also more clear on her assignment details and told Zoe that she'd be back in four days, and would then have a two-day break. Demi picked up Zoe's low level of enthusiasm, "Are you OK?"

Zoe decided to come clean and asked, "How much time do you have?"

"I have time. What's going on?"

Zoe took her through the legal issues stemming from Vijay's unauthorized access and sharing of information, despite its success, as demonstrated in Des Moines, and the comparative failure in Las Vegas when the system was down. She asked if Demi's candidate would be carrying a tracking device, and Demi confirmed that she would; then, Zoe realized that it wouldn't matter – both the candidate and Demi would be at risk without Vijay's information feed. Zoe explained that without the system, there would be no warning if an attack was imminent. Demi responded by saying that the Service had been protecting people for years without it, so it wasn't a cause for concern.

Although Zoe continued to be concerned, the call cheered her up, and they ended the conversation with both of them sincerely expressing their anticipation of seeing each other in four days.

Energized by her call with Demi, Zoe summoned up her questions of the night before and decided to call the Boston office, despite her suspension, and have them send Panova's photo to Des Moines. The Special Agent in Charge wasn't aware of Zoe's suspension and said he'd send the photo off. He also asked her if she'd received the photo that they'd sent her earlier.

She asked when it was sent, and he told her, "This morning. It was passed to us from the Boston Police, and it seems to be a link to the gang killings up here." He read the transcript that Tony Vinzano had supplied and said that the photo was of a local, small-time Russian gang member, Vik Vasin. It seems that Vasin offered to pay this kid's father $50,000 to kill someone. As it turns out, the father appears to have murdered an Italian gang member but was then killed by the victim or someone else. The money was never paid.

Zoe was pacing back and forth, seething at the bit to get into this. She asked the agent to send the photo and transcript to her phone as she was away from her office, and she waited impatiently for the message. Two minutes later, her phone pinged with a message receipt.

Zoe didn't know if she'd recognize the guy who clubbed her that night in D.C., but when she opened the photo, she was absolutely certain it was him, Vik Vasin.

Excited by this discovery and eager to get back to work, she briefly thought about what she would say and immediately speed-dialed her boss. He picked up.

Before he could say a word, she blurted, "Deputy Director, I appreciate that it will take some time to complete the investigation into the illegal data, but I have just received some critical information that may lead us to the heart of who is behind the killings, and attempts and I would like to follow up on it."

Hawke interrupted, formally, "Agent Brouet, you are quite correct that the investigation will take some time, and you will remain suspended until then."

"Deputy Director, with all respect, the system we utilized saved a candidate's life in Des Moines," she said, trying to keep her voice steady, "and without the system, we lost two lives in Las Vegas and Chapel Hill."

Hawke interrupted, "Those were both Final Notice related?"

Zoe continued even more forcefully, "Yes, sir, and if we knowingly abandon a system that saves lives and stick our heads in the sand while an investigation grinds on and the killings continue, that's a real crime. And I won't be part of it. Either we figure out a way to use the system and let me stop the people responsible, or I'll tender my resignation with immediate effect."

After a long period of silence, and painfully long for Zoe, Hawke replied, "OK. You win, for now. But we better act quickly. How soon can you get here?"

***

CHAPTER 20 – AGENT DOWN

Quincy, Massachusetts. Alek Belikov was watching his screen with the same stillness and intensity as a nature lover admiring a rare bird or animal – holding his breath so as not to interrupt the activity. He was so intent on watching that it took a while for him to realize that the operation was being carried out from within VitalTech.

The process took less than ten minutes, and it created a new feed, almost identical to the mystery version that he'd deleted earlier, but this time there was a clue about the destination of the feed, as well as a couple of strings that appeared to be commands that could be actioned externally. He'd need to dig further to understand what they were, but first, he needed to call Vijay.

***

Chestnut Hill, Massachusetts. Alek's call boosted Vijay's spirits enormously. It was the first good news he'd had in a while. They discussed the next steps and agreed that the FBI should be informed as they may have the tools, and the authority, to search the location in more detail. Alek had quickly identified Washington, D.C., 20007 as the location, but that was still a big area. He heard Vijay typing and then ask, "Guess what zip code the Russian Embassy is in?"

"Holy shit!" was Alek's rather crude reply.

Vijay knew he needed to call Zoe, despite her status. "Let me talk with Zoe, and in the meantime, look for breadcrumbs in that hack."

***

Washington, D.C. Zoe answered in a much more upbeat way than when they last spoke. She'd been reinstated, and they had a lead on the guy who clubbed her and was behind at least one of the murders by Final Notice Recipients.

Vijay shared his news about the mystery feed that Alek had found, along with the fact that the data was being sent to the same D.C. zip code as the Russian Embassy.

Zoe asked if she could have someone from her cybercrime unit contact Alek, and she thanked Vijay for re-establishing the data feed.

Vijay was puzzled. "What do you mean? I didn't re-establish it."

Zoe replied, "Ninad told me that he'd spoken with Alek and that it was up and running. It was down for a short while, which was why we were blindsided in Las Vegas and Chapel Hill."

Vijay smiled when he realized what had happened. "The thanks go to Alek. He took the risk and re-established it and didn't even tell me ... to protect me."

Zoe was thinking ahead and out loud, "So, whoever is on the receiving end of the new data feed has the same information we do."

Vijay cut in, "Except for the behavioral probability aspects and the locations of your field law enforcement personnel."

FINAL ACT

Zoe said, "Hopefully. But Vik Vasin, the guy involved with the gang killings, was waiting for me. Was that just luck, my VT2, or did someone alert them?" Zoe's mind flipped back briefly to that night and Demi's twisted ankle, and then a light clicked on in her mind.

Zoe tried to contain herself as she described her new understanding of the situation. "Vik Vasin was involved with both the Boston gang killings and the D.C. Supreme Court justice. He was tailing Connelly and heard me shout out! Could he also be involved with the incidents in Des Moines, Las Vegas, and Chapel Hill?"

Vijay weighed in, "If this is indeed the Russians, they may also employ social media in their selection process. Right-wingers, if the target is a left-winger, and vice versa if it suits their purposes."

Zoe added, "Hmm. What is their purpose? Are they trying to tactically get rid of certain individuals or sow discontent and let the masses rise up against each other?"

Eighteen-hundred miles apart, she and Vijay both shuddered.

***

Manchester, New Hampshire. Vik Vasin had finished briefing his Final Notice Zombie as much as he could, and he was reasonably confident that this mission was going to be a success. He parked his car a safe distance away from where they would intercept the target so that they wouldn't get caught up in traffic, and as they began walking, Yuri called. It was brief, as usual, but it prompted Vik to alter his plan.

He asked the Zombie for his VT2 watch and instructed him to proceed to the target as planned. Ingenuously, Vik told him that he would meet him back at the car after he'd completed his task. Vik then walked away from the target, dropping the watch in a trash can, before circling back around to the target in a 180-degree direction. He wanted to get into a good position to ensure that if the Zombie was in danger of being captured, Vik would be able to silence him. As Vik got closer, however, he realized that it would be difficult to get a clean shot at the Zombie. He thought quickly, stepped away from the gathering crowd, and called 911.

***

Washington, D.C. Zoe was going full speed ahead, trying to get caught up from her brief, but disruptive, suspension. She checked with the Des Moines field office to see if anyone or any security camera recognized Panova – both negative – and she sent them Vasin's photo as well.

She was still in her office when a call came from the Bedford, New Hampshire office. A Secret Service agent protecting a presidential candidate had been shot. The identity of the agent was not yet known, but it was a woman. Zoe's heart seemed to stop and then race ahead, and she felt a strange sense of disorientation and dread. She felt pressure in her chest, and it took an effort to breathe.

Everything seemed to be in slow motion, and she asked if there was a Bureau agent at the scene. The agent replied that there was, and Zoe was patched through. The Bureau agent at the scene confirmed Zoe's fear and identified Demi Magray as the Secret Service agent who'd been shot at 7:02 p.m. She was in critical condition and en route to the Elliot Hospital in Manchester.

Zoe looked at her watch and looked at flight schedules from Reagan Airport to Manchester. On her way to the airport, she called Ninad and asked if he could see anything on his App that would have suggested an attack between 6:55 and 7:05 p.m. He re-wound to 6:55 and saw a Recipient in an orange emotional state, in a stationary position. As he fast-forwarded, he could see the Recipient moving away from the target area and stopping again at 7:03. He reminded Zoe that because the Recipient was moving away from the presidential candidate, it didn't trigger an alert.

Just before boarding, she called Vijay to see if he could see anything from the information at his disposal.

"I do see one Recipient who had been in an elevated state, but he's stationary. Wait, that was the last reading. There are no readings coming through. The watch is not being worn!"

***

Elliot Hospital, Manchester, New Hampshire. Zoe had managed to call the Bedford Bureau with her arrival time at the Manchester, NH, airport and the resident field agent met her flight.

When they reached the hospital, there were a good number of local police visible. At reception, Zoe showed her ID and asked about Demi. The receptionist waved to a man standing nearby who immediately came over and asked Zoe about her interest in Agent Magray. Zoe showed her ID, and he relaxed, but he persisted in understanding her interest.

Zoe couldn't very well tell the Secret Service Agent that Demi was her girlfriend, so she explained that she was the point person coordinating efforts among the various enforcement authorities to stop Final Notice attacks on presidential candidates.

The agent was aware of the threats and asked, "So was this incident one of those? We never got any advance notice."

Zoe told him that she wasn't sure and asked for details of the shooting. The agent explained that the local police had received a 911 call that someone would be trying to shoot the presidential candidate at a rally in Manchester. The protection team had been alerted just minutes before a suspect had been spotted in the act of shooting. At the last second, Magray had shielded the candidate, taking the round herself. The agent was obviously consumed with admiration.

Zoe asked if Demi had been wearing her bullet-proof vest, and the agent sadly shook his head, "No." Zoe realized that she had been sidetracked from her inquiry at the front desk and asked about Demi's condition.

The agent told her that Demi had been 'lucky' in that the bullet went through her chest, missing her heart and lungs. She's stable now and should be fine.

Zoe explained, "Agent Magray and I met a while ago to develop the coordination between agencies. Since I'm here, I'd like to say hello if I can, but first, tell me about the shooter. Was he caught?"

"A local Manchester cop returned fire immediately after Agent Magray was shot, killing him."

"Was there anything unusual about the incident or the officer's return fire?"

"I was there, and it all happened pretty quickly. I give a lot of credit to the officer for spotting the shooter so fast. At first, we all thought it was the candidate who'd been hit. Agent Magray reacted so quickly after someone saw the shooter."

FINAL ACT

Zoe got the names of the shooter and the police officer, and the agent said that he thought the officer was here at the hospital. She asked him if he could find him for her, and Zoe returned to the desk to see if she could see Demi.

She was told that the doctors were almost finished with her and it should be OK in fifteen-twenty minutes. A very young-looking police officer approached her and introduced himself as Officer Barton, the one who shot and killed the shooter. He'd just finished being debriefed by his lieutenant about the incident.

Officer Barton had been on the force for only a few months, having returned from active military duty in Afghanistan.

Barton explained that he had been deployed on the perimeter of the spot where the presidential candidate would be speaking. Shortly afterward, he was alerted that a 911 call had reported an assassination threat. They were looking for a male with gray hair, wearing a red baseball hat.

Barton went on, "This is Red Sox territory and also rural, so there are a lot of red baseball hats out there. I noticed a guy fitting that description moving toward the podium just as the presidential candidate was approaching. He raised his arm, and I was pretty sure he was holding a gun, so I yelled, aimed, and as I did, it was clear he had a gun, so I fired. Too late, I guess, and the Secret Service agent jumped – actually flew – in front of the shooter's bullet. That took some guts, and I sure hope she's OK."

Zoe told him that Demi's condition looked good and asked if there was anything unusual about the shooter's mannerisms? But there wasn't. She thought to herself, 'Robot killers and 'good-guys' to clean up? What next?

Five minutes later, Zoe was given ten minutes with Demi, and she asked the nurse if she could be alone with her.

Demi looked pale, with several tubes attached as well as an oxygen mask, and Zoe could see bandages exposed at the neck of her hospital gown. Her eyes were closed, and Zoe held her hand.

Demi opened her eyes and flashed as winning a smile as she could through her mask and pain.

Zoe asked, "Hi, honey. How are you feeling?"

Demi used her free hand to raise her mask. "OK. Truthfully, pretty shitty, but I got the job done," she added with a smile.

Zoe smiled and said, "So I hear. One of your colleagues said it was an impressive act, but promise me you won't do another Wonder Woman act again, or should I say, 'Dumber Woman'? What the hell were you thinking, not wearing a vest?"

"I was in such a hurry packing that I forgot to pack my slightly larger jacket that accommodates the vest. I promise I won't do that again." And they both smiled.

Demi asked, "Why are you here?"

To which Zoe replied, "Why do you think? I heard you'd been shot and jumped on the first flight out of D.C."

Tears welled up in Demi's eyes, and Zoe used the tissues on the bedside table to soak them up. Between the mask and the emotion, Zoe could barely make out Demi's words, "I love you."

"I love you, too, Wonder Woman."

FINAL ACT

More tears from Demi and her medication was beginning to overshadow her joy of seeing Zoe. "Get some rest," Zoe said, "and I'll see you in the morning." She kissed her on her cheek before leaving.

Zoe met her Bureau colleague in the lobby, and he gave her details of the shooter, including the fact that he was not wearing a watch, and he was using a gun without serial numbers. It was too late to call Vijay, but Zoe knew what he'd tell her. He was a Final Notice recipient who exhibited levels of anger consistent with prior Recipient shooters, who wasn't wearing his watch. That prompted another thought: Vik Vasin.

Zoe hadn't had much time since her reinstatement to decide what to do about Vasin. Find him and bring him in or find and watch him? She was pretty sure he wasn't at the top of this evil tree, but now that Vasin could circumvent the Bureau's GPS surveillance of Recipients by removing their watches, she needed to do something to level the odds again.

***

CHAPTER 21 – THE OUTING

Highway 101, New Hampshire. Vik Vasin was feeling pretty pleased with himself for outsmarting the cops … twice. When Yuri called, warning him that the cops might be able to track the assassins by monitoring the Death Watch, Vik acted quickly to make sure the watch didn't help the cops. And what Vik hadn't realized was that walking away from the target actually reduced the alert level as set-up by Ninad's app..

What really made him proud, however, was his quick thinking about calling 911. It was a 'Hail Mary' move, but it worked. Sure, it was a cop or Secret Service agent that got hit, but his Zombie got taken out, and the main objective was to sow fear and division. He'd accomplished that. The network news was already awash with the shooting, and the political finger-pointing and blaming were not far behind.

As he drove, Vik wondered how Yuri knew about the cops being able to track his Zombies. But at least now he knew how to handle it. Still, he thought to himself, there were hundreds or thousands of people who get their Notices. How could the cops cover all of them? Alek would know, but he didn't want to talk with him again. And oddly, he knew that the reason was that he didn't want to have to hurt Alek. They had been friends as kids, and Alek was always nice to him, even if later, some of Alek's friends looked down at him. And then there was the thing about having his wife and kid killed. That bothered Vik, and he didn't even have a wife or kid.

He switched his thoughts to tomorrow. Yuri wanted him to train three other handlers, and he wasn't happy about sharing the glory. His modus operandi, as the cops would say, was a source of pride for Vik, and his successes were a way to keep in the spotlight and good graces of Yuri. At the same time, he had a feeling that if any of these guys screwed up, he'd be in the line of fire as well.

He also wasn't happy about spending time at a remote cabin in the New Hampshire woods with three guys he didn't know, with strict instructions that there was to be no alcohol and no women. Plus, he didn't like driving the jeep he'd been given to use, in case of rain, which would make the country roads difficult.

Vik was a creature of habit, and he was in the habit of drinking, womanizing, and driving Cadillacs.

***

Elliot Hospital, Manchester, New Hampshire. The next morning Zoe waited while the clinical staff cared for Demi. She hadn't been able to sleep well as she mulled over plans, actions, and the other side's new tactic of removing the VT2. They seemed always to be a step ahead. And that pushed her thinking into an uncomfortable zone – Demi.

Zoe quickly reset her train of thought and decided on aggressive action on several fronts. She immediately put in motion plans to bring in Lev Panova, the 'good-guy' in one of the Italian shootings, for questioning. She put out a warrant for the arrest of Vik Vasin on suspicion of being an accomplice to the murder of Louis Vinzano and Frank DiVinci. And she requested a search warrant to look at the IT systems at

VitalTech, based on Alek Belikov's information that the code was being written from within VitalTech itself.

What she needed was enough evidence to squeeze Vasin for information. Who was he working for? Perhaps Panova could be used.

If Alek was right, someone at VitalTech was feeding information to the outside, to help someone or a group find and track Final Notice recipients. Was it an individual? And who was directing them?

A nurse interrupted Zoe from her thoughts and told her that she could see Demi. The nurse laughed and said that she was making an amazing recovery and was asking when she could return to work. Zoe smiled as she thought to herself, *"Wonder Woman."*

Demi was still attached to tubes and monitors, but she looked much better than last night. She was awake, and a big smile lit up her face as she saw Zoe walk in.

Zoe started to speak, but Demi cut her off. "If you call me Wonder Woman again, I'll need to stand up and swirl around three times, completely screwing up all these wires and tubes."

It was Zoe's turn to smile, "OK, but you look great, even without your cape."

"The docs say that the shot missed anything important, so it's simply making sure there's no infection. I'm trying to see when I can get out of here and back to work."

"So, you enjoy jumping in front of bullets?"
Demi smiled, "Enjoy is maybe a little over the top, but I actually

did something. I've been pushing paper around and never knew if it meant anything. This was real. I saved someone else from being shot or worse."

"Sweetheart, I'm proud of you, but give yourself some rest and us a little time to get our Final Notice system working again."

"Yeah, what happened, anyway?"

Zoe told Demi that the shooter had been identified by his VT2, but he removed it to avoid further tracking. Zoe also explained about the cop getting a 911 call from someone, probably the guy managing the shooter, so that the shooter would be killed and silenced.

Demi asked, "Who are they?"

"We're pretty sure we've identified the guy who's been managing the shooters, but I don't think he's anywhere near the top of the tree. Also, there seems to be a lot of Russians popping up." Zoe's internal alarm system brought back the uncomfortable thoughts about Demi, so she quickly shifted gears before she divulged any more information. "Have the doctors said when you can be discharged?"

"Not sure, but soon, I think. Not today, but maybe tomorrow. And they want me to take it easy for a few days."

Zoe contemplated a Wonder Woman reply but restrained herself and smiled.

Demi continued, "My boss told me to stay home until next week," prompting Zoe to think that Hawke would probably be as unsympathetic.
Zoe replied, "OK. First, let's see when they'll release you. In

the meantime, I'm going to the Boston Bureau office today. There's something I need to do, and then I'll stop back here this evening and, hopefully, book a flight for us if they've given you a release date. How's that?"

"Thanks. That sounds great. By the way, dinner here is at six. You can join me."

Zoe made a face and grimaced, "Ahh, that's OK. Hospital food doesn't agree with me."

They both laughed as Zoe gave her a hug and kiss. "See you later!"

Zoe called the Boston office and asked them to find Panova and bring him in for more questions, today if possible. About a half-hour later, as she was en route to Boston, she got a call saying that they found Panova, and he was an hour out. They also had a surprise for her.

***

FBI Field Office, Boston, Massachusetts. Zoe arrived before Panova and asked for her surprise immediately, hoping it was a good one.

The agent smiled and handed her a grainy picture of two men. "Compliments of the Hyde Park police."

Zoe recognized Vasin immediately and asked who the other guy was.

"Lev Panova," replied the beaming agent.

Zoe called her office to check on Vasin. He hadn't been found yet, but they found a car registered to him at the Manchester

FINAL ACT

Airport long term parking lot. So far, they hadn't traced him to any inbound or outbound flights in the last couple of days, nor had they had any matches captured by airport security cameras.

She asked about the VitalTech search warrant and learned it was still being processed; then she checked with the Des Moines field office to see if anyone had recognized Vasin, or if a security camera had caught him. Negative on both.

Zoe and her Boston colleagues discussed a plan for questioning Panova, and Zoe asked how someone with a criminal past, even though fairly minor, was able to get a carry permit. Her colleagues shrugged their shoulders and explained that any police chief could grant one, so inconsistencies were commonplace.

The agents brought Panova into the conference room used for interrogation. They read him his rights again, told him that the interview would be recorded, and introduced Zoe as the Supervisory Agent from Washington. Panova was unimpressed and repeated what he'd been telling the agents for the past hour. He knows nothing more than he explained when the shooting took place.

Zoe was polite, respectful, and apologetic as she asked him to describe what happened, for her benefit. Panova sighed dramatically, but he began to recount the event.

Zoe interrupted him early on, "Excuse me. Why did you happen to be in that neighborhood at that particular time?"

Panova hesitated and said, without confidence, "I was walking back to my house."

Zoe, puzzled, "You live five miles from there. Seems like a

long walk that late at night."

Panova recovered and, with more confidence, said, "I meant I was walking back to my car to drive home."

"But my question was, why were you in that neighborhood. What were you doing before you walked to your car?"

"I dunno. I can't remember. Is that a crime? Even presidents say that."

"Lev, where did you apply for a license to carry a gun?"

Panova replied quickly, "Hyde Park police."

Zoe asked, "Do you know anyone in Athol?

Panova, with a puzzled expression, "Athol?"

"Yes, Athol, Massachusetts. About eighty-miles west of here."

Panova flatly, "No."

Zoe was zeroing in, "Yet that's where your gun license was issued. Are you sure it was Hyde Park?"

Panova shrugged but appeared more nervous, "I dunno. Maybe I got it from Athol."

Zoe continued, "Lev, you killed Peter Mason and claimed it was within your rights because you witnessed him killing another person, and you wanted to prevent him from killing others. They have a name for people like that. Do you know what it is?"

"Yeah, a 'good-guy.'"

FINAL ACT

Zoe pressed on, "That's right. And because it was decided that you were a 'good-guy', as opposed to a murderer, or a contract killer, you are currently free. But I'm getting a different feeling about you. I have a feeling that you're not being truthful, and to me, 'good-guys' don't lie. So, are you telling me the truth?"

Panova, trying to smile it off, "I am. Hey, I shot that guy a long time ago, so I was kinda fuzzy about what I was doing that night. And I thought I picked up my license at the Hyde Park station."

"OK. That's understandable. So, have you ever seen this guy before?" She handed him the mug shot of Vasin.

Panova lost his poker face for a moment and started to recover, but Zoe interrupted him, "Remember, I'm trying to decide if you really are a 'good-guy' or a murderer."

Zoe had let Panova steal a glance at the other photo in her hand, and although he didn't see it that well, he was smart enough to know what it contained. "Yeah. I seen him around."

Zoe reminded him, "In case you forgot his name, it's Vik Vasin, and we're talking with him, too. Do you want to tell us your side of your dealings with Vasin, or is this a good time for you to call a lawyer who can work out a deal in exchange for your cooperation?" She asked her colleagues, "What's the penalty for first-degree murder in Massachusetts?"

One of them told her, "Life with no parole."

They waited for Panova as he wrestled with his decision.

"Yeah, I need to call a lawyer."

Zoe hoped that this was the break they needed. Now they needed to find Vasin before anyone else was shot, and then make a deal with Panova. She looked at her phone that she'd silenced before the questioning and saw a missed call from Hawke.

Borrowing a spare office for privacy, she called him back and tried to contain her excitement about their break with Panova.

Hawke answered, "Where are you?"

Zoe explained that when she heard that a Secret Service agent had been shot, she flew up to understand what went wrong with their system.

Hawke replied sarcastically, "And it had nothing to do with the fact that the Secret Service Agent is your girlfriend?"

Zoe had been blind-sided, and she reverted to form, telling the truth. "Yes sir, she is my girlfriend, and when I found out last night that her condition was critical, I flew up here. Thankfully she'll be OK, and I'm bringing her back within a day or two."

"OK. I'm glad Agent Magray is OK. But what happened to the VT2 system? It seems we're still flying blind."

Zoe went into further detail, her conversation with Vijay, as well as the firsthand account of the police officer who received the tip-off. "It's the same M.O., except this time they used a cop instead of a hired 'good-guy', and they had the Final Notice Recipient remove his watch."

She then took him through the questioning of Panova and her hope that it would put more pressure on Vasin, once they got him, to lead them up his chain of command.

FINAL ACT

Hawke seemed pleased but asked for her assurance that the search warrant at VitalTech wasn't any form of revenge for them filing charges against Vijay.

Zoe assured him that it was based on Alek Belikov's finding that the data sharing was initiated from within VitalTech.

Hawke then surprised her when he said, "Zoe, I want you to know that I have no issues regarding your relationship with another woman, although if it were with a male Secret Service agent, I doubt it would have ever come up."

"I don't understand."

"I got a call from my counterpart at the Secret Service this morning who was upset about the VT2 system not functioning, and that one of his agents had been shot as a result. But the real point of him calling me was to stir up some shit that you and she were in a relationship.

"I got to my position because my bosses didn't care about the color of my skin and so, I'm telling you that my only concerns are that we do our jobs to the very best of our abilities. And I think that you are. Period. Now, get Vasin! Let's find out who's behind this, and let's stop these shootings."

Zoe stood there with the phone to her ear for almost a minute after Hawke had hung up.

***

CHAPTER 22 – SPARRING WITH THE ENEMY

Elliot Hospital, Manchester, New Hampshire. Zoe missed dinner at the hospital, but she didn't have an appetite – neither for food nor the necessary conversation.

Demi was happy to see her, and Zoe was happy that she was looking so well. Only one tube left. Demi told her that she would be discharged tomorrow morning and asked how her day was.

Zoe pulled up a chair and sat down close to Demi so that they could not only keep their voices down but also so that Zoe could read Demi. She began, "I received a call today from my boss, Eric Hawke. He had received a call from your boss, Miller." Zoe could see a reaction washing over Demi's face.

"When I heard about the shooting yesterday, all I could think about was you, and I flew up without thinking about much else and even without telling anyone. I was so relieved this morning that you were OK that I shifted gears and set in motion some actions to find the people responsible for the shootings. I never had time to tell Hawke about the VT2 system problem, yet when he called me late this morning, he knew about it and … that I came up here because the Secret Service Agent was my, quote, 'girlfriend.'

"No one else knew about the system failure, or us. What's going on, Demi?"

FINAL ACT

Tears welled up, and Demi was choked up and struggling to talk, "I'm so sorry. I've made a mess of everything, and now I've jeopardized your job."

Zoe clarified, "Hawke doesn't give a damn about our relationship. He was a little pissed off because he didn't know that our VT2 system had faltered, but he was more upset because Miller was taunting him about our relationship."

Demi began composing herself. "A few years ago, at a big party with lots of enforcement people, Miller came on to me, and I rebuffed him. Later, he saw me flirting with another girl, and he flashed me this look – part smile, but part evil. About a week later, he told me that the Service didn't like or trust gays and that I'd better be careful if I wanted to keep my job.

"And that was the end of it until I met you. Somehow, Miller found out about us. He told me that he knew about our secret and that the secret would stay between us if I kept him abreast of developments at the Bureau. I asked him what kind of developments, and he said anything that might push Hawke into the limelight. Miller is very ambitious and was concerned that Hawke would outshine him and be in a better position to lead the joint agency group that's under discussion."

Zoe was astonished, "And so you looked at my computer and tried to eavesdrop?"

Demi was choking, and tears were streaming, "I did. I was as much concerned for you as for myself."

Zoe shot back, "What about the sprained ankle?"

Surprised by the accusation, Demi exclaimed, "What? Why would I fake that?"

Now it was Zoe's turn to be embarrassed. "I was pretty sure you were snooping, and as you can imagine, given the lives we lead, my imagination drifted to entertain thoughts that you might be working for the other side."

Demi started laughing and crying, but Zoe still heard her say, "I love you, Zoe Brouet. Please hug me!"

After as much hugging as the hospital bed, injuries, and decorum allowed – and an unlimited amount of tears and laughter – Zoe felt a huge weight lift, and she realized she was famished. She scarfed some snack food from the lobby vending machine and then sat with Demi as they laughed and cried some more, and even discussed ideas about how to catch the bad guys, until the nurses finally threw Zoe out.

***

Reagan National Airport, Arlington, Virginia. Zoe and Demi disembarked from their short flight from Manchester. Demi was assisted in a wheelchair, and Zoe switched on her phone. There were a dozen messages, and Zoe checked the one from the FBI Boston Field Office, first.

They got Vik Vasin. She called the Boston office, and they told her that, ironically, they got him at the Manchester Airport parking lot when he was picking up his car. He was saying nothing and demanded to see his lawyer.

Zoe told them to bring Vasin to D.C. His lawyer could meet him there. She asked about Panova and was told that his lawyer was coming in later today. She reminded them not to let Panova or Vasin or their lawyers know that both men were in custody.

Zoe then checked the message from her office. It was confirmation that agents were on their way to VitalTech to search for the source of the new data feed. The others were Ninad's automatic alerts of Final Notice Recipient updates and one message from Vijay.

Vijay's call reminded her that their tracking system was useless if a killer removed their VT2, so she called him while she and Demi waited for their ride.

Vijay acknowledged that there was nothing they could do about the watch removal gambit, but he and Alek had put an alert in place if a Recipient's watch was removed for fifteen minutes; or, if someone else started wearing the watch. Alek was talking with Ninad to suggest filtering those alerts if a Recipient was within a specified range of a potential target. Zoe hadn't fully appreciated that – since the VT2 system was monitoring blood characteristics 24/7 – the system would always know if the watch was removed.

Vijay added that when a VT2 removal alert was received, Ninad could relay the warning to law enforcement personnel at the location, along with a photo or photos of the Recipient. A VT2 removal alert occurring close to a target should serve as a "high risk" warning to everyone in the vicinity, given the New Hampshire incident. Equally, if the 'robot' killer was showing any telltale profile signs or was registered as having a gun, a watch removal alert could be triggered at any time.

Zoe surprised Vijay with the news that they would be serving a subpoena on VitalTech shortly to see if they could find out who was writing the code for the new feed and where it was going. She felt a little more in control, especially with Vasin in custody.

After the call, she happily and openly shared it with Demi as they rekindled their relationship.

Zoe got Demi settled in at Demi's flat and then headed to the office. She got word that her agents were currently confiscating copies of VitalTech's data system, and Mike Kalin was screaming at anyone in his path. She expected to hear from Legal or Hawke at any minute, and she was right.

It was Sue from Legal. Mike Kalin was screaming at and into a couple of the right ears, complaining that Zoe was attacking his business for revenge. Sue demanded to know who Zoe's confidential sources were, who had advised her about the VitalTech system hack. Zoe told her what Alek had witnessed, and that the judge who issued the warrant had decided there were enough precedents to allow the search, especially given the importance of the breach. Sue was appeased for the moment but warned Zoe to be careful.

She had just put the phone down when it rang again. Vik Vasin and his lawyer were waiting for her. Reluctantly, she called Sue back and asked her to sit in on the meeting. She and Sue then huddled as Zoe brought Sue up to speed on the case; Zoe hoped that the two of them could get on a firmer footing when they interviewed Vasin.

Vasin and his lawyer, Vasily Orlov, started out complaining of the injustice of taking Vasin into custody, flying him to D.C., and then making them wait. Neither Zoe nor Sue made any apologies.

Orlov continued complaining but shifted the complaint to the legality of Vasin's custody. Zoe handed Orlov a copy of Tony Vinzano's story and a copy of the cell phone picture of Vasin that Tony's dad had taken.

Orlov scoffed and said, "Vinzano was a loser who made up a story so his kid would think he was a good father. He just happened to take a picture of Mr. Vasin. There's nothing to corroborate the kid's story and nothing to connect it to the picture. You got nothing."

Zoe pulled the mugshot of Panova from her file and slid it across the table to Vasin. "Do you know this guy?"

Vasin looked at it like he was looking at a blank wall. "No."

She then slid the picture with Vasin and Panova together and asked, "Does this help your memory?"

"Is that the same guy?" he asked, stalling for a few seconds.

"Yes, it is."

"Nah. Unless this is a fake photo, I guess I met him, but I can't remember it. I meet a lot of people."

"He remembers you, and he remembers that you hired him to kill Peter Mason."

Orlov asked Vasin, "Do you know what she's talking about?"

"No. I don't know what this guy's trying to pull. I've never hired him to kill anyone, and I don't know Peter Mason."

Zoe asked, "Just like you didn't know, Louie Vinzano?"

Orlov objected, "He's told you he knows nothing about these murders."

Zoe wasn't done. "Where were you on the night of the second, three weeks ago."

"Boston."

"I think you were in Washington, D.C., very close to the spot where Justice Jefferson Darrow was shot."

Orlov objected again. "Everyone knows that Mitchell Connelly killed Darrow."

"But Connelly was hired to do the killing."

Orlov laughed, "Jesus, now you're spouting conspiracy theories!"

"What were you doing in Des Moines two weeks ago?"

"I wasn't in Des Moines."

"And Las Vegas a day after that?"

"Wasn't there."

Orlov interrupted, "Is this travel quiz leading up to something?"

Zoe explained that in addition to hiring Louie Vinzano, Vik Pavlov, Peter Mason, and Mitchell Connelly as contract killers, Vik Vasin had hired additional killers in Des Moines, Las Vegas, and Manchester, New Hampshire. "We have flight records that place Vasin in Des Moines and Las Vegas on the dates of assassinations and attempts, and we know he was in the proximity of Manchester two days ago when another assassination was attempted." She also stated that she could place Vasin in the vicinity of Justice Darrow's murder in D.C.

Sarcastically, Orlov replies, "Those are excellent theories, but you have no proof."

Zoe countered, "But we do, Mr. Orlov. We have flight records … passenger lists. And we have Lev Panova. The guy in the picture. He told us that your client hired him."

Orlov, smiling, asked, "Is that a fact or a hope, Agent Brouet? Because if you can't show me a confession, my client and I would like to leave."

Zoe remained composed and said, "It should have been received by now. We'll be right back."

As they walked to Zoe's office, Sue said, "If the confession hasn't been received or it's not solid enough, you'll either have to let him go unless we try to hold him on terrorism charges. And that's a stretch, given what we have."

Zoe mumbled, "I know," as she picked up the pace. There was nothing on her desk, so she called Boston. She visibly sank when told that Panova and his lawyer had changed their tune. They were sticking with the good-guy story, and while Panova admitted he knew Vasin, he denied working with him. His lawyer demanded Panova's immediate release, and without an admission, or more evidence, they had nothing to hold him on.

Sue looked at the warrant again and saw that Panova's confession was part of the justification for bringing in Vasin. "So, let him go or try to get a warrant based on terrorism charges?"

She added, "Orlov was quite sure you didn't have a confession because he and Panova's lawyer are working for the same people. Panova was ready to cave, but whoever is behind all this changed his mind. Without his testimony, we have nothing. If you think he's going to change his mind, and if you're right, he'll never live to tell his story."

Zoe was down but not out. "We'll let him go. That will stop the alarms from going off, and maybe they'll get careless."

***

CHAPTER 23 – DECEPTION

Washington, D.C. Zoe was devastated. She was only a little better off than she was before Vijay started sharing the enhanced information. She would kick Vasin's case back to the Highland Park police, but she doubted that a prosecutor would take it up without more evidence. *Could Vasin be that smart to orchestrate almost a dozen assassinations or attempts and not leave any clues? Even if he's ID'd at or near a crime scene, it wouldn't be enough.* She needed a break.

Her phone rang, and it was the agent who led the team to serve the VitalTech warrant. She held her breath.

He told her that they had good news and bad news, and she chose to hear the bad news first, which was that they hadn't been able to find a specific destination for the recent hack. They were still working on it.

The good news was that they had identified the hacker. It was a former employee, Alek Belikov, who had created a pathway that allowed him to write code as though he was sitting at his old VitalTech desk.

Zoe exploded, "You must have been looking at the data feed that we're currently receiving. That was set up by two former VitalTech guys, one of whom is Alek Belikov."

The agent corrected her, "No, ma'am. We spoke with Ninad, and he confirmed that the data he's getting is from a different source than the one we found. We only found one active feed."

Zoe was beside herself. She was sure there was a misunderstanding and that the agents had been looking at the feed that Vijay and Alek had set up. But right then, all she wanted to do was go home and take care of Demi, as soon as she called Vijay.

Zoe explained to Vijay that she was convinced they knew who was managing the murders, but she didn't have enough evidence to hold them. She also related the probable screw-up with the mystery data feed and that Alek had been accused. Vijay laughed and considered that preposterous. He also added that the feed that Alek had set up was virtually impossible to detect, so the one they found must be the one that Alek had observed.

Zoe wondered if this was a clumsy attempt to frame Alek so that he could be taken out of action.

When Zoe got to Demi's, it was evident that the patient was improving. The candles were flickering, the second bottle of wine that Zoe bought the other evening was open next to two wine glasses, and Demi had ordered their favorites from their "go-to" Indian restaurant, RASA. Demi looked terrific, and Zoe did her best to leave her awful day behind, and at least end it in the warm glow of love, caring, and understanding.

***

Zoe's bad day had barely ended officially, at least on Eastern Standard Time, when she got a call at 1:20 a.m. about an attempted assassination of a presidential candidate in California. The shooter missed his intended target, was lost in the panic and confusion that followed, and was found dead minutes later from an unwitnessed gunshot. The shooter was a Recipient, and his VT2 had been removed. Security cameras had not matched his image, possibly because he was wearing a baseball cap. It wasn't clear if the shooter took his own life or had been killed by someone else. Agents from the Los Angeles field office and the Secret Service were still investigating.

Zoe tried to calculate the likelihood of Vasin getting to California in time to pull this off, but she didn't think it was possible. So that meant he wasn't the only field operator. She tried to get back to sleep, but there were too many loose ends to think about, so she decided to start her day.

Demi was still sleeping soundly, so she left a note and headed to her office. The night sky was clear, with a good number of stars out, despite the light pollution of D.C. Her problems at work faded away as Zoe marveled at the sight. A childhood memory from long ago encouraged her to select a star and make a wish. And she did.

Alone in her office, she tapped away at her computer, searching for Vasin on flights from Reagan, Dulles or Baltimore airports to Los Angeles. Finding nothing, she searched for him on flights to Boston and got a hit. Vasin was on the 5:30 p.m. flight from Reagan to Boston. Almost holding her breath, she searched the Boston-LA flights, but they came up empty.

At 6:10 a.m., she received a call from the Special Agent-in-Charge in LA. The dead shooter had been murdered. It was not suicide. They had reviewed the surveillance videos and were unable to see who might have shot him. The shooter's gun was untraceable. Zoe asked if Ninad's tracking App had been of any use, and the SAC replied, "Yes and no."

When Zoe asked him to explain, he told her that the App alerted them to a Red-level Recipient in the area, but the shooter's progress toward the event stopped about ten minutes before the shooting. When that happened, they knew that he might have stopped or that the watch was removed so, receipt of the alert certainly raised our readiness level, but insofar as tracking, it didn't help. Zoe requested that a trace be put on the shooter's bank accounts to see if a large deposit had been made or might be in the coming days.

So, here was another unidentified Recipient handler who wanted to make sure that his 'robot' assassin wouldn't talk, and that the handler remained incognito. Were there others?

At 7:00 a.m., she decided to call Vijay and see if he could add anything to the LA shooting. She knew he'd be up, although probably out running. Getting his voicemail and leaving a message, she began to sketch out where they were at the moment.

Zoe was confident that the activities were Russian controlled. The assassinations and attempts had all targeted Democrats except for the Supreme Court Justice. She was equally sure that Vik Vasin played a key role, but as a handler of assassins, not as the leader of the operation. Lev Panova was probably involved, but, at best, he could only name Vasin.

Was there another handler or handlers out there, and could they name Vasin or others higher up in the organization? Someone needed to make a mistake to give her a break. She made a note to investigate the D.C. and Las Vegas 'good-guys.'

Vijay returned Zoe's call, and she gave him an update on the Los Angeles assassination attempt. She waited while Vijay tapped away, looking into the history. Finally, he explained,

FINAL ACT

"The shooter was on red alert and moving in the general direction toward the LA Plaza de Cultura y Artes. That might have triggered Ninad's App, but I don't know what distance parameters he'd set. At about five miles from the Plaza, his watch stopped transmitting. And then fifteen minutes later, an automatic secondary alert went out, signaling that the watch had been removed.

Zoe asked if the secondary alert could be reduced to a minute. "If the watch re-connects, we'll know, but until then, we'll assume we have a shooter moving in. It's better to err on the safe side."

Vijay confirmed that was possible, and he'd ask Alek to get right on it. "Speaking of Alek, I couldn't reach him after you told me about the VitalTech search. You haven't arrested him, have you?" he added, only half in jest.

Zoe, too, chuckled and confirmed that no, they hadn't. But she did say that they needed an explanation about how his name was attributed to the hack.

Vijay promised to have him call.

After hanging up with Zoe, he tried Alek again. Straight to voicemail. He left a voicemail and then a text message. He tried e-mail, Skype, WhatsApp, and Facetime. Worry was starting to creep into Vijay's consciousness. He took Fritz out for a quick do-his-business break and headed out to Alek's house.

***

Quincy, Massachusetts. When Vijay arrived at Alek's home, Alek's car was parked in his driveway, but he didn't answer the bell or Vijay's knocking. He tried looking in through a window, and it did look like a dining room chair was overturned. He tried the front door and ground floor windows to no avail, but the back door was unlocked, so Vijay entered the house into the kitchen. It was not completely clean, as it might've been if Alek had gone away ... unless he left in a hurry. In the dining room, there was a chair that had been knocked over, but otherwise, it offered no clues. Alek's office, however, was a different story. His laptop was gone, and there were a couple of papers on his desk. An empty cup of coffee was lying on its side on the desk, sitting in a pool of coffee, some dried and crusted, some still wet. Some coffee had also dripped off the desk onto the floor. Alek had no family or relatives that he knew of, so he called Zoe.

Zoe sounded relieved to hear Vijay's voice, "I was just going to call you because Ninad is getting some conflicting and inconsistent data from the information you're sending."

"Inconsistent? Like what?"

"Like, someone is marked as a Final Notice recipient with various emotional stages, but then they are removed as Recipients."

"You're saying they as in more than one?"

"Yes. There have been over ten in the last half hour."

Vijay became very concerned, "Zoe, I'm at Alek's house right now. He's not here. His car is here, though, and I think something is wrong." Vijay detailed the scene at Alek's. "Someone has either taken him – and I can't believe I'm even saying this – or he's fled."

"I'm assuming you don't have your laptop with you to check on the glitch?"

FINAL ACT

"No, and Alek's is gone. As soon as I get home, I'll check it out."

"OK," Zoe agreed. "We're blind again right now, but can you wait there while I get an agent out from our Boston office? Don't touch anything."

Vijay couldn't believe that Alek left on his own, but he did believe that somehow, Alek was involved with the inconsistent data. He checked out the rest of the house, and there were no open drawers, nor were there suitcases lying around. There was nothing that signaled a struggle or a hasty getaway. Vijay had been pretty sure that when Alek's ID had been associated with the hack at VitalTech, it was a setup, but he didn't understand why. Perhaps someone wanted to make the FBI think that Alek was involved and fled when he'd been identified as the hacker. But who would believe that?

FBI Agent Denise McBrair arrived, and Vijay explained what he'd seen. He confirmed and stated that except for the back door and front door handles, he hadn't touched anything. She told him that Zoe had briefed her on the background, including the possibility that he might have fled, based on the VitalTech ID discovery.

Vijay exclaimed, "But that was a setup."

McBrair countered with, "That's what Supervisory Agent Brouet believes, too, based on Alek's cooperation so far. But she also said something else: that the information flow that Alek helped set up had become the central source of our defense against the assassination attempts. And now, it's not working. Could it be part of a plan to have us depend on something and then pull it?"

"I know Alek," Vijay countered. "He'd never do that. I'm afraid he's in danger, and he's already lost his wife and twelve-year-old son. If you don't need me anymore, I'm going home to have a look at why our data feed isn't working." And then, to himself, *Cease and desist be damned!*

***

CHAPTER 24 – DEAD MEN DON'T TALK

Boston, Massachusetts. Mike Kalin and Sara Huckers were breathing hard after their sexual athletics. Kalin lit a cigarette, which garnered an eye-roll, sigh, and complaint, "I thought you were trying to quit. And this is a No-Smoking room."

"After sex with you, I need something to calm down," Mike purred disingenuously. And then very coldly, "And who gives a shit about a hotel's rules?"

"Do you smoke after sex with your Russian bride?"

"None of your god damn business. And why do you keep using that phrase to describe my wife?"

"Well, she's Russian, and she's your wife."

Mercifully, for both Mike and Sara, Mike's phone rang. He looked at the caller ID and got out of bed, walking to the hotel bathroom. "Yeah."

Sara couldn't hear details, but Mike's voice rose several times with what sounded like a foreign language. An angry foreign language and a name. Yuri.

Sara was the HR Director at VitalTech. At twenty-nine years old, she'd been hired by Mike, even though she had no experience for the job. During a few "Get to know your Team Member" dinners, Mike revealed that he and his wife were having marital problems. She drank a lot, and they really couldn't communicate. He compared their problem with the ease that he and Sara had, talking about a wide range of issues. He shared that he was planning an imminent divorce. That was some months ago, however, and Sara was starting to question his sincerity.

She enjoyed her job at VitalTech, although she didn't understand Mike's choices from the candidates she had recruited. But, she accepted them as learning experiences.

Mike returned, and it was apparent he was still upset. "I've got to go. I'll pay the bill, and you can spend the night and charge whatever you want to the room. I'll see you tomorrow."

Sara got out of bed and walked over to him, trying to hug and kiss him and get him to change his mind. He pushed her away with a force that hurt.

Sara exclaimed, "Oww! I was just looking forward to a nice evening with you. You don't have to take your anger out on me," although this wasn't the first time, nor was it even close to the worst time.

"Just leave me alone, or this will be the last time we see each other after OR during office hours. Understand?"

Sara assumed that was a rhetorical question and didn't answer, and he lashed out, "DO YOU UNDERSTAND?"

"Yes," she whimpered as Kalin finished dressing and left the room.

FINAL ACT

Kalin drove to the address given to him in an industrial section of Quincy. He was admitted and led to an office near the back. As he passed an open doorway, a guy at a computer looked at him directly. Kalin thought he looked vaguely familiar.

Yuri looked at Kalin and smiled, "Did I ruin your little 'get to know your employees better' evening?"

"Fuck you, and who is that guy down the hall?"

"He's one of your ex-employees who you didn't get to know better," he smiled.

"What if he recognizes me?"

"Don't worry. Dead men don't talk. Besides, he's the one who has now neutralized your friend Vijay's data transmission to the FBI. They can't stop us now."

***

Chestnut Hill, Massachusetts. Vijay was struggling with finding the problem with the data feed. He and Alek were a capable, complementary team, but on his own, he was baffled by the way Alek had hidden the feed so that VitalTech wouldn't find it. Could that have been planned all along? No, Alek was in trouble, and he needed to find him. He knew that Zoe's primary concern was protection against more assassinations. Finding Alek was important but secondary to her, so it was up to him.

Alone in his empty house, with Fritz lying at his feet, Vijay tried to focus on the missing Alek instead of the absent Jennifer and Karima. Alek's VT2 was off, and Zoe had tried to find him via his cell phone, but that too was shut off. And his laptop had been reconfigured to a virtual IP, meaning he could be anywhere. Whoever had him wasn't communicating or asking for anything. Vijay surmised that they must have forced him to make the data feed unstable with threats of torture or some other unpleasant action.

***

Washington, D.C. Zoe got the call at 9:00 p.m. as she and Demi had just finished dinner. A presidential candidate had just been killed in Charleston, SC. And yes, the killer was subsequently killed by an unidentified shooter. To her question, the killer wasn't wearing a VT2, and they were still checking his identity. Zoe called Ninad, and he confirmed her fear: According to the data feed, there wasn't an identified Recipient near the shooting.

Zoe texted Vijay and asked him to call her ASAP at any time. He rang back immediately and had seen the newsflash about the shooting. Looking at the VT2 database, there were three active Final Notice recipients, two women and a man in hospice. There was one other recorded Recipient, but he was off-line, and no signals were being received. If he died while wearing his VT2, it would show. So, either he's alive and not wearing his VT2, or he died while not wearing his watch.

Zoe replied flatly, "I'm guessing it was the latter, as the assassin was killed. Send me his details in case we have a problem IDing him. Are you any closer to getting us a stable feed?"

"Zoe, I'll be honest ... no."

Zoe asked, "Do you think Ninad can help? He worked with Alek a bit on getting the final setup."

"I'm OK with that. Ask him to call me in the morning. Any time after 8. I'm sorry, Zoe."

***

Chestnut Hill, Massachusetts. Vijay and Ninad were looking at their screens, trying to find the hidden code that Alek had written when both their screens, 450 miles apart, starting flickering and Vijay's VT2 buzzed, giving him his Final Notice.

Vijay put Ninad on hold and escaped from the system back-end into the primary VT2 monitoring system. He looked at the screen and was dumbfounded – it displayed the first fifty of 10,455,000 Final Notice recipients! Every VT2 user had received their Final Notice.

He got back on the call to Ninad and explained what was happening. Ninad hadn't seen the primary monitoring system, so when Vijay told him what had happened, Ninad exclaimed, "Oh God, thank you! I thought it was real."

Despite the crisis, Vijay chuckled when he realized that Ninad was wearing a VT2 and thought it was an authentic Final Notice for himself. They had a brief laugh, but it was very brief, as they thought about the havoc it was wreaking. They agreed it was done on purpose, but why?

Vijay knew Alek best and said, "I think this proves that Alek is alive. But did he do this independently, or was he forced to do it?"

Ninad replied, "If Alek is alive, we have to assume that he is being forced to do things against his will – for example, making the data unpredictable. So, if they already have us flying blind, why cause mass panic unless something huge is about to happen? Or could Alek have done this as a message? And if so, what did he mean by it? We need to get into his head."

And a light switched on in Vijay's.

***

Quincy, Massachusetts. Mike Kalin was raging. VitalTech's phones were ringing off the hook, and their website had crashed due to an overload of queries from millions of VT2 users who had received their Final Notices. J. Edward was even screaming down Kalin's cell phone, telling him that the alert almost gave him a heart attack and that the markets had gotten wind of what was obviously a glitch and VitalTech's stock had dropped twenty-three percent.

Worse yet, neither Kalin nor anyone else at VitalTech knew what happened, nor could they fix it. Kalin made a call. "What the fuck are you doing with our database?"

Yuri answered, "It will be restored soon. Our visiting computer expert, the one you saw the other day, thought he'd be funny. The only thing funny about it is that it just shortened his life-span."

Kalin shouted back, but he was talking into a void. Yuri was gone.

***

Chestnut Hill, Massachusetts. Vijay looked at his phone contacts and ... yes, he had it! He called Zoe. Vijay was energized and hopeful, but Zoe sounded like she was on the opposite pole.

"Are you OK?"

"No, Vijay. I'm not. Another Supreme Court Justice has just been killed."

FINAL ACT

"Same MO?"

"No. The left has gotten into the act – the Antifada. The sad thing was that the shooter was a Recipient, wearing his VT2, so we could have stopped it if the system was working. And nobody killed him afterward."

"Who was the judge?"

"The newest one that caused such an uproar over his sexual acts, drunkenness, and lying to Congress."

Vijay, seriously, "But I guess that's still a bad thing."

Zoe laughed out loud. "You could say that. But are you calling to tell me that you and Ninad fixed the problem?"

"Maybe." And Vijay proceeded to tell Zoe about the chip in Alek's head. When Alek shared his contact information with Vijay, they included the details contained in the micro-chip embedded in Alek's scalp. "I have the equivalent of an IMEI number that you may be able to trace."

Zoe's pulse quickened as she said, "At this point I'm ready to grasp at straws. Text me the details. I'm on it."

***

Vijay's phone rang, and his heart leaped when he saw the caller ID was "Jen." She had seen the news of the shootings and killings, and she realized that as wrong as she felt it was for Vijay to supply the FBI with information, anything that might stop the attacks was better. She wanted to come home, but Vijay suggested she wait a while longer to see what unfolded with Alek. Jennifer countered with leaving Karima with her parents for a while. She wanted to be with Vijay.

Vijay agreed and explained that there was the possibility of finding Alek through the chip in his head. She laughed but was worried about Alek's safety.

***

CHAPTER 25 – ASSAULT

Quincy, Massachusetts. Zoe, and her team had been able to track the IMEI number to a location in a Quincy industrial complex. She assembled an assault team, and they planned to approach the facility in the early hours of the next day. Denise McBrair from the Boston field office had surveilled the facility. The gray, one-story, concrete building was one of a dozen similar structures huddled in the small complex. It had a vehicle door and pedestrian door to the front and a single pedestrian door at the rear. According to FBI records, the internal layout options ranged from small offices and storerooms to more extensive manufacturing or assembly operations, depending on the business. They would only find out once inside. Critically, too, they had no idea how many people were there.

Zoe would be part of the team, mainly to safeguard Alek, who was their key in re-establishing the data feed. Demi, who was still off duty, asked to go along. She had undergone considerable training for breaching a facility, she was now healthy, she was bored, and she promised to wear her Kevlar vest. Zoe welcomed her presence.

Zoe emphasized that their primary objective was to rescue Alek, unharmed, and everyone was given a photo of him. There would be a total of eight on the assault team, plus medics. Local police were setting up perimeter roadblocks to stop escapes or provide backup, as required.

At 3:00 a.m., FBI agents used hydraulic door openers to breach the front and rear pedestrian doors simultaneously. The openers forced the door jams slightly outwards so that the doors could be opened quietly.

When given the signal by the breach teams, the Boston FBI team at the front of the building encountered a single guard, asleep in a chair. He was quickly and quietly disarmed and secured.

Demi and Zoe were stationed at the rear of the building and entered a darkened, narrow hallway with two doorways on the left and one directly ahead at the end. They assumed that the end doorway led to the area at the front with the vehicle access.

The first door was open and dark, and the smell coming from within it made identification easy, but keeping Zoe's gagging quiet, difficult. Her flashlight was unnecessary, but she gave it a quick scan. Bathroom cleanliness was not a priority here.

They made their way down the hallway, and Zoe, in the lead, could hear snoring coming from the next room. The door was closed, and she whispered to Demi that she would open the door and turn on the lights, which she assumed would be on the wall close to the door. Demi was to follow closely and be ready to shoot.

Zoe slowly opened the door, and hearing nothing but the snoring, reached for the light switch. She looked back and nodded to Demi and then flicked on the light. The snoring stopped and the snorer, presumably, bolted up from his chair and raised his hands in the face of two guns pointed at him.

The room had a short return opening to the left side, so neither Demi nor Zoe could see around the corner. The guy with his hands up shouted "kill him," and Demi rushed in. She saw someone with his back to her, aiming his gun at a third person near the back of the room. She aimed, yelled, "Drop your gun!" and fired almost simultaneously, a split second before the shooter fired. The shooter went down, but he'd gotten his shot off, hitting the third man, Alek.

Zoe ran to Alek. He'd been hit in his mid-section and was bleeding profusely. Zoe shouted to an agent to get medical help ASAP while Demi secured the other two. The one she'd shot was wounded, but not critically.

The medics rushed Alek to Quincy Medical Center, and Zoe sent an agent to guard him. She sent a text to Vijay advising him that Alek had been shot and was en route to Quincy Medical.

An inspection of the premises showed it was mostly empty, with six computers and associated peripherals. Zoe questioned the three prisoners, including the one who'd been patched up by the medics. They didn't get much more than their names, so they left the scene to the technical people to look at the computers, get fingerprints, and collect evidence. Zoe and Demi went to the medical center.

Vijay had gotten her text and was already there when they arrived. The hospital wouldn't give him any information about Alek, but when Zoe inquired, she was advised that Alek's condition was critical and that it would probably be a few hours before the surgeons were finished.

Zoe suggested that they all get some sleep. She would call Vijay when there was an update on Alek's condition.

***

Zoe and Demi had checked into a local hotel to catch a few hours' sleep, and it wasn't until they were in their room that their professional personas melted away. They had both performed well during the attack, and they were both proud of each other. Zoe, in particular, was immensely proud of Demi for her quick response to the situation and credited Demi for preventing the shooter from getting off a better shot. Demi, in turn, was proud of Zoe's leadership and bravery.

Despite their shared high from a dangerous mission and their pride and love for one another, it didn't take long for exhaustion to diminish their adrenalin levels. Within minutes they were sleeping soundly.

In the morning, Zoe called the hospital and was told that Alek's condition had been upgraded to serious and that the doctors would be doing some follow-up surgery later this morning. She sent a text to Vijay and then, along with Demi, went to question the prisoners.

Only one of the three had a record, and Zoe had decided not to reveal Alek's condition. She wanted to keep the detainees in the dark about their possible roles as murderers or accessories to murder.

The guard who'd been quickly disarmed didn't know anything. That was until Zoe told him that they were all being charged with kidnapping and murder. That prompt helped him remember three guys: Yuri, Stefan, and a guy from the Death Watch company. He didn't know his name.

The wounded prisoner confirmed that Yuri was in charge along with someone called Stefan and that a guy named Mikhail, from the watch company, had been in a couple of times. All he knew was that Alek was there to assist them in hacking some computer programs.

FINAL ACT

The last prisoner, the one who ordered the wounded one to kill Alek, was Fedor Boyko. He was Ukrainian and served some time for armed robbery. Zoe reminded him that even the lesser of the potential charges against him would land him in prison for a very long time. Boyko confirmed that Yuri was in charge, but he didn't know his last name; and added that another guy, Stefan, came in for a few hours most days; and that Mikhail or Mike, as he was sometimes called, had been there a couple of times.

Boyko explained that they had been receiving a report with names and information of Final Notice Recipients that would be reviewed by Yuri and Stefan. At first, they passed the Recipient information to a guy called Vik, but recently, three other people began to get the information, too. Again, he only knew first names: Peter, Leon, and Pavel. Zoe asked how the names that were passed along to the four guys were divided, and Boyko thought it was based on the location of the Final Notice Recipients. The calls to or from the four people were made through Yuri or Stefan's cell phones. Nobody seemed to have a last name, and Boyko wasn't even sure if any of the first names were real. But Zoe was pretty sure that Vik's last name was Vasin, and she hoped that Vijay could help with Mikhail or Mike.

Zoe got one other chilling piece of information from Boyko. Yuri had given him a stern order. "If the cops ever find this place, kill Alek."

***

Quincy Medical Center. When Zoe and Demi arrived at the hospital, Vijay was there with Jennifer. They'd been told that Alek couldn't receive visitors, but when Zoe inquired at the desk, she was given the encouraging news that Alek's condition had been upgraded to 'Fair' and that they would ask the lead surgeon to speak with Zoe and give her more details.

Zoe and Jennifer hadn't met before, but both knew much about each other through Vijay, and Zoe had heard some additional details about Jennifer's attack incident and the way she'd handled it. She didn't know that Jennifer had been in California, but she was a little surprised that she had come to the hospital. Jennifer explained that she'd known Alek for some time and was concerned about him.

Zoe introduced Demi, somewhat awkwardly, and hesitated slightly, as she chose the term, 'law enforcement colleague,' to justify Demi's presence. Jennifer smiled warmly, but part of that smile was a result of a 'sixth sense' and something in Zoe's eyes that told her that despite their 100% professional correctness, there was more there than just a professional relationship.

Dr. Lisa Goodhouse, the surgeon leading Alek's care, arrived and explained that Alek had come through the operations very well. Zoe was anxious to question him and have him fix the data feed, and Dr. Goodhouse gave her some satisfaction by saying that she could have fifteen minutes with him. Zoe asked if she could bring Vijay, and the doctor agreed. These fifteen minutes were more than just about Alek's health.

Alek was awake and very pale. Still, although he had multiple tubes connecting him to drips and machines, he welcomed them with a big smile, which lifted some of the weight off Vijay, whose first words were, "I'm really sorry I got you into this, Alek. I wished it was me they had taken."

Alek proved he was in good spirits by saying, with an even bigger grin, "They must have known you didn't have the skills to help them." And then he asked, "How did you find me?"

Vijay smiled and tapped the side of Alek's head. "Ninad and I felt that the blanket Final Notice alert was from you, and we wondered what you were thinking ... or telling us, which led me to remember your chip."

Zoe interrupted the reunion and said, "Your doctor only gave us a few minutes with you now, and I need some information. We have the three guys who were there with you, and we know about two people called Yuri and Stefan. Can you tell me anything else about them?"

Alek confirmed that Yuri was in charge, and Stefan was a techie who assisted, but excitedly, he said, "Mike Kalin is involved. I saw him there talking with Yuri!"

"Kalin from VitalTech?" asked an astounded Vijay.

"Yes. Yuri called him Mikhail once."

Zoe interjected, "Well, that answers that question." She then related what Boyko had told him about Vik, Peter, Leon, and Pavel and asked if Alek knew their roles.

Alek thought that these were the guys in the field who were managing the Final Notice Recipients. He was positive that Vik was his 'old friend,' Vik Vasin. He heard Yuri mention his name once, but other than first names, he knew nothing about the others.

Zoe hesitated, but asked, "What did they threaten you with to cooperate with them?"

Alek's blush was very visible, especially given his lack of color, and he spoke very softly, perhaps hoping that Vijay wouldn't hear. "They threatened to kill Jennifer and Karima unless I cooperated."

Vijay shuddered and said, "Please don't mention that to Jennifer."

Zoe hesitated again and asked Alek, "How quickly do you think you can re-instate our data feed?"

Dr. Goodhouse and a nurse entered the room, and the doctor declared, "Time's up. We need to take him for another test."

As they were ushered out of the room, Alek said, "Bring a laptop when you come back. It will take five minutes."

The doctor, anticipating their question, told them to come back at 6:00 p.m.

***

Zoe and Vijay returned to the lobby. Zoe wanted to go after Kalin immediately, so she asked Vijay if he would come back at 6:00 p.m. with a laptop. Vijay assured her that he would and asked what she was going to do about Kalin.

Zoe smelled blood, "I'm going to bring him in. I think he'll unlock some doors for us."

On their drive home, Vijay shared Alek's health progress, as well as Kalin's involvement, with Jennifer. She wasn't surprised. Vijay didn't tell her about the threat made to Alek.

***

FBI Regional Field Office, Boston, Massachusetts. Zoe had requested agents to bring Mike Kalin and Vik Vasin in for questioning. She also asked for search warrants for Kalin's and Vasin's homes, Kalin's office, and copies of their phone records. She was told that Kalin was out of the office but

FINAL ACT

expected back at 3:00 p.m. Just in case either had decided to flee, she put out alerts to monitor airports in the region and to set up credit card and toll device tracking.

In the meantime, she and other Bureau staff combed through criminal records looking for needles in a haystack: People named Peter, Pavel, or Leon with records. Pavel and Leon were the easiest, but still, there were dozens to investigate.

***

CHAPTER 26 – INTRODUCING MOKI JOE HUNTER

Albuquerque, New Mexico. (One month earlier.) "Introducing Moki Joe Hunter," blared from the massive speakers dotted around the Isleta Amphitheater, barely competing with the screaming crowd of almost 15,000 fans. They had come to hear one of America's top Country and Western singers and one they considered a favorite son.

Moki Joe was an unlikely C&W star. He was the oldest son of an African American, John Hunter, and his Hopi wife, Totsi, a member of the Acoma tribe. The Acoma Pueblo is considered to be the oldest continuously inhabited community in the United States.

John Hunter was a Vietnam vet who finished his military career at Kirtland Air Force Base in Albuquerque. Originally from Detroit, he had become seduced by the 'Land of Enchantment,' the State's official motto. He met Totsi, a full-blooded Hopi, and the enchantment continued. They lived in Acomita, not far from the original tribal pueblo of Acoma, sixty-miles from Albuquerque.

After the Air Force, Hunter found work as a mechanic, and they had a good life, raising their two boys, Moki Joe and Tocho Tom. John and Totsi had decided that their sons' names would be a combination of English and Hopi. When their first child was born, Totsi suggested Moki and John instantly thought – Moki Joe, after one of his favorite R & B singers and guitarists, Smokey Joe Robinson. By comparison, their second son's name, Tocho Tom, sounded pretty normal.

John Hunter loved playing his guitar, and he was able to transfer his love of the instrument and music to Moki at a very young age. Totsi explained that his name (the Moki part) in the Hopi language foretold potential as an entertainer.

Moki Joe liked his full name and that, along with his mixed ethnic heritage, made life a lot more challenging than if he was simply a "boy named Sue." At Grants High School, Moki Joe was a good student, an excellent multi-sport athlete, and a prolific fighter. Mutter an ethnic joke or slur within earshot of Moki Joe, and you'd better be ready for a fight or a very fast sprint. The same went for anyone causing trouble for Tom. Moki Joe was fiercely protective. Boys named Moki were also said to have deep feelings of responsibility, according to Hopi legend.

Moki Joe was somehow aware that his temper was a dark side of him, and he would try to find a quiet place to strum his guitar to bring himself back to an even and peaceful plane. Many of the lyrics that came from these self-prescribed therapy sessions would find their way into his hit songs, many years later.

Moki Joe made it through high school and enlisted in the army in time for the Gulf War. He made it through that, too, and came home to take on whatever confronted him, which included his first marriage and child. His time in the army had polished him and made him more tolerant, but partly it was the way he carried himself that made people respect him and not want to challenge him.

After his discharge, he made up for the lost time with his music and picked up his old guitar again. The music soon flooded back with surprising ease, and he began playing out at local events, and then bigger events – writing and singing songs that came from his heart, his background, and his love for his daughter, Kaya. He had what it takes, and the 'down-home' audiences loved him.

Albuquerque attracted some of the biggest C&W stars, and soon Moki Joe found himself opening for some of the best in the business. He even toured with a few before his first CD rocketed him to star status.

Even with success, the life of a musician is grueling: travel, hotels, and many temptations. Moki Joe knew them all, and some had gotten the better of him. His marriage fell apart, he helped prove that Indians and alcohol don't mix, he tried a wide variety of drugs and women, but the one thing he held on to and cherished was Kaya. Now, however, even that appeared tenuous.

Kaya loved her father and was understanding about his failings, but she drew the line when it came to his support for right-wing politics. She couldn't understand how he could turn a blind eye, and even support, the misogyny and racially unjust positions that the Republican party either endorsed or tolerated. Earlier, when Kaya was a young teen, they would argue and laugh, skewering each other's views on issues; but for the past year, their interactions had become more acrid and even, most recently, almost non-existent. When her father sent her an autographed photo of himself and the President of the United States, she tore it into shreds and sent it back. That was their last contact, and she had refused his calls and ignored his e-mails.

Moki Joe's younger brother, Tocho Tom, who preferred to be

called Tom, had gone through school quietly, always in his big brother's shadow, except when it came to academics ... especially math. He'd won a full scholarship to the University of New Mexico in engineering and left with a double master's degree in chemical and mechanical engineering. Tom was in great demand on the job front, but he wanted to help Native Americans find jobs on or near reservations and to help preserve at least some aspects of tribal life. And so, he had begun brokering and implementing projects to create manufacturing or production facilities close to several reservations throughout the country.

Tom and Kaya had always been close, and Kaya's appreciation of Tom's humanitarian efforts brought them even closer. For his part, Tom didn't approve of his older brother's support of a political party and Administration that seemed to disdain their shared racial ancestries. Still, he never confronted his brother, and he even wondered if it was all part of his act or public persona.

Kaya was living in Detroit when her uncle, Tom, was to be honored at an event celebrating the opening of a new soft drink manufacturing plant that he had helped set up on the outskirts of Mount Pleasant, Michigan, close to the Isabella Indian Reservation. So, Tom invited his niece to the celebration. The facility would initially employ almost fifty people but was designed to accommodate expansion to four times that size.

It was the first time Tom and Kaya had seen each other in a few years, and Tom was amazed at her beauty, poise, and authenticity. She was an articulate and stunning young woman. They were both surprised by the ease and intellectual compatibility of their conversation – so much so that they both re-arranged their schedules to spend another day together.

They talked, they laughed, and they promised not to let so

much time go by between meetups. But when Tom and Kaya said their goodbyes, they came away with very different emotional states. Kaya felt lighter and happier than she had been in a long time, as she was able to talk openly with a trusted family member. She even came away with some hope that she and her father might one day be close again, based on Tom's optimism that Moki Joe may not be who he appeared to be.

Tom, however, came away with a heavy heart and burden, and he wasn't sure how to handle it. He did know, however, that it was time to see his brother again.

***

CHAPTER 27 – AN IDEA

Quincy Medical Center, Massachusetts. Vijay had returned to the hospital at 6:00 p.m. with a laptop. Sophie, Alek's nurse, explained to Vijay, in no uncertain terms, that he had a half-hour with the patient. Alek smiled like a kid who'd just gotten a new bike for Christmas when Vijay handed him the laptop. It took him less than five minutes to restore the feed, and another twenty-five minutes to show Vijay how he'd done it.

Alerted by what must have been an internal timer, Sophie pulled the laptop from Alek's grip and told Vijay that his thirty minutes had expired. On his way out the door, Vijay turned to ask Alek a question; but decided against it when he saw that he'd be interrupting something that looked a bit more than a normal patient-nurse relationship, but possibly, she was just taking his pulse … for a very long time.

On his way home, he called Zoe to tell her that the Final Notice feed was live again. Zoe was thrilled and wanted to inform her team ASAP, but she quickly gave Vijay the update that Kalin hadn't shown up at work and that they were watching airports and searching his office and home. She also alerted Vijay that she'd set up protection for Alek and told Vijay to be vigilant, at least until they had Kalin and Vasin.

***

Chestnut Hill, Massachusetts. Vijay returned home with the weight of what Zoe had just told him on his mind. Jennifer asked for an update on Alek's condition and Kalin's status. Vijay passed along the good news about Alek, as well as what appeared to be a budding relationship. Jennifer was very happy for Alek on all counts. But when Vijay gave her the update on Kalin (leaving out Zoe's warning), she asked something that Vijay hadn't thought about.

"I doubt that J. Edward even knows that Kalin was involved with Alek's kidnap and presumably the Final Notice attacks. But as soon as he does, he'll need another CEO ... and quickly."

Vijay explained that J. Edward might have been made aware that something was wrong when the FBI showed up with a warrant to search Kalin's office.

Jennifer continued, "And what about a CEO replacement?"

Vijay wasn't getting the point. "I have no idea what he's going to do, but yeah, he'll need to replace Kalin, and sooner rather than later, especially if more negative news leaks out."

Jennifer smiled when she realized that her genius-level husband hadn't ever considered the obvious. "I wonder where he'd find a qualified, even overqualified replacement? Someone who knows the business inside and out. Someone who already has the respect of the employee group, and someone who J. Edward would trust?"

Vijay finally got it. "Jen, I've 'been there and done that,' and I doubt J. Edward would want me back after I hacked the VT2 system. Besides, Kalin got rid of a lot of good people – people that I hired, and worked well with."

FINAL ACT

Jennifer retorted, "If you went back, you could ensure that good people were put in place. VitalTech was your baby. Your legacy. Do you want to see it crumble? Another hiring mistake by J. Edward at this stage could sink the business."

Vijay was not convinced and offered yet another excuse. "I don't know. I like my free time, and I want to be around when Karima, and maybe a brother or sister of hers, is growing up."

Jennifer smiled at the reference to more children, but stated, "Free time? All you do with your free time is work on VitalTech stuff, anyway."

Vijay wanted to end the conversation, "I'll think about it."

Jennifer, smiling again, replied, coquettishly, "Actually, I'd like to take your mind off it and re-focus on that brother or sister you talked about." She took his hand and began pulling him to the bedroom.

Vijay flashed his amazing grin and said, "What were we talking about?"

***

Denver, Colorado. (Seventeen days earlier.) Tom met 'MJ,' as only he called him, at Moki Joe's hotel suite at the Grand Hyatt in Denver a few hours before MJ's performance at the Grizzly Rose. They planned to have dinner, and then after the show, spend the night catching up. It felt good to be in the warm glow of his big brother, and Tom was pretty sure his brother was happy to be with him. But Tom also felt that MJ was holding something back from him; of course, he was holding something back, too. So, dinner was mostly catching-up talk. The real conversations would come out later.

Tom loved MJ's performance, and the crowd's obvious love made him proud beyond measure. He, more than anyone else at the Rose, understood the meaning of many of MJ's songs, and many of them brought on tears of happiness, sadness, and just good ole' nostalgia.

MJ was ravenous after the performance, and they decided to escape back to the hotel and order room service. His suite would allow them to relax in privacy without any unwanted attention from fans who might recognize the "Black Indian Cowboy." (That label always got a smile from Tom because MJ was actually intimidated by horses, and the only cows he'd ever been close to were 36-ounce T-Bones.)

Neither of the Hunter brothers drank alcohol anymore, but the privacy and their intimacy allowed them to be open and discuss come what may. MJ asked about Tom's recent time with Kaya, and that allowed Tom to get what he had to say off his chest.

He ambled over to the mini-bar and picked up a can of cola, "Want one," he asked, holding the can up.

"That's poison in a pop-top," MJ laughed. "I'll stick with my water."

"That's rich, given all the things you've swallowed, drank and snorted," Tom retorted as he began to compose, in his head, what he would say.

He began with his assessment of what an incredible young woman Kaya was. "She's beautiful, personable, caring, and very proud of her father, despite their political differences."

MJ expressed his displeasure, "I don't understand why we can't have political disagreements without going down a path of anger and hurt. We used to spar and then laugh it off."

Tom replied, "Politics have changed a lot over the years. For everyone." To his brother's nodding, he approached the real issue. "Do you remember when Kaya entered the Miss America contest?"

"Yeah, it was thirteen-months ago, and I was touring Europe and couldn't get back. Is she still pissed about that?"

"No. She might have been a little hurt at the time, but she's a big girl and smart. Remember, her Hopi name means 'little but wise.' "

"I named her," growled MJ, still agitated. "Well, Mom suggested it," and a slight smile brightened his face.

Tom was struggling with how to explain, so he blurted out, "The beauty pageant is at the root of her political anger and hurt."

Moki Joe looked puzzled, "I don't understand?"

Tom decided to lay it out. "Kaya was raped during the pageant." He had wanted to get it all out, but MJ exploded.

"What!?" he shouted out with a voice that could have reached the very back rows of a large venue, without amplification, and with a look that would wither all, save the very brave or foolish. "Who?"

"The President of the United States. The one with you in the autographed picture you sent Kaya."

An uneasy silence began. Tom waited for another outburst, and MJ's mind was in a state of turmoil, hate, and rage, but his reply was soft, filled with devastating sadness. "Oh my god," he whispered, as tears welled up.

Teary-eyed as well, Tom completed what he needed to say. "At first, Kaya was ashamed, a common occurrence with rape victims. But then, each tweeted support from you about the President was like salt in her wounds, and the photo was almost more than she could handle."

"I'm going to kill him."

"That's a pretty natural reaction, but easier said than done, and I'm not sure that the infamy of the event and loss of you would be in Kaya's best interest."

MJ looked at his watch and said with great solemnity, "Tom, I have exactly seventeen days to live. My watch, my 'deathwatch,' alerted me almost two weeks ago. I went to a doctor and then a couple of specialists, and they confirmed that I'm dying, but they wouldn't give me any specific timing, just that it was days or weeks, not months. I spoke with someone from the watch manufacturing company, and they advised me that the device is ninety-eight percent accurate. Only one Final Notice, as it's called, has been reversed since the watch was launched three years ago.

The brothers looked at each other and hugged, the tears flowing freely. Still hugging, MJ whispered, "Exactly two weeks from now, I will be alone with the President and Vice President in Wilkes Barre, just before my last performance. And I will kill him."

They released their hug, and Tom said, "You'll have to do it bare-handed and fight off the Vice President, although he's a pussy. But the Secret Service will be steps away if either of them shouts. Besides, Secret Service will sweep wherever it is that you're meeting, so a gun is out of the question."

"I can't die, knowing what he's done to Kaya. I need to get revenge."

Tom straightened up, and a slight smile formed, "I have an idea."

***

Washington, D.C. Zoe was thrilled that the constant alerts of actual and potential Final Notice assassins had slowed to a trickle, and none of the new ones appeared to be of the same modus operandi as Vasin's or the one in Los Angeles. The re-establishment of the system had also enabled them to prevent a potentially devastating employment-related attack in Houston, Texas.

A Final Notice recipient, who worked part-time at a supermarket in Houston, had recently lost his health insurance as the company decided to eliminate that benefit for part-timers. Unable to find alternative, affordable coverage, due to a preexisting medical condition, the employee had become extremely depressed and began to express anger at full-time employees and management at the store.

As a result of Zoe's idea to spotlight potential workplace hotspots, combined with Vijay's alert system, they identified the employee, who was exhibiting the emotional signature of a potential killer. The employee was thought to possess a gun or guns, and while en route to work, in an elevated emotional state as indicated in the data feed, he was intercepted without an incident. In his possession were an AR15 with a high capacity magazine, several spares, and two loaded handguns. He was taken into custody for a psychiatric evaluation and died a day later, as predicted by his VT2.

***

CHAPTER 28 – CHRISTMAS COMES EARLY!

Washington, D.C. Domestic life was heaven for Zoe and Demi. Zoe had moved in with Demi using one small Uber to bring over her few earthly possessions. Demi was back to work and away a lot, assigned to the dwindling but still a sizable number of Democratic presidential hopefuls. She'd had a heart-to-heart with her boss who was pissed because, in a way, she had "out-outed" him. In the end, he swallowed his pride and fully accepted her for who she was. A glowing commendation from Eric Hawke helped the process.

On what was destined to become one of those days that a generation or two (or at least Zoe) will always remember – like Kennedy's assassination, the first walk on the moon, 9-11 or Obama's election – Zoe answered the phone and pumped her fist in the air. "YES!"

The Maryland State Police had picked up Vasin through a trace on his EZ Pass toll transmitter. Zoe was excited, but she did wonder how dumb a fleeing suspect could be. Seriously. He was being transported to D.C., and Zoe vowed he would not walk away so easily this time.

Two hours later, Vik Vasin was brought in. Zoe and Sue from legal met him in an interrogation room. He was smug and antagonistic, demanding to know why he'd been brought in and to call his lawyer. They'd expected as much and told him that he'd be with them for some time. So, in the meantime, they asked him questions about how the Final Notice recipients were selected and managed. Where did he get the money to pay them? Were there others beside him managing Final Notice recipients? Everything they asked was met with no answer.

Then they described the raid in Quincy and that three people had been captured, including Fedor and two flunkies. They had given the FBI their version of the process as well as the names of Stefan, Peter, Leon, Pavel, Mike, Yuri, and ... Vik Vasin. And then they explained that he was being held under the Terrorism Act and, if convicted, could face capital punishment.

Vasin shifted in his chair at that point and demanded to speak with his lawyer. Sue took delight in telling him that he would certainly be able to make that call, but given the stakes this time, she recommended he call a new one. She also added that if one or two of the seven people involved so far could be helpful, they may be able to negotiate a lesser penalty, although life imprisonment was probably the best deal they could get.

Vasin did an excellent job of looking bored, so they ended the interview and told him they'd be in touch. Zoe couldn't help herself and added, with a smile, "We know where to find you."

That immediately transformed Vasin's bored demeanor into a rage, and he demanded again to speak with his lawyer. This time, Sue had the pleasure of telling him one more time that they would let him make that call as soon as they had more information from the others. The Terrorism Act gave them a lot of latitude.

Back at her office, Zoe returned a call to the Boston field office. The Boston Police had arrested a small-time crook named Nick Felty for illegal arms sales. He was providing names of his customers for the guns he sold. Vik Vasin was one of his best.

They'd also found a possible match for Leon. The Las Vegas field office was trying to bring him in for questioning. Zoe checked the time on her VT2, which she had put on for the first time in a while, and it wasn't even lunchtime yet.

***

Chestnut Hill, Massachusetts. Vijay was toweling off from a shower after a fifteen-mile run when his phone chimed. It was J. Edward Konig. When he finished the call, he looked for Jennifer and found her in their home gym, working out.

"Guess who just called me?" he teased.

"At this hour, I'd guess Zoe."

"Wrong. It was J. Edward."

"Was he just getting home from a party?" she asked, as she gently released the pulley on the multi-function exercise machine.

"No, actually, he was up early to catch a flight to Cuba," Vijay replied.

"And he wanted to say goodbye or ask what kind of cigars you wanted him to bring back?"

"I think you know why he called. The CEO job."

FINAL ACT

Jennifer tried to hide her smile, "He offered you the job?"

"Yes, and to end your twenty-question game, I accepted."

Grinning from ear to ear now, Jennifer asked, "But what about the cigars?"

Vijay scrunched up his face. "What about them?"

"You're going to need some."

***

Washington, D.C. Zoe's early Christmas, continued while she was munching on a sandwich when she got a call from the Ft. Lauderdale police. They had apprehended Mikhail Kalinin, aka Mike Kalin, and his wife, as they were boarding a cruise ship to the Bahamas. Interestingly, they had one-way airline tickets from Nassau to Moscow via Havana, and they both held valid Russian passports.

Zoe dispatched agents to pick them up and bring them to Washington. She called Sue in legal to let her know about Kalin and Leon, and she texted Vijay.

***

Coffee Break Cafe, Quincy, Massachusetts. When Vijay accepted the position, he'd asked J. Edward not to announce it to anyone except Don Casey, VitalTech's Vice President of Marketing. Vijay then called Don to arrange a private meeting away from the VitalTech office. Don was one of the few holdovers from Vijay's senior team when Vijay owned the business, and Vijay had a lot of respect for Don's marketing acumen. Don seemed very happy to see Vijay and relished the prospect of working together again.

Vijay wanted to see Don straight away because he valued his opinion. He began by making sure that Don was fully aware of the murders carried out by Final Notice recipients, both those acting on their own and those managed by the Russians. Vijay's detailed account shook Don. Kalin kept a tight lid on the Recipient killings, and although Don had heard the rumors, he had no idea of the breadth and severity of the incidents.

Vijay posed the two questions he had specifically wanted to ask: "What would be the ramifications of removing the Final Notice feature?" and "What is your assessment of Kalin's personal assistant?"

***

Mohegan Sun Arena, Wilkes-Barre Township, Pennsylvania. The event organizers and the Secret Service had just left Moki Joe's spacious 1,000 square foot RV after a detailed briefing about the following day's schedule. The organizers explained that they would pick him up in a golf cart at 2:30 p.m. the next day to take him into the arena green room. That would give him a final few minutes before going on stage promptly at 3:30 p.m. when the opening warm-up act finished. Following the show, they'd bring him back to the RV the same way he had come. That would give him one hour to 'unwind' before his meeting with the President and Vice President.

Moki Joe was OK with all of that, but he flatly rejected the attempts of the event organizers, facility staff and the Secret Service, to hold the session with POTUS and the Vice President, inside the arena. He told them that they could eat their burgers in the arena if they chose, but if they wanted to eat with Moki Joe, it would be in his 'house.'

The Secret Service team asked his permission – although

asking was just a formality – to allow them to thoroughly inspect his RV today, at his convenience, and then again tomorrow, while he was performing in the Arena.

***

Alone again in his RV, Moki Joe smiled at the irony of the venue – the Mohegan Sun Arena. The entertainment complex was owned by the Mohegan Tribe of Connecticut because the Pennsylvania Indians had all been murdered or forced out of the state many years ago. They had to buy their way in, and now Moki Joe was helping them to pay it off.

His thoughts shifted to his own mortality. He only had two performances left – though only one was musical – and he was looking forward to both of them. To begin with, he wanted to blow away the 8,000-plus fans so that they'd remember him as an entertainer, not just because they were there 'that night.' He wanted to hear the roar of adulation and bask in their approval. And as he thought that, he realized just how important that approval was. It meant so much more than the beatings he'd given countless idiots who had insulted him and his brother. And it partially made up for all the looks of disapproval, suspicion or even fear that he'd received almost every day of his life until he was recognized as Moki Joe Hunter.

After his meeting with Tom in Denver, he had tried to contact Kaya, but she never picked up and never called him back. He'd written and re-written a lengthy letter to her, apologizing for the hurt that he had caused her, trying desperately to tell her how much he loved her. It was to be given to her when he died. At last, he had finished it, and it was on his 'office' desk in his RV.

Tom had called him earlier that morning to check that everything was going as planned, explaining again how events would unfold. He had also cautioned and coached MJ on his letter

CHAPTER 29 – THE CHAIN OF COMMAND

Washington, D.C. Zoe's hot streak continued. The Las Vegas field office had Leon Ivanov in their possession, and just like Moki Joe would soon be doing, he was singing his heart out. He positively implicated Vik Vasin, who trained him, along with Pavel Krupin and Peter Sobol, in the woods of New Hampshire. Warrants were being issued for Krupin and Sobol.

Ivanov had spoken with Yuri and Stefan, but he didn't know their last names. They were able to get two cell phone numbers from his phone that appeared as both inbound and outbound calls. They'd let her know if they found the owners of those numbers.

***

Coffee Break Cafe, Quincy, Massachusetts. When Don Casey fully absorbed and considered the implications of Vijay's first question, he mentally had to take a step back. *He had always championed the Final Notice feature as their single most significant differentiator. Did the VT2 have enough to compete without it? How would they handle the ten-plus million existing users?*

"Vijay, I never thought I'd willingly be thinking of alternatives to the Final Notice feature, but knowing the full extent of the damage it's caused, I don't see how I can defend keeping it in. I imagine, given the havoc it's wreaked on the electoral process, you'd like to act quickly, but I have a few questions."

Vijay smiled and said, "I'd be surprised if you didn't."

"From your perspective as a doctor, how does our clinical technology stack up with Apple, Fitbit, Garmin, etc.?"

Vijay thought and replied, "We're ahead, but it's like an ongoing combination of sprints and marathons. We need to run flat out to keep ahead, and the race is a very long one. The biggest commercial advantage we've had so far is the technology of the Final Notice and our ability to predict end-of-life trends."

Don perked up, "You said 'commercial advantage.' Are there others?"

Vijay explained, "Actually, that commercial advantage has been driven by two very unique technological advantages: first, in the way, the device analyzes blood, and second, by the algorithms that convert those analyses to diagnoses. I hold the patents for those processes which are licensed to VitalTech."

Don asked, "So how do those advantages help us?"

Vijay replied, "That's the marathon part. We have an underlying advantage that helps us add new functionality, although we then need to sprint occasionally to match the competition."

Don was excited, "So, in other words, you feel confident that we should be able to remain market leaders, even without the Final Notice."

Vijay confirmed, "Yes, although we might suffer an initial,

short-term disadvantage."

Don asked, "Is there any way we can continue to utilize the underlying capability of the Final Notice functionality of the VT2 to help users detect issues earlier, enabling their doctors to intervene and prolong their lives?"

Vijay paused for a couple of seconds, and excitedly replied, "Absolutely! Of course! We can alert users that there are general or even specific issues with, for example, their cardiovascular, renal, digestive, or pulmonary systems and provide insights, using our algorithms, to their physicians. That's much better than receiving a Final Notice, which, by definition, means 'too late.' "

Vijay then started thinking out loud about how they could interface with doctors and hospitals to provide the minute clues that the VT2 was picking up.

Don raised his hands and said, "Whoa! That is all way over my head. But putting on my marketing hat, what I think I hear you saying is that the VT2 is the premier health watch that can help spot health issues earlier ... maybe even early enough to fix them."

Vijay smiled. "Spoken like a great Senior Vice President of Marketing, and the 'Senior' is intentional. Congratulations on your promotion!"

They discussed the communication issues and agreed that the legal department would need to advise them on how to communicate the change to all users. In the meantime, Don would begin preparations for the launch of the new VT3.

Vijay then asked Don for his opinion of Kalin's personal assistant, and Don seemed impressed with her. He explained that with Kalin running the show, it was pretty risky for people to be candid – those that were found themselves out of a job. Hannah Ford seemed efficient, and although cautious, he didn't think she was one of Kalin's stooges.

After he met with Don, Vijay called J. Edward and asked him to contact Hannah Ford and tell her to expect Vijay the following day. He also requested that his visit not be broadcast just yet.

***

VitalTech HQ, Quincy, Massachusetts. The next morning, Vijay arrived about two hours later than he would typically arrive when he 'officially' resumed his role as CEO of VitalTech. The lobby security guard recognized him from the Board meetings but had no idea about the nature of his visit. Vijay simply told him that he had a meeting with Hannah Ford. The guard called, and a minute later, Ms. Ford appeared.

Hannah appeared to be about 'thirty-ish,' with short brown hair, freckles, and blue framed glasses. She was dressed more formally than he expected, possibly because she was meeting her new boss. She greeted him with a cheery smile and greeting. "Good morning, Mr. Patel."

Vijay held out his hand, "Good morning, Hannah. I'm Vijay."

Vijay explained that he would officially be starting on Monday and that an announcement would be sent out by J. Edward shortly. Vijay asked her how things were in general, and Hannah confessed that it wasn't the happiest place she'd ever worked. Also, that there were rumors that Mike Kalin had been arrested.

Vijay comforted Hannah with his view of a more open and informal culture, doing his best to boost her confidence in light of all the current uncertainty.

Reflecting on his meeting with Don and the need to get his legal team involved with the scrapping of the Final Notice, Vijay asked who comprised the legal team. She listed John Riley as their Chief Legal Counsel and three additional names. He didn't know any of them and asked, "When did Liz Glass leave?" Liz had been the head of Legal when Vijay was CEO.

Hannah thought for a few seconds, "Four months ago."

Vijay thought and said, "Hmm. OK, can you see if John Riley is available?"

Hannah picked up Vijay's desk phone and dialed, "Hi Mary, is Mr. Riley available? Vijay Patel, our new CEO, would like to see him. Sure." She covered the mouthpiece and said that Mary, Riley's secretary, was checking. She uncovered the phone, and nervously spoke, "Oh, Mr. Riley, yes, Mr. Kalin has left the business, and Mr. Patel has been appointed as the new CEO."

Hannah listened, although she held the phone away from her ear, and then replied, "I understand. Well, he's here right now, can you meet with him?"

Hannah jerked the phone further away from her ear, and Vijay could hear Riley's loud voice, "Tell him to make an appointment after I've been advised that he's replaced Kalin." Vijay could hear Riley's phone being slammed down.

Hannah had turned bright red and apologized, "I'm sorry, Mr. Patel."

Vijay smiled, "You've nothing to apologize for, and please, my name is Vijay. Do you have a phone contact for Liz Glass?"

FINAL ACT

Hannah went out to her desk and returned with a number. Vijay asked her to arrange a meeting with all department heads on Monday at 9:00 a.m. He then called the number Hannah had given him. It was her cell phone, and Liz picked up.

It was nice to hear Liz's voice again, as Vijay replied, "Hi, Liz. It's Vijay Patel."

"Vijay! How are you?" she replied cheerfully.

Vijay explained, "Kalin has left and I am coming back."

Liz was thrilled and inquired about Kalin's departure. Vijay told her that he'd explain later and asked what she was doing.

Liz explained that working for Kalin had been pure hell and that she finally gave her notice to protect herself from breaking laws. She was pursuing a couple of opportunities and expected to accept one of them shortly.

Vijay asked if she'd like her old job back starting on Monday. He smiled as her quick response contained not even a hint of Liz's trademark two to three-second delay as she exclaimed, "Yes!"

Vijay told her about his meeting with Don and the details behind it, along with Don's enthusiasm for the launch of a VT3. Their concern now was how to handle the elimination of the Final Notice feature – with the ten million current users – as soon as possible?

This time there was a three-second delay as Liz took in his question. "First of all, we'll need to advise all users before we pull the plug on the Notice, and users who have already received their Notice would not be affected. I think we can then delete the Notice for the others and excite them with the positive health reasons for the change, using Don's marketing speak. Can the existing watch software be upgraded to the new VT3 capability?"

Vijay nodded and said, "Yes, although at some point, they will need a new device, I'm not clear about how long it will take to pull the plug on the Notice, legally?"

Liz thought for a few seconds and said, "We're connected to all users electronically, and we've established that as our legal communication method. Technically, you can simply … like, press a button to stop it?"

Vijay laughed, "Not actually a button but almost as fast. Yes."

Liz thought some more and mused, "I understand the sense of urgency, so what about this? I know that there was just a technical glitch of some sort that sent out Notices to everyone – hell, I was on a treadmill, and it almost scared me to death. So, what if we send out a message to all users that we're taking the Notice offline – immediately – out of concern for everyone's safety, while we evaluate new and improved functionality. The alert will provide information about how to air grievances and perhaps include a questionnaire about how important some of the planned enhancements are perceived."

Vijay exclaimed, "Brilliant! What about refunds and upgrades?"

Three seconds later, Liz continued, "OK, so we could offer a full refund or trade-in if they got their watch within the last six months, fifty percent refund if purchased within a year, or a free upgrade when the new VT3 hits the street. Or something like that."

Vijay was OK with that, although he thought that perhaps the

FINAL ACT

VT2 could continue to function with some enhanced features; to take advantage of all the new features; however, an upgrade to a VT3 would be required. But at the moment, he was focused on removing the Notice. "OK. I'll have Finance run the numbers. Thanks, Liz. See you Monday."

Vijay called Hannah in and asked for a copy of Riley's employment contract. She came back a minute later and handed him a single page, "I think this is what you want."

The letter was addressed to John Riley and read, "This letter, when signed by both parties, supersedes any and all employment contracts regardless of date. Your contract may be terminated without notice or cause at any time."

It was sent and signed by Mike Kalin and accepted and signed by John Riley.

Puzzled, Vijay looked at Hannah, who said, "Mr. Kalin got tired of executives questioning him, so, about three months ago, he had everyone sign these."

On one level, Vijay was tempted to inwardly thank Kalin, but instead, he said, "Please prepare a letter, dated today, to Riley, that says, 'You are terminated with immediate effect in lieu of thirty (30) days' notice.' Please do that now so I can sign it."

Hannah returned immediately with the letter. Vijay signed it and asked her to put it in an envelope and hand-deliver it to him. He then asked who headed up Information Technology.

"Dimitri Pavlova, but he hasn't been in for a few days."

"Who's next in charge?"

"There were a lot of changes made after Dimitri arrived. I'm not sure, but I'll find out."

Vijay changed his mind, "OK. Let's do this, Hannah. Deliver the letter to Riley tomorrow morning after you bring a copy to HR. And here is my cell phone number to call if you have any issues with anyone. I'll have J. Edward announce my appointment first thing tomorrow. And one more thing: please have HR prepare an employment contract, without the 'no notice' feature, for Liz Glass. Same salary as Riley or the salary she had when she left, whichever is more. She'll be joining us on Monday as our new head of Legal. Thanks, Hannah."

J. Edward had left it up to Vijay as to when he wanted to formally start, but between the two of them, he asked Vijay to at least informally begin ASAP. Vijay had just terminated one employee and hired one, in his informal capacity, and now, he was about to invite someone to hack into his company's IT system.

***

CHAPTER 30 – HIS BEST EVER!

The Green Room, Mohegan Sun Arena, Wilkes-Barre Township, Pennsylvania. Moki Joe was ready and raring to go. He looked at himself closely in the full-length mirror and flashed his familiar smile. He took in the cowboy hat, shirt, kerchief, jeans, and boots on his still athletic frame, but there was no hiding the sorrow and fatigue in his eyes.

The stage manager came in, smiled, and said, "Showtime!" Standing off-stage, Moki Joe was introduced, and then he literally sprinted out to a thunderous roar from the 8,000-plus fans. It took close to ten minutes to quiet them. He began by saying, "I want to thank all of you for coming out today ..." and that was enough to bring on yet another roar.

"Thank you, and I know you all came out to have some fun" ... big cheers again. Moki Joe held his hands up, and the audience quieted down. "This is my final act." Boos broke out, and Moki Joe waited until it was quiet again. "It's been a great thrill for me over these many years, and I want to leave you all with something more than my music to remember, so please, hear me out. All of you, and millions of others throughout the country, have supported me, embraced me, and I have felt your love." Cheering again.

"Thanks, but I wanted to remind all of you about something obvious. I'm half black and half Indian, but I could have been all black or full Indian, or Latino or anything else, and I think that you'd have the same feelings for me and my music. Right?" Cheering again.

"OK. So, my career made me famous. But that doesn't define who I am as a person. I see a whole lot of white, tan, brown, and black faces out there, and I'll bet that not all of you can sing, strum, or write music." Laughter and shouts from the crowd.

"And if you can't, that doesn't define you either. Who you are, comes from here," he said, placing his hand on his heart. "And we all have the same hearts, regardless of the color of our skin." Cheering.

"It's our hearts that make this country the greatest in the world." More cheering.

"So, do old Moki Joe a favor, and when you look at someone, try to get past the color of their skin and look into their hearts." More cheering.

"Thank you! ... OK, I want to dedicate this show, my Final Act, to my amazing daughter, Kaya," and with that, he signaled to his band to let it rip. The crowd went wild, and when the show was over, if you were to ask Moki Joe or most of the fans in attendance, they'd all tell you, it was his best ever.

***

Quincy Medical Center, Massachusetts. Vijay thought that Alek must be progressing well, given the relatively easy access to his room. After Vijay's name and ID were checked against an approved list by an armed officer, he was free to stay as long as he wished during visitation hours.

FINAL ACT

Alek was happy to see him and confirmed his good progress. He hoped to be out within a week. Vijay quipped that he would then miss his first day at work, and Alek looked puzzled.

Vijay added, "OK, I guess you haven't formally accepted yet."

"Accepted what?"

"The position of Vice President & Chief Information Officer at VitalTech."

"And you're offering me that job on what authority?"

"As the new CEO."

Alek grinned, "That's awesome! Fantastic! What's my job pay?"

"Seriously? You want me to negotiate with a guy in a hospital bed? An unemployed guy at that! Let's wait 'til you're off your meds and in an environment where I have less pity on you."

They laughed, and Vijay filled in Alek on Kalin and his own soft entry back into VitalTech. He told him about Dimitri being MIA and the changes in IT. He pulled a laptop out, looking around for the watchful eyes of Sophie. "Where's Sophie?"

"It's her day off, but she'll be here soon."

Vijay smiled, "Now, that's dedication! But before that minor distraction, as your first unofficial act, can you hack into the VitalTech system and cut off John Riley's and Dimitri Pavlova's system access?"

Alek returned the smile and said, "Happily! I already love my job!"

***

Mohegan Sun Arena, Wilkes-Barre Township, Pennsylvania. Moki Joe emerged from the shower in his RV. He put on his VT2, ignoring the flashing Final Notice warning to see that in just under an hour, the President of the United States and the Vice President would be ushered in for a few photos, and then the cheeseburgers will arrive for an early dinner. The plan was that the two politicians would then hold a rally in the arena before a lot of drunk, tired, potential voters.

Moki Joe thought about the past two weeks, realizing that he'd hardly thought of his impending death. He didn't feel much different physically, but he had an eerie feeling that his watch was right. In fact, his biggest fear had been that he might die before today. He looked around at the living room area, smart deep brown leather and polished wood. The soft drinks were chilling in a large bowl of crushed ice, and there were plates, silverware, napkins, and glasses set up on the low tables in the seating area.

There was a sharp rap on the door, and it was the Secret Service Agent in Charge, giving him the ten-minute warning for a bathroom break or wardrobe adjustments.

And then another knock. Moki Joe opened the door and welcomed in the President of the United States and the Vice President, with the same smile he had just practiced. A couple of photographers followed closely, and they started shooting away as the ingenuous small talk, handshaking, and arms around shoulders took place. And then it was over. The photographers were ushered out, and trays of huge cheeseburgers and cartons of French fries were brought in and placed on the low tables. And then they were alone.

***

Moki Joe motioned for his guests to sit side by side on the settee across from him and offered them the cheeseburgers and fries, placing a burger and fries on his plate after the guests helped themselves. From the bar area, he retrieved two cans of diet cola for them and a bottle of water for himself. Settling onto his settee, as they popped the tops of their colas, Moki Joe cautioned, "Those colas are poison," invoking a comment the President had used in the past, and the three of them laughed together. He held up his bottled water and pronounced, "Mister President and Mister Vice President, I propose a toast to an even greater next four years." As he sipped his water, he watched with great interest as the two men across from him took the last healthy gulps and breaths of their lives.

The President turned very red, his eyes bulged, and it looked like he was trying to say something. Then he started turning green and finally a lurid blue, before he crashed sideways, knocking a secured lamp off its base. Moki Joe had been so mesmerized by the contrast between the President's skin color changes that he almost missed the Vice President's death throes. His pasty white complexion went through similar color variations, although the colors were more vibrant, before he fell forward, smashing his face onto the low table while making fairly loud gurgling sounds.

The egregious sounds were heard by the Secret Service agents standing outside the door, and they burst into the RV, guns drawn, and observed the two slumped figures. One of them quickly spoke into his microphone. "Mogul and Hoosier are down; I repeat Mogul and Hoosier are down. Request urgent medical assistance!"

The agents then looked at Moki Joe, who was still sitting down, holding his bottle of water. One of them asked, "What the hell happened?"

Although Moki Joe knew what was supposed to happen, he

was taken by surprise at the speed of it. "I, I don't know. They popped the tops, took sips of their drinks, and keeled over."

The agents quickly took in the scene of the two opened cans of colas on the floor next to the lifeless men and Moki Joe holding a bottle of water. One of the agents checked the bathroom and bedroom. The other one, who seemed to be in charge, nodded toward the remaining cans of cola nestled in the crushed ice. "Where did these come from?"

Moki Joe then made three true statements: "One of the people from the arena or event organizer asked me ... it was either yesterday or this morning ... if I wanted beverages." That was true.

"I asked for six diet colas, cause I know that's what the President drinks, and some bottled water." That was also true.

"When I returned from my show, the colas and water were here." True.

The medics took the bodies away. They were quite dead. The secret service agents then began to ask dozens of questions to which he truthfully answered, "I don't know" most of the time. Somebody carefully collected the two open cola cans and the unopened ones, as well as the water bottles.

The Secret Service Agent in Charge told Moki Joe to leave everything as it was. He was being held here until further notice. Moki Joe asked if he could watch TV, and he was given permission.

He turned on his TV and was surprised to see how fast everything was happening from the public's perspective. He chuckled to think that he and his brother were the only ones who really knew.

FINAL ACT

There were the initial shock headlines and main newscasters bringing in their on-the-scene local affiliates to describe what happened: "Apparently ... poisoned." And then the newscast broke away to Washington, D.C., where the Speaker of the House was being sworn in. She appeared solemn and respectful in her white dress, but from everything that preceded today, he wouldn't have been surprised if she whooped and hollered. Sadly, he could never tell Kaya that he was responsible for the first female President of the United States.

***

Washington, D.C. At 6:15 p.m., Zoe got a call from Hawke. He told her that the President and Vice President were both dead, along with the few available details. It appeared to be poison, but it was not known how it was administered. He shocked her when he asked if the VT2 data feed had resumed. She confirmed it had and asked if Hawke thought a Final Notice recipient was responsible. He said he didn't have any reason to believe that, but wanted to cross it off the list of possibilities.

Zoe re-checked her VitalTech report, and although she could see a Final Notice recipient in the Wilkes-Barre area, he wasn't tagged as a threat. She called Vijay, and when he answered, she immediately asked, "Can you get into the VitalTech system and see if there are any Final Notice recipients in the area of Wilkes-Barre, Pennsylvania?"

Vijay and Alek had heard several shouts and people running around, but they didn't know what had happened.

Vijay knew something wasn't right and motioned to Alek to turn on the TV while he asked, "What's going on?"

"The President and Vice President have been killed."

Vijay saw the glaring headlines on the TV, and he asked, "Do you think a Recipient was involved with the President's murder?"

Zoe replied, "I have no reason to think so, and the killings weren't by guns. I see one Recipient in the immediate area but not in an elevated state. There are two others close by, also in normal states. Can you double-check and look at them and their history?"

Vijay tapped away and said, "There are three within a radius of twenty miles."

"Any on high alert?"

More tapping and then, "There's one that seems to be displaying the typical post anger calm that we've seen with earlier killings. Let me look into the history …Yes! He was on high alert a couple of hours ago. Hmm, he also had a huge anger spike about two weeks ago, but then dropped, increasing slowly until the recent alert."

"What's the recipient's name?" But she already knew the answer.

"Hunter. MJ Hunter.

Zoe's heart sank, but she shot back at Vijay, "Why didn't the data feed alert us?"

Vijay muttered, "Just a second," while he looked at the history … "I can't see any reason why it didn't. It seems to be working." She hung up with Vijay and called Ninad. He was immediately aware of the situation. "This morning at 10:55 a.m., I received a call from Secret Service Agent Gilmore in response to a

FINAL ACT

Final Notice Alert that had been pushed out to them. He was acknowledging receipt of the alert, as set up in our protocol, and said the situation was under control."

Zoe clicked some keys on her computer to find the FBI Agent-in-Charge on the scene at the Sun Arena. She called and explained the situation with a suspect named MJ Hunter, and the agent was surprised. "You mean Moki Joe Hunter, the entertainer?"

Now Zoe was surprised. She knew who Moki Joe was but hadn't realized that was MJ Hunter. "Moki Joe Hunter is there at the scene?"

The agent explained what they knew so far, which was that the President and Vice President were with Hunter in his RV when they both died from what appeared to be poison, possibly contained in cans of cola. Hunter had been questioned by the Secret Service but claimed that the cans had been delivered while he was out.

Zoe explained Hunter's Final Notice alert and the changes in his emotional readings, and that a Secret Service Agent Gilmore had said that the situation was under control. Zoe told him that Moki Joe Hunter was considered a prime suspect and needed to be held.

She hung up and called Vijay back. "How long does Hunter have to live according to the VT2?"

Vijay tapped some keys and replied, "Two days. Three at most."

She called Hawke and gave him the news. There was a moment of silence, and then he said, "So we might have stopped him if he'd had a gun. I'll get the on-site team to put more pressure on him."

***

Mohegan Sun Arena, Wilkes-Barre Township, Pennsylvania. The FBI at the crime scene were briefed regarding Moki Joe's Final Notice status, and they intensified their questioning. They were fighting an uphill battle, however, even though the circumstantial evidence pointed to him as the perpetrator. The combination of Moki Joe's celebrity, his apparent lack of motive or inclination, and his spiritual serenity – along with the absence of any evidence that connected him – made him unlikely to be a criminal.

Moki Joe confirmed that he was aware of the watch's prediction and explained that he had probably gone through the same stages of dying that most people in his situation had experienced, including anger. But he had come through that and was now at peace. He also didn't doubt that his emotional levels would have seen some pretty steep peaks and valleys, but he countered by asking them if they'd ever performed in front of 8,000 screaming fans?

He had always been a supporter of the President. He showed them a photo of himself and the President at the White House, with the President's signature and inscription, "To a great friend and true American."

They asked him the same questions, over and over, regarding how the cans of cola had arrived. And Moki Joe explained, over and over again, that they were there when he got back from a walk. As far as he knew, the only people permitted to enter his RV while he was performing were the Secret Service.

***

Washington, D.C. Hawke called Zoe. "We'll need to talk with Vijay to get a statement of how his system works, along with his interpretation of Hunter's physical and emotional state, based on the VT2 readings. I'll have someone from the team carrying out the investigation give him a call. You can tell him to expect one.

"In the meantime, we have a public relations dilemma: A Country & Western superstar and supporter of the President whose only provable 'crime' so far is that he was there when it happened. And, he'll be dead in a couple of days."

***

Chestnut Hill, Massachusetts. Within an hour, Vijay did get a call asking him if he could provide some information and make a sworn statement. He agreed, and two FBI agents were with him within another hour. In a recorded interview, Vijay explained how the VitalTech system worked and how he had developed a new analytical process that would assess the emotional state of Final Notice recipients. They wanted to know its degree of accuracy in this situation, and he explained that it would be impossible to measure it until there were dozens, perhaps hundreds, of similar situations – i.e., murders by a highly energetic, emotional performer preparing to entertain 8,000 fans. Even then, he doubted that it would be foolproof. The system could only forecast a likelihood, not an inevitability of violence. In reality, it could only explain why someone might have acted violently.

***

CHAPTER 31 – FINAL, FINAL NOTICE

Mohegan Sun Arena, Wilkes-Barre Township, Pennsylvania. After another almost full day of questioning following the deaths of the President and Vice President, the FBI had made no further progress in understanding why Moki Joe would want to kill the President or how he did it.

There had been a brief peak of excitement when they found the letter to Kaya, hoping that it would establish a motive:

"My darling daughter, Kaya:

I've had some time to write this letter, as I found out I was dying almost a month ago. I didn't want to burden you with the knowledge that I was dying, nor put pressure on you to abandon your views about me, given our poor relationship of late.

Your Uncle Tom explained some of the reasons you were upset with me, and you were both right and wrong. I went along with the views and behaviors of many of my fans, even though I didn't approve of them. Why? Partly because I've never been too interested in politics, but mostly, I didn't have the guts to speak out, as some of my fellow musicians have done. They suffered commercially, but now I see that they were the winners. They can hold their heads high and know they did the right thing.

FINAL ACT

I really screwed up and lost a big chunk of time that we could have had together, but I will cherish what we did have up until I draw my last breath, and I promise you that you will be my final thought.

I wrote a song for you, but every time I try to sing it, I choke up and break down in tears. I'll leave you the lyrics.

I love you more than you'll ever know,

Love, Taata"

The letter prompted widely divergent points of view ranging from it explained nothing, to it explained everything. The evidence was simply inconclusive.

Moki Joe made an impassioned, and as it turned out, a compelling plea to leave so that he could die where he was born. Weighing the law against public relations, the FBI made a sensible compromise. They charged Moki Joe with two counts of suspicion of murder. (They knew he'd be dead in a few days so he would never be convicted; they also knew that news of him dying while in custody posed a greater public relations risk than letting him leave.) In the end, he was allowed to leave the Mohegan Arena wearing an ankle bracelet tracker so they would always know where he was.

***

Acomita Lake Campground, Acoma Pueblo, New Mexico. Moki Joe's road team wasted no time driving the big RV straight through from the Mohegan Area to Acomita Lake. And so, two days after his brief meeting with the President, as his VT2 had predicted, Moki Joe Hunter died in his sleep, not far from where he started his life's journey.

***

Washington, D.C. The FBI interviewed Tocho Tom and Kaya, but neither could help them with their investigations, and over the ensuing weeks and months, there were no breakthroughs. There was no video footage to identify who brought the colas. There were no fingerprints on the cans that led anywhere, and it remained a mystery as to how the poisoned cans of cola found their way into Moki Joe's RV. Unusually, the cans had no markings or codes, making it impossible to trace them to any facility. News reports did leak that the composition of the poison was very similar to one used by the Russians in the UK and Europe, involving a Russian double agent and his daughter. Moscow denied any involvement, and Tocho Tom Hunter smiled.

***

Quincy, Massachusetts. Everyone arrived on time for Vijay's first senior management meeting, except for Alek. He wouldn't be released from the hospital until later in the week. However, he was already doing more work than Sophie thought was good for him. With the exception of Don and Liz, Vijay didn't know any of them. He had reviewed all of their resumes, and with a couple of exceptions, he was comfortable with their backgrounds. Time would tell.

His first orders of business were that everyone at VitalTech would be known as and called by their first name, and informal dress was welcome. There were no opposing views.

The next item was the Final Notice. As he had done with Don, Vijay took them through the background and history of incidents. He even included the fact that a Final Notice recipient was a suspect in the murders of the former President and Vice President, even though the charges were dropped after his death.

FINAL ACT

Vijay introduced the revised health benefits approach that he and Don had brainstormed as a better and more socially responsible option. He then asked Don and Jenni Chen, the CFO, to present the numbers along the lines that Liz had suggested. Don summarized that the number of people who would ask for refunds was expected to be relatively small, and Jenni's numbers demonstrated a minimal financial hit, if anything.

The more important news was that the revised health platform would be a major announcement, with projected sales of over five million VT3s within the first six months. Don had already put together a very compelling message that would go out with the Final Notice suspension e-mail.

Neither Vijay nor Don had expected any opposition, and they didn't get any, so they were able to send out the message removing the Final Notice feature almost immediately, and by the close of business, the Final Notice was history.

***

Washington, D.C. Zoe was ecstatic about the news from Vijay, but like everyone else, her emotions were tempered following the two recent high-profile murders, despite the victims' unpopularity.

All of the suspects connected with the Final Notice 'robots' had been arrested and charged, with one notable exception, Yuri Chernyshevsky. Zoe and her colleagues had been able to play everyone against each other, all of whom hoped to escape long prison sentences or worse. The CIA identified Chernyshevsky as an SVR operative (translated from Russian as the Foreign Intelligence Service of the Russian Federation), suspected of election interference in several countries. There was no record of his arrival to the U.S., and U.S. intelligence placed him in Russia.

The end of Final Notices did not mean the end of problems for Zoe, the FBI, the Secret Service, or any of the law enforcement agencies. The news networks were sizzling with non-stop stories about alt-right groups taking revenge on left-wing groups and gatherings, assuming that the 'Left' was somehow responsible for the death of the President and Vice President. And the Antifada responded, not just in turn, but also out of frustration with right-wing judges and politicians who carried out their roles with what was considered to be hyper-partisan zeal. Guns were being used with increasing frequency, but the Senate seemed incapable of acting. The nightmare that Eric Hawke had spoken about with Zoe over a month ago - "guns and bloodshed" – was now a reality.

The newly appointed Democratic President was considered an enemy by the Republican White House, Cabinet, and Senate, effectively neutralizing her effectiveness; but given the very short time remaining before the election, she decided to just tough it out and use her veto power to stop things from getting worse.

Political chaos, civil chaos, and economic chaos ripped through the United States in ways many described as similar to the Civil War era. With the presidential election drawing near, many wondered if it could be carried out effectively. And even if it could, what would it take to restore the nation to some form of civility, to reduce the divisiveness, and put some meaning into the name, 'United States.'

***

Chestnut Hill, Massachusetts. Unlike the rest of the country, Vijay and Jennifer's lives began to settle into a new and comfortable normalcy. Karima had returned home, accompanied by Jennifer's parents. Jennifer assured Vijay that their stay would be a short one, but they wound up staying two weeks. Vijay's weekday mornings still started very early with his pre-dawn run, and he was usually the first person to arrive at the VitalTech offices. That schedule protected him, somewhat, from enduring Nicole and Bill's presence, but unencumbered by the pressures brought about by Final Notice murders; he was in a much better frame of mind to handle their challenging habits.

He had become a student and accomplished practitioner of delegating, ensuring that he always left the office in time to pick up Karima from pre-school. And one of his hard-fast rules was that his weekends always belonged to the family. And on the subject of family, Vijay had just spoken with his brother, Sanjay, giving him the news about the VT3. He also told him about the earlier threat from Kalin that he'd kept from Sanjay.

That made Sanjay laugh. "Do you know how many job offers I get? Almost one a week and most offer a lot more money … but none of them included working for my brother."

Now Vijay laughed. "Well, as the new CEO for VitalTech, and as your brother, make sure that Father is healthy before he goes to the bank next month. He's going to see a big jump when your raise comes through."

Sanjay chuckled, "Thank you for the raise, and the warning. I'll prepare him. He's healthy, and he's happy. Every day, after the bank visit, he walks with a bunch of other retired friends to the park where they discuss and argue politics. Mother is also well. She has many friends, and they can sit, sip tea, and gossip for hours on end. About what I haven't a clue. She has asked about when you are bringing Karima to visit?"

Vijay had been thinking about that, too. "I need a little time to get the business where I want it to be, but Jen and I are both anxious to visit, and Kari is old enough to make the trip now. We'll start thinking about dates, soon."

***

Jennifer had realized that Vijay had been a bit lost when VitalTech went public, and his role was downsized, but she could never have guessed how events would play out to put him back into the business. Nor had she realized how the new normalcy of their lives would give her so much more time to get involved and really help some local and national progressive organizations. What she did know, however, was that the current normal would soon be replaced when a new member of the Patel household arrived.

Until then, they could only hope – and vote – for a better world for children everywhere.

***

Washington, D.C. Demi had picked up their dinner at RASA, and she and Zoe were preparing to eat, drink some wine, and cross their fingers as they watched the Presidential election. They had voted, and they hoped their candidate would win; but even more than that, they were holding their breaths that whatever the outcome, widespread civil violence would not consume the country.

Their departments and all others – from federal agencies to states, counties, and cities across the country – had each developed contingency plans to contain violence, should it break out, and everyone was on call. Also, many agencies had developed detailed cooperative plans to help each other, should the need arise.

National Guard units across the country had been called up to respond, and the Joint Chiefs had plans in place to protect the

Constitution, if necessary, to ensure a smooth transition. The likelihood of this latter concern was now much less since the former President – who espoused staying in office because of rigged elections – was dead, and the current POTUS was essentially a 'caretaker.'

Zoe knew the political and judicial murder tallies to date, and they were significant. Despite those losses, she and her team, with a lot of help from Vijay, Alek, and Demi, had put the Russian 'robot' operation out of business. Now, without the worry of more killings motivated by Final Notices, they could focus on the more significant and less predictable threats, which unfortunately were also the least preventable.

The threat that posed the greatest catastrophic loss of life was the growth of militias or private armies. Most were borne from the right-wing and white supremacist groups with corollary 'defensive' groups popping up around the country. Weekend training or "MilSims" (Military Simulations) were being held around the country, and quite a few businesses had sprung up, many by veterans, who put together war games and provided military-like training.

You could think of these groups or individual violent events as powder kegs and the extensive Russian social media disinformation efforts as the fuses to detonate them and the fans to whip up the rhetoric, actions, and flames.

And so, against this very eclectic, emotional backdrop, the otherwise happy couple took deep breaths, sat down with their New Zealand Sauvignon Blanc, 'Sexy and I Know It' salads and 'Tikka Chance On Me' chicken dinners and pressed the 'On' button of the TV remote.

***

VAN FLEISHER

(Almost) THE END

***

CHAPTER 32 – FAST FORWARD

Zoe Brouet was commended for her efforts and her successes in keeping the Final Notice body count down. She got an additional assist from Vijay when he agreed to her request to continue to send the behavior report, even though it didn't include the Final Notice indicator. His agreement was limited, however, to the period up through the election and then for thirty days after. They would discuss an extension at a later date. Vijay's risk-taking agreement had helped prevent five high-profile murders as well as many others.

Zoe's personal side was flourishing, too, as she and Demi continued to enjoy their newfound love. They had even discussed formalizing it through marriage, and Demi had hinted that she might like to trade in her badge for a motherhood role.

***

Vijay Patel led VitalTech to a resurgence in growth, at a pace equal to, if not better than, the launch phase of the VT2. An extremely health-conscious America eagerly embraced new devices to monitor and improve their well-being, and the VT3 – featuring Vijay's patented blood-tracking process – was the leader of the pack. The associated VT3 App was able to tell its wearers what their blood chemistry strengths and weaknesses were so they could change their diets and/

or supplements accordingly. If, for example, a user's data showed a B12 deficiency, he, she, or they could simply tap it on their app, and an array of dietary changes would be suggested along with specific recommended supplements.

With the approval of J. Edward and the Board, Vijay also reconfigured VitalTech's compensation plan, making all employees eligible for profit-sharing. All employee pay scales would be harmonized with those above and below, including the CEO, so that Vijay's salary would be no higher than ten times that of the average employee.

Despite his new 'day job,' Vijay continued to excel athletically, posting his personal best in the Boston Marathon at 2:15:13. He also cast his first ballot in a U.S. election. This was his first tangible act as a U.S. citizen, and his pride could not be over-estimated.

His biggest joy, however, was being with his family. His new son wasn't old enough for splash parties yet, but Karima still enjoyed them, and Fritz liked catching some of the splashes and helping lick the water off the floor.

The Democratic Presidential debates and news coverage had called attention, as never before, to the enormous income and wealth disparities in the U.S. – gaps that not only existed but worked against less well-off families who were ever trying to dig themselves out of their situations. So, Vijay and Jennifer joined the Giving Pledge, promising to give at least half of their net worth to philanthropy, either during their lifetime or upon their death.

***

Jennifer Patel had already recognized that the Foundation that she and Vijay had set up was too narrowly focused to address an ever-changing variety of social demands. She understood, also, that regardless of how big or powerful an organization became, without the support and decisive action from government, nothing could ever be accomplished. And so, she became an active supporter of Emily's List and became involved in local government. Of course, if you asked her if she was considering politics, she would probably say, "Definitely not." But in politics, that means don't be surprised if you see Jennifer Andrews Patel on the ballot.

In the meantime, and of much more importance to her, Jennifer gave birth to Jason Andrew Patel. She and Vijay had arrived at the name for two reasons. First, Jason is a name recognized in both India and the U.S. Secondly, its origin (Greek) means 'He that cures.'

Jason's birth also helped bring about a change in Jennifer's self-assessment. She asked her mother to give away the old jeans that she hadn't been able to zip up.

***

Fritz, the Patels' shepa-doodle, may not have had a starring role in this book, but he did have a key supporting role, as most dogs do. He was a loving, non-judgmental playmate and friend for Karima and Jason, and when he barked, it was enough to give any unwelcome guests something to think about.

***

Alek Belikov blossomed on many levels. He became an extremely effective leader within the VitalTech group and instrumental in the success of the VT3.

On a personal level, he transformed his grief over the loss of his wife and son into cherished memories of great times. It was one of the hardest things he'd ever done, but he had his new wife, Sophie, to help him. She encouraged him to talk about them, and she never exhibited any signs of jealousy. She even remembered their birthdays and always made gestures to honor them.

Sophie had also given him another reason to shift firmly into the present and future. She was pregnant.

***

Tony Vinzano, the boy who reported his father's 'Zombie' crime and first brought Vik Vasin into the picture, stayed with police detective Sean Lombardi for almost a month. That short stay seemed to ignite his high school academic performance and his goals. He decided to attend junior college to go into law enforcement, particularly to work with underprivileged kids.

***

Vik Vasin was found guilty of numerous murders, accessory to murders, several federal felonies, and a whole lot more. He was given a number of life sentences, which he is serving at the Berlin, New Hampshire, Federal Correction Institution. He was not charged with the more serious crimes relating to terrorism, however, because he became the key witness against Mikhail 'Mike' Kalin and Yuri Chernyshevsky.

Vik wrote a note to Alek Belikov, congratulating him on his marriage and apologizing for his involvement that led to Alek's kidnapping and injury. Alek was moved, and he regularly visits Vik in New Hampshire.

***

FINAL ACT

Mikhail 'Mike' Kalin was found guilty of terrorism charges by working with foreign adversaries to interfere with and influence U.S. elections and to kill U.S. citizens. He's serving multiple life sentences with no chance for parole. Sara Huckers does not visit him.

All other members of the Russian 'robot' team, except for Yuri Chernyshevsky, were apprehended, tried, and convicted of various acts of terrorism and federal felonies. All were sentenced and will remain in prison for a very long time. Chernyshevsky remains at large. Russia has refused extradition.

***

Moki Joe Hunter's role in the poisoning at the Wilkes Barre Arena was never discovered, nor was the role of his brother, Tocho Tom, in providing the poisoned colas.

And so, after a while, and without any real leads, dozens of conspiracy theories consumed the cable channels, blogs, and tabloids. Russian involvement of various types and for different reasons were the dominant ones, including: "Putin felt that the President had become more of a liability than an asset," and "An oligarch killed him because the President screwed him on a real estate deal."

Others speculated: "The President's wife wanted to get out of the marriage without the prenup taking everything away." "The Democrats were afraid he'd be re-elected," and along that theme, any one of hundreds of other names could be inserted instead of 'The Democrats.'

As for why the Vice President was included in the assassination, it just appeared that nobody was even interested.

***

Marianne Abbott's bravery did more than eradicate two despicable family members. It turned out that when the London police received Marianne's letter, they acted on her information, and a reporter for the London Sentinel Echo, Anita Jackson, heard about the story. The Sentinel Echo might not have been a Pulitzer Prize winner, but Anita was passionate about her work and started to dig. What she found was startling and heart-breaking. Knowing exactly how many girls and women are trafficked each year is difficult to measure, but two-thirds of the victims in the USA are thought to be U.S. citizens, and the total number is estimated to be 25,000-50,000.

Anita found out that a Federal measure to help crack down on trafficking was introduced in 2017, but it failed to pass, just as gun laws do. Most states have taken up measures to root out and stop trafficking, but a few still lag behind. In some states, a trafficked woman or girl may even be charged with a crime that she was forced to commit.

Thanks to Anita's interest and energetic investigation, Marianne's story shed light on a monstrous crime. And as a result, more and more people came forward with additional information both in London and beyond, helping law enforcement agencies to blot out a disgusting stain.

***

The United States' Presidential Election was ... well, you'll see.

Remember, this is a work of fiction.

***

THE VERY END

ACKNOWLEDGMENTS

I dedicate this book to my mother and father, who passed along sufficient intelligence for me to write the FINAL book series. Their more significant accomplishment, however, was guiding me to develop the wisdom to view people through their deeds, rather than the color of their skin, their religion, their political beliefs, or their financial or social status. I confess to finding it increasingly difficult to understand why some individuals and groups seem to go out of their way to hurt others, especially those less fortunate than themselves.

I want to thank my partner in life, Jackie Morris, for her love, encouragement, support, and editing, which helped make FINAL ACT a reality.

I also want to thank my beta readers: my daughters, Heidi and Amy, along with Bonnie, Diane, Leda, John, Peter, and Roseann, and suggest they re-read FINAL ACT again. It's a much better book than the one you read ... thanks to you!

Last but certainly not least, I want to thank the many (more than expected) readers of FINAL NOTICE for their acceptance, liking, and particularly their openness in considering new and different positions on important issues raised in that book. That encouragement drove me to write FINAL ACT.

Writing a sequel is tricky because some readers may not have read the first (or earlier) books. I've tried to make Final Act read as a stand-alone story, and leave out spoilers in case you decide to read Final Notice later. Hopefully, I've achieved the 'write' balance. If you liked either or both of my books, I humbly ask that you leave a review. Reviews are critical for independent authors and I thank you, in advance. Feel free to contact me at van@vanfleisher.com or visit my website: www.vanfleisher.com.   ***

ABOUT THE AUTHOR

My journey to becoming an author took over seventy years, and it started in high school – a requirement if I wanted to play football and baseball. Mr. Smith, my literature teacher, was intrigued when I aced his essay test after six weeks of saying nothing in class. And so, he asked me how I did so well. My answer was simply that, "I'd listened." He asked if I read books, and I answered honestly, "No." So, he handed me a copy of a book, "The Catcher in the Rye," suggesting I might like it. I took it and actually read it, anxiously waiting for the baseball part that would surely be in a book with that title. I'd been tricked but kick-started to a lifetime of reading.

I've enjoyed two careers over fifty years that afforded me not only the opportunity to read voraciously on my thousands of flights (seriously) but also to learn so much about people, cultures, business, and life. I worked for an international airline and lived in five U.S. cities, three countries, and worked all over the world. My other career was as an international management consultant, working in and flying between thirty plus countries.

Not surprisingly, upon retirement, I decided to write. FINAL NOTICE was my first thriller, followed by its sequel, FINAL ACT. A third book in this Final Series is in the works.

I live in Carpinteria, California with my partner (and editor), Jackie Morris, and our goldendoodle, Yogi.

Comments welcome at: van@vanfleisher.com

Visit my website at vanfleisher.com

***

FINAL ACT QUESTIONS FOR BOOK CLUBS

Following are some suggested discussion questions for book club moderators. The author is happy to consider special book club rates and engage in discussions, as possible. I would love to hear about your conversations and any comments you may have. van@vanfleisher.com.

1. Overall, do you think that the author was too one-sided, or was he fair in his dealings with the major issues?
2. What did you like, love, or hate about Final Act?
3. How would you feel about knowing when you will die, and what would you do with your last days? Could you envisage a situation where you could kill, knowing you would never live to stand trial?
4. Based on the premise of the Final Act, what do you feel are the country's most significant issues?
5. What are your views on guns and gun control?
6. Based on Vijay's and Jennifer's differing views on cooperating with the FBI, whose view is closest to your own?
7. How do you feel about law enforcement surveillance?
8. What are your thoughts on the treatment of immigrants?
9. Did you like the author's writing style?
10. Would Final Act (along with or independent from Final Notice, if you've read it) make a good movie? What actors would play the main characters?
11. How did you feel about the event at the Wilkes Barre Arena?
12. Who were the most likable characters? Least likable?
13. Did Final Act influence your views on anything?
14. Your overall rating: 1-5 stars.

Sneak Preview from FINAL CHANCE

Chapter 1 – Winter Wonderland, 2066

Camp David, Frederick County, Maryland. Friday, January 15th, 2066. The First Family were looking forward to their weekend at the Presidential Retreat in the wooded hills of Catoctin Mountain Park. The entire two-hundred-acre retreat had been protected from the inhospitable environment under two inter-connecting glass domes. The Aspen Lodge – the main residential building, Laurel Lodge – used for meetings and conferences, the swimming pool and the one-hole practice golf course were under the main dome. The other smaller dome covered an adjacent area of forest. The domes were connected via a secure tubed corridor, also of glass. Outside the domes, the unprotected areas were covered with a heavy white blanket of snow, artistically hiding the dead or dying trees and bushes.

The forested dome had a number of cleverly engineered panels that could be opened to capture a great deal of snow. The panels were then closed, and the temperature brought down to what would once have been normal outdoor temperature, so the snow kept its fresh powdery texture and appeal, waiting for the young Family members to enjoy.

The Presidential chopper, "Marine One," flew over the bleak landscape, punctuated by the domes protecting towns, cities, agriculture hubs and an occasional forested area. There were also a number of cemeteries, a stark legacy of the many pandemics that claimed so many lives.

FINAL ACT

As the chopper approached Camp David, the two youngest Family members were squealing with delight. At eight and nine years old, they had been coming to the Retreat for most of their lives – five years – and they knew that the staff at Camp David would have let in the snow.

After a quick change into snow gear, the President and family, along with the ever-present Secret Service detail, who were also dressed for the activity, headed to the forest dome.

Almost two hours later, all of them, including some of the Secret Service agents who had joined them in the snowball battles, trudged back to the main dome and the Aspen Lodge. The President had decided to unwind with laps in the enclosed pool. The enclosure had been retained, even after the dome was erected, so it could be kept warmer than the coolish temperature preferred for their other outdoor activities.

Enjoying the warmth of the water along with the calming quiet of solitude and swimming, POTUS was more relaxed than he'd been in days. His gut opinion, and that of his military advisors, was that the Russians were bluffing. But it was unheard of and unnerving that there had been no communication between the two countries' governments in over ten days.

Still, there were two positives for him to draw solace from. First, the perpetrators and architects of assassinations and thousands of American deaths were behind bars and would cause no further problems. And second, the leadership of the United States in spearheading the effort to save the planet.

It was almost twenty years ago that the doming plan was conceived and announced. It was audacious and dismissed by many, at home and abroad, as an impossible headline grab. But the United States could never be counted out. President Joe Biden, the forty-sixth President had reminded everyone, as he took office amidst the first Coronavirus pandemic in 2021 that during World War 2, a single car manufacturing plant had retooled to make a new four engine B-24 bomber every hour. And on the west coast a group of shipyards built a new ship every day for four years.

It was with that memory, that vision in their rear-view mirror, and the reality that there was no alternative to avoid the complete destruction and devastation of humanity, that drove three U.S. Presidents to do the impossible. It was their final chance.

Sanders reflected on the successful plan, rapidly constructing thousands of domes worldwide, from Washington to Los Angeles to Beijing to … . The thought was never finished, as a "Switchblade" UAV – unmanned aerial vehicle, or drone – smashed through the dome and enclosure at over a hundred miles an hour, exploding just yards away from the President. The explosion killed POTUS and the Secret Service detail instantly, even before it released its toxic gas. The gas then killed another three agents rushing to the scene before a lucky one radioed to others in the Lodge to take the Family to the bunker.

***